Setting in Roots:

Part I

Dymphna

BISAC Categories:

FIC027120   FICTION / Romance / Paranormal / General

FIC031020   FICTION / Thrillers / Historical

FIC031070   FICTION / Thrillers / Supernatural

Copyright © 2021 Dymphna

All rights reserved.

ISBN: 978-1-954779-07-5

Contents

Dedicated to my parents, who taught me there is nothing useful in a hidden talent.

And to my grandmother, who never blinked at constant adversity. May you rest in peace and may your legacy reign on.

I was born sometime around what I was taught to believe was "The War of Northern Aggression" on a date of little to no importance, to a family with neither a consequential name nor a religious contract of marriage. A man brought me from the South and raised me deep in the middle of nowhere, all those I met in my nowhere only came to go. So I was grounded all-to-quickly in alliance with a man in a location he found most fit. His decisions were not to be second-guessed or questioned, as I owed him my life. My mere existence was indebted to him.

Trouble tends to follow when you've got a debt you didn't consciously dig yourself into. That guilt somehow becomes tangible. Perhaps it has the power to affix itself like old bubblegum to the bottom of a well-worn tennis shoe, catching ever so slightly with each step. Nonetheless, such guilt wears until you're chained to your creditor.

Most folks who acquire that all-consuming guilt simply run to God and lay it all on Him. Which is good and fine and makes heaps of sense because He gave us lowly group of sinners His only begotten son. But my chains were inherently independent of the forces of God, leaving me nailed to another man in all my lonely. My evening prayers went first and foremost to my so-called knight in rusty armor and then drifted begrudgingly to Jesus H. Christ. Tail between my legs all the while. I say that not with a light heart, but a blackened one riddled with turmoil and blasphemy. Because with that knight of mine came plastic freedom and false pretenses. Penances were silently expected through thick air that suffocated any dreams of differentiation.

Still, I lie awake at night, tormenting myself by questioning all the decisions made and how they were shaped by circumstance. *Had I been born later, would things have been different? Had it been the twentieth century, would I have stood a chance?* Perhaps someone would have stood for me, back when I was too small and young, and saved me from the most kind-hearted abduction that side of the Mississippi.

But my coming-to-be did not occur from how I began. Therefore, I ought not to place the blame upon my benefactor out of spite. He isn't to take on the burdens of my autonomous actions. But, oh! How wondrous those actions were! At the time, I hadn't known my innocence was so tightly attached to my soul. As if the two were privately bound by a thick cord and could together tumble out of my body with a proper tug.

No, I am to blame for my timelessness. I am the sole creator of my continuous demise. I and the devil that I successfully tempted.

My name is Beatrix Chanteloup. In the winter of 1886, perchance my ripest year, my soul was stolen by the very devil himself, along with my God-given right to die.

"Write this: Blessed are the dead which die in the Lord from henceforth."
—Revelation 14:13

Chapter 1

Colorado, 1886

he familiar yet shocking rap on my door tugged me from my dreams. The soft warmth that accompanied my blackness was pulled back by the garish color of reality. My eyes flashed open at the sound of Ms. Liz murmuring something or another, followed by her footsteps trailing off. My first conscious gaze of the day met a full glass of water sitting on my bedside table, shimmering in the morning light. Immediately, aromas of rose petal–infused soaps vanished like smoke in a windstorm. I stared at the glass as if it could shatter beneath my glare. For the life of me, I could not recall bringing that up late last night. The sun shone brightly, and I rolled to my back; the worry of the glass proved fleeting at best. My head was fuzzy and heavy from sleep in a delirious way that made me yawn and smack my lips like an infant.

I hadn't felt so refreshed in what seemed like months—a reasonable assumption due to my conflicts with standard sleep schedules. If my sleep patterns were drawn out like a map, they would mimic how I assumed the Rockies presented themselves as a series of soaring mountains and deep valleys. The highs were nights filled with sleep terrors, screaming, and sweating, while the lows were a sleep so deep, I might as well have been amongst the dead. Since puberty, Ms. Liz had wanted me to see a doctor for my bouts of restless nights. But Mr. Jim warned her the only diagnosis a doctor gave this far west was hysteria. Neither wanted me haunted by such a diagnosis in writing.

I crawled out of my much too warm bed and sat with my feet on the hardwood floor, toes barely reaching. I stretched my neck to shake off the lingering sleep and got ready for the day. It was almost June, and the summer heat spread over Wicker Soul, my small town, like a piece of butter left in the sun. Indeed, by July, we would all be sorry little puddles. The morning still held the cool evening air, but I was dewy from the mild exertion of undressing to redress. A breeze blew through my open window and danced around my naked flesh. It was a caress, and my eyes closed momentarily as my attention drifted from the task at hand. I slowly ran my hands over my flesh, soft from that long night's sleep. I stopped before the curiosity of my own anatomy got the best of me and made me late.

An enormous clatter and high-pitched holler echoed from the kitchen below my room. I rushed toward the drama below with my lovely black silk hair ribbon still in hand, a gift from Billy on my last birthday. I attempted to straighten my olive-green skirts at the staircase landing where a grand gold-trimmed mirror hung.

I endeavored to tie up my mess of hair with the fine ribbon. Nearly black, familiar, but somehow untrustworthy eyes reflected from the mirror as I righted myself. I quickly rolled white sleeves up to my elbows, mobility outweighing any sense of propriety. I glanced back suspiciously at my neatened reflection, wondering how different the world in the mirror was from the one I unhappily inhabited. Certainly they contained more than a simple reversal of what we provided. Perhaps just through that glass lay some mystical insight into the future. Or instead pristine clarity of the past, which for me was always drenched in a humid fog. Even better, just beneath that glass was a world without said future or past. A glorious, untouchable now. Where the sluggish air moved like a soft summer day, and everything shone like the bright pools and gentle lapping tides of the sacred spring just north of where I stood. That had to be it. In the glass, the world was left to its own without the pressure of the future or shame of the past. Which left one question: *How could I get in?*

My dark eyes blinked in response to my sleepy musings. A boom of familiar laughter echoed from below, and I dashed down the steps and rounded the staircase corner to discover Billy, laughing with his large head thrown back while Ms. Liz fussed over a batch of burnt biscuits. They stood around the large island of a table in the middle of the sunny kitchen. The island was hallowed. A neutral territory where we came together in familial discussion that sometimes tricked me into believing I really *was* one of them. I worshipped that handy workspace. Ms. Liz, the sole owner of our grand boarding house, waved a towel over some blackened bits of butter and flour while Billy had a tin cup of warm coffee. The steam rising from the cup swirled lovingly, blending into his curly, dark blond hair.

"Oh, Billy, this is all your fault!" Ms. Liz hissed in her lazy, western drawl.

He wiped a tear from his eye and shook his head. "Momma, I won't be taking the blame for your burnt biscuits," he laughed as he noted my arrival.

Billy's voice was slow and low, and when words came out of that mouth of his, they were unbothered, as if molasses sat in the back of his throat. The word *Momma* sounded much more like "mawl-muh."

"Well, good morning, Trixie-girl." His gaze went from comical to weary as his dull hazel eyes clouded over like the warning signs of a tornado-stricken sky.

"The water?" I murmured, gingerly walking around the island toward the kettle of coffee. I avoided eye contact with both.

"It's been a while," Billy murmured.

I gave a polite hum in response and focused on pouring. "Did I disturb you?"

"Nah, girl. I heard you when I was coming up to bed is all. Thrashing about. I tried to wake ya, but you wouldn't." He shivered comically. "I tell you, scares the life outta me to see you like that." He had a dramatic tongue like his momma, and I fought the urge to roll my eyes.

"Well, thank you for that. I felt fine this morning." I blew on my coffee.

Rarely did I blush due to the man-made barriers of my personality. But at that moment, my cheeks felt warm. The attention my terrors brought was not welcome. Such exposure, the airing out of my dirty laundry, was a stark, albeit kind, belittlement.

"So why is Billy at fault for a batch of burnt biscuits, Ms. Liz?" I broke the silence, smiling and sipping. Mr. Jim had retrieved some finer coffee grounds on his most recent trip to Denver, and I made a mental note to inquire about getting more.

"He was jabbering on and on about Mr. Jim having come in late last night, and by horse! Lord almighty, that's a journey and a half from Denver, though you don't need me to tell ya so. Well, I never. We both know Mr. Jim wouldn't ride through the morning on a horse if his life depended on it. And having all his deliveries brought in this morning's train by some stranger? I told him there was no use gossiping about Mr. Jim's business; it isn't the Catholic thing to do. But he kept on, and I lost track of time and burnt my here biscuits! Oh, the older ya get..." Ms. Liz huffed and sighed with her chubby hands curled into fists on her plump waist.

I frowned as I mulled over her tellings. Annoyance, along with something else possessing sharpened teeth, sunk into my skin. "Mr. Jim is back?"

He had very specifically told me he wouldn't be back until Monday at the earliest. I did miss Mr. Jim when he went into the city on business. Dearly, sometimes, in my own sort of way. But his untimely arrival had me feeling no such relief.

"I met with him this morning at the post office. Had a fella by his side. I didn't have time to chat with 'em." Billy scratched at the back of his neck with a terrifyingly large paw.

I hummed in response. Mr. Jim always sent for me the moment he returned to Wicker Soul. Our relationship was unorthodox at best, suspicious at worst. But he was all I had. He, in a way, was less like a father figure and more like a guardian. Perhaps not even a guardian. Instead, a rock or birthmark that stuck around through the wear and tear of adolescence and whatever followed. There was something to be said for those who stayed in your life because they chose to, contrary to blood, contract, or conception. Mr. Jim had none of such with me. He was a reliable presence who stood by my side as I grew up and keenly understood my tendencies. He implanted a metaphorical (and sometimes very real) rod of control in my life to help balance the ever-shifting tides that roared within. There was never an option not to trust Mr. Jim. The thought of where I would be without him struck the fear of God into my scrawny self, faster than any flash of lightning ever could. He simply was to me as I was to him—a companion, loyal to the brink of madness.

I leaned forward on the well-worn table, settling my coffee and drumming my fingers impatiently as I boiled like a forgotten kettle.

"Oh, Trixie, don't you start feeling any sort of sorry for yourself. That's a nasty, selfish thing right there, and the good Lord, as well as I, will have none of it. I'm sure Mr. Jim was just too busy with this new fella. You know how fussy that man gets. Say, why don't you just run on over to the General Store? He oughta be up and about by this hour. I bet he is missing you mighty big." Ms. Liz babbled at me as she bustled about her burnt biscuits. One could do few things in her presence that didn't receive some form of criticism from "the good Catholic Lord."

"No. He'll come for me," I replied coldly.

I straightened myself and bit back the petty thoughts I was chided for entertaining. I felt uncomfortably foolish, and the last thing I wanted to do was wander on over to the General Store and knock on the door leading up to Mr. Jim's apartments. Another day of freedom was something to be grateful for. I drank down the last of my coffee with a sizeable unladylike gulp. But annoyance and green curiosity still itched at my skin like a rash.

I turned to Billy, who was unusually quiet. "Help me with Butterbis-cuit 'fore you head off with Mr. O'Toole?" I asked. Mr. O'Toole was the rancher just outside of town that Billy was a hand for.

Butterbiscuit was a horse.

He nodded at me, his curly blond hair bouncing childishly.

"Now, Trixie-girl, where do you think you're goin' off to? And Billy, you neglected to explain why you were meeting Mr. Jim so early." All too quickly, the biscuits were no longer Ms. Liz's main concern. "I ain't having any form of sneaking about in this household," she continued, a soft, plump hand finding its home back upon an equally plump hip.

Ms. Liz ran her "good, Catholic" boardinghouse tight as a whip. She claimed that nothing happened under her roof she didn't know about or approve of. Which sometimes had me wondering exactly what she *did* approve of. Billy's face was beet red with impatience. The way his eyes blinked told me the moment that mouth of his opened, an atrocious lie would rampage out, tearing the walls down with it. Whether we were related by blood or not, in my heart, Billy was my brother. I knew his less-than-clever mischief like the back of my own hand. So, I stomped on Billy's foot swiftly—thanks to the island, out of view of Ms. Liz's shifting gaze. Billy tried and failed to mask a light groan with an odd cough.

"Ms. Liz, you know good and well there ain't no nonsense going on under that sharp nose of yours. Now, if Mr. Jim isn't needing any of my help on this fine day, I figured I would have it to myself. You know just as well as I do that when Mr. Jim does send for me, he'll have me working sunup to sundown," I said in a slight rush, hoping my tone would be mistaken for exasperation as opposed to calculation.

I continued before I took a full breath. "As for our mysterious meeting of the morn—weren't you listening at dinner last night? Now, I know Billy was telling us how he had to wake up early to fetch a wire for Mr. O'Toole. Something 'bout a new feed for the cattle?" I gave him a knowing glance.

For an almost unregistered moment, Billy's eyes widened. Quickly that expression was replaced by a sharp nod in agreement toward Ms. Liz.

She sighed in acceptance, whether she believed me or not. "Trixie-girl, don't be stirring up any trouble running wild as you do. More folks are coming through town each day."

I took her dramatic statement with a grain of salt. Sometimes I wondered if Ms. Liz thought me some form of a pagan god, the way she hammered on with her descriptions of my uncontrolled self. Or perhaps she just had a couple of novels hidden away in her room, underneath the large family Bible she treasured. I was different from my birth, conceived in debauchery and therefore ever-tainted by it. All my life, it seemed the weight of whatever roared within me and wreaked havoc upon my soul was a strictly personal ailment. My internalized turmoil did not balk at the orders of man or the structures of expectation. Instead, it burned in my belly like fuel to a locomotive that could one day rush me miles away from my sleepy little nowhere. And although I was welcomed into my strange mash of a family with ease, I could not forget my origins, a heavy burden on shoulders as unremarkable as mine.

"But," she whimpered sadly, her aged face pulling into a pretty pout, "who's gonna help me remake all these biscuits?"

I grimaced at the thought of staying inside.

"Dev is still sleeping, but I'm sure she will help you with the chores today, Momma," Billy chirped. "She sang pretty late last night and got back just around midnight. But I reckon she will be up soon."

No one had the energy to inquire *why* Billy knew what time Miss Dev came home. Dev was Billy's one and only. She was raised outside town, and at seventeen, came to Wicker Soul looking for work and distance from her family. Her parents were almost always sick with the drink. It was never made clear if they ever came to long enough to notice her departure. Mr. Jim got her a spot singing at the saloon, a fancy sort of establishment and the only place in town to find whiskey that wasn't tucked away in some cupboard. Ms. Liz was always one for a charity case, so she put Dev up for free at the boarding house.

Dev was a soft soul; the selfish, harsh words and thoughts that I was sure came with humanity never plagued her. She radiated a subtle glowing halo of feminine goodness. With a tall stature, red hair, and delicate features, her inner beauty leaked out of her soul and onto her physical form. Her presence was calming, as if she were the embodiment of a passing storm, serene and welcoming. In her eyes was a stillness, the type that almost reassured someone. But beneath it all, there was something quietly horrible about that sort of *still* that left me wondering what exactly went on in that pretty little head of hers.

She kept Billy's heart tightly locked away, just as he kept hers. They had been in a slow sort of courting since their formal introduction roughly four years ago. If Ms. Liz disapproved, she had misled all of us, for she had welcomed Dev into her home and heart with the same undeniable care she welcomed me as a child.

As if her ears were burning, Dev rounded the corner with sleepy eyes and slow steps. A smile danced its way onto her lips as she took in our small gathering.

"Speak of the Devil," I muttered lightly, returning her smile.

A blush delicately slid across her soft cheeks, nearly matching the color of her hair. "Good morning. All pleasant things, I should hope," Dev practically sang back. She offered her hand to Billy as a greeting, and he leaned his lips into her knuckles.

"Nothing but," he murmured against her flesh.

I quickly shifted my gaze from their shockingly intimate moment. Ms. Liz cleared her throat with kind but suspicious foggy green eyes.

"Dear," Ms. Liz began, "wouldn't you be so kind as to help me with the baking today?"

It was evident in her tone that she wasn't exactly asking, but the gesture of a question was there nonetheless. Light and pleasant morning small talk buzzed around me. The room suddenly felt tiny. Four walls and four beating hearts could truly take a toll on someone's health. A tiny amount of turmoil bubbled within me. It was simple moments like these, surrounded by people who cared for me, just as I cared for them, that the overwhelming loneliness seized me. Like it could seep into my skin, inversely to how sweat on a summer day seeped out. It was unjustifiable, illogical, yet somehow entirely consuming, like a deafening ringing in my ears that I couldn't shake. It was something that I could not fight, no matter how hard I tried.

I had no reason to feel lonely, yet in these times, it was clear no one could understand what plagued me so horribly. And I wouldn't let them, even if they believed they could. For it was my ailment to address—crouching on my shoulders, not theirs. But each time this loneliness reached for me, it became stronger, growing from whatever penances I granted it to leave me be. I feared that one day, with that strength I had provided, it would permanently latch onto not just me, but everyone around me. I knew deep in my gut, past the stomach acid and butterflies, the only way to save them from the utter ruin that would one day consume us all was to leave.

How often had I considered closed doors? Wondering if the soles of my feet were brave enough to take the life-altering steps forward. The only thing more terrifying than the possibility of loneliness consuming us whole was the contradicting fear that I would never be brave enough to act against it.

My teeth independently gnawed at the inner left corner of my bottom lip as Billy's voice pulled me out of my trance. "You ready?"

I slowly met his gaze, nodding at the same speed. His practically permanent smile remained, though his brows furrowed when our eyes met. I shifted to instead meet Ms. Liz's questioning stare. She didn't push for details of my plans for the day. When I was younger, Ms. Liz had tried to exert authority over me, especially when Mr. Jim was not around. He played the disciplinarian, with his constant threat of skinning me alive and all. By the time I was fifteen, Ms. Liz had told me that I was as stubborn as the rocks and as unpredictable as the summer rain. In return, when I had rudely explained to her that this analogy was contradictive, she went about her business, muttering, "Just like you."

I gave Liz a grin. "I'll be at the Lil' Big."

She looked at her biscuits—fascinating things they must be—and smiled lightly. I rarely granted her the knowledge of my whereabouts. It was uncommon to find a moment away that was mine to do as I pleased. Before another tiresome distraction arose, Billy and I exited. The boarding house was a great place, at least to my small-minded eyes. Thanks to the steady rush west since the end of the war, Ms. Liz could keep the home as up to date as possible this far from Denver.

The wraparound porch was freshly painted white last August, along with new cream lace curtains in each of the twenty boarding rooms. The house was two stories, with an endless front and narrow hallways inside so that each room had a window. Overall, it was nothing too memorable, other than Parthenon pillars that sprung up from the first floor to support the porch roof. But to my eyes, it was great. As a child, I shimmied up and down those pillars, imagining I was anywhere but where I indeed was. The front door was a lovely dark oak, engraved with symbols of crops and foliage, smooth with nooks in the design that a child could nearly get their fingers stuck in. And no matter the temperature, the door was always cool to the touch.

Flowers were planted at the entrance, though with the current drought, fat luck they were. Yet, the ivy that sprung every spring curled around the pillars in full bloom, as if water held little to no importance. The bright color contrast was lovely and had Ms. Liz bursting with pride. She had placed four rocking chairs, all picked out by Mr. Jim four months ago in Denver, on the porch with a couple of end tables. I got to keep the fifth chair in my room. Boarders liked to play cards and such in the early evening on the porch. It made the perfect reading spot by candlelight on warm summer nights when sleep denied me. A second only to the roof above the porch, accessible through my bedroom window.

The sun beat down, a welcome relief as we left the porch. My skin tightened against the bones of my face as it greeted the familiar warmth.

In my dreams, rays of sunshine were strings that attached me to the sun, and I danced and basked in the glory of it all with a passion and eagerness to obey. But when I woke, I faced the disappointing reality of who actually manipulated my limbs. I tilted my head back as I tried to absorb more of the dry heat. A breeze picked up and cooled my dewy flesh. When it died, I rejoined reality from my small moment to find Billy a good twenty feet ahead of me. I rushed to meet his long strides.

"Hey," I grabbed his shoulder.

He had fixed his hat almost over his eyes so they couldn't meet mine.

"What's the story with meeting Mr. Jim? I ain't keen on lyin' to Ms. Liz for you," I continued, my left eyebrow cocked with curiosity.

Billy-boy side-eyed me. "Since when do you not like lying to Ms. Liz?" he grumbled.

"Well, I don't like it when it ain't my lie. If I'm lying for you, I got a right to know what about!" I snapped.

He sighed and took off his hat. He wiped at the sweat that beaded his forehead. A moment passed, and I attempted to be patient. "I, uh, I was looking through one of them nice catalogs for a store down in Denver. Saw a ring I thought I'd have Mr. Jim pick up for me. To give Dev for...well..."

The finality in his statement hammered home. He attempted to pull his arm out of my grasp and return to the deed at hand. I held him back with whatever strength I had.

"Whatcha needin' a ring for, Billy-boy?" Joy and surprise pumped through my veins directly from my heart.

Of course Billy and Dev would wed. Rationally, I always knew what lay at the end of the road for those two. But marriage wasn't something I thought of regularly. In fact, most formalities of life in a small town did not plague my mind. This town had shrunk away from my touch since I was a child, so naturally I had done the same to it. I was unbothered by its rules and expectations. Happy to flow in and out of sight and straightening up only at Mr. Jim's command. Marriage felt groundbreaking.

Perhaps we were older than I felt. In the thick of our springtime youth, age was as unmoving as molasses. But now it was clear that the molasses had warmed up nicely under the steady coals of patience and was spreading with ease. So they hadn't lied. The older and wiser folks who chided us with the belief that good things awaited those with such a virtue as patience hadn't lied to spare themselves the horrors of rowdy children, after all. The brief thought made me dizzy. My mind raced with childlike frenzy at his silent confirmation and then halted like the final stop of a train.

"Why now? Why so soon? Billy, she isn't...?" I stammered in fear.

Ms. Liz would keel over dead if Dev had Billy's babe out of wedlock. Billy's eyes widened in shock.

"It ain't soon. It's late, for crying out loud!" he exclaimed with cheeks flushed.

I fought the urge to hush him. His hands were in his hair as if pulling at the strands aided exasperation.

"No. No, she isn't. But she might as well be. We can't keep... I mean, it's been enough time. I won't put her at risk anymore. She's been mine for long enough, time to make it fair in the eyes of God," Billy stammered in a stern rush.

I knew how physical their relationship had been for quite some time. With them living so close, one had to be realistic about it all. Propriety or not, humans sought comfort. I didn't need circumstantial experience to comprehend that.

I nodded and grinned in response. Billy-boy reacted wildly and picked me up by my waist to swing me around like a sledgehammer. I laughed as the world spun around me. His laugh mixed with mine whimsically like the sound of wind chimes. Once he set me on my feet, I was breathless and gripped his arm so I didn't tumble over.

"Congratulations," I murmured breathlessly as I righted myself.

He scoffed, "That's a little premature, Trixie-girl, I haven't even ask—"

"Hush," I interrupted and continued to the stables. "Don't be a fool. All will be good and fine, and you know it."

The stables smelled strongly of dung, sweat, and hay. It burned my nostrils like the first smoke from the strike of a match. We kept the stables open to the guests, and since we had a couple travelers come in earlier last week, the stables were fuller than usual. Dim light broke through the barn, and certain spots where the roofing gapped allowed patterns of spotlights. I walked under their warmth, still whirling from Billy's news. With their marriage, a large, new foundation of kin would be created. One that would be strong and grow upon deeply set roots blooming in the fertility of blood relation. Whatever familial foundation we existed within no longer required me at the base, ironically supporting more than I was supported. A sense of freedom came from the realization of how much attention, as well as raw human nurturing, Billy would be responsible for.

He saddled up Butterbiscuit for me. The horse was a gentle, aging thing. In a year or two, I would no longer be able to take him racing to the Lil' Big. Billy hoisted me on top of the beastie but clung to my hand.

"Keep this news to yourself, Trixie," he commanded with a smile.

I nodded, and he brought my knuckles to his lips and placed a warm kiss.

"Need anything else?" he questioned, releasing me but holding onto the reins.

I shook my head, and he let go. I clicked my tongue to turn Butterbiscuit and was off with the wind. Silent laughter came from open lips as we galloped through town. The eyes that burned holes into me were easily dismissed. There was nothing new about their chronic case of curiosity, and it was a waste of time to pay them any mind. Everyone knew to steer clear of *the wicked thing of Wicker Soul*. I passed Mr. Jim's saloon and general store and saw no sign of life. So, I pushed on until I was beyond the small jail and out of the town limits altogether.

The Lil' Big was named because in the minds of the children Billy and I once were, that's precisely what it was. A small oasis, not big enough to even be a lake, but somehow, to us, grander than any ocean. Or so we had decided. It was located outside of town, further up in elevation, surrounded by a quiet wood, with one abandoned cabin. Surely it was once the home of a failing miner, long before I arrived.

In our youth, Billy and I ran away to the Lil' Big to fish all day and then stayed in the cabin when we were full of anger and childishness, building fires to roast our catches. We danced around the flames shouting different languages that someone wiser and older must have forgotten to make up. Then, when the moon was full, we ripped off our clothes and climbed on the boulders that surrounded the west beach and jumped into the water, fighting and splashing about like wild heathens. Which I had no issue with since according to Mr. Jim, my father very well might have been. Or a pirate. Perhaps a descendant of a dark-eyed conquistador who ravaged lands further south than here. Potentially even a tradesman from warm lands much further east. And while Mr. Jim made no effort to mask his disgust with my birth father's certain *mystery,* I could not help but delight in the adventures I was determined he experienced. I cherished the possible freedom man could possess when he was unweighted by either earthly or familial chains. Even when such freedom came at my own expense.

Nonetheless, the mornings came too soon. Billy and I would return with heavy heels to Wicker Soul, him awaiting the wrath of Ms. Liz and her harsh ear-tugging, and I, the thick, choking fire of Mr. Jim.

But as each summer passed, Billy and I found less and less time to spend at our beloved Lil' Big. Work took priority. While Billy was set on providing for a family in Wicker Soul, I dreamed of saving up every dime to take further west than this. So far west that the Lil' Big would shrink in the face of the Pacific Ocean.

The wind pulled at my face and hair as I climbed the mild elevation with Butterbiscuit. The air increased in dry comfort with each boulder we climbed, and that wind, though gentle, was laced with a quiet sense of urgency. As if the air wanted me at the Lil' Big as badly as I wanted myself there. Just as the trails became treacherous, the little green oasis with the familiar cabin came into view, and I pushed Butterbiscuit as fast as he could go.

We broke through the brush on an overgrown path that led to the cabin at the eastern beach, and I yanked my dear beast to a halt and jumped recklessly from him. I didn't take the time to tie him up, as the old fellow was too tired and loyal to cause any trouble. He wouldn't wander far; he never did. The crowded brush and branches pulled my horrid clothing from me without effort. My bare feet curled around the rough forest floor, and I was off. Sprinting toward the softer sand lapped up by the Lil' Big's clear, cool waters. I gave myself no foreplay, but instead, ran straight into the waters until I was knee-deep, then dove to the darker ends.

A thousand loving needles stung my skin from the water temperature. I resurfaced in the middle of the eastern bank. The sun immediately warmed my head, and my body balanced itself into a comfortable temperature. With care, I allowed myself to drift up to float contently on my back. Bits and pieces of my flesh hardened with the altered exposures, and my bones felt like they had turned into fresh cotton. Though my ears stayed under the water, I heard the gurgling echo of birds chirping to the surrounding life. In the comfort of my mind, I was a part of those conversations. I belonged. Around me, trees and critters whispered their greetings. They offered an unspoken acceptance I couldn't find in the perimeter of the town where I had been raised. Here, in my tiny oasis, no one asked me questions I didn't have the answers to. No one looked twice at me unless in relief of my return. Here I was missed. Here I was not *wicked*.

The Lil' Big ran her cool, wet fingers through my hair as a mother would a young girl after a long day's braid had caused an ache to her scalp. The trees told stories that a father would grumble in the lazy afternoon sunshine. I wasn't home here; I knew that. The itch beneath my skin and prick at the tips of my toes told me that I still had many miles to go. Despite that nagging, one-dimensional belief that home was a distant location, the Lil' Big told me, here, I was close. I could have fallen asleep just like that. Perhaps I did, for a small bit, but my eyes flashed open as I felt the powerful rays of the sun upon my breast and stomach. An echo erupted, low and only for me under the waters. It was a hollow, blue sort of sound. The boulder was calling to me—no, *groaning* to me. I swore by it.

I dipped back below the surface and pumped my legs hard under the cool water. The temperature clung to my naked flesh deliciously—an ideal relief from the warm, May day. When my eyes opened, I made out shadowy shapes of land and rock. The water was usually dark this far in, no matter the weather. The harsh angle of much rockier land jutted out before the west beach, possessing a singular large sitting boulder protruding from the cool waters. It was there that we had played king of the castle. We stood stark naked, screaming the laws of our made-up lands, proclaiming victories once earned.

My elbows and kneecaps still held jagged, aged scars from those childhood antics. They painted across my body with a placement so miraculous it nearly seemed intentional. An air bubble escaped my lip as my memories resurfaced with scattering, yellowed images that clouded my view. A skinny boy with floppy blond hair ran naked in front of me, arms flailing about like a madman. At the time, I was fascinated by his mix-matched skin tones; the difference between where the sun regularly met and where it did not. How odd it was, to have such an extreme range in color. Perhaps odder than the ugly thing that bounced between his legs. Poor, partially pale little Billy tried with all his height and strength to wrestle me off the boulder, but the boulder reached up and gripped my feet every time. I won each game, except when he cheated and held onto my arms as he fell into the Lil' Big.

My lungs burned as I pumped my body through the sparkling abyss, the boulder of my childhood in sight. When I all but burst, I broke the surface of the water with a large gasp. Air relieved my aching chest as I smoothed the water from my face, sliding my hands up and back to push the damp hair out of my eyes.

My reprieve from the much-needed air disappeared as I realized something was amiss on the childhood boulder. Worn boots that led to long legs dangled in front of me. Boots attached to a large man. A small noise came from my throat, not as loud as a scream nor as lovely as a gasp. Immediately my brain pieced together how very naked I was and submerged the upper half of my body underwater. I pushed myself back from the boulder and its new king.

Chapter 2

I put about ten feet between us, not looking away from where his eyes should be, were they not shadowed from the sun by a hat pulled low. I stopped moving, and the water around me stilled, sinking lower until my chin brushed the glassy surface. My undeniable femininity pumped an odd shame throughout my body.

The stranger remained still. He held a long slender fishing rod in one hand. His knees were bent, and his arms rested on them in a pensive sort of squat. His right arm was slightly reached out in my direction, though he still made no move. His mouth opened and closed a couple of times without a word slipping out. I stayed low and quiet, stunned at the discovery of unsuspected company. Folks never came around here and I had never paid much mind to any threats that extended past Wicker Soul or Mr. Jim's disapproving glare. I lacked something from all those un-had experiences. My gut churned, though not out of fear. Instinctively I knew to back up and swim as far as possible without exposing myself for the sake of my safety and virtue. As my heartbeat pounded in my ears, I couldn't recall the importance of either of those things. No, my gut churned with interest in such an unprecedented experience. Mr. Jim said my curiosity would be the end of me. I cocked my head, stared, and waited.

He cleared his throat and murmured over the quiet livelihood of my Lil' Big. "Are ye fantastical?"

I furrowed my brow at his familiar words and fought the smile that danced over my lips.

"*Macbeth*," I murmured.

I noted the water that clothed me. I barely saw my naked form's outline, so I assumed that he saw the same. My eyes flashed back to him at the rustling of movement. He had leaned forward in his positioning but hadn't moved off his rock or let go of his righteous fishing rod. His right hand had drifted back down to the boulder, and I watched his fingertips twitch as if he fought the urge to reach out once more.

"Act I, scene III," he murmured in a deeper version of my own bewildered tone.

He had a funny, barely-there accent like a mother who clutched onto the back of her grown son, desperately demanding recognition despite his dreams of differentiation.

"Tell me, Siren, where did a creature like ye learn a wee bit o' Shakespeare?" His voice floated like music.

In the stillness of the Lil' Big, it vibrated off the calm waters and lonely, looming trees. The birds were silent as if they, too, were listening for the proclamations from their newfound king. I rolled his question around in my head so it could get nice and comfortable. It was a stupid question, I decided. Rude, even. I lowered my chin into the water and took a cool mouthful. With puffed cheeks, I squirted the water directly toward the strange king. He smiled as the stream hit just before the boulder, leaving my attempts to scold him for undermining my intelligence less than fruitful.

"Why wouldn't I know a little Shakespeare?" I retorted.

A bark of a laugh came from his handsome mouth. "I, dear thing, am not a naked creature in a mountain spring. Dinna try to proclaim civility or a dutiful hour o' readin' before bed now."

I scowled. "Perhaps I had thought I was privileged to privacy."

Further down the shore, I saw a black horse tied to a low tree branch. I should have heard him coming.

"'Sides, we call it the Lil' Big," I added.

"There are more o' ye?" he asked incredulously.

I avoided his gaze.

"Tell me, my fondest find. At midnight, do ye walk upon the shores like Christ, singin' with the lot o' yer horrible, wonderful sirens? Do the fish jump at the sound o' yer voice, then line up all formal and fine like royal guards? Tell me, do ye talk to the moon?" His words came out in a rush of excitement.

He wore a curious expression. It was a memorable face indeed—broad, masculine, and sharp. I was fond of the way he spoke. It was fast and lyrical, effortlessly demanding an audience. He spoke with familiarity and ease, like we had done this all before and would do it again.

I released a breathless laugh as I mulled over his whimsical inquisition. "I am not a siren."

My body was in a constant treading motion in the dark pools. A warm silence surrounded us as the summer breeze whistled through the crowded leaves of the trees.

"If ye are telling me the truth, which I highly doubt since I know to never trust a beautiful naked woman, then might I be so bold as to ask who waits for ye?"

I bit my bottom corner lip at his comment, but the second half had me lost once more. "Waits for me?" I questioned, almost to myself. I tested the odd phrase in my mouth while attempting to dissect it in my brain.

"Yes, nymph, waits for ye. Who waits now for ye to come home? Take it that ye have a home? Creatures like ye are rare. Therefore, I have great difficulty picturin' ye within clothes and four walls. But nonetheless, who does, if ye claim normalcy? A beau? A lover?" His mouth formed around the word like smoke. "An older sister, perhaps? Or a grumpy father? When the night falls, who lies awake with ye on their mind, tossin' and turnin', fightin' off the plague o' yer figure? Whose thoughts have ye poisoned by yer mere existence? Who. Waits. For. Ye?"

My eyes narrowed into slits. I had no one waiting for me. Or so it felt. Mr. Jim's name shimmered in the way back of my mind, but for unexplainable reasons, it did not rush forward. Instead, it bubbled in my throat, incapable of gaining the necessary momentum to pass over my tongue and through my lips.

"No one."

"So, ye are free?" he demanded, leaning even more forward.

"Yes." *Liar.*

"Then, perhaps, there is a God."

My face pulled together in thought at his senseless way of speaking.

"Tell me yer mortal name."

I glanced back up at him with a sly smile. "Shouldn't I be the one asking all the questions? This is *my* Lil' Big. *My* home. You're the stranger," I sighed. "Intruder, more like it."

Another broad grin spread across his face. But it was not innocent or kind like the flirtatious blush of a young man or woman. It was twisted in a way that was as beautiful as it was terrifying. "Ye should be, yer right. But yer nae. I dinna ken why that 'tis." He murmured thickly, his funny accent becoming nearly another language in the blink of an eye.

I wrinkled my nose as I attempted to translate his blurred words. It took me longer than I liked, and I shifted in my insecurity. The man had all but accused me of illiteracy, and here I appeared slow due to his funny talk.

"Speak up now, won't ya? You sound like you've got molasses in the back of your throat," I snapped.

For a moment, everything was eerily still, then the man burst out laughing. As he threw his head back and hollered for the trees and God to hear, I flushed. The sun blared down on my scalp so intensely, I was sure the top of my head was dry. Without further thought, I dipped myself below the surface of the water again. Momentary relief licked across my flesh, and I was warm from more than the sun. My thoughts were contradictory. The urge to flee, not out of fear but something stronger, pulled at me. While at the same time, a new, unfamiliar desire to bare myself to this beautifully spoken stranger shot through me. If only to have him feast upon my unknown flesh with his gaze. To show him—no, to show *someone*—what I was. Perhaps afterward I would slap him.

Under the waters ahead of me was the end of his rod with a large fish poking around it. My lungs burned, and I resurfaced, making sure to not reveal myself as indiscreetly as before, despite my foreign desires. My stranger stood, boots gone. I laughed at his tense stature upon my great boulder. His face was still slightly blocked by the large hat, but the bottom half looked relieved at my return. He discarded his boots quickly.

"Had you worried I drowned?" I giggled and pushed my long, soaked hair out of my vision and down my slick back.

He fussed about, and I raised a hand to pause him, looking in the direction of his rod. Like magic, the thin string tugged. He reached for it and claimed his prize with no struggle at all.

"Did you tell him to latch on, nymph?" he asked breathlessly and pulled his large bass into his hands. "Tell me, if I may not know your name, what of your friends who I have just caught?"

I noted his words were now more carefully, more clearly spoken. I laughed again as he effortlessly pulled the larger-than-average fish out of the water. The creature flopped around messily but shimmered like a rainbow under the bright Colorado sky.

"Tom," I murmured aimlessly as my stranger touched the flesh of the scaly friend. It was as good a name as any. Besides, I didn't know any Toms in town to mix him up with.

"Ah, Tom. Tom who? A friend of yours? Clearly, you sent him to me when you went below, yes? So, we call him Tom... Tom Beau," he said quickly and fluidly while examining the fish. He spoke like a novel and moved like the wind.

I hummed in response, looking down at the familiar water. The stranger was staring at me too intensely, a sloppy fish wiggling in his large hands. The poor, scaly thing looked awfully uncomfortable. Perhaps his hand was calloused on the inner palm like Billy's? Or were they somehow strong yet weathered like Mr. Jim's? I watched those hands bring our new fish friend up to his face.

"Mr. Beau—" he paused with his face pulling together in a frown and then glanced over at me to make sure I was listening. "May I call him Tom?"

I allowed it.

He raised his eyebrows, then returned to the fish. "Tom, I will not keep you. Despite how satisfactory I do believe you might be, I set you free. Know that I am a weary traveler who is famished beyond any man of my stature should be. It has been a long journey to this grand middle of nowhere. But that is neither here nor there. In fact, we can discuss more later. I free you because you clearly are the beau of my newfound friend. And perhaps with such a glorious act of kindness, this nymph will fall into my arms, leaving your waters evermore."

My eyes widened at his speech. *Where on earth did a man like this come from?* He was clearly mad. The stranger dramatically kissed *my* Tom Beau—lips outstretched and all. Poor Mr. Beau wriggled in what could only be described as a fish-like manner. He released the creature to the cool, wet home we currently shared. My annoyance at this flamboyantly spoken intruder was subsiding. Perhaps the day was not a total loss. Though I still ached to stretch naked across my now occupied boulder to sun dry my hair and body. I longed for my skin to tighten across my bones under the familiar beating rays and praise the sun, my coveted but phony marionettist.

"The air is thick with decision, or the impending need to make one. Is it not?" His voice pulled me back to reality.

I gave him a lazy *hmmm* in response.

"What to do next...?" He grinned like the devil himself.

I involuntarily leaned forward out of not-so-innocent curiosity. His fishing rod was on the rock, and he stood only to remove his large hat. His eyes were serious, but details such as color were lost to me at such a distance. Quickly, he shrugged through his suspenders, and his arms reached behind his body. His dark underarm sweat stains made everything feel like summer. He pulled his light gray shirt over his head, tossing the thin fabric to the boulder at his feet. My brows furrowed immediately, and I squinted as if my eyes were playing tricks on me.

On the left side of his chest, a horribly noticeable black marking lay as if it was painted on. The shape was large and unfamiliar, a perfect diamond, with lines that extended for a couple of inches unbound by their point of intersection. When I was young, Mr. Jim had told me stories of the type of folks he knew from a life before me through his trade work. He had tale after tale of adventures on the bayou and beyond. Those stories included a fair share of altercations with pirates. He explained in grotesque detail all the markings these men put on their bodies after traveling the seas. Tattoos were permanent and painful to endure as the ink was pounded into their flesh for decoration. Like a new gown on a pretty woman, only instead of wearing a frock, she had sewn it to her flesh forever. I wrinkled my nose at the smelly thought, and I tore my gaze from the dark odd mark as he spoke again.

"Mayhap, I should join ye," he smiled wickedly as both of his hands found rest upon the button of his breeches.

I met his dark eyes, unfazed. The male anatomy held no power over me, of course. *But, oh, what would Mr. Jim think if he found out?* I knew it was irrational to think he would. We were alone in a highly secluded bit of wood. But that "what if" struck cold discomfort in the pit of my gut, causing an untimely frost over the wings of the butterflies who lived there.

"There is quite a bit of impropriety to that idea."

"In accordance with whom, nymph?"

The breeze picked up again, and for a moment, filled the silence. I now felt the decision he spoke of. The temptation of whether to continue or flee was a fog washing over our small world, too sweet on my tongue like honey and sweat. I continued to observe the dark water below me. Fleeing came back to mind. But this shirtless stranger on the rock was a large man. He could catch me. Swirling thoughts that I didn't quite understand bloomed as I wondered if that would be a bad thing. Nudity was honesty. But that wasn't a popular opinion, was it? It was indecent. Maybe that was what Ms. Liz meant when she referred to that thing inside of me that took everything a bit too far. Indecency. Wild indecency. A wildness that I had no intention of controlling. A wildness that my current *family* lacked.

"To whom?" he prompted me out of my indecision.

"Society...myself...," I murmured in a bored tone. "God, probably." At the mention of God, a bellow of laughter came from his mouth.

"God, you say? He created the naked form. What right has He to then expect it to be covered?"

"Well, ain't He always watching?" I asked, honestly.

The man scoffed.

"Besides, there's something in the Bible about all that," I reminded him even though part of me couldn't help but agree with him. He flicked open the button of his breeches.

"She's read the Good Book, has she?" he muttered to himself.

I sighed at his teasing, annoyed that he still believed me illiterate, and I was unable to prove him wrong as I was naked in a mountain spring without a book or pen.

His fingers drummed along the planes of his stomach and unbuttoned breeches. My mouth dried. If his pants came off, it would take more than God to save me from whatever followed, I suspected.

"I would prefer to be alone, thank you." My tone held finality.

A smile danced across his momentarily silent mouth, and a pair of white teeth reached out to bite his bottom lip—the action of a hungry man. "And if I insist?" he probed as he released his poor, gnawed flesh.

I let out a frustrated breath. This situation was beginning to feel out of my control. A smile stayed upon that mouth of his, but his eyes narrowed. Finally, like a storm that had held out all spring, the fear came. Those shadowed eyes whispered something I did not understand. A warmth spread that made my hands shake like an avalanche was inside me. I was acutely aware of the weight of my fingernails, and I pushed further from the rock. His smile grew like a wolf's. I set my jaw tightly to hide my growing anxiety. I was ill-equipped for this circumstance, and much to my own shame, slightly ignorant. He let out another bark of laughter as he reached down and regarded his shirt. He leaned over to pick up both of his boots with a large hand and then finally looked back at me.

"I bid you, my newfound lass, farewell." He made the too-large-for-my-small-form jump from the boulder to the dry shore. He stepped out from the blockage of the boulder, placing his hat back on his loosely queued dark hair. "Be seeing you," he softly called with a last, hard look.

I stayed still, not knowing what to say or if I wished to see him again. The closest town was Wicker Soul, and I suppose he was aware of that. I panicked at the thought. His strides were long as he made his way to his tied-up horse. His movements were fluid, almost like he was in the water, not I, and before I knew it, he was off.

With his departure, the world regained some form of predictability. The breeze still blew, and the birds called out in their tongue to whichever god or feast called back. The world around me continued to spin 'round, yet there was a tilt in my vision. My lungs were tight as I silently waded in my waters. My whole body was stiff and locked up, and I wondered if I would drown in this familiar spring. I was unimaginably condensed. Not exactly unpleasant, but unfamiliar. And despite the tightness, excitement pumped through my veins. But then the water was cold. I swam carefully to the now-abandoned boulder, childishly looking both ways before hoisting my naked figure onto the rock.

The sun was heaven sent. I held my wet legs against my chest, protecting my nudity for merely a moment more, checking that the former king had indeed left. Slowly, I uncurled, stretched, and laid across the rock. I was a desperate offering to the sun. He warmed my chilled bones, and the small water droplets evaporated from my flesh—payment for such a delicacy. With my payment, that beloved sun of mine smoothed out the trouble worn on my furrowed brow. He pulled at the muscles in my face until it was continuous, even skin once more. Unbothered by man entirely. My arms raised and rested above my head as I sank into the warm, calm nothingness.

Chapter 3

ord only knows how long I dozed. But like with most unplanned slumbers, I awoke with a jolt of confusion and dizziness. My disorientation was not unlike how it felt when, as a teenager, I awoke after sneaking whiskey with Billy-boy the night before. I covered my eyes while trying to shake the sleep from my bones. It was late. Much too late to even consider slinking back into the boarding house unnoticed. Sitting up, I swung my wobbly legs over the edge of my reclaimed boulder with fuzzy vision. I leaped off the rock into the shallow waters. A sharp pain rocketed through my foot, and I immediately retracted it from the water, balancing on the other like a dancing fool. I pulled the injured foot up into my hands, staring in shock at the black feather and other unnamed bits sticking out of it.

I made quick work of yanking at the carnage, and blood trickled out of the deep but small gash in the sole of my thick, labor-roughened foot. I held the piece up to the sun and leaned my bare backside against the boulder. A damp stickiness rubbed against that bare flesh as I tried to analyze the invader of my foot. I pulled my back from the boulder in confusion.

A darker colored stained where I had leaned. I straightened my figure, and keeping my injured foot out of the water, ran my fingers over the damp spot. Red appeared on the pads of my fingertips. It was an odd contrast to my pruney fingers. And then I noticed below me in the shallow a blackbird, or what had once been one, shimmering through the reflective waters. The feathers' stark coloring was outlined by the blues and sunlit yellows that played on Lil' Big's surface. My curious face reflected over the bird.

I leaned closer to study the pitiful sight. The skull reflected horrifically, crushed under the moving waters. Mr. Jim had told me that blackbirds, ravens or crows, were clever beasts and that I ought to always watch my belongings around them for they would sweep down and snatch them faster than the devil. I wondered how a bird so intelligent could have been misled enough to fatally ram itself into my beloved boulder.

I took a deep breath and tossed the beak back into the waters, dipping my fingers in above the dead creature to wash the blood off them as well as my backside. Then I reached to cup a small amount of water in my palm and gently washed my foot. It stung for only a moment. I studied the bird, simultaneously transfixed and horrified. With the water softly stirring around me, the bird almost seemed to move. The eerie sight had me slowly wading away from it, despite my morbid curiosity.

I walked lightly, wary of my foot, from my beloved Lil' Big and journeyed through the root-infested beach. I trekked proudly, naked as birth, back to Butterbiscuit, who couldn't be bothered with my distressed attitude or limp. The cabin shrugged at me in its less-than-glorious stature. The horse groaned as I dressed in haste due to the sun's low placement in the sky. My mind raced as the bird and the man and the day I had let go to waste circled about it. Once fully clothed and properly suffocated, I untethered the patient beast.

Everything felt rough to the touch. It was odd, as I wasn't sensitive to much, other than a raised voice here and there, which really just grated my nerves more than anything. My anxious thoughts leapt while I slowly took the familiar path back into town. I had knots in my stomach but couldn't find the proper motivation to race to the *comfort* of home, late hour or not. I decided no matter what Ms. Liz hollered at me for how long I'd been gone, another quarter of an hour wouldn't make a difference.

I focused on the breeze and descending rocky lands. Butterbiscuit needed no guidance back to Wicker Soul, and the cool air cleared my mind. My head lolled back as I absorbed the last bits of sunshine the day offered me. The sound of the train brought me back with the realization we were near home. The train only made it out here Monday and Friday, once at nine in the morning, once at six in the evening. My spine straightened as I tried not to whip my head back and forth curiously for a new face in the lightly trafficked town. Perhaps he had already left. The thought sent waves of relief along with utter devastation through me. I rolled my shoulders, shrugging away the invasive curiosities I didn't have the spare time to entertain.

The grand house came into view, painted an eerie blue thanks to the nearly sunken sun. Billy's large figure stood on the porch. A low whistle came from him. I sped past toward the stables.

Billy hollered towards the house he entered, "Trixie-girl is back!"

I growled at his comment, knowing Ms. Liz was more than likely putting up a fuss. I made haste tying up Butterbiscuit, rushing before I took in a full breath. I made a beeline to the water pump and splashed my face, then rubbed water into my hands, washing off the day as quickly as my fumbling hands could manage. I scrubbed underneath my nails so that my hands looked as presentable as possible. I dried my face on the sleeves of my shirt, rounded the house, and approached the porch. I froze on the final step, my palms twitchy as I searched for some object I could use as an excuse for my tardiness. Wildflowers or fish would have been enough.

I muttered to myself in a depreciative tone at my thoughtlessness, pushed into the house, and followed prominent voices into the kitchen. My slow pace was inspired by the discomfort of Ms. Liz's impending disappointment. Still, like an old loyal mutt, my ears perked up at the recognition of one male voice echoing out of the kitchen. My eyes immediately met dull, tired blue as I entered the loud, laughing room. A smile broke its way across my lips as Mr. Jim faced me, a stubborn look on his face. I rapidly assessed the room and saw only familiar faces. Relief flooded me.

"Damnation, child, where have you been running around to?! You've got all of us waiting on ya."

I interrupted him by sprinting into his ill-prepared embrace. The abnormal day melted away as I threw myself at the man I hadn't even realized I missed. He huffed and hugged me. His scolding dissipated immediately. His hug was stiff at first but softened slowly like butter. I inhaled deeply his familiar scent of stale tobacco and dust.

"Got a thing or two for ya." His odd southern accent vibrated warmth. "Though now I don't feel like you deserve it. Dammit, girl! I went looking for 'bout an hour. You wasted my time this afternoon."

Mr. Jim had a rough way of speaking, and words took time coming out of his mouth, even when he was angry and hollering. He had spent most of his life in New Orleans, where he says it's so hot you can fry an egg on your skin. Suppose I was from there, though I couldn't remember it for the life of me.

I pulled away and smiled. "I was gone for a day and you weren't expected till Monday. What *are* you doing back early? Why didn't you send for me?"

I stepped away from him and placed my hands on my hips, my lips dry from my retort. His eyes turned into shadows as if he was trying to work up a good glare. My frustration from earlier resurfaced. He chuckled, but it was forced. He ran a weathered hand over his matching weathered face. I had rudely yet to acknowledge anyone else in the room but decided they could wait.

"Quit bossing me about," Mr. Jim snapped at me with a comical sneer.

Behind him, on the island, sat a parcel tied together with brown string. Dev and Billy stood on the other side of the island. I quickly assessed their positioning, wondering if Billy had furthered his proposal. Their casual stance answered my question. His arms were folded across his broad chest, and she stood tall, her delicate hands folded politely on the countertop. Her pale, undecorated left finger burned my eyes.

My brows furrowed deeper at Mr. Jim's lack of response. He touched the parcels. On the bottom, it looked like some form of fabric. The print was deep brown, black, cream, and red, designed in a vivacious pattern including fringe at the corners. It was soft and thick to the touch as I picked it up. Tied securely on top was a blue, clothbound book. The golden title sparkled under the fading light.

A grin pulled at my cheekbones. I met Mr. Jim's eyes. "Thank you, Mr. Jim," I murmured.

"Got that blanket there at a trading post just outside o' Denver. It should be good and warm for ya when winter comes 'round. Thought you'd like it, too," he replied in a rough, oddly clipped tone. His gaze flickered back and forth between the gifts and my face enough times to make me feel much too aware of myself. For a brief moment, his gaze felt analytical, as if I were that jigsaw puzzle he couldn't quite get. It wasn't uncommon for Mr. Jim to stare too long at my countenance, quietly picking out the parts of me that reminded him of my dearly departed momma and disregarding the miscellaneous remainder. But I couldn't help but shiver in silent contemplation as to which gift was reminding him of my father—the adventure novel or the brightly colored blanket.

"Book's good." He finished with a set in his jaw.

I nodded at his rationale for giving me gifts, repeated my thanks, then turned on my heel.

"Trixie-girl, where ya off to now?" Billy hollered impatiently.

"To put this all up in my room. I'll not have the likes of you spilling whatever's for dinner on it," I replied, rounding the corner and up the stairs.

"Well, hurry up, now. Supper's already been announced. Folks are waiting," Mr. Jim called.

I waved my arm so that he knew I heard him, whether he was watching or not, before letting out a final sigh of relief.

Once alone, I rubbed my hand over the blanket and book, held them to my face, and sniffed. They smelled musty, but other than that, nothing familiar about them stood out. I pushed the lost, confusing disappointment that perhaps matched the odd look in Mr. Jim's eyes out of my mind and opened my door. I quickly set the items on my small table and rushed out of the room.

As I re-entered the kitchen, Ms. Liz did the same from the grand dining room. She gave me a very pointed look. "Well, there you are. Funny, you come right in time, now, don't ya? You know I can't expect Miss Dev to set the table and clean up when she's been working hard with me all day on this meal. Really, Trixie-girl," Ms. Liz said sassily.

"I just got back. I'll handle the dishes this evening," I replied quickly.

She *hmph*ed in response, and I inspected my nails as if I had dirt on them, even though I knew I did not. She stopped her movements and observed me with her hands on her hips, clearly waiting. I said nothing.

"Well? Where were you, girl? It's late. I 'bout sent Billy searching for ya!"

I responded with a halfhearted smile and a muttered apology.

When I finally straightened to meet her eye, hers widened a bit. "Heavens, you're a sight. Hadn't you tied your hair back 'fore you left?"

I reached up and was surprised by a mess of locks. I squeezed the hair by my scalp out of frustration, closed my eyes, and let out a soft, "Damnation."

I had been wearing my best silk ribbon. Ms. Liz let out a cluck of disapproval at my swearing and drab appearance but said nothing more. Dev rushed over and made work of me. She hummed as she bound my hair into a loose braid, giving my shoulders a squeeze.

I scowled at her over my shoulder, "Couldn't you have given me a warning?"

She shrugged. She was close enough that I felt her shoulders move behind me.

"You've come back looking much worse. I suppose we didn't notice," she teased sweetly.

I jabbed her lightly with my elbow, and she giggled.

"Well, go on! Get in the dining hall, the food'll get cold, and folks are waiting," Ms. Liz ordered as she left the kitchen.

Billy bumped his shoulder with mine, sending me a goofy wide-eyed grin, and offered his elbow to Dev, leading the way. Mr. Jim offered me his arm, and I automatically gripped the nook of his elbow.

"What's going on with you, girl?" Mr. Jim's breath was close to my ear. The sheer irony I found in that comment had me shooting him a glare equal to his own.

"Me?"

"Yes, you. You're acting suspect."

I let out an unladylike snort. "I thought I always did."

"Now, I'm serious girl, what wer—"

"What are you two whispering so fiercely about?" Ms. Liz interrupted.

My eyes flashed to hers. She wore a confused and worried look. Her eyes flickered to Mr. Jim as if she could, with him, create some sort of parental council for my obvious distress. But Mr. Jim paid her no mind. Instead, his gaze stuck to me like the oil on my skin. I fidgeted and shifted my gaze around again. My stomach was tight without reason, and my bones ached like a storm was on its way. Ms. Liz reached out to touch me in concern, and I flinched away.

"What? Oh, uhm...nothing," I muttered to no one and broke from Mr. Jim to take my seat next to Billy near the end of the table, away from those I didn't know. Though I made sure to nod at the elderly fellow I had seen last night sitting on the porch. He touched the brim of his hat in response.

The table felt sparse despite the three travelers with us that evening. Ms. Liz sat at her rightful spot at the head of the table. Dev sat next to Billy, and Mr. Jim, not wanting to let my agitated mood go, sat close by me. I leaned an impolite elbow on the table—a certain amount of exhaustion tickled at my nose and my toes. In my seat, I finally sank back into the softness of my body.

Ms. Liz cleared her throat, gathering everyone's attention. "Let us pray," she murmured, ducking her head automatically.

I glanced over at Mr. Jim, who bowed his head and offered his hands lightly on both sides. I knew not to take that hand. A hug was enough affection for Mr. Jim to last at least a month. I leaned both my elbows on the table. With almost all the company's heads now bowed and eyes closed, I rested my forehead against my thumbs.

"Bless us, oh Lord..."

The sound of quick, heavy footsteps, as well as a chair scraping, stopped her. I heard a light reaction around the table to the new guest, followed by Ms. Liz's stern but polite words. "We've just started grace."

"I apologize. Please don't stop on my behalf," said a deep voice.

I heard a smile in the voice, and it was suspiciously smooth. Ice shot through my heart, and my gut plummeted. "Well, it's a little late for that, isn't it," I mumbled around gritted teeth, reluctantly lifting my head because I wouldn't be a coward at my own dinner table. I slowly opened my eyes to face our tardy guest before closing them immediately.

Mr. Jim nudged me and whispered, "be polite."

I opened one eye, and everything felt very far away, as my gaze met the most curious shade. Dark gray. Much like how a summer storm rolled in and taunted a well-planned picnic. A smile as slow as molasses spread across the sharp face of our new tenant.

The rock king had joined us for dinner.

Chapter 4

Grace continued around me like the mundane buzzing of a beetle as I held the gaze of the rock king. Shallow, quiet breath rang impossibly loud in my ears. Warm anger formed in my chest as he inspected my person. He glanced at Mr. Jim, who sat quite close to me, and then back to me and cocked his eyebrow.

"Amen," the room echoed with finality.

My lips numbly moved around the word. A light chatter ensued, and I stayed transfixed on the rock king. Stillness was a guise, a survival skill. My mind frantically spun to create an excuse for my behavior from this afternoon as I waited to see the character of this man. Would he speak up about it? Surely not, for it was just as severely scandalous for him to have stayed and spoken to a naked woman as it was to *be* said naked woman. He was at fault, was he not? Hadn't I, to a certain extent, been taken advantage of? I was an innocent young woman, minding my own. I inwardly winced because that was not true. I was no innocent thing. I was the wicked thing of Wicker Soul. And therefore I would be at fault.

Mr. Jim was going to slaughter me.

"Please forgive my interruption. I must have dozed off in my room after such a long day." He directed his words at Ms. Liz, though his eyes stayed locked with mine.

She responded with a cute *psh* and a flick of her plump wrist.

"And forgive me for not making an introduction prior. The day got away from me, you could say." Mr. Jim quickly glanced in my direction and continued roughly, "This here is Mr. Jayson Wallace. He has come to work with me."

My jaw audibly snapped tight with a low click. Mr. Jim's words replayed like a wobbly wagon wheel, bouncing off the hollow walls of my heart. The casualness of his statement stung. I was mildly aware of the chorus of polite acknowledgments. One by one, my family joyously responded with their own introductions. I watched his eyes meet theirs with eager interest and then return to mine with each new name learned. I looked away from his childish mockery, noting the left-hand corner of the room that flickered with the combination of candlelight and the almost entirely sunken sunlight. Shadows danced, begging me to join their slow sway, and the vapid words became a breeze on a chilly evening.

I felt the pressure of a separate gaze intensify. Mr. Jim's eyes darted from me to Mr. Wallace and then back again before he gestured with his chin to Mr. Wallace. Mr. Wallace expectantly regarded me. I cocked my eyebrow with a dismissive attitude. I reached for the cornbread in front of me, grabbing two servings as I was suddenly starving. Mr. Jim *hmph*ed at my gluttony, and I passed the bread to him before he complained. I spread the butter over my still-warm bread. Mr. Wallace took note of each action, every bend of the elbow and shuffle in my seat. I turned to Ms. Liz and gave her an appreciative smile, or the best I could muster, for making cornbread. She knew it was a favorite of mine. She smiled back, lovingly. A rough clear of the throat next to me had me shrinking.

"And this here, surly thing, is our Trixie-girl. Trixie Chanteloup," Mr. Jim announced as I continued to eat.

My eyes found Mr. Wallace as he made an approving *ah* in response.

"Charmed," I mumbled moodily around a large amount of cornbread. I lifted a corner of my mouth in a halfhearted grimace.

"The pleasure, truly, is all mine. Trixie...Girl, was it?" His smile made mine slide off my face.

I eyed my water glass, wondering how much damage it would do to his smile with a harsh throw. I didn't like how the childish name of endearment used by the entirety of my makeshift family sounded in his mouth. The word *girl* had that slight accent and came off more like "gehl." Oddly, his accent was much less apparent than during our previous encounter. Though it still danced in the shadows of his conversation, he held it back intentionally. Curious.

"Just Trixie," I corrected before a painful swallow of thick cornbread. A discomfort caused once again by me surrounded the table, reaching even the strangers at the end. However, no such discomfort could outlast the presence of the mighty Ms. Liz.

"So, Mr. Wallace, tell us more about yourself. We are so happy to have you in Wicker Soul; I hope you do know. And excited! Why, Mr. Jim has never brought someone into town for business. Feels like a successful sign, though I wouldn't know entirely, I suppose. Do tell us how long you'll be here?" She conversed pleasantly, leaning one elbow on the clothed grand table impolitely.

Mr. Wallace wiped his mouth from the bite he must have just taken. "Thank you, ma'am, but please call me Jayson." She nodded at that. "As for how long I'll be around here, well, I guess it'll be indefinitely."

I heaped food onto my plate.

"And have you any family waiting for you? Perhaps a bride you'll send for once you're settled?" Ms. Liz probed between bites of stew.

The man put down his silverware and leaned his elbows on the table, resting his chin where his hands met and folded. I chilled at her chosen words.

"I'm afraid even if I had much of a family, they're long gone by now. I've been on my own since before I can remember," he answered cheerfully.

I shoveled food into my mouth, trying to look like the conversation fell on deaf ears.

"No family? My, oh, me. But you can't be much older than my boy, Billy, here," Ms. Liz gestured to Billy, who had stew dripping down the corner of his mouth.

Mr. Jayson Wallace grinned in response. Billy swallowed at the mention of his name, wiping his messy mouth with the back of his large paw.

"Huh. Well, that's too bad, but welcome. We got plenty of wanderers coming and going, plus there's Trixie-girl, so you'll fit right in!" Billy welcomed with a friendly grin.

I elbowed him in the side for the mere mention of my name and muttered, "Hush."

Dev quietly scolded him with the volume of a mouse. The mouse might have been a bit more robust. Billy looked back down at his food like a confused child in trouble.

"Oh?" he piped up in interest. "Trixie is not of relation?"

My skin was warm under the inappropriate amount of attention. I tried to tuck in my food, but anything other than cornbread tasted like sawdust. Mr. Jim looked at the man with a bored yet annoyed stare, something that I had grown accustomed to in my life. For a moment, I considered feeling sorry for the fellow. He grinned knowingly at Mr. Jim, then me, then his plate of food.

"Oh, heavens, no, Trixie-girl is not of kin. Our Mr. Jim brought her and himself here a little over eighteen years ago from New Orleans," Ms. Liz began. "My, she was such a funny little sight! I still remember big gruff Mr. Jim walking into our home with this wild running little girl dressed up as a boy. 'Course most people probably couldn't tell her sex, but I saw right through Mr. Jim's disguise he had her in."

My eyes widened in disbelief at how large Ms. Liz's mouth had become in such a short period.

"I reckon no one pays much mind to an older man traveling 'cross country with a young boy. But when you got a little girl with ya, not to mention one rambunctious as Trixie-girl, you'd find yourself dealing with an opinion. Might as well have called the mercenaries to get that child from me. 'Sides, the girl was too wild for dresses, what with the way she ran about. Lil' pair of britches fit her behavior better," Mr. Jim explained.

Mr. Wallace nodded in full understanding. But I couldn't help but note the wrinkle in his brow. I looked up to the ceiling, praying that perhaps the floor would open and swallow me whole. God was punishing me for not helping around the house today. I was sure of it. Or for running about naked. Probably a bit of both.

"So's," Ms. Liz continued to my astonishment, "I weaseled my way into knowing what kinda man Mr. Jim was, and what kinda business he was pursuing. My, oh, my, did it take a long time to get him to even talk to me. Surly is as surly does, I'm sure you know. He finally tells me that he is a man of all sorts and that he is taking the girl with him as far as California! Just stopping here in Wicker Soul on account of the child growing restless with the journeying and such. I tells him he hasn't got any further to go. The saloon was for sale, and with the war just ending, it ought to be bringing in plenty soon enough. The rest, I have to say, is history. Well, that, and I also got my way into having the child raised here at the house. Told Mr. Jim I didn't care where she came from. A child like that needs some mothering."

I met Ms. Liz's tender eyes intending to glare so she would keep that mouth of hers shut until Judgment Day. But the gentle look on her face and everything she said was all in honor of me. So, I swallowed my pride, not the cornbread. Ms. Liz had a low, enunciated speaking tone that gave every word more syllables, sounding a bit like comfort and a lot like prayer. She was from somewhere in the South, further east than Mr. Jim and me, but had spent all of Billy's and half of her own life here in the foothills.

"Yes, of course," Mr. Wallace acknowledged.

His blatant stare continued, and I focused on anything else with a certain sort of hyperactivity that had my hands shaking.

Mr. Wallace shifted attention to the innocent Mr. Jim. "You *brought* her, you say? Might I ask as to how you came to *have* her if there is no relation?"

"That's enough about me, thank you," I interjected sharply, wiping the back of my hand across my mouth for crumbs.

I grabbed my small glass filled with water and downed it with the same passion I had the cornbread. I reached for Mr. Jim's once mine was empty and poured his water into mine. He reached into his inner coat pocket, producing a silver flask. He filled the now empty cup with whiskey. Mr. Wallace watched our interaction with amusement and suspicion.

"What about yourself, Jayme? Jordan, was it?" I leaned back in my chair and sloshed the water around in a circular motion, childishly hoping for him to be as irritated as me.

"Jayson, actually, Jayson Wallace," he replied with a smooth smile.

Clearly, he was happy to have my attention. *How could the smile have been alluring only a handful of hours ago?* Now his teeth looked menacing, like a wolf. Perhaps *he* killed that crow with those wolf teeth. At the very least, he might have shown those pearly whites and tempted the bird into a fit of suicidal blindness. Poor thing probably didn't stand a chance.

"Oh my, that feels much too intimate upon a first introduction, if you were to ask me. We'll go with Wallace for now," I mused after a beat.

His eyes gleamed.

"Where ya from, Mr. Wallace?" inquired Billy.

"New York, as of recently."

"They all talk like you in New York?" Billy asked. He was referencing the way Mr. Wallace spoke around his *r*'s and his vowels.

"For the most part. Though more than likely, the 'talk' I've got is from further east than New York."

I inspected my glass, thinking about *r*'s and *e*'s and *i*'s and *o*'s.

"And where, might I ask, were you before New York, Mr. Wallace?" Ms. Liz prompted.

"Heaps of places, ma'am. I've been on my own travels for a while. And again, please call me Jayson."

"And you've really got no one? Not even further east?" Ms. Liz continued.

Mr. Wallace gave a thoughtful chew to his food before glancing back at Ms. Liz. "To be completely honest with you, ma'am, I've been without them longer than with." His repeated proclamation of solitude finally seemed to sink in.

"Is that so?" Ms. Liz pondered with a sort of forced laugh. "How old are you, Mr. Wallace, if I may?"

I leaned forward, resting my elbow on the table impolitely and ate as if I could not be bothered despite the sharpness of my ears.

"I've known Mr. Wallace now for most of his life here in the States," Mr. Jim interjected in defense of the man on trial. "I've been needing help with the store as well as the saloon for quite some time. He will be stepping in the running of the general, while I focus on other ventures."

Mr. Jim took a long drink of whiskey as if it were a universal handshake to the whole of the table. Wallace broke his gaze from me with new interest in the drink as he nodded at Mr. Jim. Wallace's notion was wordlessly acknowledged as Mr. Jim reached back into his breast pocket to retrieve whatever was left of his flask. As if he were a young man once more, Mr. Jim tossed the flask across the table into Mr. Wallace's coordinated hands. He sent a friendly wink to Mr. Jim and helped himself.

Bile filled my throat at the garish show of male bonding. The obvious inferiority of my existence pounded in my head. *How foolish was it to think that perhaps I could achieve more than what my reproductive organs claimed I could?* With the toss of that damned flask, I envisioned my own chance of a future, one that didn't include this godforsaken town, being tossed away all the same. Because Mr. Jim had yet to discuss any "other ventures" with the likes of me.

The room was too small. My skin felt like it was stretching toward the walls behind me, blending and bleeding into the background. The threat of the noose couldn't get me to eat my now cool food. My hands tingled and ached as I clenched them to keep a consistent blood flow. I wanted to leave. I was too warm. My neck was itchy and damp, and the moment I scratched at it, a rash would bloom. That rash would be evidence that I was not only up to no good but that my no good had become bad enough my own body was rebelling against me. I would then be expected to explain myself, and I never did like any of that nonsense.

"Trixie-girl, why you staring at your food like that? Are ya sick?" Billy asked through packed cheeks. He was going to get his ears boxed if he made one more comment. I shifted my eyes to Ms. Liz, seeing the small hurt at my apparent distaste of her cooking.

"I'm not partial to it today," I answered honestly, looking at the mess I'd made.

"Perhaps the girl is partial to something else?" suggested our new guest. He was proving to be a nosey bit. "Perhaps fish?"

Was this it? Would he truly wait through that ordeal of a dinner-side conversation only to damn me now? A rush of air flew out of my nostrils. Caution was just about to the wind.

"What an odd thing to say," Ms. Liz noted.

Mr. Jim's shrewd glare, now very much directed at me, made my skin blister. My mind went blank besides the drumming within me that chanted *gotta get away, gotta get away, gotta get away.*

"Why, we rarely have fish in this household. Almost never, unless someone brings a catch back from the spring a couple miles north of here. The girl and my Billy used to run wild up there! Called it the Lil' Big, they did. Supposing, we all still do. Say, Trixie was there today, if I am not mistaken," Ms. Liz prattled on.

The next thing I knew, my chair came out from beneath my rear, and I stood. No one moved, and I grabbed my place settings, exited the room, and then the house.

Chapter 5

The summer air was cool against my agitated flesh. I made my way to the porch railing and caught it, nearly hauling my entire frame over the edge. I dangled like that, wood pressing harshly into my stomach for a couple minutes. My head swirled from the positioning, and I was swimming. I straightened myself and replaced my stomach with my elbows.

I was surrounded by a peaceful night with a full moon on display, much like a spotlight. Wicker Soul was Her main attraction. She painted the town an odd gray, making it look celestial in its sad lack of color. The slow bustle of human noise around me was almost overpowered by the sound of the lazy breeze. I breathed deeply through my nose, getting a small sense of relief just as the scent of burning tobacco hit my nose. I sighed.

Mr. Jim's steps were too soft for a man of his stature and age, so I barely heard him walk up behind me. He leaned against the railing to my left and regarded the sky with me. "Mind telling me what's going on in that head of yours?" His words formed around a cigarette. He took a long drag. When he exhaled, the smoke matched the tired gray of the dirt road in front of us. That road led south and eventually to the train tracks. It was the most direct route out of Wicker Soul, and it looked damn fine to me, dry and lonely or not. He passed the cigarette to me. I gladly accepted as he put another between his lips and struck a match.

I took an equally long drag, allowing the sweet smoke to spread all the way down into my lungs. The familiar heat slid into my chest and traveled to the souls of my feet. I let it out slowly through my nose and felt a touch more grounded. We stood in silence as I attempted to put together what I wanted to say. Mr. Jim gave me time. My attention flickered back to the moon we both faced. She was glorious with Her broad, understanding expression. When She was full and round, I stood on the verge of confessing all the wrong I had done and all the wrong I planned to do.

"Do you think Mary lives on the moon?" I asked abruptly, as I slowly exhaled a graceful plume of gray smoke.

"Well, I reckon that depends."

"On?"

The air shifted a bit as if we caught Her attention.

"On which Mary you are referring to, of course."

My eyebrows shot up in intrigue as I assessed the moon. *That was a great question, wasn't it?* I contemplated whether the moon was pureness or redemption. Mr. Jim smoothly elbowed me.

"What's really on your mind, girl?" he prodded gently.

I blinked myself back into reality and fought a grimace. "I suppose I'm trying to figure out what's going on in yours," I finally stated, taking another drag. Technically, I was not lying.

Mr. Jim changed his stance, turning so his back was now against the railing and Mary Moon. He folded his arms and looked up at the wooden ceiling of the porch, puffing on his cigarette. I kept contemplating Mary, keeping a respectful quiet. I knew good and well folks weren't supposed to chatter in Mass too loud. I believed that being in the presence of Mary (it didn't matter which) was just as hallowed as the mundane scripture spewing endured every Sunday, and I wasn't ashamed in the slightest.

"You're referring to my bringing in Mr. Wallace?" he drawled.

I gritted my teeth to force myself into a patient response like he taught me. I unclenched my jaw to take another long and slow drag, refocusing my gaze on Mary. "What do you need someone new for?" I asked coldly.

The porch roof was weighted down with the thousands of words that couldn't be formulated that I thought it could squash us like bugs. Mr. Jim said nothing as if he thought the crickets or the breeze could speak for him. They did not come to his aid.

"Like I said at the table. Help."

I brewed silently. Uncertainty was a bitter taste in my mouth. "You can't handle the work?"

He rolled his eyes. "It's not a matter of what I can or cannot do."

"What is it a matter of?"

"What I want to do."

"You don't want to be here?"

"Not particularly, no."

My stomach sunk. Mr. Jim would go. *Why wouldn't he? What did he have here that he couldn't recreate somewhere else? Somewhere better. He would go, and I would be here.* Thankfully, fury masked my heartbreak. "So that's it, huh? You bring back someone new and train him, then hightail it out of here? Leave us with only the dust your heels kicked up?" I hissed wildly.

He just listened, and the disinterest in his vacant eyes nearly destroyed me.

Was I such a fool to have believed he wouldn't leave? Or, at the very least, allowed me the dignity to leave first?

I whirled around to face him. Mary Moon, be damned. My temper rose due to the innocent attitude he dared to take. I stood as tall as possible and jabbed my pointer finger into his chest. "Well, then what's the timeline we're working with, hm? Hell, will you even last the weekend? It won't take long for our Mr. Wallace to pick up where you'll leave off.

Say, I'll pack your bags for ya. Anything sounds better than watching you play fucking patty-cake with your good ol' boy like I'm just a part of this goddamn, godforsaken scenery you've grown so tired of." I jabbed his chest harshly with each profanity.

My poking hand was snatched and squeezed so tightly the knuckles felt like they were grinding on each other. Mr. Jim stepped closer to me, his eerie pale eyes shining with annoyance and frustration.

"Bite that tongue!" he snarled.

I tried not to flinch. I didn't shy away from much in life, but when it came to fights with Mr. Jim, the bickering was short and usually left me cowering. I clenched my jaw until the muscles in my face bulged. He raised my hand up to the level of his face, stretching me to an uncomfortable stance that straightened my entire arm. His grip slid from my palm to my wrist, and he squeezed so tightly that my fingertips tingled and pulsed. The look in his eye sent me back to my childhood and despite my pride, scared me to my core. We stood like that for a long moment, breathing in the other's exhalations. The pain in my wrist added fuel to my fire, helping my frustration burn and crackle tempestuously. His gaze was sharp and unflattering as I hoped mine was in return.

"Where is all this coming from? It ain't like you to be so sensitive," Mr. Jim whispered.

I huffed through my nose like a bull.

A cough coming from the door interrupted us, though Mr. Jim still held onto my wrist. The noise surprised me enough that I dropped my cigarette. Mr. Wallace leaned against the side of the home, all cavalier in his stance, and through the darkness, I thought I watched his attention follow what I had lost. The man would have been invisible if it weren't for the fading light from the window next to him. A candle flickered deep within the home.

"I hope this quarrel hasn't got anything to do with my arrival."

Automatically, I opened my mouth to respond, but Mr. Jim's grip tightened on my wrist. I hid my wince with a pleasant smile.

"No, sir," Mr. Jim muttered.

I refused to look away from Mr. Jim, despite the pressure of an unrequested audience. I had never heard Mr. Jim refer to someone as a "sir" and for some reason that realization itched at me. Our position was not exactly flattering. I'm sure it looked as if I held something in my hand that Mr. Jim had not permitted me to grasp and that he was squeezing my wrist until I gave it back.

Mr. Wallace took a very long, deep breath, and the sound held judgment, layered in his attitude as buttercream in a cake. "Glad to hear it. I'll be saying goodnight then."

He looked at me with inexplicable emotion. He touched the brim of his hat with his fingers, glanced at my hand still much higher than my head, and retreated inside. With the door shut, Mr. Jim finally released my hand, tossing it back to me with disgust, as if it wasn't only a moment before his lifeline. His decision to hold my wrist in front of Mr. Wallace, to prove a point to us, made me feel cheap. I fought the impulse to grip my aching wrist, to massage blood flow back into it, and averted my eyes.

"Have I truly spoiled you so?" he finally questioned. His angry spittle lightly sprayed my face.

I didn't flinch.

"Have I led you to believe that you are the sun, and it is us, the measly nothings which circulate around you and all your glory?"

I ground my teeth.

"I have been stuck in this goddamn town years longer than I planned. Hell, this country," he said slowly. "If I was going to abandon or jade you, don't you think I would have done it by now? I gave my word to your momma, and as far as you know, my word is law."

His words softened whatever had chilled and hardened within me.

"I ain't spending the rest of my life here, and I am doubting you will either. Now you listen to me, and you listen good. Your Billy-boy is gonna be asking for Miss Dev's hand any time now. They'll be married 'fore the winter hits, hear you me. And she'll be expecting, if she ain't already. Once that baby is born, ain't nobody gonna have the time for the likes of you, including Ms. Liz. It'll be the perfect time."

"For what?"

"Blasted! To get you out of here. You and me both. I promised your momma you'd be taken care of, and this town ain't enough. She wanted more for ya, and so do I." His words softened. He leaned against the railing in a more relaxed position, his arms now folded over his chest. I mimicked his position. "We'll go to San Francisco, and then turn right around and head east. Head east, and don't stop. Cross the water and get you straight to Paris, France. We could get you a proper education there. Make a real lady out of ya. My French is a little rusty, but it'll do. We could get you speaking like a queenie, just like your momma, in a year, I reckon. We could get you out, Trixie."

I smiled at the contagious hope in his words. But something tugged at my heartstrings at his casual mention of my late momma. "And Mr. Wallace?"

"I can give my business to him." My eyes widened slightly. "The man's a loose cannon. He'll be needing some quiet life in him 'fore he goes and catches another city on fire."

My eyebrows raised at this information about his seemingly prodigal son.

"If you're concerned about the cost"—I wasn't—"I've got more money than God. These bits here in Wicker Soul ain't gonna change that."

I nodded and once again allowed the blanket of quiet night to wrap itself around me. I let the embarrassment of my initial reaction out with a large huff. This was it. The words coming out of Mr. Jim's lips were all I had ever wanted, and I allowed them to sink in. He stood so sturdy in my presence, handing me everything I had ached for. Dressed and trimmed on a silver platter. And yet with his kind, blunt, rough words—so like him—a hollow aching crept into my stomach. Chilling those butterflies I held so dearly. I took in the length of the dirt road, and despite the dark, it looked like it could go on for the rest of forever. Mr. Jim would be by my side for my entire life. My own bitter self-hatred grew, knowing despite all he had done for me, that was not what I had wanted. *Had I not been devastated only moments before at the thought of him leaving me?* I fought the urge to spit, and I reached out to gently place my hand on his arm, the only gesture I thought would express the gratitude I owed him.

A quick grin spread across his weathered mouth. "It's getting late." I pulled my arm back, glancing at the Mary Moon shining high.

Amen.

"Best you go on inside and see if Ms. Liz left you the dishes."

I nodded and turned to head back inside, stepping on the surviving embers of the cigarette Mr. Jim had rolled for me. I stopped as my hand rested on the wood of the cool front door. My fingers still fit into some of the grooves, despite my age. "I understand now, Mr. Jim. But you of all people know to be wary of a mouth as smart as your dear Mr. Wallace's."

"Pay you no mind to him, Trixie-girl. And I mean that. He is here to work alongside myself, nothing more. Be ready for stocking and inventory at eight."

I entered the house without a second glance. Though what he promised had not been precisely what I longed for, I tucked a small blossom of hope deep within my heart. And silently begged that God would do good on it.

Indeed, the dishes were left for me, along with a lone candle to aid me up the stairs. I made haste of the sloppy mess, my supposedly well-deserved punishment. By the time the great-grandfather clock struck ten, I was finished.

The stairs creaked on my way, as I was too tired to walk gently. The pressure of the day was like a devil crouching on my shoulders. On the top floor, there was a small gleam of light coming from a cracked door, newly occupied, just to the left of my room. I walked slower and attempted to silence my movements, more so than when I feared the disturbance of those sleeping. The door was cracked open, wide enough to fit my face. The room appeared entirely moved into. On the desk were piles of books and papers in a certain disarray that feigned years of occupation, not hours. Multiple candles burned and an oil lamp shone, as if the resident paid no mind to the night. As I pushed my face in the crack just a fraction more, I was hit with the scent of lavender along with something almost like pepper. It was enticing, and I fought the urge to give a large, unladylike, and damning inhale.

A closer view found the naked back of a man, bent over a basin filled with water underneath a hung mirror. I heard the sloshes and breathing of the creature who inhabited the room. Suddenly, the head swung back, and dark, damp hair followed in a fluid motion. The small, rapid movements across the flesh of his back contracted and released with vitality. His muscles and skin moved together in a dance, like an over-excited creek after a May storm. Each movement and flex of his body held a specific, remarkable intention despite the unhurried nature that leaked from his long fingers. God did not control this man. And my, did it show.

The naked intimacy of his movements represented concrete livelihood, as opposed to a stuffy glimpse of it. Life, finally, *life* bloomed amongst the weary, dusty earth that surrounded this town. Fractious life that, for a moment, seemed to match the heinous wicked lurking deep within me. *If we were made in His likeness, what then explained the phenomenon of when likeness called to itself, within someone else?* I was paralyzed by these thoughts as small droplets ran down his planes.

"You're a liar. But you already know that." The statement came from the mesmerizing Mr. Wallace, as he faced the door to find my head invading his quarters.

I jumped a little at his statement. His eyes were not kind, despite the playful disregard in his tone. Maybe they never were. Once again, I did not run from him. I would not be the child with her hand caught in the cookie jar. Instead, I leaned entirely into the doorway, pushing it further open with my foot. My hip rested against the frame, and my arms crossed my chest defensively. He raised an eyebrow at me as he walked closer to the door.

The marking upon his left chest shone starkly as it was no longer evaded by bright, blinding sunlight. It was pitch black and thick but perfectly symmetrical, as if it came from a well-crafted branding iron. It reminded me of the patterns on the blanket that Mr. Jim had recently bestowed on me. The lines were basic and sharp, yet there was something very old about it. And despite their cut, the acute angles that made up this horrible marring of the flesh, the blackness rippled as if it were one with its backdrop. A harsh contrast, it seemed, to be upon something as languid and soft as flesh. It matched the dark hair smattered around his chest in what I assumed to be a usual masculine way. I had never seen the bare chest of a man with dark hair. I told myself the image's novelty was why I found it so fascinating and nothing more. He was close enough to touch, half nude with firelight dancing over him in all his glory, and my eyebrows furrowed at his proximity. He innocently reached for his shirt, which rested on the dresser by the doorway I occupied. I relaxed until he proceeded to not, in fact, put the shirt on, but instead crumpled it in his fist.

I cleared my voice. "A liar?" It was raspy but did not quiver.

He placed his large palms on the edge of the dresser, leaning a little forward but still looking sideways at me. He was much larger than me. He couldn't be but an inch smaller than the bear Billy had grown into.

He looked down at me with an unfamiliar expression. "I asked you very clearly who waits for you. And you lied."

My mouth opened at his accusation, and a little laugh came out. "I stand by my answer. 'Sides, I'm not sure if you can start pointing fingers after the... mess of today."

"Ah, but I can!" he sang. "You asked nothing of my comings, or my goings, or my pastings. And equally revealed none of your own. I had no way of knowing that you were Mr. Jim's *infamously* innocent stowed away creature. Therefore, I will not allow myself to be condescended into the wrong for not answering questions I was not asked. But you, oh, you, my dearest little devil, you lied through your teeth. Naked as birth all the while."

A flush crept over me, but I did not flinch.

Though his tone was light and sounded like music, a lingering, altogether ugly emotion hid behind it. I didn't recognize it, and I thought myself quite familiar with all things ugly. *Was I ignorant of other sets of emotions?* None of his were predictable nor recognizable. I could not categorize them into an easily accessible box in the back of my mind, should we converse again. I didn't like that. I had spent most of my life absorbing others' intricacies and comparing their emotions and dreams and motives to my own. One might assume I was a good listener, but that wasn't true at all. I was a horrible listener. Manipulator was more like it. I turned surrounding folks into large walls I hid behind through falsified interests. Raise others up, so I might sneak away through the trenches we had all started in. That would be difficult with Mr. Wallace. I couldn't catalog what he was about to do. Nor did I seem to even comprehend what he was talking about.

I set my jaw before responding. "You asked..."

"I asked who waits for you. Do not tell me that our dear friend Jim isn't lying awake at this most pristine moment, tormented by the thought of you. You, his stolen nymph of this dusty town. You, his original sin who stands naked on the rocks and shouts to the sun gods or her people before her. Perhaps even calls to the spirit of the land, those forgotten Titans to whom she truly belongs. You run to them unknowingly as a grown child. Such a selfish little thing, you are," he tsked lightly. "That man lies and waits for you so patiently while you dance naked under the sun. Don't you tell me he does not, and even more, don't tell that to yourself. You're smarter than that. And if somehow you aren't honey, you better get learnt on being so."

The last sentence was said in a mocking drawl, eerily like Mr. Jim. The combination of that and his words nearly knocked the wind out of me. Without thinking, my arms unfolded, and my right hand swung. I think it was the *selfish* that set me off the most. Because it was true. He caught my open palm just before it contacted his flesh. I immediately flinched as his fingers wrapped around the tender wrist that Mr. Jim had squeezed too tightly only hours before. His grip slid down, away from the bruising, and he pulled my hand to his mouth. His eyes softened but still clung to a glimmer of indescribable darkness. I yanked at my wrist, but he only tightened his grip. He gently kissed my hand, keeping my eye. My brows furrowed in confusion.

"This is the mark of a man who waits for you," he whispered against my wrist.

I gnawed at my bottom lip as his lips pressed small touches all around my hand, which involuntarily clenched into a fist. His slid gently up to my palm. He spread out my fist and then took each finger into his mouth. Biting each pad lightly, making another type of mark on me comparative to the one left from Mr. Jim's temper. I jerked my hand free and cradled my wrist against my breast as if his touch burned more than any bruising. I glared up at Wallace, but he looked bored and a little hungry.

"But you do not belong to someone just because they wait for you. You may have been misguided into that angry, selfish mindset in which you wallow, but you are not a spoil to be reaped, assuming you have yet to have been so?" He raised his eyebrows and crossed his arms across his chest.

I closed my eyes as a flush washed over my body from the vulgarity of his words. Everything was hot. "My relations with Mr. Jim are little to no concern of yours. You ought to bite your tongue at such horrible words." I whispered through gritted teeth. My stomach ached.

"That may be true, but lucky for you, I've decided to make anything that remotely involves you my most personal concern." He flashed a quick and wide grin.

My hands held my face in fantastic horror, and my hair fell out of the makeshift braid. His gaze lingered. *Was a man expressing... interest in me supposed to be desirable?* I ought to have been relieved. Even a bit empowered, because wasn't a match the light at the end of the tunnel for any young woman, let alone one as unfortunately born as I? But in that moment, as this strange, beautiful man indirectly declared that certain interest, I felt less than. My stomach sank, and the butterflies plummeted.

"For someone who claims to worry about my person, you seem to be hell-bound on compromising it. I won't be bought or bargained for by anyone. Especially not some yuppy, pretty dandy from God knows where." I kept both of my hands against the sides of my neck to cool the warm flesh.

A bark of laughter escaped the devil of a man's mouth. "Oh, girl, I won't be needin' a cut o' ye. I've got nae a doubt in me mind, with time, ye'll come to me all on yer own. And I'm more than glad ye find me bonnie."

I simply scoffed at that. Something in the way he spoke changed a bit at that statement. That sometimes-accent was weaseling its way back in, yes, but it was more. A certain emotion had come into his speech, piggybacked on the burr around his words. It annoyed me. This man, intrigue be damned, had no idea who he was dealing with. I turned on my heel to put as much distance between us as possible while still living under the same roof. A hand on my shoulder stopped me.

"Before you go, I almost forgot." He sauntered over to his disastrous desk and produced a beautiful black silk ribbon. My mouth fell slightly ajar.

"I noticed your hair was loose. I personally don't have an issue with it, but something tells me I'm alone in that vote. I found this stuck in some brambles on the east end of your sacred dancing grounds." He held the ribbon up for me. I snatched it and quickly departed his room. Slamming his door, then my own.

Chapter 6

I couldn't breathe.

Air that had once been effortless and unnoticeable was as heavy as stone within me. It crowded in my lungs like the aftermath of a rockslide. But rock piles from violent slides still had pockets and hope. This was less forgiving than stone. Like molasses. Yes, because stones could be broken up into tiny pieces and then become dust, and once they were dust, I could cough them up. But molasses stuck. Molasses stood the test of time with rubber defiance that put fossils to shame, and as I opened my mouth to scream, it only expanded. I was drowning. Wherever I was, however I had gotten there, it no longer mattered because death knocked at my door. Foolishly, I allowed it to rush in like an agitated spring and fill up my lungs as I gasped at its intrusion. The attack worsened by thickening once inside and taking up all the empty space within me until whatever it was, I also became.

"Trix!"

The voice pulled me out of the blackness. I screamed through my molasses-coated throat to find relief in the cool night air. My body shuddered as harsh coughs ran through me, finalizing my departure from the swirling nightmare that had nearly conquered me. I faintly noticed another body in the room as I was tucked neatly under their shoulder while my head spun. Everything burned. I wiped the coughs and sweat and tears from my face with shaky hands. When the liquid was clear from my eyes, my sight was interrupted by an alarmingly close Mr. Wallace, clad in a concerning disposition. He rocked me back and forth like one would a newborn.

"Can ye breathe?" he whispered urgently, his large hands going to my throat to massage it.

I closed my eyes and took a ragged breath. The action ached, but the air was a welcomed relief. My throat had only moments before been full and clogged with a heaping serving of stinky, sticky syrup. His other hand rubbed my bare arm up and down to soothe me. My skin turned to gooseflesh at his foreign touch.

A light, followed by a Billy, rushed into my room. He froze at the sight of Mr. Wallace. He nodded slowly like he was still waking up, and the scene was halfway acceptable to his drowsy sense of propriety. I pulled my legs up to my chest and tried to inch away from Mr. Wallace. The shockingly casual nature of our position heated the blood in my veins. I detangled myself from his grasp, and his hands fell on my bed.

"Trixie-girl, are you alright?"

I cleared my throat and nodded. "Yes," I croaked. I turned to Mr. Wallace. "You don't need to be here. Go away." I was harsh as my cheeks flamed.

His eyebrows shot up high. "Yer girl...the thing 'twas screaming. I thought ye were dyin'." The latter was directed at me almost as an accusation.

Neither Billy nor I spoke. The atmosphere was, as expected in such an unfortunately familiar situation, tense. This wasn't the first time a boarder had woken to my terrors, nor would it be the first complaint or demand for money back.

"What's wrong? Dinna tell me ye didna hear her," he said in a tittering rush.

Billy sighed as he leaned against the doorframe. He stared at his feet as if he felt the weight of my shame. "She gets these nightmares. Come every couple of months. Has since she was a little girl."

"Nightmares," he repeated. "'Twas a nightmare?" He looked incredulous.

I folded my arms over my knees and rested my cheek on top of them. I bit my lip and flinched as his hand stroked my back gently. My movement caused Mr. Wallace to pay no mind, though.

"My momma can set you up in a different room, so that her thrashin' won't bother you, if-ing you would prefer," Billy offered.

"That won't be necessary, but thank you, Mr. O'Connor." Mr. Wallace cleared his throat, his accent fading into the background once more as he burned holes into me with his stare.

"Mr. O'Connor was my father. You can call me Billy," Billy piped in, followed by a heavy yawn. "You want me to stay up with ya, girl?"

I shook my head against my knees. "You both can go now. I apologize for disturbing you," I mumbled miserably.

The weight of the two worried souls inhabiting my chambers was the real nightmare despite the lingering terror of my dream. Breathing was horribly overrated, as my throat still felt ripped to shreds.

Mr. Wallace's hand stilled on my back, and he removed it. His weight lifted from my bed, and Billy leaned over to gently kiss the top of my head. I reached out to pat his face, the best emotional gesture I could give.

"Get some rest, girl. I'll come back if need be."

"I'll see you tomorrow."

Billy exited the room at the finality in my tone. I hoped my message was clear that I ought to be left alone. His steps were followed by Wallace's. With the sound of my door shutting, I took a large breath and lightly coughed. I winced as I rubbed my sore throat and stayed tucked around myself, afraid to make another sound.

Perhaps I was more afraid to fall back asleep. It was rare for me to recall my nightmares, but this one had shaken me. I drummed my fingers in a slow pattern while staring off into the night. The stillness was a comfort compared to what I had experienced in the trappings of my mind.

I gave a large, long sigh at the sound of my door reopening. "Billy, I told you I'd be fine. You best not have Miss Dev waiting on you now." I forced a smile though he likely couldn't see.

The door shut. I perked up and saw Mr. Wallace leaning against it, shirt draped open and hands behind his back. A candle that he brought flickered across his features. My face cinched together at the intrusive Mr. Wallace, as well as my damning words the man had no business hearing.

I pulled my blankets closer to my chest, protecting the bare skin that peeked through the chemise. "That wasn't for you to hear. You'd be best off letting it fall out of your mind."

He nodded and inspected his nails.

"What are you doing here?" I pulled myself tightly together.

His gaze was too personal, like he saw into me. Past the clothing, and then the flesh that clothed my supposed soul. Disgusting.

"You can't be in here. What could you possibly want at this hour, Mr. Wallace?" My voice was still rough around the edges. I danced on the edge of hysteria despite my low tone.

"Quit with the *Mister*. I came to check on you. I couldn't much do so with your Billy-boy hovering." He didn't move.

I groaned, burying my face in my hands. "I am fine. I am exhausted. I want to go to sleep. I'm sorry for waking you, truly. It won't happen again." I couldn't hide my own grimace at the words, though.

He pushed off the door and walked to my dresser, eyeing the random items on it. "There you go, lying again. You really ought to work on that, girl. You promising me it won't happen again indirectly means that you won't be sleeping. Therefore, despite claiming you want to go to sleep, you won't be doing so."

I stirred in my nest of sheets, and his brows furrowed.

"You're bleeding."

Bleeding? I pulled myself up tighter. Frantically, I looked for a blood stain from an unplanned monthly. *Oh, I could die.* He slid beside my bed.

"No, not that. Lower." He looked annoyed and referenced to a light stain near where my foot had been and grabbed at my ankle. He yanked the limb gently out from my nest to look at it. I had forgotten about the small wound from earlier in the day. He sat on the side of my bed and pulled my foot into his lap.

I murmured a quiet, "Hey!"

He gave my ankle a slap as if to hush me. Then he turned the foot back and forth, looking at the cut as I tried to pull my leg away. "What happened? And would ye quit it? I'm looking at yer bloody injury."

I stilled a little at that.

"'Tis small, but deep. What happened?"

I cleared my throat and surprised Wallace with a harsh tug, freeing my ankle from his grasp. He really needed to stop taking hostage of my appendages. "I stepped on a bird."

A bark of laughter, set at a higher pitch than one would expect, escaped his mouth, and I quickly moved forward to cover it and hush him.

"I'll not have Billy-boy rushing back in here to find you so comfortable," I scolded.

He nodded, composing himself with another cruel smile. "Stepped on a bird?"

I nodded.

"How did you manage to do that, girl?"

"The blackbird was already dead and in the water. The thing must've flown right into the boulder you so rudely stole from me." I eyed him with a quick, angry glance. "I didn't see him and jumped right in. The beak pierced my skin."

My stomach tightened as I returned to the terrifying dream. I suppose I had been trapped beneath the swaying water. Stuck at the bottom of the Lil' Big, decaying as only corpses do. Drowned in the beloved water that had once held me closer than any human. Full to the brim with her, burning through my too-full lungs. Staring up at the ever-moving world that I no longer was part of. As if whoever had left me here had not taken the time to shut my poor, dead eyes. *Hadn't they always said death was the final rest?* I shuddered.

"There was a dead blackbird near you?" He got up from my bed and paced, but his shoulders looked bunched.

I nodded.

"That's peculiar."

"I thought so as well. Mr. Jim always told me blackbirds were clever creatures. Killing yaself ain't too clever." I watched him from beneath my eyelashes.

"Au contraire, my girl. Plenty would believe *killing yaself* to be the cleverest of all. But I digress. Tisn't normal behavior for a blackbird. A dead bird usually means death is near."

I didn't quite like his mockery of my drawl. He examined the mis-shaped bits and pieces that cluttered my dresser once again.

"Says whom?"

He whirled around. "Not your God, that's for certain."

I furrowed at his words.

"Just watch for a fever with a sore such as that."

I nodded. I hadn't considered an infection.

"You've had these terrors your whole life, hm?" He set my hairbrush down, not too gently, and fiddled more.

I rubbed the soft skin beneath my eyes for a moment, hoping it would ease my exhaustion and nerves. I nodded as my head buzzed from the alternating conversation.

"You've never seen a doctor?"

"Mr. Jim says I'll be written off as hysteric," I whispered the damning word. "'Sides I don't need any more attention drawn toward myself."

"Because?"

In his hands was a photograph that he attempted to show me as if I had never seen it myself. The photograph was of a woman. I let his assumptions be whatever they were about a photo of a single woman on my dresser and the information given to him against my wishes at the dining table.

"Well...A family tree never helped me much," I said quietly.

He stared intensely and then looked back to the photo. Picking out the pieces that matched the girl in front of him, no doubt.

He held the photo closer to his eyes. "You look like her, you know."

"Don't," I whispered.

The woman in the photograph was remarkably lovely, and notably fair in coloring. He let out another rough bark of laughter. "Where's yer da?"

"My what?"

He rolled his eyes. "Yer *daddy*. Where's yer photo o' him?"

I glared at him. The transition between mocking my vernacular and his foreign accent that only came out when he wanted left me confused concerning his real attitude. "Don't be stupid."

"Stupid? Am I to believe ye have occurred to us with nae a father? Tell me, girl, are ye the second comin'?"

I picked at the lovely threads of my blanket.

"Shame doesn't suit you. That there is an ugly thing on something pretty like you. You can only control your hand's touch. So that pathetic little bit about wherever you came, I would let go of it right quick. Same goes for guilt," Wallace said quickly, setting down the photo, not too gently.

A stammer of nonsense bubbled at my lips, but nothing useful came out.

"When you were younger," he offhandedly continued, "did anyone ever try reading to you as you fell asleep?" He now sauntered over to my desk to examine the heaps of books scattered across it.

"No. But Mr. Jim used to stay up with me."

Mr. Jim indeed used to even rent out a room, despite his own apartments across town. He would stay with me until I fell asleep and then sneak into the nearest room, hoping, I'm sure, that I would sleep soundly so he could too.

"He used to stay in the room you have...enchanted," I continued, picking at a ball of nothing on my blanket.

Wallace slammed a book shut at my statement. He gave me a tight-lipped smile. "How kind of him."

He walked closer to me, grabbed the rocking chair in the process, and pulled it up to the side of my bed. He plopped down in it with dramatic exhaustion, and the beautiful chair groaned in protest. A thick book with shimmering letters sat in his lap. I inched further away from him. He leaned back and rocked without a care in the world.

"And when did he stop all of this?" Wallace continued, staring at the ceiling above him.

I shrugged. "Suppose when I was fifteen."

His eyes met mine. "How respectful of him." His tone was back.

I nodded slowly. *At what point did having a man unwelcomed into your chambers require a scream? Probably upon discovery...*

"So, shall I read to you from your Good Book?" he purred.

I shrugged without thinking. He created an unusual distraction with these continuous assumptions I had some form of possession over God. *It was He who possessed me, was it not?*

"I promise it won't hurt. Besides, something tells me that in a town like this, I really ought to be freshening up on these silly verses." He winked.

"Ain'tcha got any faith?" The words came out quickly and did nothing for my defense.

A slow, slow smile paired with a coy glance beneath his lashes. "Oh, girl of mine, that's a loaded question. But do know that I am not *that* self-absorbed to lack an *acknowledgment* of our Good Lord."

A small smile pulled at my lips at his teasing tone. I snuggled lower into my bed, making sure to give my back to Wallace. The chair lightly creaked as he rocked back and forth, fumbling through the pages of the

Bible. I closed my eyes as the sound of his voice blended with God's so intricately, I fought sleep only to figure which was which.

I woke to an empty room, a bright morning, and the blanket from Mr. Jim wrapped securely around me.

Chapter 7

It was rough waking up. My bed was too warm, but still the sheets clung to my body like a dear friend pulling me down to relax a moment or two longer. Everything was so soft. Another crash and holler from below, more violent than yesterday's, along with the grandfather clock striking eight, had me scrambling out of bed as I wrapped the new blanket around me. I was late. A harsh swear came out of my mouth. I threw open my door and rushed down the steps to investigate. My foot ached as it landed flatly on the first-floor wood, and I rounded like a bullet into the kitchen. Laughter erupted as I assessed what had shocked me from my slumber. The room smelled like burnt coffee beans, and Wallace stood next to the stove, waving his hand around like it had a mind of its own. A tin cup lay on the wooden floor surrounded by a pitiful puddle of burnt brown liquid. Wallace whirled to face me with brows painfully furrowed. Still chuckling, I covered my mouth. His face slowly relaxed, and his hand stilled. He nearly blushed in amusement.

"Did I wake you?" he questioned in a hushed tone to match the shy morning light and glanced around at his mess.

I composed myself and gave a little shrug and set about getting him a cleaning cloth. I handed one to him and took a couple steps back as he immediately squatted to wipe up the coffee.

"What were you doing, Wallace?"

There was something captivating about the way this large, intrusive man cleaned up such a childlike mess. I clutched the blanket tighter to myself when he looked at me from his low position.

"I suppose, just looking a little like an ass, eh?"

I nodded and wandered over to the island, eyeing some biscuits. They must have been made at the crack of dawn without any assistance from me. I gnawed at my lower lip. Guilt settled in the pit of my stomach, much like clockwork.

"Where's Ms. Liz?" I reached for a biscuit. I brought it to my lips, unable to stomach a bite but indulgent to the flaky texture.

"She's settling up with the wash out back," Wallace stated before slapping his thighs and standing.

He appeared comfortable in his surroundings, and I was envious. Distrust and insecurity plagued every step I took in this town. Yet, this

Wallace character walked on in without a care in the world. Must've been nice.

I nodded and looked out the window facing the rear of the property. I saw a flash of Ms. Liz hanging up linens to dry in the sun. *How many hours of rest had she gotten?* I worried my lower lip, causing my biscuit to crumble. Wallace leaned over me to grab a biscuit. He didn't step back to return my personal space, and I attempted to mind my own.

Ms. Liz continued to bustle about with the laundry, wiping flyaway hairs from her face. Gone was the wild, golden blond that radiated through my childhood memories. What was left was a finer, duller head of hair resembling an old sheet of paper, carelessly tucked away. Tucked, not hidden. No, Ms. Liz, despite all her glory, had not become the coveted love letter she deserved to be. Instead, through the waning years, she became forgotten like a wrinkled newspaper.

As the sun shined down, it was as if the bright light stole color from her, washing her out. She faded before our eyes. The grand battle between the fiery blond matron and the sun, which raged for years, was slowly ending. I pondered that walking relic of motherly goodness and wondered at what age the sun stopped bringing life and started taking it away? *Could we feel it? Did it hurt, this silent, uphill battle for vibrancy? Or was it slow, like falling asleep? Was the battle woven so tightly into our existence, the exhaustive aftermath was mistaken for a long day's work?* Perhaps we as humans simply didn't realize that's what it was all along. We slept, not to rejuvenate ourselves from the day-to-day efforts of the body, but to recover and fight off the sun another day.

I couldn't remember when her hair had last been golden. I spent so much time growing up I forgot to pay mind that aging doesn't stop once you are grown but betrays and stays until its welcome is well overdue. As one grew closer to a life that one could finally *live*, those above who helped lay the tracks were all the while nearing something much less promising.

"What did I tell you about guilt?" Wallace's mouth was close to my ear, hovering over my shoulder, and following my gaze.

"If I didn't feel guilty, what would that make me?" I whispered.

"Alive," he breathed.

He took a large bite of his biscuit. Crumbs landed all over my shoulder, and the proximity to his munching sent me into a fit of giggles. I pulled away and brushed off his leftovers. He smiled down at me. I took a bite of my biscuit. The crumbles of the dough dropped down my chin. He reached forward to brush them off. I tucked my chin in before he could touch me. Wallace dropped his reach but regarded the blanket. The air in the room shifted quickly.

"He was adamant about getting you that. I almost missed the train to stop at the correct trading post. I wonder why that is."

I shrugged, holding the newfound treasure as closely as I could.

He continued, "Why that trading post? Why a blanket? For him to tuck in his *little girl* at night, hmmm?"

I didn't respond but narrowed my eyes, suspicious about the direction of this conversation, as I took another bite.

"I think you might be too old for that," he continued bitterly as he looked me up and down.

The change of pace in his tone was as abrupt as being kicked off a horse. It was unnerving how he could switch his playfulness to low boiling anger. His words were dirty, and I knew he wasn't really asking questions that he wanted me to answer. He said them because he liked how those words, so horrible without reason, felt around his lips.

"Mr. Jim isn't my father."

"Aye, I ken."

Damn that grin.

"What are you getting at, Wallace?"

"Nothing in particular. I may not be from around here, but I have a hard time believing any father, cultural differences aside, would let his wee girl go without a blanket. This shouldn't be your first. It's hard to believe it is. You know that, and Mr. Jim knows that."

I glared at him, and a chuckle slipped from his cruel lips. He turned on his heel, tossing the dirtied towel haphazardly on the kitchen island, and headed toward the door. My blind loyalty kicked in without a moment of hesitation.

"You're quick to bite the hand that feeds, ain't ya? Whatcha doing now, Wallace? Running to shine the shoes of that there hand?" I snorted at myself, satisfied.

That got him to freeze. He slowly turned back around, a sadistic smile pulling at his lips. "What in heaven's name has you believing that *I* am the one doing the shining?"

I raised my eyebrows humorously.

"Excuse me?" He stepped closer. "Are you under the impression that I am working *for* your Jim?"

I stammered a little in confusion.

"Well..." He advanced more.

"Well, what?" I gnawed at my bottom lip, squeezing the biscuit to the point of crumbling in my hand.

"Well, I had assumed as much. What with you coming here and being a loose cannon," I quoted Mr. Jim's words from the previous night.

"Loose cannon?!" A howl of laughter came.

I stepped back at that, but he didn't let up.

"Girl, ye best open those big ol' eyes of yers to see what's happenin' around ye. Assumin' makes an ass out of *you* and me."

Mr. Jim used to always tell me, "You assuming makes an ass outta me, and if you know what's good for you, you'll know how much I hate feeling like an ass." All usually grumbled around a half-smoked cigarette paired with that stern look on his face that told me if I didn't shape up soon, I would pay for it plenty. I had been chided with this mindfulness since before the word *ass* struck a blush of naughty across my soft, child-like face, to well after when the term had become one for everyday use. Now, twenty-something years old, I still couldn't figure out what was good for me despite that gentle education.

So, I informed Wallace precisely what I *assumed* he could do to himself.

His jaw dropped, and that goddamn howl of a laugh erupted once more as expected. "Oh, girl, that's a treat right there. I'd pay money to hear to such a phrase come right out o' yer bonnie yap for the rest o' me days."

An animal growl rumbled in my throat.

"Maybe I ought to go find a certain Jim. I'll explain to him that his ward is wanderin' about the house nae entirely dressed for the day, with the mouth o' a sailor, botherin' me as I attempt to go about me business. Causing quite a mess o' everythin'..." He referenced the crumbs on the floor and the dirty rag he had thrown on the island.

I could picture it now. Mr. Jim, mad as a hornet on a hot summer day, grabbing my arm as tightly as he did last night and hissing, thinking I was bothering his new business "partner." Or even worse, him hissing about why I was acting so *ungenteel* around a fella. The things in my life that felt so certain just a day prior spun rapidly like a top on a smooth wooden table. Any sense of power I once had slipped through my fingers, and damnation, it made my hands ache. I clenched and unclenched my fists to get some blood pumping properly to them, in hopes they wouldn't start tingling. I reached to grip my blanket once more.

"What are you doing here, Wallace?" I hissed like a knee-jerk reaction.

He stepped closer. "That's as rich as molasses. I was gonna ask you the same damn thing."

"Anyone ever told you that you're as intrusive as thistle weed?" I asked sharply.

He smiled down at me, leaned a hair closer, and brought his hand up to my chin. I kept eye contact despite the unease and white-knuckle clench I had on my blanket.

"Probably, but never to my face." With that, he gave the soft part beneath my chin a gentle knock with his fist and finally left the kitchen.

"You meant invasive," he called back, turning his head halfway, "I believe."

Heat boiled in my stomach as a frustrated holler penetrated my clenched teeth. I threw my biscuit at the back of his head. He laughed and exited the house. The clock struck a quarter past, bringing another holler from me and a dash upstairs to get ready for the day.

My tardiness was the dust around my feet as I dashed into the general store. I was met by the lackadaisical eyes of Mr. Jim behind the counter. I gave him a nod, knowing that his boredom with my unnecessary existence was much better than any other reaction. I inhaled and clapped my hands together to discard any lingering, small bits of earth or untimeliness.

"Get to the back and help with the organizing. Be quick about it, ya hear? Make up for some lost time." Mr. Jim called over a book he was looking at on the counter next to the register.

I nodded at nothing and headed to the back through the swinging doors. The heat in the room was my so-obvious punishment for being late, among other things. Sweat prickled on my lip like a mustache as I surveyed the wreck of a storage room. In the southwest corner were piles of grains, which I understood needed to be transported to the dry cellar for proper storage. I took a moment to scan everything else that needed settling. I decided that it was better to start with the tough and end with the easy while the coolest part of the day was here and fleeting fast.

I approached the large woven bags, grimacing at them like an old pal I really hadn't cared to visit with—the second half of my punishment. Mr. Jim knew clear, clean, and well that I would struggle attempting to lift one of these, let alone a whole damn pile of them. More likely than not, I would need to ask for help. I didn't like doing that. I glared back through the swinging doors, hoping Mr. Jim felt it. I mumbled a couple words of encouragement before heaving up the first of many bags.

I just needed it on my shoulder. Surely, then I wouldn't struggle to get it down the narrow steps into the cellar. I grabbed the full yet obnoxiously malleable bag in the middle and attempted to lift. I got it about a foot above ground before stumbling a little when it slid out of my hand. My foot throbbed under the pressure of additional weight.

I took a deep breath and licked the sweat from my upper lip and ignored my foot. I strained but had a better grip on it. My arms almost immediately ached as I waddled like a duck toward the floor cellar door. I made it halfway there before the bag slipped from my hands again. I kicked it with an impatient good foot. My forehead was already slick with perspiration, and there was a ringing in my ears. The soft, whispering movements of dried grains within the heavy bag mocked me. I inhaled deeply and tried to haul the bag up to my shoulder. I acted quickly, figuring if I was fast enough, I could outrun the fatigue that seized my muscles.

"Sisyphus."

I startled, and the bag fell from my grasp. I followed it, landing on my rear end. I placed my sweating face into my hands that smelled like dust and horse.

"What?" I responded through clenched teeth.

"Sisyphus," Wallace repeated lazily. There he stood, comfortable and unbothered, in the door frame. "Well, sort of. I suppose." He gestured to the bag next to my feet and then to the pile in the corner. "You have an impossible task, by God. Or at least your god. A punishment of mental and physical means. Your boulder is the grain, and a bit of ignorance. He is planning on that."

I hummed in response, sitting pathetically and embarrassed by my obvious shortcomings. He came over to me and offered a hand. I tried to blow the loose strands of my hair out of my face with a big huff, then took that hand only to be jerked to my feet. I stumbled. He looked at me hard, studying, but his gaze told me he was not thinking about me. The way his eyes flittered to each side of my face made me feel like he couldn't see it at all, but instead something in his own mind. My face was merely a blank canvas for his daydreams or plans. *And folks called me fanciful.*

"He is making a point with this."

I nodded, keeping my chin high.

"You're going to hurt yourself if you keep at it this way. Lift with your legs." He squatted down next to the bag of grains. He gestured with his head for me to do just the same. I followed his squat right next to him.

"Now," he straightened his back, "you want to keep your back straight like so. And the point is, lift with your legs. Not your arms or your back." He hoisted the bag of grains on his shoulder, then slowly stood.

I watched the fluidity of his motions, cataloging. The bag was comfortably on his shoulder as he nodded and dropped it next to me with a soft thud. "Now, you try. Use just your legs, Trixie-girl."

I took a breath and got closer to the bag. Getting the bag on my shoulder was tricky, but I stayed low for a moment to compose once I did. Then, I focused on my legs. I focused on the soft dirt beneath my heels, the pressure up my calves to my knees, thighs, and rear. The pain reminded me that my foot was on the ground, and that is where it all started—strength and a sturdy form. I focused everything there and slowly lifted my body. I tried to focus on myself, not the weight that seemed to be sinking me further into the earth. Pain was good, pain was familiar in my body, and it further proved my capability. Finally, I was straight, as if a long piece of string was attached to the crown of my head and led to the heavens. *I suppose one was, wasn't it? Wasn't God one master marionettist? And we, His lovely little creations, just waiting on our turn to dance?*

"How do you feel?" Wallace prompted. He had his arm bent around his waist, and the other arm rested under his chin as he analyzed me. Breathing slowly, I tested my stability and took a small step. Easy.

"Stable," I confirmed and walked with purpose to the cellar door. I took the steps minutely and made it down smoothly due to that slow care. I released the bag from my shoulder and tossed it to a dark corner. I smiled to myself in that dark, damp cellar.

"You gotta get stronger. Takes practice. Do it every day. What is the strongest part of the tree?" he fired off quickly.

"The trunk," I stated breathlessly.

"You got it, girl. The parts of your body that hold you up are the strongest. Your neck and arms are just there to look pretty. Keep the weight in the base, like a tree, and you'll find yourself much stronger in no time."

I nodded, looking over at the pile. One down.

"Now, do the rest of them. Do this every day if you can. Arse'll be sore, but that's good. Means the body is building. You practice this, and you'll be stronger." He was repeating himself, but I didn't point that out. Primarily because there was an air of frustration in his repetition. Perhaps to him, I was not the only person in the room. So, instead, I nodded and enjoyed the vulgarity of his reference to my backside. He looked at me for a moment longer, then strode out behind the shop. I gazed over my shoulder in the direction he left. I huffed to blow the hair out of my eyes once more and got to work on the rest of the bags.

Sᴡᴇᴀᴛ ᴅʀɪᴘᴘᴇᴅ ᴅᴏᴡɴ ᴍʏ ꜰᴀᴄᴇ as if a bucket of water had been poured over my head. The heat that I created alone was proof of my completed task. Not without difficulty, though. I was crawling up the cellar doorsteps, shamelessly. My foot had long ago gone numb. My lungs burned and felt abnormally tight. Once I made it back to proper sea level (whatever that was), I braced myself on my knees and let out a long string of coughs. The coughs racked through my body like hundreds of dull needles. Bright flashes of lights danced behind my forced shut eyelids as the coughing continued.

Someone was beside me, whacking on my back like they would a sick baby. I coughed more at that and struggled to take in a full breath. I blindly wiped at my face to clear all pathways for air to enter and exit. Finally, the coughing subsided. I stumbled some more—the numbness in my foot was causing me to be more off-balance than usual. Mr. Jim's arm wrapped around me and stabilized me. I then took a smooth, deep breath and forced a breathless laugh. I wiped back the sweat and hair from my forehead.

"You all right?"

I nodded.

"Your grain is stored," I smiled at him sarcastically.

He glanced at the empty corner where he had piled up that grain. A look of surprise as well as chastisement swept over his aged face. "Well, if it was too much, you should have asked for help. Are you hurt?"

I suppressed a roll of my eyes and shook my head. "You asked me to sort the room, and I did. What else you got?"

My challenge had Mr. Jim straightening and looking stern. I raised my chin toward him. Mr. Jim placed his hands on his hips, and I leaned a bit over to catch my breath fully.

At that moment, Billy walked into the back room. Concern flashed across his face as he rushed toward us. "Is she faint?"

I shook my head no and backed away from them.

"Why would she be faint?" Mr. Jim glared at Billy.

Billy looked more confused. "You dreaming poorly again, girl?" Mr. Jim's tone was clipped.

I shrugged and took another step back.

"Everything all right in here?" Wallace inquired, clearly drawn into the back room by the commotion.

I wiped at my face one more time and straightened.

He took a tiny step. "Is it your foot?"

I backed away from his beeline advance and shook my head.

"Her foot? What's wrong with her foot?" Mr. Jim's voice was sharp. "What in the hell is going on?"

I headed to a corner full of boxes and textiles and opened them to figure the proper organization to it all. Avoiding the attention altogether like it was as easy as breathing.

"She stepped on a bird," Wallace muttered and continued toward me. He grabbed the back of my neck, pulled my face up to his, and placed his other hand on my forehead. "Have you got a fever?"

I pulled back violently and turned my back to him and Mr. Jim. My flesh was still grimy from my exertion, and Wallace's actions were damning.

"A bird? You stepped on a bird? And how do you know this, Jayson? Trixie-girl, what's going on?" Mr. Jim drew closer.

Billy looked confused and helpless. I shrugged and peered in the box to see beautiful white lace. I lifted it and headed toward the front of the store through the Dutch door.

Mr. Jim grabbed my arm. "You stepped on a bird?"

"A blackbird, sir," I answered matter-of-factly.

Billy smothered his laughter, and the corner of my lip kicked up.

"And what has that got to do with Mr. Wallace?" This question was through clenched teeth, quiet enough for only me to hear.

There was an accusation in his tone. I shrugged. If we hadn't had an audience, and I were five years younger, I may have earned a slap. Mr. Jim hated my shrug.

"He saw me limp and asked. Guess ya didn't notice," I answered cool-ly and rolled his grasp off my arm. He looked angry. I walked toward the storefront, and Billy held open one saloon door for me and followed.

"You're gonna get yourself in trouble, Trixie-girl," Billy taunted.

I rolled my eyes and hung the lace in an orderly fashion. "Yeah, yeah, yeah. What are you looking for?"

He paced around the produce, smiling at a ruby red apple. "I can't remember," he laughed. He reached for the apple and shined it as if to help me.

"Take it, and get going." I clapped some dust off my hands, walking back to the storage room and pointed at the front entrance. "We are busy."

Billy let out a whoop.

I paused outside the doors to the back, barely seeing Mr. Jim's back to me, and Wallace caught my gaze. Mr. Jim was shaking his head.

"You do the grains for her?"

"Did it herself, just like you asked."

"Why would you let her do that? She could've hurt herself." Mr. Jim scolded senselessly.

Wallace let out a bark of a laugh. "Why did you have her do it if you thought she couldn't?" Wallace's eyes danced at mine.

I entered the room. "What else you got?" I asked with my hands on my hips.

Chapter 8

ime carried on much like risin' bread. It grew in the summer heat slowly and softly, shaping delicately to the new environment. The alterations were invisible to the naked eye but evident by the time night had fallen. Swollen from unnoticed efforts.

The rain held off consistently, which left everyone praying to God no matter what they had done the Friday before. The warm, dry air had the whole town restless. The water level of the Lil' Big had sunk a good foot, or least I had found it had the one time I made it out there since Mr. Jim's glorious return. Suppose the heat and the drought were our punishment for trying to live out in the middle of nowhere. God was ashamed of our little town, so it was clear He had decided to dry us out until no water was left, and then perhaps, we would all catch ablaze. Sinners burned quicker than dried-out pine anyways, according to the word of the Lord, and they didn't call where we were the Wild West for nothing.

Despite the new help from Mr. Wallace, Mr. Jim worked me tooth and nail. Senseless busy work that left my mind wandering as far as the ocean. I was distracted by my personal hopes and dreams that perhaps, one day soon, I could baptize myself in the sea while Mr. Wallace fell into our patterns with charismatic ease that baffled me as much as it intrigued me. From the first day working together, it was clear that I had been wrong. What had developed with his new residency was much worse than my initial fears.

Mr. Jim did not simply train Wallace and slink off into the night, but instead, a partnership unfolded. A partnership that left my scrawny self tossed to the side. The constant need to prove myself to Mr. Jim now fell on deaf ears; with Wallace present, there was no competition. He had walked into our lives higher than where my short legs reached. Wallace became a consultant to Mr. Jim, and I remained a glorified errand girl. Boredom with my position had me, on slower days, wondering if perhaps I had already perished in the surrounding warmth. The horrible heat of the summer, coupled with the constant reminder of my uselessness, felt a bit like a test to my moral soul. And I was failing. Or already had failed and was left to pay penance. In whichever ring of hell was set aside for bastard children with impolite tongues and a wild streak that drove them to tear their clothes off any chance they got.

But alterations that occurred to my body grounded me back down to the reality in which I resided. Wallace was correct; I got stronger, and my backside hurt weekly. These little aches were all the proof I needed to know I had not perished since I was fairly certain there was no room for growing pains in eternal damnation. Beneath my skirts, and unnoticeable to the general public due to them, my backside had grown sturdier. Each morning as I dressed, I ran my fingers over my slightly altered body. I wondered if perhaps I resembled Dev in figure. At least moderately. Something in the back of my mind reminded me that no matter what, the stuff that made me up would always be sturdier and less soft than her lovely bits. My foot had healed without a fever, and the scar was a funny pink that wrinkled in an odd way when I flexed it in the candlelight. But that was the extent of it. Overall, my survival and my newfound strength had me feeling a little more stable in the body I was trapped in.

Nonetheless that stability did not protect me from the insecurity of my entity. Never had I been so acutely aware of my size or sex. My coloring and lack of family, yes, of course. Those insecurities had followed me around and were hammered into my upbringing, synonymous with my name. They had always been a target on my back that kept me from small talk as well as most social gatherings. They and they alone had earned me the title of *the wicked thing of Wicker Soul* though nobody admitted it. My sex never held anything back. I had played with Billy and worked alongside Mr. Jim, never caring much what was between my legs or theirs. But now, with Wallace around, well.

Never had it felt so inferior to be myself. The constant awareness of my unnecessary womb exhausted me each day. And every night, I faced the cause of my misery, coaxing me to sleep with terrifying tales from the Good Book murmured gently as I drifted off. I was almost sure that Mr. Jim had no idea that Wallace snuck into my room each night to read to me sleep. I hoped to keep it that way. Nothing sordid happened, though I wasn't foolish enough to think that the basis of it all wasn't sin itself. Yes, Mr. Wallace was the cause of all my problems and distress, and to take comfort in him was hypocrisy that knew no bounds. It caused me to pray deep and ponder deeper. But there was something about it all—the secrecy and the intimacy and the quiet of it. It was something entirely my own. Untouched by Mr. Jim, or God, or anyone else. It was my little moment of divine carelessness that I couldn't help but revel in each evening. I listened to the stories of our Lord and Savior in despicable mockery. It was wonderful.

The promises that Mr. Jim made at the beginning of the summer did not progress. No move to leave was initiated, and Billy had yet to ask for Dev's hand. So, I sought comfort in what I read and placed my hopes in the words that I whispered to God during the few moments of quiet time that weren't spent in humor at His expense. He had yet to reply, and I was growing weary of my trust in Him. Perhaps Mr. Jim had struck a deal with our Lord in which they traded off control of my strings once the other was bored or busy. Because with each passing day of my life, it grew clearer that God was too busy for me. Though I kept this theory to myself.

On Mondays, Mr. Jim liked to spend the day in his upper office, above the shop, to go over his books and finances and such. This was a well-respected habit only to be interrupted by his not being in town. He entertained an intrusion by me from time to time, but overall, I steered clear of Mr. Jim on Mondays.

By noon one Monday, I had sorted out the store to a perfect semblance, front, back, and cellar. It was an explicitly warm day. More than once, I rubbed some of the lavender oil that Wallace had insisted the store sell on my neck to prevent the odor of my most human nature. Never had Mr. Jim taken consideration of any goods I thought would be nice for the small community. The shop was alive with colorful textiles from the East that Wallace stated were first brought to New York City, then here. Ms. Liz was exponentially fond of the little pots of face and hand creams and those oils that made everything smell lovely and feminine. So unlike how we had all felt for the duration of our lives in Wicker Soul. The morning train brought nearly no one into town, and everyone was a touch grumpy over it. Colorado's drought was scaring most passers quickly through, instead of the slower meandering, which we enjoyed economically and socially.

During the hot, dull day, I was at the counter with my newest book (which had been snuck into my room by three-guesses-who). Outside of reading to me each evening, Wallace and I had struck a deal of sorts. One morning, I woke up to find newspapers and article clippings from all over the world slipped under my door. Wallace told me if I read up on all the current events he provided, he would gift me a book every two weeks. He said the more I read up on the world and could discuss with him, the naughtier the books he gifted would be. This was a challenge that I couldn't turn down. He happily fed my morbid curiosity of not only all things naughty but the world that lay beyond the outskirts of this dusty barren town. And while I adored the naughty novels he provided, I was more drawn to the discussions he expected as payment.

In the corner of my mind, I knew he was in the backroom fussing, or building or organizing something or another, and I tried to push that small awareness away. *Tales of the Grotesque and Arabesque* was clenched in my sweaty palm and sent a shiver down my back. It joined the trickle of damp from the heat. My attention was glued to the pages, intrigued and slightly disgusted. For the life of me, I could not put it down. I was transfixed by *The Fall of the House of Usher*, rapidly ingesting the story as it played out across each page. I felt myself dashing through the dank, dark halls with no light and the fear of something much worse than God at my back. My lungs burned a bit, and my breath came out rough. I almost heard the breathless building of a blood-curdling scream echoing throughout abandoned halls.

The sound of the knock on the glass elicited my very own scream, and I nearly jumped out of my skin and coughed. The beet-red face of Ralston, Mr. Jim's barkeep for the saloon, peered in anxiously from outside the glass. I mouthed *what*, and he motioned for me to come out. I tried to still my coughing and heart rate with the hand that had held my book, which now was at my feet.

"Trix? What's going on?" Wallace said as he rushed through the swinging doors, only to pause there as my coughing cleared.

I waved him off, despite the confused worry on his face. I bent down to pick up my book, and Wallace grinned. I huffed, figuring precisely what the turning wheels behind his eyes explained to him. I dusted off the cover, and he let out a boyish giggle, high-pitched and foolish. I had noticed he made this noise when he was utterly delighted.

"You're too smart to get scared of that," Wallace clucked at me before heading back once more.

"Ralston, what has gotten into you, scaring me like that? I ought to smack ya," I hissed as I exited the shop.

"Trixie-girl, I need your help. Watch over at the saloon for me? It's the missus. The neighbor boy just came to the saloon saying that the baby is coming. She's screaming for God to come, and I...well, I'm worried His plate is a little full today. Please, girl, it'll be our first." His eyes were panicked and wide as sweat dripped into them. He didn't even bother to wipe it away. His whole body vibrated.

I frowned a little. "Ralston, Mr. Jim ain't ever gonna let me work the bar. Besides, who's gonna watch the shop?"

"Trixie! I'll get a customer in the bar 'fore you'll get a chicken clucking for eggs in this shop when it's this warm. Please, girl? She needs me."

"Go on then, I'll handle it," I muttered.

He sprinted off as a cloud of dust collected from where he started and followed where he headed. I coughed a little more at that, and I leaned through the store's open door, stood on my tiptoes, and saw Wallace's back. He was deep in conversation with someone I didn't recognize from either the distance or our lack of introduction. I waited. But when three minutes had passed and Wallace had yet to stop for a breath, I decided to head on over to the saloon and make sure nothing happened while Ralston was away. *It couldn't take too long for a baby to be birthed, could it?*

It had been a very slow day, with Wallace busy in the back. He could help if someone wandered in. If he couldn't, then that just proved he wasn't worth the skin off his own ass. I took off to the saloon. I kept my head down and tried to not think about Mr. Jim. *If he found out...* well, I would just have to make sure Mr. Jim didn't find out. I quickened my pace, not that anyone would have stopped me, but I didn't want to take any chances. I pushed my way through the saloon doors, relieved to find it empty, which was a good sign.

Since I began working for Mr. Jim, he explicitly stated that I was to never, never, never, *never* enter the saloon. Once Dev started singing there, I had been permitted to watch a couple of her best performances with the supervision of Mr. Jim. And I had run supplies over to Ralston on busy days. But I was in and out, sometimes with Mr. Jim trailing behind me both ways.

The saloon had high ceilings and red velvet curtains. The tables, chairs, and bar were all polished to a rich walnut color with intricate detailing. The bar was fancy, like the type you would see sketched out for an advertisement in a big city with a large, dirty, unfortunate-looking mirror hung behind. I couldn't help but think that the mirror was dirty because God wanted the customers to witness their inner devils while they wasted away. And those devils pounding on the other side had soiled hands. *Would drinking be considered sloth or gluttony? Perhaps a bit of both?* It was fair to think that the tarnished mirror reflected the sins of man. That or it had not been minded by a woman to polish.

The saloon groaned at my entrance. "Oh, hush," I muttered under my breath.

The floorboards squeaked as I meandered over to the bar. "Don't you be giving me away to Mr. Jim. We gotta keep this our little secret." I chided the elusive building that I had been so diligently kept from.

Rationally, it made sense that Mr. Jim didn't want me around a mostly male-infested establishment that served drink, and a particular type of merriment young women ought not be involved in. All the same, his ruling sat high on my list of things that left a bitter taste in my mouth, which we did not discuss. Behind the bar looked as I assumed it should, and I observed the less-than-vast new world. Clearly, a step out was not always a step up. I missed my book, but I was thankful for the surprisingly cooler temperature of this building. Perhaps it was the higher ceilings. My fingers drummed as I half-turned to glance over the inventory of the mostly amber liquids. It looked well enough stocked. I saw a white apron hanging and reached for it. I put it on just as a creek of the floorboards echoed throughout those cool high cool ceilings.

Chapter 9

I waited for the holler but defiantly continued to tie the apron around myself. I would look guilty if I acted as such. I smoothed down the front of the apron and held my breath, becoming very uncomfortable. I avoided looking in God's mirror and kept my face turned just so that my expression could not be seen.

"Say, you open?" an unfamiliar voice called.

I exhaled, wiped the sweat from my hairline, and placed both hands on the low of my back. I hummed a response and listened to the steps come closer. The scrape of a barstool pulled out resembled gunfire. I turned to face my customer, focusing on keeping a neutral but classically couldn't-be-bothered composure—something that had once come to me effortlessly.

He was very clean-looking. A dark, neatly kept mustache framed a friendly mouth. His clothes were plain but new. A little more expensive than what was usually worn either in this town or by anyone misled enough to pass through. He wore small spectacles, and his face was heat flushed. His dark, bushy brows furrowed a little as we made eye contact, and he looked long enough that I would have blushed had I not already been red from the heat.

"Thirsty?" I questioned.

"Parched."

I nodded and grabbed a squat glass and a bottle I recognized. I poured the glass to the level Billy and I had when we had snuck a bottle back in our youth. I pushed it to him as his brows shot up and down in response to the fill. I put the bottle back behind me, then walked the length of the bar to tidy up a bit. I found a rag further down and squeezed it in my hand. I kept the façade of confidence despite my inner turmoil. I had absolutely no idea what I was doing.

Chewing on the bottom of my lip, I attempted to look busy. I should have smiled more at the fella, said "welcome," or something polite along those lines. I wandered back, placing myself in front of him once more, aiming to be more hospitable. Or, at least, should he speak again, I could turn my cheeks up like a pleasant young lady ought. While I kept my back to the man, I polished a glass I had discovered left on the south end of the bar, clearly overlooked by Ralston. The thought his child coming was probably a little distracting, so I forgave him.

I had one eye on the fella as slyly as possible via the dirty mirror. I was so busy wondering if the man could tell I was thinking too hard about doing my job correctly that I couldn't do much of anything. I wondered intensely enough that the glass nearly fell out of my hand. I fought the urge to give an exclamation of anxiety. The sound would have resembled that of a dying animal, I had no doubt.

Luck favored me because the man wasn't looking at me at all. After a while, he took a very long and slow drink, and I watched his Adam's apple bob in completion. He found my eye in the mirror, and I looked down at the glass in my hands that somehow was still there. *Fuck*. At the very least, I could have grabbed a new one.

"From around here?" He adjusted awkwardly in his seat despite his pleasant tone. Something about wood and its echo made everything louder. I fought the urge to hush him. His question was stupid. He clearly had no idea where he was.

"Someone force you on that train?" I drawled.

He shook his head slowly with a confused smile.

"So, you got yourself here by your own volition?" I continued.

He nodded, and I gave him a breathless little laugh. Gold was running out, and the West continued to be flooded with folks in search of a better life than the one Mr. Lincoln's war had left them. Back East, Mr. Jim said they were making some kinda romance story about the lands this far out. I had been here long enough to know there wasn't any romance here, and if there ever had been, it had dried up by the time I arrived.

"You and you alone watched Loveland pass by through the window of what I only assume was a lonely train and just kept on chuggin'?" I asked with a slow raise of my brow.

He nodded.

I scoffed. "If you are looking for some story of the Wild West you fancy city folks read in your magazines or cartoons, you've come too far north. This is the last stop before those mountains. This is a town where folks stock up before traveling over and further west. Across those mountains and toward a better whatever-may-be. And this ain't a popular route, hear you me. Anything worth finding was already found further south and further west. It gets colder up here and earlier. So, mister, to answer your question, no, I am not from here. You are too far in the middle of nowhere to find anyone who is *from* here. This town is a bear trap you best not fall into."

"Fair enough," he mumbled into the glass. I picked up a new glass like a real professional. "So, where are you from then?"

"Further east," I responded vaguely.

My gut tightened and gone was the fear of his judgment of my overt lack of experience. It was replaced by a slow, sinking discomfort. Folks who drink like to talk, I supposed. He idly spun his glass, causing a dull clatter to speak for him.

"How 'bout yaself?" I asked slowly.

He smiled at his glass once more, and I decided it was a nice smile. His eyes flashed up, and the way he looked made me wanna smile right back despite it all. Someone who had that kind of smile had practiced it. Wallace had that kind, but only in large groups, I had noticed.

"Further east."

I put the glass away. "Another whiskey?" I called over my shoulder, reaching for the bottle.

He rolled his small glass intricately between his fingers. His hands were big, and on his ring finger, a thin gold wedding band glimmered in the low light.

A married man couldn't be much of a threat to me, could he?

"Sure thing, Miss... Say, I think I forgot your name."

I grabbed his empty glass a little too harshly. "No, you didn't," I replied with a tight smile.

He put his hands up as if to show he was unarmed and smiled again. I ignored the gesture, silently pouring his glass and sliding it back to him, as I had seen Ralston do once or twice before in my quick passing. Thankfully, the glass did not topple over.

"So, how old are you?" His words echoed in his glass and he downed the liquor quickly.

Beneath the bar top, my hand squeezed the cloth. Curiosity killed the cat, after all. Mr. Jim always said a sign of my immaturity was my constant inquisition. Adults did not bother each other with the ridiculous questions that plagued my conversation. Questions were ignorant, uneducated, unimportant, and, most of all, untrustworthy. Or so he had said.

Besides, I understood why no one would take an interest in anything about me in this life or the next. I had slid by, clinging to the shadows and sides of buildings all my days. Running to the furthest destination from a town that kept me at arm's length. Which was not very far if one brought out a proper measuring stick. I wasn't the one to be noticed. The war of freedom for an American man, and who exactly that included, was over. But not much had changed with that victory. I didn't know much about anything, but I did understand it was not yet a welcoming world out there. Especially for a young woman without a proper, *traceable* family tree.

So, I folded my arms over my chest with the towel in my fist. "Old enough to know what questions are polite and which are not."

He leaned toward me at that. I couldn't move further back if I tried.

"Gentlemen don't ask ladies such things," I added.

"Who says I'm a gentleman?"

I clucked my tongue at that and his devilish grin. I glanced back at the ring on his finger. Despite his attempts to be charming, there was something very off about his flirtations. They were calculated. Each question was planned and much too smooth.

"Well, I'm still a lady."

"Well, Miss no-name, no-age, no-home, you move out here from further east with a family?"

I shrugged, glancing down at my nails as if they had some fault.

He gave a *harrumph*. "Well, you got a man out here? Make a family of your own?"

I shrugged again.

"I can't win, can I?"

I gave him a mean look. "Sir, what exactly are you trying to win? Are you gonna have another drink? You're starting to bother me." I swung the rag over my shoulder, placing both hands on my hips as Ms. Liz did when she wore her more authoritative hat.

"All right, one more drink. But I insist you have one with me."

I huffed and rolled my eyes but grabbed another glass and the bottle. A little voice in the back of my head, the one that went off when I got myself in the most unusual circumstances and sounded an awful lot like Mr. Jim, whispered a warning. I poured the whiskey anyway.

We both lifted our drinks, and he asked, "So who's the owner of this place?" He shot his entire drink once more.

I held the glass of whiskey before me as if, at any moment, it would reach out to bite me. Mr. Jim wasn't the friendly type and didn't need to be meeting every Tom, Dick, and Harry that walked in. Especially one as talkative as this fellow. And even more, he did not need to be pulled away from his Monday paperwork to find me behind the bar against all orders. But right as this questionnaire of a man asked who the owner was, Wallace walked in. He looked confused and a little grumpy, only to pause, settling in the doorway with a devil's smile.

"Well, there's the owner right there, sir." I pointed to Wallace.

Wallace's eyebrow rose, but for just a moment. He quickly pushed back some stray hairs of his and walked toward my new friend, who had turned halfway to take a gander.

"Afternoon, girl—" he did not say my name "—and afternoon to you as well, sir. How may I be of assistance?" His funny little accent was gone, and I had gooseflesh. His voice sounded more like a grumble, more like Mr. Jim. His immediate reaction to the situation had me noting how thick the air was with unspoken emotion.

Questionnaire looked skeptically at me. He threw a thumb in Wallace's direction, saying, "You're telling me this is the owner? It doesn't even look like he's got hair on his chest."

"Well, he does." *I should not have said that.*

Wallace's eyes were wide with sheer delight as he looked at me in shock.

"He is older than he looks," I corrected.

I shot my whiskey and winced at the awfully sweet, hot taste. Wallace's smile couldn't have been any bigger.

"The girl ain't wrong. The name's Jesse Williams."

I turned around with my glass to clean it up as the heat of the whiskey lingered in my nose. I watched Wallace place himself between the fella, who was straightening up, and me through the mirror. The fella twisted his mustache and gave "Jesse" a sharp eye. "She said she didn't have a man."

I stilled at that.

"Well, then I'd take her word on it."

"She your regular?" Wallace shrugged. "Seems a little young."

"We take care of our own 'round here. What can I do for ya?" Wallace inquired smoothly.

I headed over to the other end of the bar and straightened up already straight glassware. "Well, Mr. Williams, how long you owned this place?"

Wallace looked relaxed, leaning against the back of the bar with his arms crossed, looking interested. Questionnaire was leaning forward, nearly panting like a dog after a bone.

"Been involved with it for a while. What brings you into town?"

"Business."

"What sort of business? Heading further west, I suspect."

"Suppose I could. Been on the move for a while now. You bring her here with you?" He gestured his chin toward me. I unashamedly polished glasses facing the man who insisted on discussing me, but kept my distance.

"You know her?" Wallace looked over at me as if he were seeing me for the first time, from the perspective of our nosey new friend.

"Not sure. Someone I know might. Those eyes..." He looked down at his empty glass and downed whatever droplets remained. "I must say, you don't forget eyes like those." I fought a scoff at his melodrama. I didn't know anyone.

"Girl, come on over here," Wallace said with ease.

I obeyed with my head held high despite the discomfort that ravaged my gut. Those butterflies had grown teeth and gnawed away at my belly.

"You know this man?" Wallace inquired with a kind, unreadable face that paired nicely with my bored one.

I studied the man hard like I was genuinely trying to place him and play along. I squinted with those eyes of mine he swore he knew, then shook my head. "Not from this lifetime."

Questionnaire cracked a smile and nodded, then rummaged through his pockets until he produced a fine watch with a shiny silver chain. "Next train?"

"Heading back to Denver already, are ya? Leaves at six. Hope ya find whoever you're looking for," Wallace said politely.

He added a light chuckle as if I were some pretty young thing that folks asked about all the livelong day, and he had grown accustomed to the curiosity. I was sure he thought himself a clever bastard, my Wallace. But if we all were to turn and take a good long look into God's mirror, I wasn't sure if "pretty" would be what we found. The man continued to nod as he fished out his purse. He placed a coin down for the whiskey then looked at me. He tightened the strings and tossed it to me. I caught the surprisingly heavy bag.

"Thank you. I do as well," he said to Wallace. "They don't call me Saint Anthony for nothing." The man stood, touched the brim of his hat toward me, and walked out of the saloon. Beneath, where one of his hands lay, was a small piece of paper that Wallace reached for as I jingled the bag.

"What a funny thing to say," I mumbled.

Wallace turned the small paper over in his hand, then smoothly pocketed it. He glanced at the bag in my palm and gestured with his eyes to my pocket, and I nodded. I gestured toward his pocket with my eyes, mimicking him. My curiosity burned.

"I have no intention of letting you go after him, girl. Now, you mind telling me what's going on?" Wallace yanked at the cloth that rested over my shoulder and grabbed the empty glass. He polished off the leftover tawny liquid.

I inhaled and let it out dramatically, letting my lips flap together as my face vibrated with the movement. A sense of relief slowly coated my gut with the man's departure. "Ralston's baby is coming. Figured it made sense to just head on over. Didn't have the time to ask permission."

He rolled his eyes at me. I leaned my hip against our side of the bar and watched him smoothly handle the glassware. "What did he say his actual name was?" Wallace asked, turning and nearly overpowering me.

I took a small step back and shrugged.

He leaned back and let out a bit of an angry laugh. "Christ, Trixie, do you ever take the time to ask anyone their name?"

My head buzzed from the whiskey, and I couldn't help but reflect on my carelessness of our first encounter, which I had no doubt he was referring to with his amiable annoyance. Despite the chide, I preferred Wallace's comical exasperation to Mr. Jim's short fuse when dealing with my general nonsense.

"Was he in here waiting for you?"

I shook my head. A droplet of sweat slid down my spine. He took a step closer, and I wiped my forehead. It was like he brought the heat from the summer into the saloon with him. *I had been comfortable before he came in, hadn't I? Well, at least temperature-wise.*

"You sure you don't know him?"

"Yes, *Jesse*, I am sure I do not know him," I drawled.

He took another step closer, and I held my ground. Partially because I was stubborn and didn't like his condescending tone. And partially because my back was pressed as tightly as it could be to the lip of the bar.

"What are you doing here, anyway? Who is at the shop?" I prompted with worry and waved my hand in the direction of the general store.

He snatched my hand, and I involuntarily waited for a punishing twist or swat or squeeze for being rude. Instead of lashing out, he pressed my hand against his chest. Gently he held it there, so it was enclosed in a warmth that I really didn't need.

"Now, now, Trix. 'Twas lookin' for ye, girl. Figured with a day as hot and slow as this, and Jim tucked away with his papers, that we'd have a wee picnic. Maybe ride over to the Lil' Big and get our toes cool. Say a hello to our Tom Beau. I suspect he is missin' ye somethin' awful."

I pulled at my too-warm hand, but he held on tight and kept an easy face. I glanced at my boot-clad feet and pictured my toes, a bit swollen from the heat and the leather and the standing all damn day, sunken in the cool waters of the Lil' Big. And I pictured his larger pale feet next to mine as the birds chattered and the wind cooed, pushing hot air on the backs of our necks. He tapped his fingers against mine, quietly demanding a response.

"That sounds nice."

A hand interrupted the view of my feet as Wallace lifted my chin with his knuckles to force eye contact. Evil wasn't red or black. No, evil was the color of Jayson Wallace's eyes. They shone like the all-too-still waters of Lil' Big on a hot and cloudy day, shamelessly wrapped around my naked body. I chewed on my bottom lip, and he shifted his thumb so that it could rub at it, not too gently. The motion was invasive, but I enjoyed it.

"Girl, I think ye'd be shocked at just how *nice* I can be."

I raised my eyebrow and pushed the bar to its limits with my body weight. The rib of the tabletop dug into my back with a bite, and I relished briefly in the controlled, familiar feeling. His gaze was as hungry as the first day I met him, only now I could see the whites of his eyes.

"How's that whiskey treating ye?"

I stopped myself from moving to wipe at the sweat dripping down the back of my neck caused in part by the whiskey in question.

"Warm," I said bluntly. I wouldn't let him rattle me.

"Mmmm," he hummed in response, stepping closer.

His leg pushed through my skirts, and I was inordinately aware of it. I kept his eye despite the urge to look at the leg and see just how close it was. His breath fanned across my face. It didn't smell like much, and that was nice.

"Wallace," I began with nowhere to go conversationally.

His hand slowly slid from my chin over to the high of my cheekbone. His face was, somehow, contorted with a lack of assuredness as well as his cocky spirit. I leaned into that hand and watched his face make expressions I didn't understand. The feeling of his rough hand against my skin was unexpectedly pleasant. He leaned an inch closer. My breath stuttered in my throat at his final proximity. Just as I comprehended his intentions, his eyes flashed to the door.

A mean and familiar smile bloomed, shattering the beautiful façade he had painted for me across his countenance. "Afternoon, Jim."

I clenched my eyes shut and swore horribly.

Chapter 10

Wallace leaned against the door of Mr. Jim's office with his arms crossed behind him, looking bored as ever with a pipe tucked between his lips. I glanced down at my feet to avoid Mr. Jim's gaze. I quietly wished they were in the Lil' Big, with or without Wallace's big ol' pale man feet next to them.

"You mind explaining to me what was going on behind the bar?" Mr. Jim's voice was low.

I took in the messy office around us. My attention rested on a big brass tub that sat in a far corner. Something tugged at the back of my mind as the summer sun shimmered across the tarnished tub that could barely fit a grown man. Something about the way that bathtub glimmered...

Mr. Jim cleared his throat impatiently.

I crossed my arms over my chest and held my chin high. "I—"

"I was just teasing her, Jim," Wallace cut in, his words coming off rough around the wooden pipe. I fought the urge to whirl around and smack him.

Mr. Jim looked over at Wallace with venom. "Well, don't."

Wallace laughed at that, but he nodded. I was flustered about being the center of the discussion. Wallace had been closer to me than any man ever had, and to have Mr. Jim catch us made my skin itch.

"Why weren't you at the store, Trixie?"

I moved my jaw around a bit as if it was sore, buying myself time to word my reasoning properly. Although it was shocking, Mr. Jim allowed me time to organize my thoughts.

"Ralston's baby is coming. He asked me to cover for him. Bit of a rush."

"Anyone come in?" His tone was deadly.

I nodded.

"Who?"

"Some mister from outta town. Clean. Chatty sort." I wanted to cover my mouth as the unnecessary details tumbled out before a second thought. Nerves had me rambling.

"Chatty how?"

"He was asking about Trixie and who owned the place. He was very focused on how long Trixie had been here," Wallace said, taking a step closer to us but still from a reasonable distance.

Mr. Jim bowed his head and took a deep breath. "Did you get his name?"

"No, sir," I said without hesitation, unable to fight the boredom in my voice.

No reason to prolong the inevitable hollering. The room was too still, only interrupted by the sound of the train blowing. It was southbound in ten minutes at the most.

"I'm docking your wages," Mr. Jim finally said, glaring at me.

"Excuse me?" I retorted with a step toward him. "I am not the one who left mid-shift. Need I remind you?" I noticed Wallace turned his back to us and rested both hands on the top of his head as if to pull out the hair upon it. As if he were as frustrated as I was. Mr. Jim paid him no mind, per usual.

"Are you suggesting I withhold pay from a man who has a family to support on accounts of him needing to be with his wife for the arrival of their firstborn child?"

I stomped my foot out of frustration.

"I think not," he said with finality.

"A situation presented itself. I handled it. I broke nothing and caused no unplanned expenses. I didn't stir any trouble. Why would my wages be docked?"

"You were ignorant and irresponsible. You need to just ask for help. You got too much pride for having nothin' between your legs, girl."

I was silent as the day repeated in my head; I was looking for my detrimental error. I had broken a rule. I had to give him that. But in my defense, the man clouded me with so many it was hard not to break one or two in my daily routine. Wallace slithering into my room each night broke at least the top three, and I fought the urge to look over to the man at fault with butterfly-wrecking nerves. *I could trust him to keep our secret, couldn't I?* I shook my head as if it would clear my racing thoughts. I sifted through myself as well, in search of the pride he accused me of being filled to the brim with. I was dog tired and couldn't shake the awful taste in my mouth.

"That ain't right, Mr. Jim," I settled with, through clenched teeth.

"Right?! You wanna know what ain't right? You incessantly and mindlessly disobeying every godforsaken request I give you. And expecting to be paid for it! You risked the reputation of my business today due to your selfishness and arrogance. I provide income and a roof over your head, and this is the thanks I get? I have half a mind to fire you. Now get your scrawny ass out of my sight before I really lose my temper; so I can sort out this mess you've made for us."

"What mess, Mr. Jim?" I finally hollered loud enough that the veins in my neck throbbed.

He took a step toward me, and I immediately grew light on my feet so when he swung, I wouldn't fall. I hated to fall. I hated looking up at him as he stood over me and stared like I was to blame for his violence.

Another step from Mr. Jim, and Wallace quickly slid in front of me, placed his hands on my shoulders, and walked me backward out of the room. His face was uninterested, and he didn't make eye contact, but his grip on my shoulders could bruise. The pipe looked as though it would splinter between his clenched teeth.

He stopped when he was in the door frame, and I, the dimly lit hallway. "Go," he mouthed, still looking over my head.

I took another step back, and his hands fell at his sides. I tried to meet his eyes, but he, in return, slammed the door so hard the air rushed against my cheeks. I wiped at my clammy face, then dramatically stomped down the steps loud enough to echo throughout the warm, quiet building. I made it to the bottom and waited a beat, saying one rushed Hail Mary in my head. *Would a prayer fall on deaf ears if my once memorized words began to stumble? Which saint was responsible for translating the messy pleas that came from minds so lost and desperate language seemed to only be a barrier?* Ought to light a candle for that one once I figured it out.

Then I crept up the steps with the sensibility of a church mouse. The door was shut tightly, but a lifetime of sneaking about told me the wood was good and hollow. Walking only on the balls of my feet, I leaned my right ear against the cool wood. My cheek was damp with sweat and liquified anger.

"Damnation!" Mr. Jim grumbled.

I heard glasses clinking and pictured Mr. Jim pouring himself a couple fingers too many of whichever amber liquid happened to be within reach.

"You—" Wallace stopped short.

The floorboards creaked closer to the door that I hid behind.

"Best you check and make sure no creatures are lurking in the hall. You do it—I'll slap her if I see her," said Mr. Jim's voice.

I bit the bottom of my lip and swiftly turned to flatten myself against the wall next to the door. I held my breath as it swung open a little violently. It seemed we all were in bad spirits. Wallace poked his head out to look down both ends of the corridor. When our eyes met, it was as if he saw right through me. I flashed him my most pleading look.

"All clear!" he called and turned to casually place himself in the open-door frame.

I was blocked, out of sight, should Mr. Jim come closer to the door. His stance created the illusion that Wallace kept watch for Mr. Jim. To my amazement, the lookout was for me. I inched toward Wallace. His crossed arms made his back a little more intimidating. I gazed too long at the sharp mountains of his shoulder blades. The hand that tucked under his right elbow waved at me slightly.

"Continue," Mr. Jim finally said.

"You were too hard on her."

"Bah! I wasn't hard enough!"

I almost saw the spittle that flew from such an outburst. I listened to Mr. Jim swallowing and noticed that Wallace's hand had turned into a fist.

Mr. Jim let out a sloppy, "Ah. That girl is going to be the death of me. Truly."

Wallace snorted at that. "She did exactly what you or I would have done."

"But she ain't you or I, is she? It ain't right having her work the bar."

"I agree, Jim. I don't want her working the bar either. But she was just trying to help."

"That girl is never 'just trying to help.' That girl is a vain, immoral beastie sent to me from whichever ring of hell she was conceived in. A wild thing, running around and causing a muck of everything I have put together for us. She cannot keep her place."

"And what exactly is her place? You'll have the girl store grains until she's faint, but she's too good to pour a couple drinks, is it?" A tense silence followed Wallace's sharp question. "Jim," he sighed, "I'm just trying to understand. Who is she to you?" Despite Wallace's calm and condescending tone, his fist tightened.

I angrily bit my lip. The skin around Wallace's broad knuckles was lighter with the stretching. That image of unexplained anger tugged at my heartstrings. I couldn't help but reach out to try and ease that fist. The man was putting himself between Mr. Jim and I, something that no one had ever done before. At my touch, his fist loosened. I tried to pull away, only to have him smoothly snatch at my fingers. He tangled them together and took both of our hands to fake a back scratch—a smooth disguise of his impulsive movements.

"We've already discussed this," Mr. Jim said solemnly.

My stomach quickly sunk at the confirmation that this was not the first time the two had spoken of me behind false pretenses of privacy. I pulled at my hand to distance myself from Wallace. To be this close to him suddenly felt like treason.

Mr. Jim cleared his throat to continue his lazy condemnation. "I have spent my entire life teaching that girl to not bring any attention to herself."

"What is so wrong with anyone ever noticing Trixie-girl, eh? You plan on keeping her forever?" His fingers got a little tighter around mine.

I observed our intertwined hands a little dazed, wondering if my palm would start to get clammy. Nerves did that to me sometimes.

Mr. Jim didn't respond. I heard another loud and rude gulp.

"This isn't about the girl working the bar, is it, Jim? At least, not really."

Silence.

"Should Trixie-girl know the man that came into the bar today?"

I tried again to pull my fingers away from Wallace, becoming a little more frustrated. He yanked at my wrist harshly and covered the movement with a cough. I was pressed against his back with a tumble that, thankfully, he withstood. I fought the urge to bite him. Gone were those warm feelings my heartstrings were creating. Back was my piping hot annoyance.

"No."

"Do you?"

Mr. Jim said nothing again.

I pressed my forehead a little harder into Wallace's back even though in the moment, I violently hated him. I once again dug through my memories, trying to recall the mustached man from anything other than this day's greeting. I had nothing. I only knew folks in Wicker Soul, and even them, I didn't know so well. I had no connections outside of Mr. Jim, and he made sure I knew it. So, the question of if or why I would know that odd fellow passing through upset my stomach.

"There's something you're keeping from me, isn't there?" Wallace's tone was unnervingly low.

I tried to pull away. My stomach dropped, and if the butterflies drowned, I really didn't know what I would do with myself. I had been ordered out of the room by perhaps a grace of God, and not just Mr. Jim's command.

"I don't know what's going on, but you can't blame the girl for acting how she does. She is completely ignorant of what is and is not appropriate to occur between a man and a woman, and you're to blame. You've kept her in the shadows for too long. One of these days, she is going to get hurt," Wallace continued.

"You telling me this out some kind of firsthand experience?" Mr. Jim growled.

I didn't breathe.

"Not exactly."

A cold silence fell.

"I did not bring you onboard to advise me in the matters of my girl."

"Yer girl, huh? And yer sure about that? Because dealin' with her seems to take precedence o'er just about everythin' in yer life."

I buried my face deeper into his back as if to say, 'don't push.' Our intertwined hands crushed against my breastbone, and he held on tighter.

"Back off, *boy.*"

Wallace tensed, almost pulling away from me. I gripped his shirt with my free hand.

"Is Trixie in danger?"

Another large gulp from Mr. Jim. "I don't think so." My breath was warm against Wallace's back. "But I have my concerns. You said the man was headed for Denver?"

"Left his card with her."

I pinched Wallace's skin as if to hush him, and he squeezed my hand tighter.

"Called himself Saint Anthony. I've been away from the church longer than I'd be comfortable admittin' around these parts, but ain't that the patron saint for lost things?"

I ground my teeth so harshly my jaw could have burst from both sides. There was a pause in the room, then chaos. Drawers were opened, and things shuffled around haphazardly. Mr. Jim doing anything in a rush, let alone pack, made my teeth grind. It took a lot in me to keep my breathing low and my panic at bay.

"What're ye doin'?" Wallace inquired.

"You can handle everything here. I gotta get to Denver. Gimme that card." Mr. Jim's voice was hushed but urgent.

Wallace paused for only a moment, then with the hand that wasn't wrapped in mine, he fished in his pocket for the slip of paper. He produced it and rearranged himself so that I was even more tucked behind him. I pushed myself so close that we could have been one person, and his thumb tenderly stroked my hand. I pinched his back again.

"Ye plan on tellin' me what this is all about?" Wallace fired.

Mr. Jim's footsteps approached us, and I made myself as invisible as I could with the corner Wallace had created for me. Wallace's free hand held the card up for Mr. Jim. His weathered hand reached out and snatched it. He hurried on.

"I'll explain when I'm back." And he rushed down the steps.

Wallace turned so that I stayed behind him, and his back pressed my back into the wall.

"I'll be waitin'!" Wallace hollered.

I didn't move until I heard the slam of the door. With that reassuring sound, Wallace stepped away from me. He leaned his back against the opposite wall and folded his arms across his chest. I mimicked his stance and relished in the cool air that replaced his warm body. It was too warm out for any of that nonsense.

Chapter 11

Mr. Jim had been gone for the better part of a week. Unsurprisingly, Wallace, left in charge of just about everything, had no problem keeping up with the business necessities. The hour was late, and the night was warm. We had trickled to the porch, unable to take the heat that lingered in the boarding house's walls. The air was dry and thin and ought to have been cooler this time of year. It had been a hot summer.

I sat on the railing, one knee bent with my book resting against it, and the other dangling. Very ladylike. My hanging foot swung lightly as if my subconscious attempted to stir the air enough to create a breeze. The stillness of the air made my book more unrealistic. I had read the same line about four times by the time Billy-boy gave a grumpy sigh and fidgeted in the large rocking chair.

Dev was quietly working on her needlepoint to the right of him, and Ms. Liz had drifted off to sleep to his left. Her mouth was opening and closing softly, as soft snores escaped. I was happy to see her resting. Not even a cricket chirped, and my mind wandered to Mr. Jim. The air of his departure was an awful taste in my mouth. I had foolishly been waiting for a letter with some form of explanation all week. My gut clenched tightly. Something wasn't right. The promises he made to me that night he had last returned faded. Whatever planning I assumed was necessary for leaving come spring was yet to be discussed. I waited for Mr. Jim with the same desperation as a farmer for rain.

Colorado's drought remained.

Billy sighed again, and I looked at him. Dev did the same with a secretive smile on her face. "Well, it's hot as dogs, isn't it?"

We both sighed in lazy agreement.

"Seems about time for a rain, don't ya think?" he grumbled as if reading my thoughts.

"Probably. We're in the heart of August," I agreed, gently folding the page I had pretended to read and closed my book.

Our voices were low, as we were keenly aware of Ms. Liz's slumber. It was true, the end of July was a typical time for a storm to pass through, and that storm hadn't shown. The moon was growing full, but She was not quite there yet.

"Man, this night is too hot, I tell you. I cain't be the only one feeling so. How's about a drink, girls of mine?" Billy smiled handsomely at the both of us.

Dev smiled back a little secretly, and I let out a laugh and leaned my head against the pillar.

"Ms. Liz has a bottle of good sherry stashed behind her canning. Grab it, won't you?" I breathlessly reported as I winked at Billy, who stood but gave me a look of disgust.

"Sherry? What about something a little less..." He trailed off, gesturing with his hand as if I understood what he meant.

I rolled my eyes. "A little less what?"

Billy scratched behind his neck. "Wells, if-ing we are gonna have a little indulgence, why wouldn't we just head on over to the saloon?"

"You wanna go get whiskey drunk? Fine by me, but you'll be going on your own," I huffed.

"And why is that?"

"Well, Dev and I wouldn't be going."

"And why in hell wouldn't ya? Girl, you been drinking whiskey since you was sixteen and still had braids in your hair. Dev makes her livelihood singing her pretty little heart out there for Christ's sake!"

I said nothing.

"It's 'cause of Mr. Jim, innit?" Billy pushed.

I set my jaw and noted the saloon's faint light. My body was still, despite the roaring in my head. The urge to leave gave me a headache—to remove myself from this exact place and moment, so I wouldn't be subject to such vicious amounts of attention.

"Trixie-girl, don't you think it's about time you stop being so afraid of Mr. Jim? I mean, he ain't even in town," Billy added.

The night couldn't get any quieter, yet after his words, it did. I ground my teeth. Because he was right. But not in the way he thought he was. Mr. Jim's wrath still put a shiver down my spine. As a child, I had been braver. That was the only conclusion I had arrived at this week. In my youth, life hadn't seemed like it could really dig its filthy claws in deep enough to scar. So, a slap in the face here and there from an angry caretaker rarely slowed me down. But now, as a grown sort of woman, those slaps had decreased.

I was not a child, and life had been good to me. Especially considering my circumstances. But the older I got, the larger and less inviting the world seemed. The circumstances I was born with were much more apparent than in my youth. As a child, running around in the sun all day explained my *unkept* appearance. But now, excuses for my appearance were more transparent. Everything about me was a shade too close to suspicion. And out here where law was a three-letter word, most folks hadn't taken the time to learn—suspicion could be dangerous. The dangers had grown from a scary story to something palpable bubbling just beneath the surface. Those dreams and plans of simply taking off one day felt ignorant and childish now. As much as I hated to admit it, Mr. Jim made me feel safe.

My Billy-boy was correct. I feared Mr. Jim. But that fear of him was not so much that he would return to Wicker Soul only to find me up to no good. That, at this point, I would relish in. Now my biggest fear, the one that kept me up without a wink of sleep almost every night since he left, was the fear that he wouldn't. I needed him to take the brunt of the world for me: that, or a goddamn miracle.

Thus, I was confident God had turned a blind eye to me, despite how much I tried to discuss such a miracle. Despite how much I yanked at those strings that attached me to His will. I couldn't tell if He was mad at me for all the naughty I had gotten into lately or if He hadn't ever bothered with me in the first place. I pictured the wooden base of my marionette, up in that white and fluffy heaven of His hung on a door hook like a well-worn coat. Secure, forgotten, not going anywhere.

Those worrisome visions of mine made me just about as lonely as possible and reinforced that I could not lose Mr. Jim. My desires to flee were squishing like a bug under Christopher Columbus's boot. Because my chances of drowning in a world without Mr. Jim, as a no-name female orphan who couldn't seem to ever behave, were high. And so I sat on a porch, waiting for him to come back so I could start living again.

I thought I'd been pretty good about keeping all that private, though. My face and chest grew warm and itchy. I quickly swung myself off the railing and walked right up to Billy, jabbing my finger into his chest. "I ain't afraid of no Mr. Jim."

Billy smiled a big toothy grin. Lying for me was as easy as breathing, it seemed. "Oh, yeah? Prove it."

"Billy, how about you find that bottle of sherry, hmmm?" Dev reminded as she stood and gently placed a hand on his shoulder.

He went into the house without a second word.

"Thank you," I murmured just above a whisper.

Dev settled herself back into her rocker. It squeaked lightly. "To be entirely honest with you, I am not sure I could stomach any whiskey or whatever follows tonight," she offered quietly, focusing on her needlepoint. Dev sat in front of me, but she was miles away. I felt her distance in the warm summer air.

I stood in the middle of the porch, quite awkwardly, with my book in my hand and stared dumbly at Dev.

"Quit that, missy," she grumbled.

I slowly walked back to my preferred seat on the railing. I studied the shy Mary, bright like the harvest moon, but not round enough. I'd start praying again once She was. Ms. Liz's soft snores, as well as the bit of rattling from inside the house, were the only noises of the night. I closed my eyes and leaned my head against the pillar, getting a little lost in it all.

Running most of the business with just Wallace in charge had me working hard enough that my mind shouldn't have been on anything other than the time to wake, eat, and sleep. Instead, I was in a constant daze of nerves. My gut told me that Mr. Jim wasn't just going to leave me here, but my heart ached at his departure. After he left his office in a rush, I ran to the window only to see him walk straight for the train. No stopping to look for me with an update of his going. His head was down, and he rushed to catch a departing train. The train that I had never been invited on.

Clinking glass pulled me to the present and briefly away from all the worry. Billy returned to the porch with the bottle proudly in one hand and four small glasses hanging between each finger of the other. I hopped off my seat and helped him. I set each glass down on the railing and reached my hand out to pour for everyone.

"The girl works one shift and thinks she's our bona fide barkeep, does she?" Billy teased.

I simultaneously snatched the bottle out of Billy's hand and smacked his head hard enough to know I didn't want it brought back up.

He grumbled, and I poured two-thirds of each glass full and set the bottle down to disperse them. "I poured the fourth for Ms. Liz in case she wakes."

I raised my glass to cheers, and they joined me. The clink of the glasses sounded like they shattered in our hands with such a silent night, and we all giggled, glancing worriedly at Ms. Liz. But she slept on, so we drank. The light, tawny-colored liquid was much more pleasant than any whiskey. It wasn't sweet, but salty and nutty where whiskey felt sticky. It was warm going down but didn't leave a streak of fire that made me choke. More so, as of late. I closed my eyes to savor the taste just as a small, short-lived breeze picked up.

"That's nice, hmmm," I purred.

They both murmured in the affirmative.

"Really, that ain't half bad, now is it?" Billy-boy added, a little surprised.

I swatted his shoulder and giggled, taking another small slip. Dev just held hers close to her breast. She looked a little pale in the evening light. I cocked my head at her as if to prompt her to explain what I didn't exactly know, and she turned her shoulder to me. I furrowed my brows and stuck my nose in my glass to give it a good inhale. It smelled hot, and my nostrils crinkled up involuntarily. Billy reached around me to snatch the bottle, now half-full. He had already downed his glass and poured himself another, and I scoffed at that.

He gave me the eye and a bit of a *harrumph*. "I've seen you drink double the amount in a quarter of the time."

I smiled. Unfortunately, Billy was correct. It wasn't exactly acceptable in the eyes of God, Mr. Jim, or society. Still, as Billy and I entered our teenage years, I found I enjoyed a drink as much as the boys my age.

"Man-zan-nella. Huh," Billy read as he held the bottle against the bits of light and sipped his second glass slightly slower.

"In Spanish, when there are two *l*s, it makes a *y* sound," Wallace announced as he slowly walked up the porch steps.

The man took one final puff on his pipe before regarding it to his shirt pocket. "*Manzanilla*," he pronounced for Billy.

"Well, ya don't say?" Billy seemed impressed with that, so impressed a small fly could have floated right into that mouth of his.

I felt Wallace's gaze on me as I took a calming, deep sip. He had kept clear of me since Mr. Jim's departure. None of the *teasing* that had gotten us into trouble last week reoccurred, and I enjoyed the predictability of being held at arm's length once more. Alone, at least to an extent.

"Evening, Jayson. Care for a glass?" Billy placed a friendly hand on his shoulder.

"I suppose it couldn't hurt. What have we got here, anyway?" Wallace reached for the bottle to analyze. His eyes widened. "Where on earth did you lot find this?"

"In my momma's cupboard. Where'd ya learn Spanish?" Billy-boy asked while passing Ms. Liz's glass to Wallace.

Wallace didn't break his focus from the bottle as he reached out to take the glass, not even as he lifted the glass to his nose and inhaled deeply. He closed his eyes briefly, and I couldn't help but mimic his actions. His face was so serene.

"Spain."

None of us said anything, and he noticed us waiting for a better answer.

"Traveled quite a bit in my younger days," Wallace said with boredom.

Billy hummed at that. I shoved my nose back into my glass and closed my eyes. I smelled more than a nutty aroma. I smelled apples, hay from a horse barn, orange peel, walnuts, salty gravy, and something that reminded me a bit of the damp earth.

"You get all that?" Wallace murmured.

My eyes opened to Wallace, staring at me intently, his mouth corners lifted and slightly ajar. He looked excited. I nodded, then took another sip.

"Swish it around in there," Wallace suggested gently.

I froze but did as he said. My cheeks felt comically puffed out as I gurgled the liquid. It coated all the corners of my mouth with flavor. It was surprisingly potent for the relatively small amount of sherry I had consumed. My body felt a little warm, and the taste was as intoxicating as the alcohol it possessed.

"Now, swallow."

I did as instructed and flushed. Wallace raised his eyebrow at me with anticipation, and I licked the remnants from my lips.

"Delicious," I answered truthfully.

He refilled my glass.

"What're you talking about, Jayson?" Billy-boy asked as he shoved his nose into the glass.

"The complexities of the sherry, Billy. Its layers."

Billy's mouth twitched in a lack of understanding.

Wallace continued. "They are there, like a cake, but a bit less obvious. You've got to search for them, work for them, have patience with them." Wallace made eye contact with me, despite the direction of his conversation.

I gestured to his glass with my chin. Wallace took a sip and swallowed quickly, following with the smile I had grown accustomed to.

"They are past the initial appearance, past that garish temptation of alcohol. You drink the sherry to experience the sherry first. The reward for your patience with her is the stupor." Wallace took another sip.

Billy sniffed deeply and then quickly downed the liquid in his glass. I couldn't help the laughter that bubbled out of me. I covered my mouth with the lip of my glass as Billy grimaced for swallowing a fair amount of alcohol so quickly. Billy let out a rude, "ah" in satisfaction, and Dev giggled. "I don't know about all that, Jayson, but that damn sherry sure does taste good."

Wallace chuckled and nodded before taking another sip. He refilled Billy's glass and handled him the bottle. Then he leaned against the railing near my book. He picked up the book he'd slipped into my room nearly three weeks ago. I hadn't progressed much.

"Honey, haven't you tried yours?" Billy softly asked Dev.

I wandered over to Wallace as Dev reassured Billy. Wallace quickly flipped the page to where I had dog-eared my place, then looked up at me as I approached.

"You stuck?"

I shrugged.

"Don't tell me it's boring you," he smirked.

I shrugged again, and a hot breeze picked up and pulled at my loose hairs. Wallace put down the book and mimicked me leaning over the railing. His shoulder lightly brushed mine. We were silent as Billy and Dev spoke in hushed love behind us, and Ms. Liz's snores scared off any bugs.

"Do you want another book?"

"Where all did you travel?" I ignored his question and provided my own. I was still thinking about his brief mention of his "youth."

"The shorter answer is where haven't I traveled." His hands slowly twisted the glass.

"Have you been everywhere?"

He laughed. "Well now, that would be a lot of wheres, wouldn't it?"

I said nothing at his jest and attempted to be patient.

"Not yet, I'd like to."

"Is..." I began but stopped myself.

I wanted to ask him everything about everywhere, but the words caught in my throat and lingered there. I leaned in to smell my almost empty glass again and desperately wondered what the ocean smelled like. What it sounded like. But I felt insignificant as those questions began to claw their way out, so instead I took a final sip of my drink. I felt Wallace's eyes, and I didn't bother wiping the sweat that trickled down the back of my neck.

"It's hotter there." I stilled at his words. "Hotter than here. Where this sherry comes from."

I nodded slightly to encourage him to continue.

"It's this little area called Sanlúcar de Barrameda."

I loved the way his mouth moved around the foreign-sounding region. No one spoke like him around here, and it made me look closely at his mouth.

"It's close to the water in the southwest of Spain. The region is called Andalusia. Everything is brighter there, like everyone's got a little more life in them. Maybe it's the ocean influence or the heat. I haven't quite figured it out. They've got these red capes, and I tell you, Trixie-girl, the red is so bright it shocks you a little. Makes your stomach feel funny. The air is so thick there sometimes it feels like someone is pushing back on you when you try to walk forwards. It's too close, that air, and it tastes like the ocean. It helps make that sherry of yours taste salty."

"Saltwater really does taste salty, huh?" I asked quickly.

"Yes, girl, it's saltier than anything you've ever had."

I smiled at the thought.

"It can sting your skin, but it's nice. It ain't anything like your Lil' Big. Days are hot and seem endless in the summers, and everyone's settled into this slower way of going about life. Your meals are long, filled with wines and sherries and salty meats and sweet fruits and creamy cheeses. And they've got these spices that make Christmas morning smell like dried-up leaves. It's all just so much slower there. But then, at night, everyone sort of comes out of that lazy, and there's music and dancing. You start to be happy that the air is so close."

I tried to imagine it. "You make it sound like a story."

"It is a story, Trix." His eyes were bright.

"That's what life is supposed to be, a story. *Your* story. And it's up to you to make it the best it can be—you alone control how grand the story is. You have the world at your fingertips, girl. You just don't see it."

I looked away from him.

"You could go, you know. That money Mr. Saint Anthony left you, plus whatever you've made working for Jim, you could buy passage. Easily." He spoke urgently in hushed tones.

I closed my eyes for a moment as I tried to swallow down my immediate *no* and basked in the tempting *yes* that momentarily chorused in my heart.

"Mr. Jim wants to head west first. Then to France. Is that close to Anduloosa?"

"*Andalusia*. That would be another trek, but of course, it's closer than here. What's Jim got to do with this?"

My throat tightened as my mind twisted to find a way to explain it to him. So, I said nothing. My hands tingled and ached with nerves. As if my fingernails had become too heavy on top of my fingertips. I focused on Billy and Dev as she prompted him for a glass of water. The door quietly shut, and I wanted to invite Dev to join us and divert the attention off myself. But she was already walking past us and around the corner of the house quickly, with a polite "excuse me." I followed her with my eyes until she was invisible and well on her way to the outhouse.

"Trix..." but Wallace was interrupted by a strange sound coming from the direction Dev had just hurried off to. It almost sounded like retching. We both waited a moment, but the sound was gone as quickly as it occurred. "Trix, girl, I could help you get out of here. I could..."

I whipped my head around to give him my most sarcastic look.

"I mean it, though. If you want out, we could..."

"Wallace," I practically pleaded.

"...find a way. There is always a way."

My heart broke a little at his kind words. He saw that and reached out as if to touch me. I jerked back.

"Drop it," I said quickly.

Something icy glazed over his eyes in response to my rejection.

"Why are you not upset?" he shot at me.

I looked out across Wicker Soul. A faint smell of rose petals hit me, and I glanced down at my empty glass. I ignored the emotion his question evoked from deep within. He took a step closer, and I flinched, squeezing my eyes tighter. I could practically feel his hot breath on my skin.

"You know something is going on, and after last week, you know it isn't good. You are smarter than this, and you are deliberately putting your head in the sand. I want to know why. Where is that rage of yers? I canna understand why yer nae more upset," he whispered fiercely.

It was funny how his accent sometimes slipped up in the most random scenarios, always paired with that rattle of emotion I had no name for. Suppose it was an excellent way to keep my attention. My eyes flashed to his. Of course he didn't understand. How could he? He didn't know what it was like to be born into debts and contracts you didn't sign. I didn't have the energy or patience to explain it to him and didn't feel like he deserved it anyway. I swallowed down the tears of rage that collected in my eyes and met his gaze with my head held high.

"I am always upset. If I took the time to entertain all the reasons why I'd never get anything done," I snapped.

I pushed down all the emotions from such an attack as quickly as I could. I turned to snag the bottle of Manzanilla from the little table between Billy's seat and Ms. Liz's still snoring form. The moment my fingers touched the cool bottle, a harsh voice called out to my surprise. "Can't get enough of the drink, can you, girl?"

I froze as my heart pattered with relief at Mr. Jim's return, and with a flash, Ms. Liz's eyes opened. She snagged the glass from my hand. "Oh, Jim, leave her be. I was asking for a refill. Hotter than whatever lies below us is this evening. So, we all are having ourselves a little fête 'fore we go crazy."

I shared a small smile with Ms. Liz, and she winked. I poured her glass calmly and then turned just as Mr. Jim walked up the steps. I fought down the urge to stride up to him and wrap the familiar man in an embrace, as I had done months prior. But those months between then and now felt thick, full to the brim with lifetimes in-between. I had missed Mr. Jim. I bit my lip and smiled at him. He, in return, sent me a soft smile that took a brick off my chest.

"How ya been, girl?" He leaned against the railing and fished into his pocket and started rolling himself a cigarette.

"Just fine," I answered nonchalantly.

I casually walked over, attempting to rediscover my countenance of not having a care in the world. I folded my arms across my breast. Mr. Jim struck a match, lit his cigarette, took a long inhale, and then passed it to me. I could have broken out into the smile of a child on her birthday if I hadn't such an audience. I took my peace offering and inhaled deeply.

I only smoked with Mr. Jim. And he only offered when his spirits were high. Or at least, higher.

"Mr. Jim, you're back!" Billy exclaimed as he came out of the house with a glass of water in his hand. He shot a quick glance toward me as if to say sorry. He clapped Mr. Jim on the back, and Mr. Jim just nodded politely at Billy-boy.

"How was Denver?" Billy inquired obliviously.

I rolled my eyes and took another deep drag.

"Oh, just fine, Billy-boy, just fine." Mr. Jim looked at me and snapped his fingers, indicating to return his cigarette.

I promptly obeyed.

"Where's Dev?" Billy looked around as if he just noticed she wasn't on the porch.

"Ran off to the outhouse, be back any minute, I'm sure," Wallace offered coolly. He came out from his leaning posture in the shadows and approached Mr. Jim. The two shook hands, and Mr. Jim gave him a sharp smile, which Wallace returned.

"Keep my books tight?" Mr. Jim asked a little gruffly.

Wallace nodded and slid his hands into the pockets of his worn trousers.

"Mr. Jim, you must have a glass, as we are so happy to have you return to us," Ms. Liz proposed joyously, turning to rush into the house for that glass she insisted on.

A funny silence fell upon us, and I kept my eyes on Mr. Jim. He looked a little tired, but his spirits were much higher than when he had left. Dev slowly returned to us, floating on up like every step lifted her a little closer to the heavens. She always seemed to float about, but I could have been hyperaware of it due to the stark contrast between us.

"Ya alright?" I asked.

"Of course, Trixie-girl." She happily took the glass from Billy's outstretched hand.

"Nice to see you again, Mr. Jim."

He waved that off with a smile. "You all set for tomorrow?"

She nodded and took a large drink of water. Dev sang Saturdays, but it had been slow this summer, so she was scheduled most days of the week as of late. Polite conversation buzzed as Ms. Liz returned with a glass for Mr. Jim and all cheers, excluding me as I was playing the innocent. Mr. Jim continued to be cordial, and my heartbeats fell back into a comfortable pattern.

"Well, I've decided to pay a little listen to Miss Dev tomorrow, and I think we all ought to. Be a bit supportive of her talents and such," Ms. Liz said with finality upon her return.

Billy chorused in agreement, and as Dev blushed prettily, disappointment settled in my belly. I watched Mr. Jim, hopefully. Ms. Liz was aware of the tension behind Mr. Jim's abrupt departure last week. Still, she had not taken the time to discover any details behind why. And if she had, her ability to sneak about had reached new heights that would be as impressive as it would be terrifying.

"I'd love to go. Mr. Jim?" I was polite but steady with my questioning. I waited with patience, and Billy awkwardly finished his glass with his third loud gulp of the evening.

"Now, Jim," Wallace started with a singsong tone, and I wanted to slap the smile right off his sharp face. "What's the harm with the girl spending some hard-earned time with her family, hmm?"

"How's that, Jayson?" Mr. Jim's tone was icy.

"The way I see it, Trixie-girl is working-class, yes? The girl is working nearly every day to support herself and no one else; that isn't the sort of lifestyle for anyone above the working class," he continued, almost as if he were twisting a knife directed at Mr. Jim.

"What is your point, Jayson?"

"My point is, despite your view, the thing isn't technically a lady of much. My point is, my dear partner, if you are gonna leave Trixie in the working class," he smiled at that and looked at me before taking a slow sip of his glass, "she might as well enjoy the perks."

Chapter 12

I immediately left the gathering, nearly incapable of controlling my elation at the granted *permission* to hear Dev sing the next day. Part of that elation was rational. It didn't want to be squandered by me putting my foot in my mouth to upset Mr. Jim something awful and have this gift taken away. The other part was kept warm by the sherry Mr. Jim was under the impression I didn't consume, which went to my head quicker than I had planned.

Upon closing my door, I heard the faint echo of steps that followed. Heavy from a day's work and the stress of having to carry a larger form reverberated throughout the halls. The steps grew closer to my door, and my lightheadedness had me scrambling from the midst of undressing to lock my door. I stood pressed against the wood with my blouse almost entirely off. A soft knock vibrated against the cool wood. I gnawed at my bottom lip, realizing with an odd, sinking feeling that I really couldn't know who it was. I was a little ashamed since someone like Dev always knew who was knocking at her door late at night and she wasn't nearly as saintly as she looked.

Maybe worse, I didn't know who I hoped it was. So, I stayed silent and placed the hand that wasn't holding up my blouse over my mouth to quiet my breathing. My face was warm. Billy always said the best way to make up your mind was to flip a coin, and I fought the urge to quickly go rummage for one to calm my gut.

"Trix?" Wallace's gentle voice whispered.

Unexplainable tears sprang to my eyes as disappointment flooded in. I wouldn't need that coin to flip after all. Of course Mr. Jim hadn't come up to converse with me after such a time apart. *Why on earth would he need to?* He didn't owe me explanations for anything, and that was made abundantly clear. I should be happy. My elation should continue with the confirmation that Mr. Jim was so comfortable with his decision that he felt conversation unnecessary. But instead, I felt a cold dismissal. I had been prepared to rage. The wildfire that had been consuming our relationship was extinguished with a soft breeze instead of the storm I meticulously built by hand. My efforts weren't even necessary. I was not a storm, but instead a pulse of air, as useless as the changing tides in a landlocked location. Fucking meaningless. I was hollow with disappointment. A small sob slipped from my covered mouth as my mind tore at itself with claws sharpened by each passing second.

The knock repeated vigorously. "Trixie-girl, let me in."

I removed my hand from my mouth and placed it against the wood as if to hold the locked door shut. The doorknob slowly twisted an entrance attempt, but the lock held. Another quiet sob bubbled.

"Och, come on now. I dinna want ye alone. I'll just read to ye, girl." The doorknob jiggled once more. I pushed harshly against the door.

"Don't—" was all my thick throat mustered.

I leaned my head against the cool wood. A soft thud echoed above where my head rested, and I imagined Wallace mimicking my posture. My chest hurt as everything behind my breasts and lungs screamed to rip open the door. To stand before the man who tormented me in the daylight and made me pray like my soul was for sale in the moonlight. But the aching in my head that desperately tried to rationalize Mr. Jim's actions latched onto my heart and yanked it tightly against my spine.

"Please dinna start this..." His voice was strained as if somehow he was as choked by emotions.

I ached, lower than my heart and lungs. I was hollow at the thought of this large man outside my room, broken by the inability to enter, just as I was broken by not allowing him in.

"Go." Another sob broke through my lips, and in that moment I understood that there was something very wrong with me. Something terrible had grown like weeds within me, something that made me cling to one man and shove another away. So, I turned my back to the door and put myself to bed.

I **WOKE UP EARLY, JUST AT THE BREAK OF DAWN**, my head pounding from lack of sleep. After putting myself to bed, I listened to Wallace settle outside my door, lightly knocking every now and then as if I would change my mind. He stayed until my crying was no longer audible. He whispered a sweet farewell, and I shoved my blanket into my mouth, silencing emotion that threatened to spill over again. I tried desperately to sleep, but my body kept me up. I was awake until the wee hours of the morning. Sitting in the middle of my bed, arms tightly wrapped around my knees. When my cries settled, I experienced an unfamiliar sensation that started in my heart and spread down to the lowest pits of my belly.

I was hot and hollow in parts of me that I had always tried not to pay any attention to. The foreign feeling, both emotional and physical, made my jaw ache from grinding my teeth. I couldn't say why something warm and very private in nature made me clench tightly. Still, it was almost as if I knew someone would somehow witness my discomfort despite my solitude. And that possibility made me feel ashamed and clench even tighter. I dozed off about two hours before dawn, only to wake with a dry mouth and the lingering hollow feeling.

I rose undeterred by the desire to hide under the covers for the rest of eternity. The water left in the basin from the previous afternoon was cool and felt nice as I quickly splashed it on my face. I washed down parts of my body that held any stench and dressed with the same speed before stumbling out of my room in a sleep-deprived daze.

I discovered Billy-boy down the hall, leaning down to kiss a sleepy-looking Dev, snuggled tightly in her wrap outside her bedroom door. I froze, unseen in the darkness of my doorway. How strange that even at dawn, with sunshine sneaking into almost every nook and cranny of such a loving home, the shadows still found a way to pull me back into their sinister embrace. The tender visage of affection that I had grown so immune to over the years struck me. I watched as Billy-boy gently stroked her cheekbone before going back to his room. Dev smiled to herself and quietly re-entered her room.

When Dev had first joined us in town, overnight Billy became a confusing and unfamiliar thing. Perhaps that discomfort I had felt for the closest thing I had ever had to a brother could have been blamed on my own immature, adolescent mind. But when she entered our lives, everything changed. He had changed, and so did our sweet relationship. Not for the worse, but sometimes, in private, I had wondered if it was for the better. With her arrival, those last pieces of innocence and childhood wonder were ripped from Billy and me. Though I had stayed innocent, Dev's arrival brought sexuality to the table with a side of previously untouched human nature. Her introduction into our lives forced us to put away those childish things and walk forward into the life we were expected to create. While that brought her and Billy together, I was left very much alone, ripe for the shadow's plucking.

The hallway was empty once more, and I stayed put, worrying my bottom lip. *I had wanted to be alone, hadn't I?* When I was alone, I was not expected to explain. There was no tearing myself apart to fit into a mold when I was alone. So yes, I had coveted a life I would never have to answer questions I didn't know the answers to, which indirectly pointed me into a shimmering lonesome. But for reasons beyond me, witnessing Billy and Dev's love reignited that warm feeling from the previous night, which spread down to my lowest belly. More accurately, it went straight to the core of my entire, and unfortunately female, body. Something about that ache didn't sit right with my lonely. Contrarily, a cold feeling pumped through my veins. Cold, like regret.

I wondered what would have happened if I had opened my door last night. And allowed myself to accept comfort from a male counterpart that I obviously craved attention from. *Would he have sat in the rocking chair and read to me from the Bible with a voice much older than his body portrayed? Staying only until I fell asleep, or at least pretended to?* The pretending was only on occasional evenings when an itching in my toes told me no matter what man or God had to say about it if I slept, the terrors waited for me with open arms.

Or would last night have been different? Would he have been able to see the aching feeling within me, as he seemed to see everything else? Would he have the words to explain the desperate and mindless sensation that had me feeling warm and so alone that I might collapse upon myself? If so, did that mean he would provide a thorough explanation of the baser needs that seemed to have developed overnight? Needs that all and all probably would take an entire night to satiate, as they always seemed to with Billy and Dev. Would Wallace have been bidding me a sweet farewell in the wee hours of the morning? Would I have flushed cheeks and a sneaky look in my eyes that could make all the girls envious? Was I ready for all that?

My mind screeched to a halt. *Was I ready to walk into the womanhood I had worked so hard to ignore?* I had viewed my own body as a sexless being that fit neither here nor there, never taking the time to look more than twice at a handsome boy. For some reason, I was now oh-so-acutely aware of perhaps why that feeling within me was *hollow*. At the sound of the room-closest-to-mine's waking, I darted down the steps.

Chapter 13

I paused outside Dev's door. My fist lifted to knock quietly, but the nerves in my stomach held me frozen in place. As if God Himself was tired of my lazy, the door swung open to reveal a flushed and casual Dev with her hair down.

"Oh, Trixie," she breathed with a giggle, "I thought I heard someone at the door. Well, come on in, won't you? I'm just getting ready for tonight." She ushered me in.

I stalled for a moment with anxiety bubbling in my belly but snapped back into myself, rushing in and shutting the door softly.

"Feeling better?" I asked the door nonchalantly, clearing my scratchy throat afterward. She and I both knew I heard her sick last night, and I wasn't gonna let that slide on by.

She hummed in response to that.

I nodded to the door, dissatisfied.

"Trixie-girl? You all right?"

I spun at that and gave her a genuinely awful smile. She was taken aback by whatever face she saw, but I approached her as she sat in front of her vanity. "I'm fine," I murmured, moving to sit on her bed behind her. "I sure am excited I'll be getting to see you perform tonight."

She regarded me with an excited and nearly scandalized look. "Aren't you just? Oh, I'm so happy Mr. Jim is letting you loose!" She fell into a fit of giggles, but something beneath her tone felt a little tight.

Something was grounding about watching a woman prepare herself. Dev's deep red hair cascaded down her back as she glanced between herself and me in the mirror, slowly arranging it in a style. In the moment, with the late summer sun sinking, the beautiful woman who readied herself was given an unearthly glow. It was as if I had seen this all before. I squinted, almost waiting for her to start humming a tune I couldn't quite place. The image reminded me to swipe a bar of that rose-scented soap we had at the general store for her. I blinked at that abrupt thought. *Did Dev even like roses?* I fought the urge to shake my head and refocused on slowly attempting to put together the words I needed.

"Dev?" I finally said.

"Yes, Trixie-girl?"

"How..." I paused to lick my dry lips.

My hands shook slightly. *Why had I waited so long to have this conversation?* She had worry in her eyes, and I couldn't hold her gaze for more than a few moments. I hated myself, feeling foolish and ignorant. My embarrassment rushed in like the Great Flood. The flushed girlishness that I had repressed for so long flourished through me without expectation like a risky crop finally setting in roots.

"Brush out my hair, won't you?" she requested brightly, pulling me from my dark spiraling and allowing a break for my poor, abused bottom lip. She held out a fine brush to me. I gently brushed out her soft red locks, making sure not to catch on any knots. I listened to her breathing for a while and allowed the familiarity of her small movements to comfort me. She seemed better than last night.

Last night...

My head spun like a twister. Each object caught in the windy cyclone was how to begin my sentence. Dev was a very patient person, thankfully.

"Dev?" I finally mumbled.

"Yes?" She coaxed gently.

I felt her gaze through the mirror, but I stared at the task at hand. "When...when did you know?"

She politely waited, clearly aware that I had more. I stopped brushing to think for a moment. I gazed at my hands buried deep within her rich hair. It took serious effort to not just yank on that beautiful mane and scream what I meant. Now simply wasn't the time to be childish. *This was the most significant part of being human, wasn't it?* I finally met her eye in the glass, and I prayed my question wouldn't require any further explanation.

"How did you know you were ready to have...relations?"

Her mouth fell ajar.

"With Billy, of course," I finished in a rush.

That giant, curious, and perhaps even a little bit hopeful hole was filled with disappointment. Disappointment was a cold, shrewd witch that I knew far too well for most of my life. Dev's eyes drifted downward. There was no need for any further explanation, despite her silence. She knew exactly what I was talking about. I swallowed my shaking breath and continued to gently comb her hair, hoping to work out the cold feeling closing in around me.

"Trixie-girl, you shouldn't be thinking about such things. I shouldn't..." She took a shaky breath. "I shouldn't have told you. It's not decent. Especially for a young woman such as yourself. I've been a bad influence."

I closed my eyes tightly and counted to ten to calm the rage toward my dear friend. "We are the same age."

She reached back to grab the comb from my hand, then turned fully to look at me. She touched my hand in the same gentle manner. "Trixie-girl...we don't know that."

I yanked my hand back from her. I wanted to spit, and I began to pace.

She turned to me a little desperately. "Besides, we are different. Me and Billy, it's just something...well, you wouldn't understand 'cause you never..."

"Don't you start with that," I snapped and saw red. "We ain't that different, ya hear? And if this has got anything to do with my... my *father*, Dev, I swear! We don't know what he...well...my insides are made up of the same stuff as any other woman. With the same feelings and, and..." I gasped for breath.

One hand was over my heart, and the other was over my gut. One beat quickly, and the other churned, bubbled, and boiled to the same rhythm. "I may not know where he went, and my momma may be dead as a doornail, but that doesn't mean I don't deserve to feel something for once! I came here to talk to you to understand. I am a person, and I've got those warm hollow feelings, and I refuse to have them dismissed because I am below you or..."

"Trixie!" Dev cut me off with tears in her pretty eyes.

I stopped, and she took a deep breath to steady herself and slowly wiped the few tears from her eyes. "Trixie-girl, when on earth did I say you were below me?"

I gaped at her like a dumb fish.

"I *don't* think that, and I never did, so drop that real quick." She reached out and placed her cool palm upon my cheek. I scowled at her, but the tears continued to pool.

"I know you ain't below me, and that's what I am trying to say. You are so far above me. I am craning my neck to see right up your nose." Her voice cracked with a breathless laugh.

My jaw loosened.

"You, girl, you are gonna get yaself outta here. Me? I'm good-for-nothing. Nothing other than singing and making sure my tits look round and creamy under that cheap stage light. Now, I love your Billy-boy with all my heart, but that man is not just the best thing that is ever gonna happen to me. Trixie, he is the only thing that is ever gonna happen to me."

I inhaled to speak, but she held up a dismissive hand.

"You ask me how I knew or when I knew, well, let me tell you this. I knew the moment that boy laid his pretty, lazy eyes on me that I had one way to keep him. And I did what it took to accomplish just that. I'm lucky, 'cause it seems like we've got something real here, an honest sort of love. But I would have done all of this without love, and I would have done it just the same. And that is the difference between you and me. You ain't ever gonna have to do that. You've got some gumption in that belly of yours. You'll never need a man to take you in. You ain't ever gonna need to lay yaself bare on a bed when you are scared and desperate." Her tears spilled over.

A small, deep, and damn her for it being beautiful, sob came out of her red mouth. I bit my bottom lip. "That is how we are different.

You wear your lack of family like it is some smudge, but it ain't. Trixie, you don't belong to anybody. You are free. When I brush your questions aside about a warm feeling or the boudoir, don't take it incorrectly. Those feelings are a waste of time because you're worth so much more than your fuck." Her words were harsh, but the expression in her eyes that pleaded with me, the stark honesty of it all, had tears catching in my eyes just the same.

I wiped at mine quickly and pulled my hand away from hers. Dev was fragile. This I had known. But I never knew how deep that fragility had sunken into her. She could break. She *would* break, and I or anyone else would not be able to fix it once she did. I slid a hand over my face and took a deep breath. Her emotions were heavy, and I opened both my palms as if to offer consolation.

"Dev—" I murmured, but she faced the mirror once again.

She wiped at her face with shaky hands, ridding the tears and pinching her cheeks to add a lovely flush. Or at least that was the attempt. Her fair skin was pale and a little waxy as if she was ill or just about to be. I walked closely behind her but did not reach out. She had been healthy only moments before.

"Dev, you don't look so good."

She met my eye in the mirror and dropped her face. She slowly shook her head back and forth. A violet shudder went through her body that had me spin on my heel and grab her empty chamber pot from beneath her bed. She was sick last night, and she was going to be sick again.

She turned just in time to grab the pot from my hand and collapsed to her knees. I rushed over to her side to hold back her hair while she retched. I hushed her as if that was comforting until her body stilled, and she took a rasping breath. I reached over to her vanity to grab a small handkerchief and began wiping her face. She took the cloth from my hand a little harshly, pushing the pot away, and stood to reface the mirror as if nothing had happened. Her face had regained a fair amount of color, and she leaned into the mirror, tucking back loose curls into a lovely style.

I stayed on the cool, hardwood floor, looking up at her dumbfounded. I grabbed the pot and stood, ignoring the smell. "Dev, what are you doing?"

"I'm getting ready," she rasped.

"Dev, you're sick, you can't perform tonight. I'll bet you're running a fever. You need to rest." I approached her and placed a hand softly on her back.

She looked over her shoulder at me sadly. "I'm not sick."

I let out a bark of laughter and thrust the pot in her face. She winced at the smell. "I beg to differ. Get in bed. I'll fetch a doctor."

She gently pushed the pot away and faced the mirror. "Trixie-girl, trust me. I'm something, but it ain't sick. I'd love a good bit of indigestion right about now."

I stared stupidly at her as she clipped on earrings and fluffed some more at her hair. She met my eye in the mirror. Her eyes were just so sad. In the wake of our sobbing at the cruel inferiority of our sex and what it cost, I understood. I closed my eyes. I reopened them and saw her look of shame in the mirror. Mr. Jim had, as usual, been right.

"We gotta get you a doctor," I blurted out. *Didn't a doctor or someone need to check on all this? Or was it too early? How early was it?* My head buzzed.

Dev gave me a pathetic laugh and straightened, pulling her bosom more prominent in her gown. "Oh, Trixie, I don't need a doctor. I need a ring."

But she had one. Or at least Billy did. *Why hadn't he given it to her yet?* I gazed at her pale and bare left ring finger in the mirror. "Does Billy know?"

She bit her lip and shook her head as tears pooled her eyes. A knock at the door had us both whipping our heads.

"Miss Dev, you seen Trixie-girl? Mr. Jim is looking for her, and she ain't in her room," Wallace called through the wood.

I rolled my eyes and rushed to the door, cracking it open just enough to fit half my body through. Wallace smiled, and I thrust the pot into his hands. His face pulled together.

"Clean that up, won't cha?" I rasped and tried to shut the door in his face.

He caught it and leaned close to me. "Yours or hers?" he asked gravely, his jaw was set.

"Hers," I hissed through clenched teeth. He had heard her last night right alongside me.

"Fuck." He swore unapologetically.

He gave me a curt nod, and I shut the door, turning back to Dev. She didn't bother to wipe her tears as they slowly spilled over her sad eyes. She lost control of her emotions with gasping, quiet destruction, and I stepped back so that I pressed against the door. Probably not the most supportive stance to take while a friend faced utter peril. Her face fell into her hands, and she continued down a rabbit hole of despair. I had never seen her express any emotion this intense, let alone one of such unhappiness and anxiety. My mind froze in response.

"Dev, what is going on?"

She breathed deep and stood with a stumble. It wasn't as if Billy was running off anywhere. It wasn't ideal, and Ms. Liz would probably have a heart attack, but the situation could be worse.

"I don't know what that boy is waiting for," she hissed and wiped at her ashen face.

"You gotta tell Billy. You've got nothing to worry about, he..."

"He what?" Her voice broke.

She had a bitter tone that I did not like to hear from a mouth as pretty as hers. "If Billy was wanting to have me as his bride, don't you think the boy would have done so by now?"

I bit my tongue. Once again, frustration churned in the upper part of my belly, where anger tended to reside. Why had Billy gotten a ring if he wasn't planning on using the damn thing?

"Dev, Billy loves you."

"I'm not stupid. We ain't married. I assumed he would marry me before this happened. But now...Oh, what have I done?"

"That's why you've got to tell him. That boy just needs a kick in the pants. Men are like that, ya know. They can be real lazy. He ain't going anywhere," I assured her, though I was prickled at this situation. Billy had the ring. He was planning on marrying her. This would just speed up the process. It simply had to. Because if it didn't, I would have to clap the boy on his ears until it did.

She nodded at me, and I walked back to her, wiping her tears from her cheeks. "And if he doesn't?" She continued to get ready; her face was cold. She applied rouge to her lips with an unsettlingly steady hand.

"Well, if he doesn't, you and I will figure it out." I gestured to her stomach.

The door swung open. "Dev? You alright? Jayson said you were ill," Billy said in a rush, coming into the room at the same speed. He stopped at the sight of her. Her eyes went wide in the mirror, but she made no move to turn to him.

I stood awkwardly with my mouth a little open—nothing new there.

"Trixie, why don't you go on?" Billy said slowly, walking toward Dev.

She stayed frozen. I headed out of the room, shut the door quietly behind me, and leaned my forehead against the cool wood. I heard soft mumbling but no details of the conversation. As voices grew, I abandoned my post with heavy heels. It wasn't my business anyway.

Chapter 14

y head was light, and I wiped away any clammy sweat. I headed toward my room to see Wallace leaning against my door, ankles crossed, smoking his pipe. His face was a grim despite the cool and calm stance. I kept walking, so he was forced to open my door for me. I didn't have the energy to protest as he followed me in and then shut the door. I sat rigidly on my bed and stared blankly ahead.

"You alright?" he mumbled around the pipe in his mouth.

I shrugged.

"Dev is with child," he stated.

If I wasn't already sitting, I would have fallen. Nothing below me felt sturdy enough to sustain the weight of our situation. Suppose it wasn't exactly ours, as it wasn't mine. I felt foolish because I still struggled to fully comprehend said situation. It was all so heavy. And that heaviness perched on those unremarkable, scrawny shoulders of mine so intensely

I slouched. I leaned forward to rest my elbows on my knees. It was childish to have not considered this outcome. *I* had been childish to think that nothing could go astray with their actions. Selfish even; because it had not really affected me, and therefore, I hadn't taken the time to properly fret over it as a friend ought to have. Never had I considered what could lie on the other side of love. Never had I taken the time to understand the price that came with it.

"I always thought it wouldn't be a question." My lips felt numb around the words.

"What wouldn't be a question?"

"Loving someone." I closed my eyes and inhaled deeply.

"Righteously or... or religiously, I suppose I knew that it was meant for marriage. That... *that* was meant for marriage. It's what we're taught and all. But I suppose I found no wrong with it happening when something was real special. Figured it was a given, even. I guess I thought Dev and Billy were real special."

He hummed at that as I worried my bottom lip. I knew I wouldn't have been able to prevent what had happened, nor would I have ever had any mind to. But still, my guts churned as if the fault were my own.

"This ain't about you in any way, girl," he muttered.

It was like he read my mind. Or, at the very least, my facial expressions. "Have you ever had relations?" I shot back, dodging myself as a topic entirely.

"Yes. Yes, I have." He didn't move from the door but crossed his arms over his chest.

People did that when they felt attacked, I noticed. And my straight-forward questions tended to leave most people feeling attacked. People thought covering your chest prevented any onslaught of verbal abuse. It didn't. Those who thought differently hadn't met me.

"A lot?" I prompted.

"Yes." His jaw flexed in the most wonderful way around his silly pipe, his voice the rumble of a winter storm.

I nodded. I believed him. I felt something nasty in the pit of my stomach.

"Recently?" I challenged.

He took the pipe out of his mouth to pocket it. "That's enough, girl."

I rolled my eyes. Silence fell back over us. I tried to not hear the distant muffling of a louder conversation outside my room. I bit my bottom lip again.

"It's different for men than women, isn't it?" I pondered.

He just stared back at me, hard.

"Women think it'll make someone stay. They do it because they want the person to stay. Dev did it to make Billy stay."

"People do it for lots of reasons, Trixie-girl. But when it's right, both parties want to stay."

"I don't know what that means," I admitted.

"I know. One day I think you will."

"Has it ever been right for you?"

"I don't know," he sighed. He almost sounded sad.

"Suppose not." I couldn't help remarking nor could I control the mild elation I felt with his confirmation of solitude.

"Oh yeah, how do you *suppose* that, girl?" He pushed himself off the door and sauntered over in front of me, matching my look. His face was more gentle than usual, etched with worry. The man had a bit of kindness deep down, I was beginning to discover. I swallowed the guilt from last night's lockout and continued.

"Well, you're alone after it all, ain'tcha?"

His face turned serious. "Yes, I suppose I am."

"You never stayed."

His eyes grew a little suspicious. "No, no, I didn't."

I broke our gaze. Wallace was the type of man that would leave. Someone who would leave a girl like Dev.

"In my defense," he finally began, "I'm not quite sure anyone ever wanted me to stay."

I looked him up and down, trying to imagine myself in such a situation where I would need to decide, after relations, if I would want him to stay. I didn't know the answer to my musings, and it frustrated me. My little knowledge of relations had told me the entire experience was quite invasive for the woman, as well as painful. But Wallace without his shirt had made my body feel soft and pliable.

"Don't be looking at me like that, Trix."

Heat crept up my neck. "Do you think Billy will stay?" My voice shook as the question escaped my lips.

Wallace paused, then sat next to me on my bed. He grasped my shoulder gently, turning my body toward him as he brushed back strands of hair that clung to my clammy, anxious face. I didn't push away from him. "Yes."

"Then why hasn't he proposed to her? He has had that ring for months now, Wallace. What if the boy's got a wandering eye?"

"First of all, when will you quit with that 'Wallace' nonsense? Secondly, the way I see it, and I am sorry if I am the first to say it, but your Billy-boy ain't all that bright. Sometimes a man has got to take a punch in the gut to really open his eyes. I don't think your Billy-boy is going anywhere."

"And if he does?" I prompted.

"Then, I'll grab him and beat him six ways to Sunday."

I nodded at that, believing him. But the thought that it could come down to such a spectacle broke my heart for Dev. *Would she even want a man after he ran off? How far did love go?* Bells and whistles went off in my head like Independence Day. I was surprised at his interest. Why, it nearly seemed as if he cared about the situation. I couldn't quite comprehend why he was so sensitive to this issue, unless of course...

"You got any babies, Wallace?" I questioned abruptly.

"No."

"How can you be certain?"

He sighed, clearly a little exhausted with me. Couldn't blame him, really. "There are ways around it."

My eyebrows shot up at that. "If there are ways around it, how come no one uses them?"

"I can't answer that question, girl. And it probably isn't appropriate that you're asking."

"It's inappropriate for me to ask, and it's ignorant for me not to know. I'll have you know I am not keen on being stupid."

"What're ye so curious for, Trixie-girl? Ye got somethin' more than Dev on yer mind?"

I swiftly swallowed down the answer I wanted to give like a reflex. But the mind is a powerful thing. And mine was causing me to break a sweat at the effort to control the thoughts rampaging through it. I searched for a name to give to the emotions and physical feelings burning within me. The shockingly high burning point only added to the summer heat.

His eyes turned a benevolent shade, and his expression was nearly gentle, with only a hint of that sardonic smile. "Well, I'll be damned, lass." I shook my head. His smile spread like melting butter across the sharp planes of his cheeks. His hands slowly slid closer to my neck, and I jerked my chin to glare at it in disgust.

"It's nothing, Wallace. So, you just put an end to whatever stories you're concocting in that head of you..."

A knock on my door cut me off, and I jumped up from on my bed. Wallace's hand slid down my shoulder at my movement and tangled lightly with my fingers.

"Trixie-girl?"

I yanked my hand from his at the sound of Mr. Jim's quiet voice.

"Did I mention Mr. Jim is looking for you?" Wallace asked, barely above a whisper, staging innocence. His hand stayed in the air, fingers twisted in the angle I had left them, as if he expected mine to return.

If the repeated knock and twist of a doorknob hadn't nearly had my heart jumping out of my chest, I would have loved to slap that innocent look right off him. I was at the door, slamming it shut in a heartbeat, as my own pounded.

"What the—" Mr. Jim grumbled with surprise and rough annoyance.

"I'm indecent!" I hollered, attempting to sound more embarrassed than desperate.

The doorknob jiggled again, and I looked back at Wallace with agony. He, in return, looked sufficiently entertained.

"Well, put yaself together, girl, I got something for ya."

"Mr. Jim, really, I am right in the middle of changing." I hoped against hope that the desperation in my voice sounded more shocked and annoyed than guilty and overwhelmed. "Can't it wait?"

He gave me an annoyed sigh.

I heard a muffled sound as Wallace covered his mouth with a joyful expression on his face. He leaned against my bed in comfort. I gestured for him to do something awful to himself as well as hush in a spasmodic wave of my one free hand.

"Well, at least crack the door, so I can hand it to ya. Don't want it getting dirty on the floor."

I fought the urge to snap and remind him that the floors in Ms. Liz's House were always spotless. I rolled my eyes and said a prayer for my own virtue. Hypocrisy be damned, as I untucked my shirt and ripped it off my body, then proceeded to shuck off my boots and stockings in record time. I was left barefoot, in a skirt and undergarments so I wouldn't be caught in my most uproarious fib. I didn't look back at Wallace despite the sound of him moving from my bed. I stood in front of where the door cracked and opened it only slightly. I stuck my hand out, and Mr. Jim glimpsed his dear ward, clearly still dressing. Sharp, bare shoulders poking out in the dim light. Boney but stable; blessed without feminine curves.

I met his gaze, and he politely looked away as he thrust a soft, heavy fabric in my awaiting hand. I yanked the fabric, longer than expected, into my room and slammed the door just as I felt fingertips trail along my exposed shoulder. I kept one hand on the door to hold it firmly shut. Wallace didn't meet my eye, and I pulled my shoulder away from him. Deftly he retaliated by grabbing my shoulder and pressing my body against the door and his body against my own. I bit my lip and stared up into his unforgiving eyes. Tucking my chin into my neck, I tried to pull back from Wallace. But the door was unsurprisingly inflexible.

I glanced down at the heavy cloth in my hand. It was a dress made of fabric much finer than anything the likes of I had ever owned. I shook it out to see creamy lace detailing around the neckline, which was square and lower than I was used to. It had a pale blue pattern with small yellow flowers scattered throughout. Altogether, it was feminine and lovely— the type of gown for a woman.

"That color always looked real nice on your momma."

Wallace admired my shoulder. His hand reached out and was just a few centimeters away from stroking the thin strap of my undergarment.

"I was plannin' on gifting it to you on a holiday, but I figured with us all watching Miss Dev sing... Well, ya need something more than the skirts you been wearing, I suppose."

I clutched the dress tightly as tears sprang to my eyes. I clenched my jaw to keep them from falling. I couldn't tell what was causing my tears—gratitude or embarrassment. Wallace leaned closer to me, resting one open palm against the door while the other reached to lightly touch the edge of my left eye where the tears began to pool. His touch prevented them from trailing down my cheeks.

I wished to shove this beautiful man aside, rip open the door, and embrace the elder one who so thoughtfully worried about my aging before I had taken the time to. His actions were such a fatherly thing to do, and so unlike him. His care was so intimate and wholly mine for one glittering moment. The overtly feminine gown was ghastly in my eyes, looking not unlike drapes or someone's Sunday finest. It was something that I wouldn't have wanted to wear, yet somehow I loved it. The gown was the attention I had not felt. Now that it was making itself apparent, I could not pay thanks due to a different man compromising what might be my very soul. And I couldn't help but wonder if I liked it.

"Thank you," I said roughly, captured in Wallace's eyes. I was torn and slightly drowning. Irrationally, my heart wanted to stay in his cruel and delicious stare till what was below came above. Perhaps even bury into him, crawl under his skin and stay there.

"Get yaself ready. We'll have an early supper 'fore we head off together," Mr. Jim grumbled. And his footsteps trailed off.

Despite Wallace's intensity, he had no permanent hold on me, so at Mr. Jim's relieving footsteps, I slid out from his grasp. He made no move to readjust himself but merely turned his head. I held the gown up and over my body and looked down to see the shoulders and waistline hit the correct places. The blue made my skin look a little bit pinker and less rusty, I decided. Wallace made a noise, and my eyes flashed to his. He was laughing and not too kindly.

"You should go," I said quickly.

He looked at the door in front of him and nodded to it, still smiling angrily. "I would have bought you black," he said smoothly, straightening himself and grabbing at the door handle.

"Because I'd be thrust into the of mourning my soiled reputation by accepting such a gift from you?" I queried dryly but curious all the same.

He shook his head a little and opened the door a crack making sure no one was in the hallway, then slid out the crack he made. He held his head still in the doorframe.

"Because you like it." He flashed his eyebrows up and down and then closed the door quietly.

The room was still without his presence, and I glanced down at the gown once more. I did like black.

SUPPER WAS QUICKLY SERVED, all on account of the excitement of going to the saloon as a *family*. I was thankful for that. The funny little praise I received for coming down in a proper gown with lace trimmings and flowers galore did not please me. Billy had choked on his glass of water when I entered the room, and I noticed his skin was pale. Dev mumbled something quietly under her breath at him, and he looked at his plate. I wanted to weep at the frigid scene. It seemed, despite the heat, winter had arrived under our roof.

Meanwhile, Ms. Liz, oblivious to her son's dilemma, cried out with unnecessary excitement. "Oh, a doll, truly Trixie-girl, you look like a doll!"

I sat.

"Only thing missing are some ringlets, I'd say," Wallace added coolly.

"Looks nice," Mr. Jim said gruffly, and I forced a smile over to him.

I had caught a look of myself in the large mirror just before fleeting downstairs. The neckline immediately made me fidget. Despite my love for running amuck nude at my Lil' Big, I had never shown this much of my skin in regular company. The lace itched something awful. The top half of my body felt like it was on sale like a prized bull. Attention was a warm and stifling thing.

I kept my ears perked up throughout the quick sup, hoping to catch any conversation between Dev and Billy, but they were as quiet as church mice. It quelled my appetite something mighty. That, and the looks Wallace gave from across the table. He noticed my nearly frantic glances at Billy and Dev. His eyes softened a bit around the edges, and he just nodded in a small way.

Dev excused herself with a large, nearly cracked smile to go on over early. We all wished her luck. Her lips were shaky, and I noticed redness around her eyes she so clearly tried to cover with the powders she wore when performing. The powder looked a little loose on her skin this evening, and her cheeks a little shallower. As she departed, I idly wondered if her cheeks would plump up like Ms. Liz's once the baby inside her really started to grow.

Chapter 15

An hour later, we all trekked to the saloon. I held back with Mr. Jim, a little fearful of entering without him at my immediate left. Something stagnant in the air had me feeling like I was walking into a trap. He offered his elbow as we stepped before the saloon doors. I gave him a half-smile, and he reached out to pat my cheek. I hid my surprise at the kind gesture, and we entered.

The saloon was different in the evening glow, and smoke clung around the bar and the room's low light. Few faces turned at our entrance—some random, tacky form of a happy family. Even fewer looked familiar to me. Ralston sheepishly smiled from behind the bar and as I had not seen him since last week, I mouthed congratulations to him. He nodded, busying himself once more. I hoped Mr. Jim hadn't reprimanded him for that day. Someone, probably Ralston, had rearranged all the tables and chairs to grant Dev a more captive audience. The candles had the red velvet curtains glowing and seeming to move like waters of fire.

Men were merry with drink, and women I did not know looked comfortable with those merry men.

Ms. Liz's back stiffened at an open kiss between two folks, followed by mild cheers from the happy witnesses. The room was filled with such unashamed joy, as well as the lingering scent of harsh whiskey. I shivered at the novelty of it all. Mr. Jim released my arm, gesturing for me to take a seat. He walked to the bar with Wallace and Billy, whose shoulders looked like they pulled him down with the weight of the world, just as Ms. Liz reached for my arm. Mimicking the hold Mr. Jim just had me in, she pulled me to a seat.

I smoothed the dress that clung to me and attempted half-mindedly to pull the neckline up a bit higher. Ms. Liz swatted my fidgeting hands and held one in both of hers on the table. I tried to keep a cheery face but felt too much in the moment. My eyes searched wildly for Dev, wishing to simply sit with her. I wouldn't even expect an answer to all the questions that were rushing into my mind. At least not immediately.

I avoided the gaze of Ms. Liz's all-too-keen eyes, growing more and more worried at each odd uncontrolled fidget. "You got somethin' on your mind, girl?"

I shrugged, and she squeezed my hand too tight for comfort. I was an excellent fibber, but tonight for reasons beyond me, my talents were not shining. My heart reminded my twitching mouth where exactly my place was, and I coolly slipped my hand out of Ms. Liz's crushing grasp.

"Excited," I responded tightly.

She nodded unconvinced at that, and Mr. Jim was suddenly standing on the small excuse for a stage next to the grand piano. He clapped a couple times to create a large echo, and slowly everyone settled down.

"We've got a great show for y'all tonight, so let's hear a round of applause for the prettiest girl in town, Miss Devony!"

Around us, the crowd erupted in deafening cheers that made me wince. Billy was peering into his drink at the bar. Wallace was fixated on him, a small frown plastered across his face as if Billy had just said something displeasing. *Oh, I was gonna kill the boy 'fore anyone else got the chance to.*

Dev walked onto the stage just as the pianist sat down. She looked lovely and glittering under the lowlights of the saloon, providing a coy smile with shy eyes for the roaring crowd. Her gaze drifted over to Billy, and her face faltered only for a moment. She recovered just as the music began, but in her eyes, a melancholy I had yet to know stained the introduction. Gone was that calm-after-the-storm presence that usually surrounded those pretty pale orbs of hers. All that was left was a puddle of rain, pathetically shimmery in the sunlight, which dried her up with each passing moment.

I followed her gaze to see that Billy had left the bar and was slowly heading for the door. My eyes flashed to Wallace, who registered the same shock. Mr. Jim took the seat next to mine. Immediately I tried to stand, only to have an all-too-calm Mr. Jim smoothly press me back into my seat. I didn't look away from Wallace, and he turned from me to stare at the stage. My fists clenched.

"Not your place," Mr. Jim murmured low.

"If it's not my place to strangle the boy, then whose is it?"

"Not yours."

I switched my gaze to Dev upon the stage.

"'Tis but a little faded flow'r,

But oh! How fondly dear,

'Twill bring me back one golden hour

Through many, a many a weary year."

Her voice shook as the poignant ballad rang softly through the saloon. Her hand rested on her lower stomach with a look of longing to the distant light, as if she weren't truly with us, but instead, ahead. Amid her weary years with the small babe by her side. Alone.

I could see it. She and a small babe, in a large brass bathtub on a hot summer night. The scent of rose soap swirling around them. Devastation in her eyes as she tried to smile through the pain of what her life had become. Tears sprang to my eyes, and I blinked rapidly at the vision that permeated my mind. I blinked until it drifted back to the darkest corners of my mind where it belonged. Her voice cracked, and a warm silence fell across the crowd. Dev shook her head and smiled to herself before sharing that smile across the stage. She opened her mouth to begin again but froze.

A loud cry rang from outside the saloon. Sounding a little like anguish and a lot like an animal. Something clattered, and I whirled my head around. The saloon doors swung open, and Billy ran through, knocking a handful of chairs and mugs of ale over and leaped on stage. My heart soared for Dev. Because though the boy was the portrait of a fool, humanized for us to pay homage to and laugh in the face of, there was only one reason he would be onstage. For all to witness, he collapsed to his knees in front of Dev. Her shock was nearly comical. I let an inappropriate burst of laughter escape my softened, relieved lips. Ms. Liz swatted at me and gave me a shrill hush. She was hovering in her seat as if she were about to jump onstage to join them.

"Marry me," he gasped desperately.

Her hands covered her mouth, and one could hear a pin drop in the room. Even those merely passing through town were obviously entranced in the lovers' moment displayed in the shining lights of a cheap country stage. Muffled sobs came from our dear girl. As Dev shakily nodded her head, I nodded as well. Ms. Liz joyfully screeched, jumping fully out of her chair and raising her arms overhead. I let a few tears trickle down my cheeks and continued to nod. The relief of what I'd witnessed gave my head a feeling of being much higher above than below. As I swatted violently at my tears, I wondered when I had become so emotional. In the past month, I cried more than I had in the past four years. Mr. Jim looked over at me and winked. I blinked in the realization that the wheels were suddenly in motion for his grand plan. Their engagement laid the tracks for our inevitable departure.

DEV FINISHED HER SET with the vigor of a woman satisfied. Most satisfied indeed. I watched with pride as Billy-boy offered a hand to help her down the steps from the elevated stage, where her creamy tits did, in fact, resemble two bowls of fresh milk. Her cheeks were cherry red, and her eyes were still rimmed with the tears she had shed upon the dramatic proposal—and perhaps before her performance.

The chorus of claps and cheers created happy lines on all our faces, even Mr. Jim's, who quickly dashed behind the bar to grab a "good" bottle of something for us to enjoy. With our gift, we all settled outside the saloon at a rickety wooden table and chairs. The thick night wrapped us in a heavy quilt while the whiskey was warm in our bellies. Our chatter died down, and I watched with clandestine joy as Dev and Billy continued to make moon eyes at each other. The clouds had hidden the actual moon that evening, so I was forced to rely on them for a little light in the darkness.

"Ah, and what shall we discuss now?" Ms. Liz inquired pleasantly.

I fought the urge to roll my eyes at her need for constant conversation. Everyone around mumbled something unintelligible, and I reached for the bottle. With the taste of Mr. Jim's "good stuff" on my lips, I discovered I much preferred that hidden bottle of Ms. Liz's.

"I've always been partial to a ghost tale," I confessed into the lantern flame, just as a warm breeze picked up.

"Oh, no, Trixie-girl. Not those devil stories!" Ms. Liz cried out melodramatically.

"Ain't no devil in a story, Ms. Liz," I sighed.

"They ain't any good is what they ain't."

I didn't have the heart to inform her that whatever just came out of her mouth contradicted the point she was attempting to make. Or to confess that Wallace had been filling my head all summer long with "devil stories" blasphemously alongside tales from the Good Book, and I had yet combusted in flames.

"When was the last time you had a Bible in those hands of yours? Hmm?" she prodded.

I met her knowing gaze over the table lantern's flickering flame and could only guess what expression was on Wallace's face.

"Lord knows you need it."

"Why's that, Ms. Liz?" Wallace prompted, our conversation having caught his attention.

"Why's what, Mr. Wallace?"

"Why would your Trixie-girl here need a Bible in her hands?"

The air around us became very close. I kept my eyes loyally on the fire, but my hand gripped the bottle.

"Well..." Ms. Liz started but had trouble continuing.

"Yes?" Wallace prompted like a hungry child.

Ms. Liz didn't deserve his scrutiny. It was exhausting for me, and at least I kept up with most of the things he said. The tone in his voice felt harsh against the indulgent evening. Ms. Liz fidgeted in the corner of my eye, but I made no move to save her. Instead I took a sip.

"Well, on account of the girl's previous upbringing, of course," she finally stated.

I blinked slowly at that, feeling exposed and chilled.

"You mean her *parentage*." Wallace's retort caused me to stiffen. His words were somehow shocking despite their simplicity. The way his mouth curled around the word made it seem like he was hinting at something that wouldn't be brought up in polite conversation.

"Excuse me?" Ms. Liz replied, but Wallace was looking at me.

"Her heritage, whatever it may be. You say her past, but you mean something else entirely. You think she needs the Bible more than others because she is different than you. Because you think she *looks* different from you."

My jaw fell open at his smooth, unheard-of defense. The muddled and unspoken line drawn in the sand, separating me from those around me, now shined bright with an even a grander spotlight than Dev's creamy tits. I shuffled in my seat.

"Why, I never!" Ms. Liz said, dumbfounded.

"Tell me I am wrong." He stared angrily at her.

The hot night air licked at my clammy skin as Ms. Liz boiled from a temperature altogether different than the one that affected me.

But when she didn't reply, he leaned forward and taunted her cruelly with, "I dare you to."

"Mista Wallace," she began, already breathless. "I have raised Trixie-girl as if she was my own. In another life, that child very well should have been my own. I couldn't give a hoot what y'all think the girl is. She could be green for all I care. When I say what I say, I mean what I say, and I do not need some quick-tongued flat-footed nobody from God-knows-where telling me how I mean it!" Her angry words bled together, like a punishment of poetry.

Wallace leaned back, a frustrated curiosity playing on his features. "I apologize. How did you mean it then?" He was quieter now.

Ms. Liz rubbed the left side of her face, just below her eye, for a moment. "Happiness ain't as simple as folks like to think. And despite my most earnest efforts, it ain't all about the nurturing. Happiness, well, I suppose, sometimes comes down to blood, and it ain't in everyone's. When I say the girl needs a Bible in her hand, I suppose I mean the girl needs all the help she can get. The kind hearts of man can only go so far."

"And what exactly has you believing happiness isn't in her blood?" Wallace demanded as the firelight made his face appear to flicker.

"That's not my tale to tell."

He looked to me expectantly. "Well, it isn't mine," I grumbled.

He leaned closer to me at that. "Then whose tale is it, Trix?"

I felt the puff of his breath on my cheek.

"Mine." Mr. Jim answered gravely. He fixated on the lantern light that was slowly dying. I licked the warm sweat that trickled from my upper lip.

"Then, Jim, the floor is yours."

"My momma and pa may have been drunks, but between sips, they taught me the privilege of privacy," Dev said smoothly. She leaned down to brush a kiss on the top of my head. "You can tell me in your own time, Trixie. Thank you for the celebration."

She faced the rest of our small crowd. "I'll be heading to bed now. Thank you all for such a wonderful evening." Her eyes flashed to Billy's before returning to the ground.

I caught the signal and flushed for her, patting the hand that rested on my shoulder. Her ring was cool to the touch, and I was delighted despite Wallace's nosy inquisitions. Relieved at last.

"I'll walk ya," Billy said quickly.

Unfortunately, Billy and I were not the only ones who could put two and two together.

"And I will chaperon," Ms. Liz stated with a huff and the loud shuffle of getting up from a seat that may have been too low. Before she left, I caught the delectable sneer she sent Wallace. I coughed over a giggle, and he shot me a sarcastic glance. The three walked toward the house, figures disappearing as they left the light of the saloon.

"Jimmy, come on now. Ye've got me on me bonnie wee toes o'er here," Wallace stated gruffly as he stretched his legs out carelessly. So, Wallace was feeling... something.

Interesting.

Mr. Jim shot an annoyed look at Wallace in response to such impatience. Then he gave me a small nod and cleared his throat. "Trixie's momma, ya see, she wasn't like most folks you meet."

We waited as the lantern's light flashed across Mr. Jim's frown, creating demonic dancing features for one fleeting moment. I fought the urge to fill in the silence with whatever cruel words would follow.

Dumb.

Slow.

Touched.

Fast.

Too fast.

Shameless.

Whore.

Whore.

"She was transcendental."

The surprising word sent a shiver down my spine.

"Her father used to say she had cotton in her ears, that girl of his. When I first met her, I mistook her tendencies for a streak of stubborn, like our Trixie-girl, here."

I snorted a little.

"But it wasn't obstinacy that made her the way she was. She had a world of her own. One that we wasn't allowed into. And she had no plans of leaving that world of hers. Suppose it was prettier than what we all saw and lived through. That, or maybe God saw what he created and couldn't bear the thought of reality tainting whatever she was and put a barrier 'round her that we couldn't see. 'Cause nothing, and I mean nothing, could bother her into assimilation. She was constantly walking on clouds. Fearless, but not out of bravery. It was out of something much more worrisome. She had a gentle mind, I suppose. Childlike in her wondering while rebellious in her wanderings." He paused and looked around at us. "You had to keep a close eye on her."

Wallace leaned forward. "She needed protecting."

"I met her when she was a few years younger than what I suppose Trixie-girl is now. Her father and I struck up a fur-trading business. At the time, it was a good place to be trading—New Orleans, that is. Money was good.

"Her father wanted her married off sooner rather than later. I had grown to care for the girl, you see. Loved her, even. Figured when all was said and done, I would take her as my bride just as he wished. But at the time, I hadn't seen the rush. I couldn't feel that urgency in the air like a father does. Suppose a father always knows when his girl is up to no good. Suppose it's a little like how before a storm, all those broken bones long-healed start to ache. Suppose I was so distracted by how entertaining her no good was, I couldn't see how much she required someone to set her straight. To lay down the law. Suppose I wasted too much precious time supposing. Because by the time I could see, it was too late.

"And then along came Chanteloup. He was a big fellow. Bigger than any man I ever laid eyes on. The kind of big that scares a person. The kind of big that hurts a person. Maybe without even knowing it. He had left his *people,* thought I suspect there never had been any to begin with, and he had been on this...traveling. This...this constant wandering about for years!" Mr. Jim exclaimed like it was positively barbaric for a man to travel. Like there was something fundamentally uncivilized about the notion of moving from one place to another with ease. "He traded furs and goods like the rest of us; made himself a pretty penny. You could see in the way he decorated himself. But that *man,*" he sneered as if my father hadn't actually been one, "had no business making eyes at Magdalene. And yet like a moth to a flame, that girl sure did lean on in when he made his eyes."

There was a rambunctious holler from inside the saloon then settled.

"Where did he come from?" Wallace prompted, pinning an assessing eye on me as if he could figure out the answer to his own question from my visage. When I met his gaze, I watched his eyes flashed from frustration to acceptance. I watched him understand that any further questioning, any expectation for answers I didn't have, hurt more than the questions themselves ever could.

"Damned if I know, damned if any of us knew. The bastard didn't speak. Never spoke a goddamn word. We was the ones who named him Chanteloup...Singing Wolf. Thought ourselves as clever. No, I don't know where the man came from. All I know is that he was big, and he was as crackled as Mississippi clay."

Silence fell. When I blinked, I almost saw a warm smile and dark wrinkled eyes. So, I blinked until the image was gone. I felt naked, and I knew I was a coward. I hadn't the courage to stand up and demand that he stop. Stop the story now because we all understood the rest. And if somehow Wallace didn't, he could put it together in the morning. I needed Mr. Jim to stop airing out the secrets of my unwelcome existence like his own dirty laundry. Because if no one knew there was something amiss, it wouldn't matter who my father had been. But he didn't. And I remained silent.

"I don't know what she ever saw in him. Couldn't even speak a word," Mr. Jim repeated.

Wallace leaned back and crossed his arms; his gaze flickered to me and back like dancing candlelight.

"I won't be a liar and claim that he reaped something that hadn't been sowed. Reaped something that *I* hadn't already sowed. But that man spoiled whatever was left of her right quick. They ran off a couple counties over and were living by the swamps. Playing house of sorts. He gave her the idea that she was his wife. Ha! Can you imagine? A little thing like Maggie as that giant's wife?!" Mr. Jim let out a big, mean laugh, then reached for the bottle, taking a very long drink.

He wiped off his weathered face with the back of his hand. He spoke of my momma as if we had known her. Had known her and agreed with his opinions on the predicament she seemed to have gotten herself into. The assumed familiarity Mr. Jim utilized in his storytelling was jarring at best.

"That ain't no proper union. He had her living in sin, ravaging what was left of her good name. Her father was through with her real quick, and I told myself I was as well. We carried on without her in our lives, and a couple years passed. Planned on keeping it that way; her gone to us as we so easily had been to her. That was till I heard there was a baby.

"One of the reasons I tried to keep her away from Chanteloup, other than the obvious, was on account of his walking about. Man never seemed to stay still. Full moon always had him restless, and the man, I swear to you, would be gone for weeks on end. I told her ain't nothing was gonna keep him around. So mighty shocked was I when I paid her a little visit to find her alone with his little pup at her tit." He gestured to me.

"Oh, she sure was a pretty babe, though. Hated to admit it, but she was. What with all that swirling dark hair and those smart black eyes. Maggie wouldn't tell me how long Chanteloup had been gone for. But she let me hold the babe. Trixie-girl took a liking to me, I tell you. Made my girl smile something real big."

My hands were clenched tightly in my lap.

"I visited just about every week. I was there to watch Trixie grow. And all the time that blood-father of hers was on his *walk*."

The air grew hard to breathe.

"I started looking for him, asking around if anyone had seen him and all. He was gone like smoke. So's I head over to Maggie's and tell her the man is good and gone. Told her to pack up Trixie's things, and we would head west. I was taking her to San Francisco. She'd never seen the Pacific Ocean. The poor thing had spent her life just mucking about in the dirty air and water of Louisiana. Told her I would be back at the crack of dawn, and we would start over."

I held my breath and peeked at Wallace. His jaw was set, and while he seemed transfixed by the flame in front of him, he contradictorily leaned back, relaxed in his stature.

"Dawn comes just as surely as I did. I heard Trixie-girl screaming from down the road and was running, but I was too late. More likely than not, I was five hours too late. Maggie's body hung high, and that face of hers was a shade too dark to be considered lovely any longer. To this day, when I think back on that sweet girl, my mind betrays me. All I see is that lifeless body and puffy purple face, twisting slowly in the air. Gone, like the snap of that poor thing's neck, are all my beautiful memories." Mr. Jim's voice shook.

I coughed, tasted iron, and wiped at my lip. I must've bitten it. Mr. Jim slid a large hand down his weathered face as if doing so wiped away the memories with his perspiration. I reached for the bottle and took a very deep drink, allowing a couple of gulps down my throat. It burned like hellfire. Mr. Jim paid no mind, and Wallace continued to be entranced by the rapid dancing flames.

I set the bottle back down, my head buzzing something awful. Whiskey worked well when feelings such as those started to creep up. Mr. Jim seemed to agree as he reached for the bottle, still warm from my lips, and finished it with an impressive gulp. He let out his classic, "ahhh," which finally broke Wallace's trance from the flames.

"And?" he prompted with a tight jaw.

I looked at the dark sky in the distance; no Mary Moon came out to comfort us tonight. I wondered if God was looking back.

"And what? The rest, you know. Packed the girl up and headed west. I promised a better life to Maggie, and I wasn't 'bout to do wrong by her baby."

Wallace changed his position quickly, leaning forward with his elbows on his knees, gaze intense.

"Well, what did you do with the body, Jim? Call up the authorities to cut her down, did you? Did you go fetch Trix's grandfather before you ran off with her?" Wallace's anger vibrated in the heat of the night.

I continued to gaze at the moonless sky. Mr. Jim wiggled a bit, crossing his arms over his chest and staring down the empty streets in front of us.

"Well?" Wallace demanded.

"Well, what? The girl's granddaddy had washed his hands of her long 'fore she was even born; bastard's ears didn't perk up much at word of the babe. I wasn't about to risk anything with her, leaving her to a man she didn't know. She was small, needed protecting." There was a growl in his voice.

"Protecting her from her own kin, Jim? Didn't you say you were in business together? You got a habit of mistrusting your business partners?"

Mr. Jim said nothing, and I pictured myself sitting at the Lil' Big alone. I almost felt the sunshine on my skin.

A fist slamming on the small table we huddled around broke my trance, and the bottle fell over with a clatter. "Dammit, Jim! What did ye do?"

"I did what was best for Trixie! What I've always done! I sent word to her granddaddy once we were settled and safe. You see him anywhere?!"

My chest ached, and despite the heat of the evening, I was cold all over. With my eyes closed, my head felt like a leaf in the wind. I had not heard this part of the story before, and it was plundering through my drunken mind without mercy. Surely there was a reason Mr. Jim kept this from me. *What use would I have had with a granddaddy?*

Only, I had never heard anything about a granddaddy. There was a hollow feeling in my chest as if something I had not known I wanted was taken away from me before I had a chance to weigh it in my palm. He told me I had no one. I had lived my life thinking there was no one. Perhaps he was protecting me from the rejection of knowing there had been someone who didn't want me. Protecting me from the heartbreaking fact that my blood relations had wiped their hands clean of me for things I had no control over. Things that I couldn't change, even if I wanted to.

I fought the urge to spit and stomp my foot and holler and scream into the blank, dark sky, demanding God to tell me why. To, for once, shed a little light of hope on my unruly path of life that became more impossible each day. To give me *something* that couldn't be taken away or charge me more than I could pay. *How many times could I look up to God with empty hands before He would finally let me be?*

I wished I would have known. I wish I had known so I could have fooled myself into thinking that I rejected my granddaddy in return, a cruel and stuffy man he must have been. Nothing was ever in my control. And here Wallace was, rubbing my nose in it all. I felt a scream or vomit building in my throat. I stood up, stumbling a little. Wallace immediately stood as well, reaching to steady me. I flinched away from his touch. Mr. Jim eyed us with such palpable suspicion, I couldn't help but turn my back.

"Wha..." Mr. Jim's question was interrupted by the sound of glass shattering and a bit of an uproar.

We all stared through the saloon doors. A fight was building like wildfire in a windstorm, and I took a curious step forward. Two different hands landed on each shoulder to yank me back. Mr. Jim pushed my chest harshly, causing me to stumble back, and Wallace caught me in his warm arms. He steadied me, wrapped an arm across my chest and shoulders, and held me tight to him. Wallace backed up slowly as the shouting grew.

"Get her out of here!" Mr. Jim ordered curtly before he headed into the scene.

"Mr. Jim!" I called, but Wallace spun us around and switched his hold on me to a hurried pressure against the small of my back.

"He'll be fine. Let's get ye out o' here."

I huffed but walked with Wallace.

Chapter 16

he shouting grew fainter as we drifted further into the dark evening. I inhaled the thick air deeply and folded my arms across my chest as we walked toward the boarding house. I glanced over at Wallace peripherally, unable to make out a facial expression in the dark of the night. The outline of his profile stuck out as a lighter, but still dull gray against the moonless evening.

"Have you any memories of them?"

I slowed my walking to a stumbling stop, surprised by the question. A fleeting image flashed in my mind. There, it weakly glimmered like silverware in need of a proper polishing. I pushed it back to the shadows where it belonged, with all the other undesirable chores. I shrugged, and Wallace yanked at a loose strand of hair. I couldn't help but worry what sorts I was in if my loose hairs were visible in such poor lighting.

"What's the difference between a memory and a dream?" I asked softly.

I watched him shrug from the corner of my eye and continue to ponder.

"Well?" he prompted, digging a teasing elbow into my side as we walked.

My head felt light but jerky from the whiskey. I closed my eyes and reached out to stop him with me, forcing patience and permission to collect all the loose ends slithering about in the most random of assortments and remember.

A small, blurry picture sluggishly appeared in my mind, dragging its feet caked in thick, mucky feelings. Before I could snatch the emotion trailing behind it, a lost melancholy bubbling behind my closed lids, the image faded. I managed to grab hold of the last wispy strands, and it halted with haste. The memory gave in, playing in my head as if it were happening in front of open eyes in a fleeting rush.

The memory was a warm bath and a smiling woman. The bathtub was shined brass. A large man sat next to us, laughing with the woman and holding a pad of paper. The woman's hands were soft and warm as they helped run water through my hair. I was there for just a moment, smelling the certain heat permeating the air mixed with the rose-scented soap. I tasted graphite and the burning wick of candles and something very sweet. Then the memory, much like an old note, was tucked away in the rickety desk of my mind. But its presence flickered, nonetheless. As if a small stubby candle sat behind it in that locked drawer, casting shadows through a useless keyhole. The memory was the closest thing to a dream I ever had. It would invade my mornings just as the sun shined in through the windows, having survived any nightmares from the sleep before. I had clung to it, in secret, throughout my life here in Wicker Soul. I felt treacherous sharing even the smallest bits of it, as it was mine. Mine and *theirs*.

Wrinkled dark eyes.

"A brass bathtub." I started walking again, looking down briefly to let one single tear fall, and the rest evaporated in the dry, thick air.

Wallace caught up to me after a beat, as if he had needed time to process such a short, dismissive answer. "That's it?"

I nodded curtly. He nodded with unsatisfied acceptance as if he knew not to push me. Over the skies, a flash of red lightning danced.

"Rain's coming," Wallace announced.

"Heat lightning. Didn't you know? We are boiling alive, Wallace. Speaking of boiling, you oughtn't to have been so hard on Mrs. Liz. Mr. Jim, as well. You're in sour spirits tonight," I snapped all too quickly into the dark.

"Oh, quit. That woman is an old bigot if I ever saw one. Everybody's blood is the same color and temperature. It doesn't matter how they claim to care for you. Don't let them, or anybody else, tell you that your wild comes from your blood. That's a gift from God, and Him alone.

Being a careless little thing hasn't got anything to do with what's running through those pretty veins of yours. You best remember that."

I wrinkled my nose, figuring out if there was a compliment tucked somewhere inside such a speech.

"And you do not want to get me started on Jim tonight, girl."

I rolled my eyes, working to not allow his words to sink in. It was too hot for any of this. I reached to wipe the sweat off my brow. Ahead, just before the stairs to the boarding house, was a group of stumbling men. Wallace's arm snaked around my lower back, and he directed us toward the stables. One of the drunks hollered, and another turned toward us, and we burst out running and giggling like mad. Whatever they called out was lost to our ears. The drunken fools disappeared as we hit the stables, and I caught my breath from the running and laughing.

"Everyone's got an itch in their pants tonight, haven't they?" I queried.

Wallace shrugged and leaned against the worn wood. He brushed at imaginary dust on his shoulder and regarded the moonless sky. This far from the saloon and the lingering lights of the boarding house left us barely able to see each other in the dark. A hot wind whirled around us.

"Heat does that to a man. Can drive him to the brink of madness, as he knows deep down in his liquor-swollen belly a hot summer night is nothing next to the flames of hell awaiting him." He answered smoothly.

I nodded, ever dumbfounded with his odd little tangents, especially after I had soaked my own tongue in whiskey. Silence wrapped its arms around us. My liquor-swollen brain swayed my head, and I worked hard to focus my eyes.

"Whatcha thinking?" I finally asked.

Wallace shrugged.

"You think Mr. Jim is okay?"

Well, that got him. "If you say his name one more time, I will shut that mouth of yours with whatever means necessary."

I pushed away from him at the sudden change in his tone, and he towered over me. My back was against the barn. A flash of lightning showed the fury on his face. The thunder that followed split at my ears and had me childishly reaching up to cover them and squeeze my eyes shut. Wallace's hands fell on top of mine gently.

I opened one eye. He was close enough that I made out his face a little better in the dark. He opened his mouth but then flinched softly and frowned. Slowly, he removed his hands from my ears, and I opened my other eye. His eyes were unfocused, as if he didn't really see me. I opened my mouth, but he quickly covered it, closed his eyes, and tilted his head backward, up to the dark sky.

I wiggled my mouth against his hand for a moment, and then I felt it. My eyes grew wide at the sensation of a drop of water landing on my forehead. I reached for Wallace's hand and moved it from my mouth, mindlessly pressing it against my cheek, and tilted my head back just the same as he had, waiting. Another blinding flash of lightning hit so close I swore I saw where precisely in the foothills it landed. The following slam of thunder erupted, and the heavens opened like lazily drawn curtains. Rain fell on us with unexpected violence, and I laughed. The indescribable joy that comes at the end of a drought surged through my veins, and Wallace's laughter joined mine. I held up my open hands as if I could catch and hold onto the wonderful rain. I threw my head back even further, opening my mouth graciously.

Lightning continued to burst, and I saw him as clearly as if the sun were shining on us. Or at the very least, Mary Moon, proud in all Her glory. Faintly I heard something under all my laughter and thunder, almost like an equal celebration. Perhaps it was—perhaps the drought had affected more than just me and my restless self. I felt Wallace's large hands wrap around the small of my waist and lift me. He spun me round and round as the rain drenched us. I wrapped my arms tightly around his neck and threw my head back once more and enjoyed each touch. Liquid, solid, or miscellaneous.

At the slightly unstable hold he had me in, I instinctively wrapped one leg around him to keep myself up. I felt all his masculine pressure in such a position and couldn't hide the foreign sensation that pulsated through me. The combination of his warmth and terrifying strength (which lifted me like I was a half-full sack of flour) and the cool consistent downpour had me drunker than any whiskey. And for just a moment, there in the celebration of God's nearly forgotten town, I allowed myself to bask.

Then I was no longer spinning, physically at least. My mind continued to whirl as I attempted to focus on Wallace's somber face. He leaned closer to me, and I pressed my forehead against his, breathing in what he had breathed out, mixed with a raindrop here and there. I couldn't help the smile that lingered even after Wallace swallowed deeply and studied my face quite seriously. Unable to catch my breath or control the giggles that were so unlike me, I let myself relax. With the shift of a hand, I realized precisely which parts of me he was holding. And the specific pressure suddenly against my belly, attempting to invade an area I spent a fair amount of time pretending didn't exist.

Wallace's grip flexed at the soft but strong flesh of my bottom, and I quickly jumped down from his embrace. I backed away from him, contemplating offense, as he stood dumbly in the western downpour. I watched him shake his head, clearly having made up his mind before he stalked toward me. When he was upon me, reaching for me, my internal war was complete, and I slapped him without hesitation.

Feeling very much the mouse within reach of a spiteful cat, I tried to steady my ground. His purr was cruel, mocking laughter. I swung my right hand once more, and he snatched my wrist before I made contact. Without thought, my left swung, and he caught that one, too. He squeezed, but not tight enough to bruise. Instead, he threw my hands over my head and pressed them against the slimy, rain-sodden wood of the stables. He leaned down, and I flinched into the sturdy wall, turning my neck and straining for unavailable space. My heart pounded as his eyes taunted the closer he got. I set my jaw squarely just as his mouth pressed against the bottom corner of my own. I jerked my chin away and felt him laugh against my flesh. I yanked at my arms, but he held them firmly against the stable wall.

His slick, smiling lips against my chin were extremely unfamiliar. Despite the riot that was going off in my head to *push away,* that secret female part of me tilted my jaw to provide him with a more accessible angle. He made a noise against my skin, then proceeded to press his lips from my chin to my neck, all the way to my collar bone. His kisses were soft, but his tongue lapped at the water on my skin in a way that caused me to gasp just as his teeth closed lightly around a bit of skin that covered my collar bone. A dark laugh vibrated against my suddenly, unbearably sensitive skin.

"What are you doing?" I whispered, aching everywhere in anticipation.

My palm itched to try and slap him once again. Still, my neck continued to arch back, almost welcoming his lips and harsh teeth moving up from my collar to the tender flesh of my throat and then the line of my jaw. Then he dragged his teeth against the sharp of my jawbone, nipping and suckling, and I was losing my mind. I groaned in a keening, high-pitch tone as warmth flooded very low within me. He pulled back to face me.

I knew he was looking into my eyes though I couldn't see much of them—the lightning had evaded us and cloaked us in a shield of dangerous privacy. "Don't ask questions you know the answer to."

And his lips crashed down on mine. I gasped at the sudden expression of emotion, and he caught my tongue immediately between his teeth and suckled. I tried to pull back but had nowhere to go. He released my tongue only to press his lips against my bottom lip, then nip at that as well. I pushed my lips back against his because, despite my naiveté, his actions were causing the warm feeling within me to spread, and I liked it. He ran his free hand down my ribs and curved it around my back to crush me against him. It was too close, and it wasn't close enough. I opened my mouth to nip at his tongue and lips and teeth and chin like a madwoman. A deep noise came from him in response. That noise, carnal in nature and utterly terrifying, yanked me back to my senses.

My hands were trapped, and I was pressed too tightly against him to properly squirm away. But my legs. Before I could think any further, I jerked my knee right into his groin. He broke apart from me and groaned. I folded forward to catch my breath, bracing my hands on my knees. I was starved for air and sputtering quite unceremoniously.

Wallace turned to walk it off as I continued to gasp. He leaned over himself like me. Much to my horror, though, he recovered remarkably fast. Impossibly fast. Within seconds he was stalking back toward me, and I shrunk against the stable wall, my eyes wary. His face shone with disgust at the recognition of my fear. He took one step backward and a deep breath.

"I love ye," he all but hissed.

His eyes were ornery as if his proclamation was something I ought to apologize for. My body went rigid at his words, and the rain suddenly felt ice cold. No one had said that before. I had never contemplated love. All I knew was care. I felt care. I would like to think in my life I had provided some sort of obvious care for others. That perhaps I wasn't as selfish as my harsh manner portrayed. Because I knew care very well. I knew that I was cared for. Care was warm coffee and patterned blankets and glasses of water by the bed late at night. Care was the feeling of slipping underneath the covers after a long day and warming with languid ease.

But love?

I didn't know love. Perhaps that is why my chest filled with a cold and empty feeling at his words. *Why did the expectation painted so beautifully across his arrogant face make my body feel chilling anger that I had never experienced before?* The warmth that had so recently pulsated through me was gone. What replaced it was a jagged disappointment like the day after Christmas. Therefore, my mouth spoke for the broken heart I never realized I had.

"Well, what's that hafta do with me?" tumbled out of my mouth.

The clap of thunder, followed by lightning, echoed in response to my statement. It was God sighing in disappointment. Chiding my vanity or pride or sloth. Whichever He found fit. *Well, there He was.* All ears now, it seemed. The power of the lightning illuminated a look on Wallace I had never wished to have inspired. Gone was the devilish smirk and gone were the ever-knowing eyes. Replaced with a vast nothing. His jaw set, and I glared at him with all I had left.

Nonetheless, he slowly reached out as if to touch me. I swatted him away, and he stumbled backward at my aggression. I pressed on, pushing his chest with all my strength to get him as far from me as I could. He stumbled some more, and I pushed again, hellbent on charging him down. He had a funny smile on his face then, and I pushed once more, entirely exerting myself while, other than a small stumble, he barely moved.

"Hmmm? You think I want that? You think I need that? I don't. I don't need any of that, Mr. *Jayson* Wallace. You can keep your love," I spat through gritted teeth, rearing up to push him, hoping this time he would land on his ass and stay down.

I burned with hate. This man walked into our lives and upturned each thing he touched in such a careless manner. He was breaking everything that had made sense, forcing me to question things I had come to terms with long ago. The past was too far behind me. I couldn't afford to look back, and he couldn't understand that. And now he stood before me, asking for all that I was with his stale proclamation. Expecting a reciprocation. As if he had a right to it. As if these words meant anything. I couldn't believe them. *Because if they really did mean something as spectacular as he insinuated, then why was he the first to use them?*

He dodged my push and took a couple steps backward, breathing deeply. I breathed through my nose like a bull, shoulders hunched forward. For a split second, I longed for that hollow feeling that had ached throughout me only moments prior. It had pulsated from my core through my bloodstream. Though it had caused a specific frustration, I had enjoyed the fundamentals of it. Something about it had felt right, and now it was gone. And it was his fucking fault. He stared at me coolly, despite the breathing out of his mouth like he was as exasperated as I was. Another clap of thunder erupted, and lightning captured us in our war stance.

As quick as that lightning flashed, Wallace reached for me, gripping me tightly from the back of my neck and smashing his mouth upon mine once more. His lips were merciless against my mouth as if he were devouring me. He made my breath his, sucking my soul alongside it. I bit at him, and I reveled in the return of his low sounds of satisfaction. Our tongues danced together as each fought for power that both needed to survive. His arms wrapped around my body like a vice. The part of him which was hard where mine was empty pressed against my stomach. And the ache returned. But now it had grown in ways I couldn't understand.

Or relieve. My hands were tangled in his hair as I pulled him closer, deepening our battle of power. One hand stayed at the back of my neck with an unwavering hold, while the other moved from its gentle location at my hip. It slowly slid, leaving a trail of fire, and found its way to the top of my dress.

His hand splayed large and warm just below my collar bone on my exposed chest and rested there. His fingers drummed against my chest, and I woke from my trance. That tapping felt impatient, and I recalled with painful abruptness who I was and how inexperienced I was in all of this. And then I was slapping and hitting and pushing until he released me again. He threw me away from him, and despite being off-balance, I regained myself and stood proud. Perhaps a bit too much.

"Would ye quit?" he snarled, taking a step closer to me.

I stepped back and scrunched up my nose in disgust at his myopically masculine mind. "Me?"

"Aye, ye. Are ye frightened?" he asked and lifted two empty palms as if offering evidence that no weapons were present.

I set my jaw. He took another step closer, and I spat at his feet.

His face went from shock to fury. "Dammit, girl!"

I shook my head at him and wiped at the rain in my eyes. I crossed my arms over my chest and headed toward the boarding house. To do what, with everything that had just occurred, I did not know. Maybe I'd search for another bottle of sherry. Or at least a biscuit to munch on. But of course, I didn't make it to the boarding house. My arm was grabbed by Wallace. Clearly, his damning me was not the end of our *disagreement*. He pulled me tight against him once more.

"Who are you living for?" he whispered hotly against my ear, then his tongue traced the shell, lapping up rainwater that fell heavily upon it.

I groaned low, and the sound was unlike anything I had ever heard from myself. It was as if all those sensations in my ear were equally attached to my most hungry place. My hips needed to push forward as my mind swirled through Wallace's horrible torment. His teeth captured the fatty flesh of my ear and pulled harshly. I gasped at that. Perhaps I didn't crave a biscuit. Probably would be a bit cold and stale by now anyway.

"I asked, 'Who are you living for?'" He pulled away, and I fought against another strange noise that had begun within me, one that ached to have him back. It was suspiciously like a whimper. He looked at me, waiting, and I tried to catch my breath. "It ain't a trick question," he said softly.

With a flash of lightning, I saw his sad face. It made me want to spit all over again.

"The war is over, Trixie. Now, I'm not sayin' 'tis a perfect world out there, especially for someone like ye. But there will be a day where no one is goin' to ask where ye came from. And if ye stick with Mr. Jim, I can promise ye that ye will ne'er see that day."

My teeth ground together as another flash of lightning struck, and the skies rained down on us like it was Judgment Day.

"So, what exactly do you propose I do, Mr. Wallace?" I yelled back through the rain and wiped my face with a frustrated, shaking hand.

He took a step forward, and I took a step back. It was hard to keep our eyes open with such a downpour, but the lightning provided a touch more visibility. "I propose ye run. Ye run like the hounds o' hell are lickin' at yer heels."

I let out a harsh laugh. "With the likes of you?"

He stepped forward faster than the lightning above this time and gripped my shoulders firmly, giving me a little shake. "Aye."

He shook me so hard my head flung back a little. He gentled then. "Aye, girl, I am proposing ye run off with the likes o' me, and we start that life yer aching to live. The life yer so deservin' to live."

I tried to twist out of his arms. I was overwhelmed and angry. *He thought it was just that easy?*

"That's it? I just pack up myself, dump it all in your perfect waiting arms, hmmm? You think you're strong enough to carry all that? Slap my hands clean and tip my hat at my good ol' Mr. Jim. Hey, mista, thanks a bunch, but I'm off to Andoloochia!"

He shook me with a snarl. "Andalusia."

I wanted to bite that snarl right off his face. "I may be *the wicked thing of Wicker Soul*, the wild no-name born in the swamps, but that don't make me cruel."

He scoffed over the loud roar of the surrounding storm. "What are you talking about, girl?"

I struggled against him madly. All the while, the elements we had subjected ourselves to roared in jealousy at our own disaster. How angry God must be that His storm He so righteously had blessed us with after such a drought was paling in comparison to a much earthlier eruption. At the hands of man? Blasphemy, perhaps at its highest level. At least I wasn't alone in it. If I went down for this, Wallace was coming with me.

And yet, I still *felt* alone. I was raw and exposed to him and God. My own thoughts, crippling and filled with something unnamed which I had kept so securely hidden, now shone brightly from behind the tremendous barrier I built. And that barrier I had spent a lifetime creating—sacrificing silent blood, sweat, and tears—was being washed away in the storm. My self-preservation was crumbling, and what lay within those crumbling walls was something I never wished to face head-on. I struggled against Wallace once more, and he brought me even tighter against his chest. I could barely breathe. My eyes looked wildly for a way out. He transferred both of my wrists into one large hand, then brought the other to my jaw and squeezed my face to look at his. My soft cheeks felt strained.

"Answer me," he commanded.

"The weight, damn you!" I growled in response.

His jaw stayed set, awaiting further explanation.

"The weight of...the weight...," I stammered.

My weight! I wished to cry. But the words were too ugly, too simple, even for me. Nonetheless, their presence in my collapsing mind tore me apart as I had never acknowledged them before.

"No matter where I go, no matter what I do, there's this weight. I walk so heavy on an Earth that didn't want me. And you act as though it is fine, that my debts are so easily transferred, that my shame is a silly notion in my *feminine* mind." A cry escaped my mouth. "As if," my voice trembled as I continued to yell over the storm, "I were ignorant to the certainty I bloomed in soils drenched with regret." Sweat poured out of my body, mixing sloppily with rain.

Wallace's jaw was set in a dangerous line. "So 'tis final, hmmm? Ye stay with him?"

I wanted to sob at his simplification of my raw, exposed soul, so instead I yelled. "I'm not to be fought over!"

"Then quit making me!" His bellow put the thunder to shame.

He pressed his cruel mouth on my ear and hissed, "Ye remember, girl o' mine, when ye lie awake at night. When ye are alone with yer perfect Mr. Jim, and he is keepin' his watchful eye on ye. Ye remember when ye are filled to the brim with yer so-sorries for yeself. Filled to the brim of how *horribly* I've left ye; ye remember just one thing. One wee difference between yer Mr. Jim and me. When it came to what ye wanted, 'twas I who, at the very least, asked."

Then he smashed his mouth against mine. Just as a sob came out of me, for what I did not know, he pushed me away from him. Tossing me back to myself as if I were a dirty rag. I fell to the ground and quite pathetically into a puddle. He looked down at me and shook his head slowly, then walked toward the stable entrance. I shook my dazed head and reached to press cold fingers against my swollen, stinging lips.

"Yeah, well, good riddance to ya!" I screamed so harshly that my voice cracked.

The dark figure of a man on top of a horse rushed past me through the downpour. I watched them disappear into the ragged night. And then my tears came.

Chapter 17

Ilay out in the rain as an offering, paying a silent thanks to the end of the godforsaken draught. Or so I told myself. Deep down, I knew I lay out there with thanks that in the dark rain, my tears were felt natural, they blended in. It rained so hard I could barely breathe through it all. My throat was raw as ever, more than likely from all the emotion I tried to swallow. Mr. Jim always said emotions, more specifically a "big hurt," had a way of making your outside as sick as you were within. I hadn't thought the loss of Wallace would ever qualify as a big hurt. An enormous thunder clapped, and I opened my eyes to witness the remaining light. He was gone.

The steps beneath my shoulder blades bit into my skin harshly, and I pushed harder against them in return. Momentarily finding relief in pain I controlled. Pain that I didn't have to think about or organize or assign a proper name to. It was the type of pain that was direct, honest, and mindless. I sat up quickly as another sob rocketed through my body and slammed a clenched fist against my upper thigh.

He was gone.

The soft flesh radiated with sparks of a dull, deep ache. I hit myself again.

He was gone.

And again.

He was gone.

And again.

He was gone.

The roaring thunder and rain paired wondrously with my roaring mind. I focused on the leg pain that I created. A sweet, seductive distraction I was desperate for, and my mind was blank, except for the pain. *He was gone.*

He was gone because of me. I had sent him away with ease, might as well have packed his bags for him. My knuckles ached, and I curled myself up into a ball as more sobs broke loose. An elegant fine china vase, which was all that had occurred between us, was shattered on the floor, and I was left with the horrible mess, my clumsy hands alone to blame. The pieces of Wallace were scattered throughout the hardwood of my mind as I acknowledged that I was unable to put them back together. Not this time. Not with him gone. Not alone.

And it *hurt*. All of it hurt so very much more than the pain in my leg, and that made me angry. Primarily because I had not thought it would hurt. The surprise of my emotions piled up, one horrible thing upon another. And that theoretical weight pushed me onto the steps from which I could not leave.

As the lightning continued to flash and the thunder crashed, I counted the beats between light and sound. Calculating how long this haven of a summer storm would last. To see how long I could wallow before having to face the unwanted life waiting for me. But it seemed Wicker Soul was in the heart of the storm. Perhaps, I thought, we were the storm itself. Therefore, it would only end with our most ultimate demise. We had caused the storm surely enough. It was deserved punishment for all the naughty in such a forgotten bit of stolen land. A pathetic settlement full of cheap tricks, warm drinks, and only one, nearly rotted Catholic church.

It was my home. Or the only one I recalled. A part of me was Wicker Soul, despite its obvious hesitation toward my existence. I was the wild thing that lurked in the shadows of this town and the suspected source of all its wicked naughty. *That's what they had always said, wasn't it? Hadn't the people of this town whispered behind their hands since I was a child?* A child who didn't understand what was so strange about herself in the first place. *Was I naughty and wild by nature, by the widely unaccepted mingling I was a product of? Or did I become wild in response to how they welcomed me? What had I truly become, anyway? The horrible nymph, as Wallace had first referred to me. Perhaps. But he had never said horrible, now had he?*

Fantastical. Wallace was the only person who had ever referred to me as such. If anyone would ever again send another jolt of pain through me. I sat back up and threw my head into my hands and heaved over myself like a gargoyle. All my joints ached, and I couldn't sit still due to it.

"Did he hurt you?" a familiar, solemn voice called through the storm.

I clenched my eyes tighter and attempted a shaky breath. "No," I murmured just above the roar of the world.

"Don't you lie to me, girl." I couldn't miss the shake in Ms. Liz's voice.

I turned just as the lightning struck, revealing my rain-soaked, emotionally swollen face. "He didn't hurt me."

Ms. Liz nodded and stood her ground, unafraid of the lamentable creature I had become. "So, he's gone then?"

I set my jaw and nodded.

Her arms crossed over that large bosom of hers, and her brows knit with sympathetic, motherly worry. "Well," she sighed.

I turned back around to face the storm.

"You comin' back in?"

I shrugged.

"Well, don't stay out too long. You'll catch your death."

Over the storm, I heard her lingering presence and felt her worried gaze burning holes into my rain-sodden back. After about three more massive cracks of thunder, the door shuttered closed against the wind. I was alone once more.

Just below the pain and sorrow was the familiar frustration with myself, as I, per usual, did not have the words. In my mind, all the emotions, predominantly negative, created the most tangible and comprehensible feeling, and yet, they left a disconnect between my mind and my mouth. A torn string, perhaps. And in return, this upset caused my head to grow thick and heavy. Because behind all that mess within my mind, the young woman in me knew I should feel guilty for being so dismissive to Ms. Liz. But damnation, I hadn't the words. That had to count for something. That guilt I felt ought to add something human, something *relatable* to a nymph like me.

No one could pull those words out of my mind. Not even the man who had raised me in his likeness. At least his frustrations were as familiar as they were predictable, albeit childish. At least he entertained me, even if he lost his temper. He was there and listened to it all, the best he could. There was something to be said for that. So, I reached out and clung to all childish things and my Mr. Jim. I allowed them to sink into the cracks of my so broken heart and fill them with whatever nameless need I sought. They were the mortar between the bricks, which I would use to rebuild the walls temptation had brought tumbling down.

I stood too quickly, so not lightning but stars danced in front of my eyes. Blindly, I stumbled back into town. Mr. Jim had not returned, and my swollen eyes may have misled me, but I almost saw a candle burning in the window of his apartments. I pictured him, sitting with a pile of papers on his desk in the sickly yellow candlelight. A glass filled much too high with amber liquid.

His face would be stern, scowling even, and at my loud entrance, scowl deeper, and perhaps he'd even holler at my appearance. But then he would see my face. See the look that rarely, if ever, had taken it over, and he would stand. Offer me a seat—a glass, his glass. A blanket to warm my sodden body, and I would stammer, stumble, and chatter, making no sense in the very least. And he would growl and grumble. But he would sit with me until I fell asleep in whichever chair he had tucked me into. Then in the morning, he would call for a bath in that brass tub of his. And with that bath, perhaps I could wash off all that was weighing on me, and I could walk into the day and the life I had grown so immune to.

But I couldn't. Not really.

No amount of rose-scented soap or summer storm could ever return me to who I had been. Mr. Jim could boil that water in Ms. Liz's most trusted iron, and it still would not strip Wallace from my soul. And that was indeed going to be an issue. I was going to be stuck missing that damn man for the rest of my life, and no ocean, city, or book would fix that. He would be stained on me evermore, as those dark markings were upon his flesh.

I screamed a long strain of profanities into the storm until my voice cracked from the efforts. I stood in the middle of the wide dirt road that ran through our town, equal distances from the boarding house and the saloon, and lifted my face up to the storming sky. A small laugh bubbled at my rain-soaked lips. Agony and laughter were really the same. In my utter solitude, I had no one to remind me of the difference between the two, except maybe God. And yes, sir, I did hope that He was planning on paying me a visit.

I hoped that He took in the woeful sight of me and was sorry. I wanted my God guilty for always giving too late and taking too early. For expecting me to be a pretty, perfect marionette to Him and every other man, only to be disappointed in my so-called womanhood. Or even worse, when they expected me to be not a woman at all, but a sexless product of the original sin. I came from no Eve, but instead the speaking serpent.

I wanted Him to acknowledge me as me, not *the wicked thing of Wicker Soul* or Mr. Jim's awfully behaved ward, or the daughter of a whore and a runaway train. I wanted recognition for the person I had become, despite the circumstances He had blessed me with. But most of all, I wished to cut the strings that tied me to Him and Mr. Jim. Because those strings were silent expectations that wrapped like thick cords around my wrists to yank me with painful abruptness in whichever direction they found fit. Those yanks had conditioned me to react violently and speak with venom. To contradict all those accomplishments I insisted I had. I hated those strings.

Once they were cut, I could truly run. Perhaps then I would find Wallace. Just to leave him as he left me, and then I would keep running until I reached the end of the earth. And then I would run some more. My heels itched at the idea, and I looked to the black sky to see if my puppet strings were visible with the next strike of lightning. Once I saw them in real time, I would cut them myself. All I had to do was squint my eyes and look. I raised my arms so that I was stretched as Jesus on the cross would have been. That really ought to get some attention. Lightning struck, and my eyes flashed open.

"Release me," I whispered to the sky with gritted teeth.

God roared in response. A dismissive laugh. I stood my ground and faced His wrath. I had waited all summer for His attention, and now that I had it, I wasn't going to lollygag about. I shook my wrists and at the strings that entrapped them.

"Release me you coward!" I shrieked up to the storm-stained heavens.

There was a strike, close enough to smell before the largest clap of thunder yet bellowed. The world stood still. The rain softened a bit. Although it still fell quite freely and intended to continue throughout the night, the storm's personality had shifted. It nearly seemed sorrowful. Something close to regret as an odd relief began to fill me.

"I'm surprised it took ye this long to run over there. Unless yer heading on back after yer council. Tell me, girl: did ye at least get a chance to work up a proper wail?"

I tilted my head a little farther back as the familiar voice echoed through the storm. I whispered a hypocritical thanks to the sky as well as the Man who ruled it, dropped my noticeably lighter arms, and whipped my head toward the boarding house. His dark figure stood with fists clenched. A gentler flash of lightning allowed me to fully witness his expression. The man was furious. Lovely. I laughed breathlessly.

"Wallace," I whispered just above the storm. He was stalking me down once more, and I ran to him.

"Quit bloody callin' me Wallace," he growled as our bodies slammed into one another.

I wrapped my now free arms tightly around him. And it was I who captured his mouth with mine. He laughed against my clumsy attempt to kiss, and I growled as he pulled back and hoisted me so that he was now a tree I desperately tried to climb.

"If ye missed me that much, 'tis a good thing I turned 'round. A full night's punishment would've done ye in, I fear. Canna say I'm surprised. Didna I tell ye that first night, when I wanted nothing more than to yank ye by yer long-undone hair to me room and lock the doors for the rest of eternity, that I'd have ye coming to me all on yer own? Ought to've made a bet." His teasing chides brushed hotly against my lips, and I took his chin between my teeth. Quieting his incessant speaking.

His hand returned beneath my rump. The other snaked up just below my chin, slowly pulling my lips back to his. He kissed me gently, nibbling at me lazily like a midnight snack. Wallace whispered my name so delicately as he broke his lips from mine, somehow more tears came to my eyes.

Was it foolish to have assumed that I would be empty by now?

Once again, for more than the sake of our little nothing-of-a-town's livelihood, I thanked God for the rains, though I knew He was too mad at me to acknowledge it. I pushed closer to Wallace, to be fully reunited with him, as the long lines of his body warmed me and increased the flushed, stunning feeling deep inside. I rested my slippery forehead against his and reached to thread my fingers through his hair, yanking the tie loose. As I ran my fingers through the damp hair, something rattled him.

He pulled me tighter, if it were possible, and buried his face in my neck. His teeth came together sharply, nearly painfully, catching my skin. I cried out, and his tongue massaged the hurt. With a crack of thunder and strike of lightning, Wallace captured my mouth once again, and we moved back toward the boarding house.

I didn't waste time worrying about who might see because anyone awake at this hour must have also witnessed me in the heat of my mourning. *So surely they could turn a blind eye to the end of such a spectacle, couldn't they?* Our tongues now danced together as I heard the shutter of the front door slam. Perhaps, Wall—Jayson. Jayson, Jayson, Jayson. *God, that was something I would really have to work on now, wasn't it?* Perhaps *Jayson* had a habit of counting and memorizing steps. For I couldn't understand how in the dead of night he managed to make his way up the stairs while his lips seemed incapable of leaving my flesh. His movements were smooth where I would have stumbled, and I clung to him with all the strength he taught me to build, feeling an odd familiarity in a situation I had never experienced before. Perhaps my body was reverting to its raw, inherited, animalistic nature. *It lurked within all of us, didn't it?* It had just taken much longer to wake up within the likes of me.

His lips stilled against mine, and I realized we were no longer moving. He slid my damp body out of his hold, and we stood in front of my closed bedroom door. He reached around to open the door for me. I reached for his face and kissed him, trying to walk backward and bring him with me. I could kiss him forever, and at that moment, I had every intention to. He groaned lightly against my lips.

My fingers slid from the wet planes of his face as he abruptly held himself at the doorway. His eyes were closed, from what I could make out from the flickering candle that Ms. Liz must have left in my room, and his heavy breathing alarmingly flared his nostrils. His large knuckles were tight against the outer edge of the door frame as if his back were straining against an unseen pressure working to force him into my room. His head was down, and his shoulders were hunched with rigid effort.

"Jayson..." My voice was barely louder than his breathing.

His name was foreign on my tongue. I preferred Wallace, because realistically, how many women had been in my situation prior and whispered the name *Jayson* in the throes of whatever I was about to enter? No, I would not be like them and submit to something as easy and ordinary and forgettable as a first name. It was too used, too unfamiliar, and not any way I wished to be.

"Tell me to go," he said through a clenched jaw.

I moved closer to him as I welcomed the vibrant rationality that hid behind what he said—proximity caused his eyes to flash open. Wild.

"Trixie, tell me to go. Tell me to go. And more importantly, tell me to go and nae return. Because if I dinna...If ye give me...Ye've had a long emotional night. I will nae be angry when ye tell me to go. 'Tis...well, lass, I...I canna—"

His voice was hoarse, barely above a whisper. How odd it was to hear this man stutter. A surge of unexpected power rushed through me. I reached over to the bureau where the candle had been left, unsteady from the damp clothes, hair, skin that encased me. I held the candle level with my eyes. A leftover raindrop slid down my chin, neck, and then down the valley of my regretfully small bosom, which, even in a dress as finely made as this, couldn't help but disappoint.

Wallace watched that droplet and its path, his mouth opening by a fraction. A pale pink tongue, painted a little orange in the firelight, pushed against his sharp teeth. His words should have struck an emotion in the virgin I, unfortunately, was—something more potent than fear, the tormenting uncertainty of the unknown. But I did know. At least through books, I did. I may not have experienced the act before, but I was aware of what would transpire. Why I should slam the door. I knew what was entailed should I not. The threat against my very soul hung in the air. But God had cut His ties with me. I knew He had. Or I, Him. Whichever way, it didn't matter. And as I stared at Wallace staring at me, I didn't care. What was the point of purity if one never had the hungry eyes of a man so mystical, wondrous, and fine, memorizing your form? If I closed the door, I feared, past God or any guilt, that I would never feel this way again.

So, I stepped forward. Wallace's eyes lingered where that horrible drop of water slid. I reached out and placed my hand where his shirt fell open and felt the warm, damp skin. His breath came out as a hiss. "Tell. Me. To. Go," he whispered harshly.

I reveled in the contrast between sex and color, where my hand touched his chest: hair and skin. "I can't."

And with that, his lips formed an *o*, and quickly he blew out my candle. His arms came around me, effortlessly lifting me off my feet and wrapping around my back. The candle fell out of my hand. His lips were on mine relentlessly, and wildfire burned through my arms wrapping around his neck and threading my fingers through his hair. I pulled his hair as his teeth bit down harshly on my bottom lip. Biting was something Wallace did a lot, now that I knew him in this light.

With the pressure of his teeth closing around my lip, I groaned. His large palm traveled down my back to the lowest part of my bottom. He gripped the sensitive flesh greedily, and I threw my head back at the sensation, gasping. His lips never left my skin. They just continued gently along my jawline and neck.

His hoarse voice vibrated against me. "Hallelujah."

He walked in with me, using his foot to slam the door shut. The door closed on any purity my soul had clung to, and within were the joys of the flesh.

Chapter 18

I awoke to the great-grandfather clock striking three. Wallace's soft snores blew in my ear, and I lolled my head away from the tickling breath. One large hand cupped my breast, while the rest of his form stretched out with about half a foot between us. The sheets were tangled, and our naked selves proved it had not been some dream.

I slowly sat up so that my back was against the headboard, and Wallace's unconscious hand fell from my breast to my lap. His deep voice mumbled something incoherently lovely. I closed my eyes as it all came back with a flushing start. Human coupling was much more than I had imagined. It was much more indeed, filled with acts that had nothing to do with the altogether *male* need to procreate. No, in fact, acts that could in no way, shape, or form lead to procreation. Incredible, freeing acts that gave a feeling like the rush of running on a chilly fall day. I had enjoyed myself thoroughly.

I was old. Or at least older than I had been. I had to be—I felt age upon my skin like morning dew. As if such an act was so stupendous, it had altered the flesh. Or perhaps we were *at it* for so long, years had passed in the blink of an eye. I quickly reached to my face to check for sagged skin, or perhaps instead, leathered skin from time and the sun. But alas, the skin beneath my fingers was smooth and taut. Slightly damp with the oil that constantly plagued it.

A flash of lightning illuminated the room for a split second, and I realized the *tap-tap-tapping* of rain had ceased. Quietly, gently, I slid out of my bed, allowing Wallace's hand to fall with a soft thump, and he retracted it. I noticed the mess on the floor by the only light of the peeking moon and grasped a large cloth. I slipped Wallace's shirt on and clung the material close to me like a schoolgirl in love would with a gifted handkerchief. I managed to find both of my thick stockings and pulled them on without making too much noise as I jumped about.

On the balls of my feet, I tiptoed to the window, carefully opening it. A cool wind blew in as well as a smattering of leftover raindrops. I glanced back at Wallace's sleeping face and maneuvered out. I sat in my usual seat, feeling the damp roof immediately through the cloth covering my rear end. That part of me felt sore, and the sog of the roof availed it slightly. As I made myself comfortable, I discovered Wallace's trusty wooden pipe in his shirt pockets. I placed it in my mouth and absorbed the taste greedily.

I took in the familiar view of the sky, watching the clouds move sluggishly across the dark horizon. As if they were second-guessing the allowance to glimpse the glorious Mary Moon echoing across the town below. I pulled my knees up to my chest and watched the patterns She and the clouds made. If you stared long enough, it almost looked like they were dancing in the sliding light.

The clouds were coveting the moon. Though, as those alive through His ultimate sacrifice, didn't we all? An angry lover, those storm clouds must be. Angry at the sun and the drought that had kept them from their moments with Her, our Mary Moon. The clouds spoke with the breeze and the rain. And when the lighting lit the sky for those brief moments, it was a crescendo of clouds raising their voices.

I couldn't help but wonder if those strikes of lighting were to hit us in vengeance. As if the only way the clouds could physically take out their anger was to strike at us measly humans below—the sinful bystanders. God would simply watch with a certain approval of it all. What control did He have over something as powerful as clouds and rain and their love for Her? I had pushed His limits, pushed His control to its breaking point, and I was but a speck of dust in comparison to those stupendous acts of nature. I flexed my much lighter fingers for self-assurance. Mr. Jim said that my father would go a-walking each full moon and wouldn't be back until dawn. Perhaps he was a part of the storm now. That was a nice thought. *If he was now a part of the storm, was it so incredible to wonder if my momma had ended up with Mary on that there ever-chaste Moon?*

A warm breath fanned across my cheek, pulling me from my musings. I leaned toward Wallace as he nuzzled me. The scratch of his whiskers was a new experience that I hoped to never live without. "Do you hurt?" His voice was low against my cheek. He gently took his pipe from my mouth.

I nodded and wiggled my bottom against the cool, relieving roof. He sighed. He was still within my room but tall enough to lean out and rest his elbows next to me. I returned my gaze to the honorable sky.

"What are you thinking about?" Wallace finally whispered.

His hand delicately traced patterns on my shoulder. I inhaled a lungful of the misty air with an open mouth, wanting to taste the catastrophic love Mary Moon evoked. Taste it, and maybe inherit some of Her power, whether Momma was a part of it or not.

I swallowed my medicine with a constricting gulp. "The sky. And the moon. And God. Maybe my mother and father."

"Let's start with God then. What business has He got in this moment?"

I smiled at his speech, returning to the blasphemous flamboyancy one could really get used to. "Just about everything, one would think."

"Well, He can just mind His own... Is Ms. Liz's tedious Catholic guilt creeping up your spine?"

"No, Wallace, it isn't."

"Good. Now what of the moon and sky?"

"That first time I saw you, you asked if I talked to the moon."

"Yes, I did, and I wonder if that is what I have caught you doing now, whispering your darkest prayers and fantasies to Her. I envy that Moon, I do."

"You couldn't."

"I do," he nodded. "Because She gets your secrets and your thoughts. I want those."

I just shook my head and returned my gaze to the sky.

"And lastly, are you upset by what Jim shared?"

"I suppose I should say no; I don't know if I wanted it to be told. It sounds different when other ears can hear it."

"It all sounded awfully...convenient to me."

"It's my fault. I should have told him to stop the story," I mumbled.

"And that's just what it is, Trix. A story."

I mulled his words over, still transfixed with Her. I swallowed down any annoyances I felt toward him for distracting me from such a beauty. He was speaking too loudly, too harshly in Her presence. She was grace eternal, was She not?

"Do you love Jim?"

I kept myself still at his question, something that I knew would come. After everything, Mr. Jim was the last thing I wanted to think about. I looked back up to the sky as a gentle flash of lightning, perhaps one last scream, bloomed.

"Trix..." he murmured, running his nose along my jawline.

"Does an old dog not love the largest tree so that it may lie in its shade?"

He continued to trace my face with his own. "You are not an old dog. And he is not the largest tree."

I continued, "He was the only comfort I could find. That was enough. I don't know, Wallace. If I say yes, you'll ask why. And I don't know if I have an answer to that."

He stayed quiet.

"I suppose he was the only thing I really knew. It felt, well, it felt wrong to question him. Like I was ungrateful, so I never did. And in return, he never left. Maybe that's always been enough for me."

I turned to face him dead on, denying him the closeness he had been relishing in.

"Do you think I'm going to leave?" His voice was rough.

He recalled our earlier conversation, as did I.

I sighed. "I hope you won't."

I did. I hoped he would stay. Stay because of me. Or perhaps despite me. *But was that not the same as what Mr. Jim had done to me? Had I not been trapped by something more than just a duty, but a grand notwith-*

standing? An anchor that held my soul to the bottom of his ocean, and his alone?

"But I won't ask you to stay. I won't make you. I won't weigh upon you or...or let you become the one who waits for me." I bit back the emotion that bubbled at my lips.

His fingers wrapped tightly around my arm, and he harshly yanked my body closer to his chest. "Hear ye me, girl o' mine, I am leavin' this town in the same fashion as the warm air will retreat, and winter will arrive. But I am nae leavin' without ye. Ye give me yer sighs and yer 'sorry for yerselfs' all ye want. 'Tis a waste of breath. Dammit, girl, didna I just *show* ye that I canna leave without ye? I told ye that when it's right, 'tis the same for both, and I meant it."

I flushed as he crudely pulled me even closer against his body. His hands ran up and down me, grabbing and touching every single place, soft or not. Warmth pumped through my veins. I bravely reached up to hold his face, forcing eye contact. His eyes were narrow slits. Their wild expression made sense in the calm moonlight. Absolute desperation that was masked by a fear-fueled confidence.

"Come with us. We can all leave—you, me, and Mr. Jim. He says he is gonna take me as far as San Francisco and then back out East. Across the Atlantic and to Paris, France. I'm sure you've already been, but I haven't, of course. Say, do you speak any French? Mr. Jim knows a little, but we are gonna need all the help we can get, ha!" My voice was rushed and nearly stumbling.

Wallace's hands settled upon my upper thigh and rib cage. A slow, dangerous chuckle came from him. "That sounds a wee bit familiar now, aye?"

I furrowed my brow.

"Mr. Jim ain't takin' ye anywhere. I'll nae be sharin' ye with the likes o' him, Trixie. Ye've given yerself to me, and I'm keeping ye. And nae, I dinna speak French."

I took a deep breath. *How could I explain that nothing was that simple?* He nuzzled my neck, and his hands tenderly squeezed the flesh they cupped.

"Tell me ye love me," he murmured against my neck, his tongue tracing patterns.

I closed my eyes, focusing on sensation instead of the butterflies that rioted in my stomach. My lack of response altered his licking into bites, gentle at first, then crueler and a clear punishment. I cried out in response and tried to pull away. He was then on the roof with me, on top of my form with laughter in his eyes.

"Tell me ye love me, Trix," he murmured again, as gently as a man like him could.

I kept his eyes and took a deep breath to settle my aching heart. I reached up to trace the lines on his face as a wide smile spread across it.

"Whatever you are, to me, you are the most," I said with all the finality I could muster.

"That'll do, girl." Wallace rolled off me and back through the window, pulling me with him most excitedly.

Chapter 19

I woke to sunshine and a lightly stuttering breath in my ear once more. I nuzzled toward Wallace's warmth. His breathing evened out, and he pulled me closer into a more artistic embrace. But I was awake. I wriggled loose, not free, of the hold enough to reach over Wallace's wonderfully sleeping form, to grab my book from the side table. With the soft leather in my hand, I straightened a touch taller, attempting to comfort myself as well as to not disturb my overnight guest.

I read of the sea with such desperate ferocity that I nearly tasted the salt Wallace had whispered of on my tongue. My head was full of what I thought the sound of crashing waves was, somewhere between the splash of water and the whisper of the trees on a windy day. But I didn't know. At least not yet. That flash of hope, the potential of finally seeing the ocean, made my stomach do a small flip.

I didn't know how long Wallace had been watching me, being fully enthralled in my book. At some point, I gave him a side glance to find those eyes sleepily staring at me. I startled a little and let the book dangle limp in my hands. Somehow the romantic descriptors of the vast ocean no longer held my attention. He lay on his side, with one arm tucked behind his pillow and another still resting across my waist. He was lovely to look at when he wasn't speaking. Despite the relaxed manner he always held, that calm, collected expression of sheer uninterest, something burned in his sleepy eyes.

His hand lifted slightly, tracing the circle of my breast. Earlier, in the heat of my most educational experience, I attempted to learn his body. He had been so confident in handling mine, and in the midst of my efforts to catch up, he had laughed and swatted my hands away from his chest. He then gave me a very wonderful kiss as if to say, "Thanks, but you've got this all wrong." Nonetheless, in the present, mine puckered immediately at his touch.

"This," he whispered, leaning in closer to me, "is the most beautiful color I have never seen." He briefly kissed my confused brow.

I glanced down at his finger, softly tracing my now pointed feminine source of nourishment. The contrast of the color was quite lovely. Those parts of my body were not as sunned as my face and arms but still seemed otherworldly compared to his fair complexion. As if in some way, underneath it all, I was red, and he was green. Opposites, but perfect together. Like Christmas holly. His touch was not shaking the ground I stood upon, like some actions from last night had, but it was warm and felt interesting. It was such a secretive touch. His face appeared bored, but his eyes were dancing.

"Wallace?" I whispered.

"Hmmm?"

"What are you doing?"

He grinned and returned his gaze to my specifically puckered skin, slowing his circles so that heat pooled in my lower stomach at the same speed. I bit my lower lip.

"What's it feel like I'm doing?"

I felt playful embarrassment at that. He snaked an arm around my waist, swiftly yanking me to straddle him as if he were the horse between my legs. My arms immediately wrapped around my own bare breasts, embarrassed with the new, vulnerable position.

"Wall—" I began to gasp.

His eyebrows shot right back up with a disciplinary look. I continued to hold my breasts but bravely leaned down a little bit closer to him so that I could taste his breath on my mouth.

"Jayson," I breathed airlessly. Between the two of us, the air was too thick to get a sentence out properly. I placed one hand on his chest to steady myself, just over his black tattooed marking, the other stayed wrapped around myself. I glanced down at the mark, at the smooth, un-interrupted skin. I had assumed it would be raised, like a scar.

My fingertips followed the sharp straight lines of it delicately, worried that maybe it would hurt. He captured my hand and held it against the mark. My fingers splayed out and brushed the black hair that smattered across his chest, more heavily so in the center. It had no hint of gray and was softer than I imagined. My eyes flashed back to his gentle smile. His hair was like his ink, without any hint of gray either. I hadn't really been this close to him in full light before, to look at the soft smile lines around his mouth and the light crinkles around his eyes. All only a little bit deeper than my own. He couldn't be more than five years older than me.

"How old are you?" I whispered.

His eyes narrowed most peculiarly. For the first time since I had known this man, I saw it. More likely than not, I had seen it all along, subconsciously. Which was why I could never lock my elbows to keep him at arm's length as I knew I should have. I understood why I was so drawn to him. Behind those flickering eyes, behind their tricks and mischief, I saw the same thing that I witnessed in my own reflection. Perhaps my own soul. Loneliness. Clad identically as mine, as if it were his shadow. Connected to him, as was mine to me, through thick and thin. Even when the sun went down, it lingered in silence, visible only when a flicker of light hit it just so. But once that light did discover it, the shadow took an eerie shape. Proving it had been there all along, proud in its nature. Crouching on our shoulders.

I swallowed down a follow-up question of how he felt about open doors. I didn't swallow too hard, though, because his hand reached up to stroke the high of my cheekbone. I pushed my face closer into the contact.

"I don't know."

I nodded at his answer, feeling very close to him. The familiarity in his lack of knowledge made me feel alive. Something told me Wallace's story of coming to be in this exact middle of nowhere rivaled mine.

"Me either."

He nodded back, and I released my breasts. Both arms shot up to cage my face and brand me with a powerful and punishing kiss. I gasped at the intensity and speed of his mood swing. Instantly, I was drunk. Completely and entirely intoxicated with the moment. I couldn't breathe, and I didn't want to. Each touch and pinch and bite and lick pushed me further from my moral sobriety and deeper into whatever I was becoming. But his hands stilled with an odd jerk as I flinched to his caressing of my upper thigh. Wallace pulled back from my lips and inspected his hands while my mind spun back down to solid ground. I followed his gaze at the sharp intake of breath. His fingers gently traced the beginnings of a massive bruise, and I swore in remembrance.

"I didn't do this," he whispered to himself, his eyes giant orbs of guilt.

I whispered an unnecessary "no," watching his face as he went over every touch from last night, attempting to place the injury. He sat up swiftly, and I toppled from sitting on his belly into his lap, his fingers mindlessly tracing the bruise I had given myself.

"But I did." I bit my lip and shook my head.

He, in return, countered my shake with a nod. He closed his eyes and exhaled deeply out of his nose, then leaned forward and placed a slightly painful kiss on my injury. I hissed at that, and he bit the sensitive bruise. I clenched my teeth, immediately feeling his anger and sadness as they transferred to angry shame within me. I pulled away from him, and he left the bruise alone but wrapped an arm around my lower back to hold me still. He trailed gentle kisses up from my bruise to my hip bone where he nipped, to my belly that was stretched tight from my attempt to squirm away from him, to the belly button and then my ribs. He buried his face between my breasts, placing one kiss on my sternum.

"A pain in ye leg canna fix a pain in yer heart, girl," he mumbled against my skin.

I bit my lip and nodded, feeling much like a child caught amid a most awful naughty.

"I shouldna have stormed off," he continued.

He swatted at my almost seated, bare rear end. I gave him a small smile, which he matched. "Next time, I'll stay and just keep screaming at ye."

I laughed aloud at this, and his smile grew. He placed another kiss on my sternum. "I love ye, Trixie-girl."

My laughter died down, and I nodded despite the unpleasant tightening in my stomach. I kept nodding as tears gathered in my eyes, and I slid my hands from his neck to the planes of his cheeks to pull his face up. His lips found mine just as my tears poured over. There was a war in my mind that I was vulnerably ill-prepared for. He broke the kiss to lick the saltwater that rolled down my cheeks.

My tears did not stop despite his gentle nature. After multiple laps of the tongue, he pulled away to look at me. His face was raw and confused, and I sobbed at that. He held me as close as he could. As if he were squeezing all the shattered parts of me back together. As if I were something to handle with care.

We should have heard the footsteps. It was not like the sun was not up. In fact, we had relished in it. Using it to our passionate advantage. Which, in a roundabout way, was clearly why we didn't hear the footsteps. But we should have.

Our only alarm was the call of, "Trixie, you alright?" Then my door swung open, and Mr. Jim continued, "Ms. Liz said you were..."

Wallace quickly lifted me off him and threw his body in front of mine, so my nudity was shielded, for the most part. He held me back behind him, but I peeked under his arm at Mr. Jim, and dread pulsed through my veins. That and fear for our lives.

A father would have gone mad. Rushed a man in bed with his daughter. Beat him to a bloody pulp or at least start hollering. Maybe even pace about the room breaking anything he could get his hands on out of pure rage. It was the protective, instinctual thing to do. But Mr. Jim was not my father. Therefore, with an eerie calm, he looked to assess the obvious before meeting my eye as I peeked beneath Wallace's underarm. He didn't even acknowledge Wallace. As if he weren't involved in what had just been witnessed. His eyes burned into mine. Wallace bravely snarled some form of dismissal, and his grip on me tightened.

Mr. Jim still only looked at me, disgust evident in his eyes as he slowly shook his head.

"Just like your momma." To prove the cruelty in his words, he spat at the dress he bought for me, lying in a pool at his feet, and left.

"Hey!" Wallace hollered in retaliation. He jumped out of bed and grabbed for his pants. In a moment, he was yanking them on, jumping about. I trembled, and Wallace quickly leaned over me to cup my face. "Stay here." He ran out the door, hollering at the footsteps going on down. "Dinna speak to her like that, Jim!"

I gasped and stood, rushing to the door to hear Mr. Jim swear at Wallace. The doors within the house opened at the noise with shameful curiosity. The men's steps traveled to the first floor and out of the house. I darted to my open window to follow the fight. Wallace grabbed Mr. Jim's shoulder; swung him around to face him. Mr. Jim shoved Wallace, but the shirtless man held his ground.

"What are ye doin', bargin' into her room like that? She's a grown woman!" Wallace asked angrily.

"Oh, don't even try that with me, boy. These tables ain't turning. Not when I find you making a whore outta my gi..."

A crash of flesh against flesh cut off Mr. Jim's horrible statement. He stumbled backward from Wallace's assault. Profanities rang out so vile and tightly linked with my name I covered my ears, squeezed my eyes shut, and spun from the window.

"Looks like Mr. Wallace couldn't stay gone long, don't it?" Ms. Liz's voice had me jumping around from my place at the window.

She glanced at my lack of clothing, then around the room with a small huff. I was clad in only my stockings. I stood, nearly naked as birth, my arms incapable of acting on any form of humility I ought to have. My hands just shook at my sides.

"Oh, dear," Ms. Liz said softly as I gasped for breath.

My throat was smaller than it had ever been. She took one step toward me before I heard familiar and faint steps pause at my door. My eyes flashed wildly at Wallace, and I scratched at my throat, coughing and wheezing as if there weren't any space for the airflow. White-hot panic engulfed me. He rushed me, snagged his shirt from the floor, and wrapped it around my naked form as if to protect me from the eyes of Ms. Liz. I coughed hard and leaned my slick forehead against his bare shoulder. The perspiration caused my head to slide, and I stumbled a bit.

"She's having a fit," Ms. Liz exclaimed, taking a worried step closer.

Wallace pulled my body closer to his to shield me from her. The room spun as I clung to the shirt wrapped around me. I was freezing for a moment, and it shocked my system. My teeth chattered around any attempts to breathe.

"She's feverish," Wallace murmured, placing a hand over my forehead.

"I suppose such a scene would have me sick with nerves just the same. The poor girl might faint, Mr. Wallace," Ms. Liz sounded equally stern as worried.

I pushed away from Wallace to lean over, brace myself on my knees, and cough this fit Ms. Liz claimed I was having right on out. Eventually, I could breathe. Little black spots danced in my vision.

Wallace harshly grabbed my chin and yanked my face toward him to look at me. He put his palm back on my forehead, and I leaned toward the cool temperature of his hand, growing warm once more. "Ye been feelin' poorly?"

I pulled a little back from him as I recalled we didn't have the room to ourselves. I shrugged and clutched the shirt tighter around myself.

"Ms. Liz, fetch Trix a glass o' water, aye?"

I cleared my raw throat.

"I believe it is you who should run off to get Trixie-girl some water. Give the girl a chance to make herself presentable."

Wallace glared at Ms. Liz, and she put both hands on her hips, standing ground on the floors she so proudly owned. "Don't you be lookin' at me like that. This is still my house, and therefore my rules. Now get out 'fore I decide to throw you out!"

Wallace gently patted my cheek and rolled his eyes at Ms. Liz before exiting the room. She shut and locked the door behind him. Something more complicated than shame flooded my system. Shame tended to come with regret, and I couldn't bring myself to regret the decision I had made with Wallace. But the distress on Ms. Liz's persona, paired with the frown line that creased her forehead, had me feeling heavy with insecurity. Ms. Liz rubbed at that wrinkled forehead of hers, and I pulled Wallace's shirt closer around myself. She sighed again and reached for me with an outstretched hand. I stared at it for a beat. Then, I held out a shaky hand to meet hers as she sat me down on the bed. I got myself under the twisted covers, trying to hide my sheepish expression about how much of a wreck the bed was.

She patted my hand. "Take a bit more rest for your nerves. Then I'll see you downstairs." I stared in confusion. "Child, for your safety, I ain't letting you out of my sight today. We've got a long day of chores ahead of us," she said with a dry chuckle, then left.

Chapter 20

I rested for nearly two more hours and begrudgingly came down the steps to find Ms. Liz waiting for me, right in the middle of making rising bread. I said nothing as we worked the bread. After ten minutes of silence, the dough gained its shape, and Ms. Liz took a large breath.

"Mr. Jim's actions were not preferable, and I have half a mind to go give that man a talking to, but we must remember to be gentle with him. He has always only wanted what is best for you."

"What he thinks is best for me," I corrected tightly. I was going balmy. My ears were already hot.

"Yes, well, it's fair to say none of us thought of you to be in the market for a husband."

My kneading became noticeably rougher. I fought a shiver at the word *husband*. "Of course, it is," I muttered through clenched teeth. I broke into a sweat with my thorough working of the dough. The kitchen was silent, except for the abuse of my bread and the pounding in my head.

"Trixie, is there something the matter?" I shot her a look, and she stilled. "Other than the obvious, of course," she corrected herself. "You're not worried 'bout Mr. Wallace, are you?"

I threw the dough harshly onto the table and took a step back from it. I wiped at my sweaty forehead, trying to calm the furious buzzing that rioted within.

"Now, I have to say that I am not exactly happy with the man and have my other half of mind to sit him down for a talking to, but you ought not worry about it all."

"You gonna give anyone your whole mind? Or you just plannin' on handing halves out till everybody's had a bit of talking to?" I rallied harshly at her.

She put her hands on her hips and gave me a stern look. "Alright, what is the matter with you, girl?"

"Ms. Liz, are you in any way confused by what you have witnessed? Let me explain if so. Wallace and I did not just spend an entire evening destroying my bed from a much-too-vigorous game of chess. And now everyone in this goddamn town knows."

Ms. Liz stayed quiet for a moment, picking at her dough a little childishly. "You worried that 'cause everyone knows, Mr. Wallace won't want to have you for a bride, is it?"

I let out a scream. *How could she not understand this one moment that was exclusively mine was ripped from me and soiled? Judged and categorized and given deadlines, which then forced it into something that demanded approval.*

"Child, I have no doubt the man will want to marry you! He is a fool in love." The kindness and forced reassurance in her tone made me nauseous.

I approached the windows to observe the cloudy day in the foothills. Those mountains looming on the gray horizon mocked me. Long ago, they had nestled themselves upon my shoulders in such a manner that with each passing day I remained stationary, their weight intensified. Now the discomfort was nothing more than a loyal companion.

But over the mountains and then some distance beyond was the ocean. I knew this to be true from the maps I had studied in the quiet hours of the night when sleep either evaded me, or I was too scared to submit to it. I had traced the western route with my grubby finger, over and over, from here to the Pacific Ocean until the ink bled into surrounding rivers and roads. In San Francisco, even I, wicked and unremarkable as I was, could stand at the edge of the world where the water met the sand and endure.

I closed my eyes and imagined those elegant crashing waves come to life as they rushed upon the shore. Felt the water's temperature coating my toes as the Lil' Big had done on cool spring mornings when I couldn't be bothered by the schedule of the day ahead of me. The California air would be harsh against my face, much like a Colorado winter storm. But I imagined it would smell greener. Then I would jump on a grand old boat and just go and go and never look back. I almost heard the leaves rustling paired with the sound of gentle water babble. *There were trees in California, weren't there? Surely, they would rustle along the rush of the sea like the hum of a lullaby.*

Once I got out there, my moments would be my own. I simply had to get there. Unfortunately, with the scenario that played out this morning, it was clear my getting there was becoming much more difficult.

"Trixie?" Ms. Liz's soft voice brought me back to reality, and my eyes flashed open.

"And of mine?" I stared at those mountains, and though I knew their presence was a part of me, they seemed impossibly far away as reality wrapped itself back around my heart like a cold vice.

"Your what, dear?"

"My wants," I bit out.

The voice in the back of my head, the one that sounded a lot like Mr. Jim's, reminded me that rationally none of this was Ms. Liz's fault. But I had started, and dammit, I deserved a finish. She politely waited for what we all knew was coming.

"Has no one ever considered what I want?" I stood back at the island, which had always been common ground, where our pitiful attempts of bread sagged on the well-floured wooden countertop.

She broke eye contact with me, but not before showing the shame in her eyes. "No, I reckon we haven't."

I punched my fist into the dough violently at her confirmation. I put forward an angry exterior, fearing the interior one wilting like a too-warm flower inside me.

Ms. Liz wiped bits of dough off her pudgy hands to approach me. She kept me at arm's length. "Trixie-girl, do let me explain." She wet her lips and continued. "Is it possible for you to understand that though we have wronged you, perhaps you wronged us just the same?"

I began to speak, and she held up a hand to stop me.

"Never once did you shed any light on...well, anything. You never told a soul what you wanted, other than perhaps Mr. Jim. In your time here, never have you opened to us. Since the day I met you, even as that sweet little girl, you were so angry at everything."

I bit my bottom lip; guilt mixed with frustration and anger.

"I have loved you the best way I could. The only way I could. If you feel as though I have failed you in any manner," her voice shook, and she took a steadying breath. "Well, perhaps it is because I felt as if it were not my place. I have loved you as my own, but you are not my own. And despite all my wants to understand you, at the end of the day, it felt disrespectful to think that I could. As I watched you grow and turn angrier at the world, I wanted nothing more than to reach out and explain it all to you, as a mother does to her daughter. But what you went through, I couldn't explain. I couldn't give you the tools to help you understand things that I did not. I couldn't fix the world for you, and it was ignorant to believe I could see it through your eyes when it has always been so easy through mine. So, I did the only thing I could do. I loved you through it. I loved you instead of condescending you."

I bit my lip harder.

"If I have failed you, please know that at least I respected you."

I nodded as a tear ran down her cheek. I rubbed both of my arms to ward off the chill from such a conversation. Yesterday, no one loved me. The weight of two loves in such a short period was heavy and oddly cold.

"Trixie, what do you want?"

I shrugged.

"Do you love Mr. Wallace?"

The small child, hiding within me still clad in britches, longed to reach up and take hold of this plump, loving woman and confide in her that I didn't know. The reality was, I didn't believe I knew what love was. Or what it was supposed to feel like. But I was too proud and ashamed to ask because she loved me. She had just declared so. *And if I were to ask what love was, well then, she would know I may not return that affection in the same manner, and wouldn't that make me something awful? Wouldn't*

that mean that there really was something horribly wrong with me?

"I have to, don't I?" I whispered through the tears that quietly rolled

down my cheeks despite my hurried fingers.

"Oh, girl," she said quietly and pulled me in for a hug.

I returned the embrace, inspired by that small child within me that

simply needed the comfort of a warm, soft bosom. She hushed me and

smoothed my back with gentle hands.

"Because if I don't, what does that make me?" I continued. "If I don't,

where does that leave me? If I don't love Wallace, then why on earth did I

just ruin my life for him?"

My sobs bubbled at my lips, held back by a single, worn but resilient

thread of pride, and I buried my face in her shoulder. She kept sooth-

ing me as the tears fell. She leaned her head upon mine. I was genuinely

cushioned within all that she was and made her female, a kind mind, and

incredibly soft breasts.

"Ms. Liz," I whispered as my lungs ached with the pain from my heart

and my head, "what's wrong with me?" That sob finally broke through

me, and she squeezed me tighter.

She took a deep breath, and I felt the exhale against the hairs on my

head. "Sometimes people love each other, and it's the same. Other times

it isn't. It doesn't make their love any less and don't mean there's some-

thing wrong with you. That's just the way of it, I suppose. Our hearts don't all run at the same pace, and sometimes one party needs a chance to catch up. If he really loves you, he will let you catch up, girl."

"I...I just don't know," I whispered. "I feel as though...oh, I don't know how I feel." My mouth was too wet with tears and snot. My words got stuck in an excess of unnecessary lubrication.

"Do you want to be with him, as a man would want to be with a woman?"

I surrendered and nodded glumly.

"Do you want to be with him, as a friend wishes to be with another friend?"

I nodded again, listening to the soft pattering of her heart.

"Then let's give our Mr. Wallace a chance to wait on you, mmm?" She released me lightly to lift my chin, making our eyes meet. Hers were so gentle, I felt another rush of tears come on.

"Let that love grow good and slow now, girl. That man ain't going nowhere without you."

I nodded, and my brows furrowed.

She gave my chin another tap with her knuckles. "But if that love ain't growing, don't you get in your head that you've got to make it. Or believe that man is your only ticket outta here, ya hear? I'll not have you selling your soul just for a chance to stretch them little legs of yours. You feelin' the need to go, and you come to me. We can figure it out together."

I nodded against her and detangled myself from the warm embrace. Her words were kind, but they were too late. I swallowed down the angry question of where such a promise had been a year ago.

She switched her gaze to stern almost immediately, though. "In the meantime, I am not approving of the sharing of bedrooms without a holy union in order, understand?"

I grimaced. Something told me Jayson Wallace couldn't give two hoots about what Ms. Liz approved of. And I may have been a lot of things, but I wasn't about to be a hypocrite and deny him entrance, for I yearned to share his company all the same.

"Chin up, girl, and get back to work. We've got heaps to do," she clucked and went back to her dough.

Chapter 21

y arms and shoulders held the strain of a long day's cooking by the time supper rolled around. I trudged up the steps to my room with little energy and even less of an appetite. It was a wonder that most folks who cooked were plump; after a day that long cooped up in the kitchen, I couldn't imagine wanting to eat.

I sat in the rocking chair pulled up snug to the open window, where the cool twilight air and droplets of rain fluttered in. I shivered as the droplets landed on my skin. I was clad in only my undergarments. My skin turned to gooseflesh at the invasive kisses of damp air, but I made no move to alleviate the discomfort.

I half-heard the call for supper as I stared out the window to the gray horizon. Slowly, the sound of familiar steps grew nearer to the house in the quiet drizzle. The steps were heavy and a little more sluggish than their owners' usually light ones, proving their day had been as long as my own. I sighed and rubbed my forehead, where the touch of a headache bloomed. The steps paused with the hollow echoing of their weight on the front porch steps. The aroma from a warm meal floated up, penetrating the cool air. My mouth stayed dry.

I waited for Wallace's steps to enter the house, and when they did not, I looked down at the porch. He was paused halfway up the steps looking to my open window. He smiled one of his wonderfully sardonic smiles, but something about it looked forced. His eyes were tight. He pointed down with a long pale finger that was almost as bright as the sun while gray light crept in around the edges of the town. He wanted to know whether I would be going to dinner. I pulled the wrap that was pooled at my hips closer and shook my head. He gave me a half-smile, accepting my answer. He then puckered his lips as if a kiss could take flight upon the soft, damp winds to land on me, and he entered the house. I warmed a little at the sound of his steps, confirming entrance. I would never admit it aloud, but his presence gave me comfort. However, I did not move from my seat.

The night continued to grow colder as more rain came. All the while, the sky took on an eerie, but somehow equally lively, gray-green hue. Droplets grew and fell upon my windowpane. They sprinkled a loving kindness across the planes of my face. Only through temperature could I tell the difference between them and the silent tears raining from my eyes.

Mr. Jim did not come to dinner. The light burned from his office apartments, flickering through the haze of the evening, and I willed him to come. The last bits of light from the lackluster day diminished as the conversation of merely existing through this day echoed up from below, yet I did not falter my gaze. My squinted eyes and wrinkled brows ached. My hands were on the window with my chin resting on top of them. Everything I had, including the bits that I so desperately wanted to save for Wallace, was focused on Mr. Jim in that moment. I pushed as hard as I figured God could push the winds to will Mr. Jim for once to understand me. To forgive me. And to love me through it all, even with my transgressions.

Despite the love that Wallace had offered, tied in a ribbon and blessed with good intentions, I yearned so powerfully for the love I didn't have. It was tender and asexual, with instead much more intimate caresses of the soul. Though Wallace had taken it upon himself to fill the hollow aching within me that burned so deliciously, I recognized something was still missing within me, which would ache forever. Unless, of course, I could find a way to will Mr. Jim with the desperate power of a wild woman's mind.

I wiped at my rain-clad, clammy forehead, and my hands shook. Everything hurt. It was as though the breath had been knocked out of me. Or perhaps I was falling down a deep dark hole with no comprehension of where it led or who had pushed me down it in the first place. It was the helplessness that seized me, trickling into my reality so that the hole and the situation I attempted to deal with bled into each other like damp ink. The hot, ragged air that came in my lungs felt pressurized as I finally broke my gaze from Mr. Jim's flickering window to cover my watery eyes. Just like the night before, I sobbed. Snot bubbling, gasping and gagging sobs.

How predictable of God, to bring me the man I had begged for, only to take away the other who had always been there. A repercussion, it seemed, for standing up for myself against Him. Or instead, perhaps it was the punishment for what lay between my legs and seeking to satisfy it. The real curse of womanhood. The inevitable decision between the man she wished to love and the uncontrollable love she had for her daddy. No matter what type of man that daddy happened to be. Women were expected to tear their love in half. Separate violently from what she was born into, born of, for the chance at life her godforsaken soul begged for. Men truly got it all. I sobbed for heaven-knows-how-long until my hiccupping grew so aggressive, I had to straighten my posture and rub my throat to ease the passage of air.

"Bless you," Wallace's quiet voice called.

I opened my swollen eyes to find him leaning against my closed door, hands behind his back.

"Oh," I said slowly and stupidly.

He shifted his weight from one foot to another.

"How long have you been there?" I questioned quietly through a thick, raspy voice.

"Long enough," he said firmly.

The quiet rain echoed in my room as the last bits of sunlight faded behind mountains or clouds. I hadn't any idea of the hour.

"Are ye hurtin'?" His brows were pulled deeply together, but his jaw was set.

"No, Wallace," I reassured him.

My heart warmed a bit at his concern.

His tone stayed in a dangerously even tone. "Are ye regrettin'?"

I held his brooding eye and was greeted with familiar loneliness that matched my own unspoken emotions. I mulled over his question. Despite the sorrow I was all but vibrating with at the thought of losing Mr. Jim over something as predictable as another man, I still couldn't bring myself to regret anything that had happened between Wallace and me. But I didn't have the right words to explain that, and my tongue was rather thick with my attempts to find them. So, I simply held his worried, steady gaze, and shook my head.

Wallace sighed deeply, then sauntered over to where I sat. He plopped down on the cushions of my bed, very quickly taking up the room and making it his own. He ran a large hand over his face as if to wipe away the remaining bits of anxiety that had spent their time stomping about in that dear mind of his.

How endearing did the man look now? Love and hate were truly two sides of a coin, interchangeable once tossed into the air. Left only to the fate of whichever direction the air blew in the very last moment. Despite the animalistic intimacy we had shared earlier, Wallace did not touch me. I even pulled my wrap closer around my chilled frame. He leaned back with his feet still planted on the floor as he held himself up by strong elbows on the soft bed.

"Is it anythin' I can fix?" he prompted gently.

My nose felt tight and twitchy at his care, and I fought back the tears. I was endless, and I needed to rein it in. But my chin continued to quiver with a lack of control I had never experienced before. I took a shaky breath and tried to speak, but a croak came out of my mouth. My chest burned. Suppose that was what I got for being such an emotional ninny for hours on end.

He made a sound in his mouth that had the character of a *tsk* but sounded more like "tach." "Och, girl," he murmured.

I shook my head and attempted to reassure. "I'm fine," but it all came out as a gurgled mess.

He sat up and gently opened his arms. He didn't make the initial move but waited for me to push myself forward, permitting me a false sense of power in the moment. I steadied myself, then stumbled into large arms. He caught me tightly and fell backward, allowing me to curl up like a babe on his chest. He held me as I slowly lost my mind all over him and his poor shirt. Somehow, he was able to hold the weight of it all. Body and mind alike. He provided classical cooing noises and soft rubs and pats against my back.

"Och yer warm, Trix," he murmured against the soft parts of my neck before providing a tender kiss.

But he said no more. He didn't fill the small amounts of empty space between us with questions that the Lord and he both knew I couldn't answer. Or perhaps just didn't want to. I couldn't figure out which one was worse, to be stubborn or ignorant. By the time my body ran out of tears, the room was fully enveloped in darkness. I stirred and mindlessly rubbed my face into the chest of his soiled shirt. Another kiss was planted on the top of my head and lingered. The lack of access to his own toilet for the past couple of nights had provided a scratchy amount of facial hair that caught slightly in my hair. I oddly enjoyed it. I sighed, and the sound was surprisingly content, even to my ears.

"Let's get ye to bed," he murmured gently.

Fluidly, he sat up with me, and I caught a dizzy spell that left me stumbling. He steered me to my vanity and dampened the cloth that was haphazardly thrown next to the basin. He dabbed and wiped frigid water against my face. I flinched, but he held me in place, spending a bit longer on my eyes, gently pressing the coolness against the sensitive skin. "Twill help with the swellin," he murmured, re-dampening the cloth and applying a touch more pressure.

Goodness, I must have looked a sight. Nonetheless, I allowed him to continue bathing my skin. He muttered a quiet, "there," and dropped the cloth, only to quickly splash some water on his face. He let out that high-pitched giggle, and the corners of my mouth turned up despite the effort it took. He dried his face with a sloppy shirtsleeve and steered me back to my bed, where I was quickly swooped up and tucked under the covers. I opened my mouth to mumble my thanks and a kind goodnight, but I frowned as he stripped down to his undergarments. I flushed, undismayed by the previous night and morning. I strained to look away and felt the weight of my bed sink as he climbed into it with such ease, I wanted to throw an elbow.

"What are you doing?"

"Don't ask questions you know the answer to," he chided and confidently made himself comfortable by tucking in all snug-like.

He took up quite a bit of space and turned to his side, propping his head up while his elbow was buried into the pillow. He looked perfectly content within my most intimate surroundings as if he were a cat who had found the nesting spot in the heart of someone else's barn. Give a man an inch, and he has already gone a mile. I folded my arms across my chest over the covers, tucking myself a little deeper in. I stared, blindly, up at the ceiling. The room had taken a chill, and gooseflesh erupted upon my exposed skin.

"Ms. Liz ain't gonna be happy if she finds ya here," I mumbled blandly.

"Ask me how much I care what Ms. Liz thinks." He silently drummed his fingers against the bed cloth. The faint shape of his nipples peeked through his chest hair and the dark.

I closed my eyes, frustrated at his comfort as well as my lack thereof. I had given him my all—the only part a woman had to give, and he had taken it kindly. *So why did it matter that he returned to my bed now? Why couldn't I allow my body to reach out and burrow within his warmth?* All the fears of rejection had come and gone in a relatively short period. For a woman in the circumstances I was born into, that ought to be a comfort. But my mind chanted propriety and my previous conversation with Ms. Liz over and over as a default. My heart suspected something else was at play that led to my resistance, but that bit felt more disturbing, and I just didn't have the energy to confront it.

"Trix?" Wallace prompted softly.

"Hmmm?" I faked a sleepy tone.

"You really worried about what Ms. Liz thinks?"

I shrugged, and he let out a chuckle. The rain pattering softly through my window triggered Sleep's gentle arms to reach out and pull my body tighter against the bed in a much-needed embrace that gave more than it took. Such a tradeoff was more delicious than man's touch. My head was heavy on the uneven pillows, and it felt like one thousand gentle lips laid butterfly kisses across my body. It was rare for her to pay me a visit, this lovely sleep. She evaded me night after night, for so long. Sending her angry brother, Nightmare, in her place for years on end. To have her visit with me was a treat that warmed my toes. Slowly I was drifting, gently falling...

"What if you married me?" His words shocked Sleep before they shocked me. Her arms quickly retracted deep within my bed, leaving only the cold air to rush in as her disappointing replacement.

I squeezed my eyes tighter, desperate to bring her back. But she was gone, and probably for good. At least that evening. The crushing and intrusive reality of his question added to the chill on my skin. His breath was steady and patient, waiting for a response I didn't have.

"It's not exactly how I pictured my life, I'll admit. But if I have to marry you, I will," he stated.

I turned his melodramatic confession over in my head as the cold, sinking feeling intensified in the pit of my gut. "Have to," I repeated dryly.

I didn't know why I was acting or feeling this way. I understood deep down that in no way did I desire the opposite of his proposal. I did not want to be apart from him, perhaps ever. Such a realization had me feeling as if I was standing on the edge of a cliff. Swiftly Wallace straightened a bit more in his positioning, bringing himself closer to me. He smirked, but his eyes were troubled.

"Yes, have to. If marriage is the only way I will be able to rightfully keep you, I'll do it. Whatever you want me to do, girl, if it ends with me having you wholly, I will do it."

I turned on my side to face him. His words were laced with pride and trimmed with desperation. I reached out and placed a shaky hand on his forearm. His gaze fell on that small hand of mine.

"Wallace—" I stopped.

I didn't know where to go. He gave me a funny little smile and furrowed his brows. He then, thankfully, hushed me. "Just think about it, hm? I won't force you into anything. But it'd make just about everything a lot easier."

Nothing said romance like convenience. I rolled onto my back. "Goodnight," I sighed and closed my eyes tightly.

The bed shifted as he mimicked my adjustment. The still night taunted me. Despite the room temperature, my core was heated to be in bed with Wallace. I tried to hold still and keep my body to myself. But my efforts didn't last long. It was perhaps only a handful of tense minutes before I launched myself on top of Wallace's patiently waiting form.

Chapter 22

r. Jim stayed gone. Each evening, the seat next to mine at the dinner table sat vacant, and everyone pretended not to notice while I stared at a full plate of food. With Mr. Jim absent, my appetite followed suit. I was too tired to eat.

Whatever bits of a civilized mind I previously possessed undoubtedly had slipped out the window throughout the week. Each morning as Wallace left my bed, he told me to give Mr. Jim space. Then, he pranced off to work right beside that very man. Goddamn traitor, that's what he was. I couldn't take one more night of Wallace sneaking into my room only to tell me that another day had passed without change. Such anticipations met with crushing disappointments couldn't be good for anyone's health. At least, that is what I told myself as I slowly walked up the steps to Mr. Jim's apartment office. As I approached the shut door, I tightened my shaking fist before rapping.

"Ya?" his voice grumbled.

I let myself in. Mr. Jim simply stared at me without a hint of recognition. I straightened my back as tall as I could and kept his eye. He made no move. Memories of the last time I had been in his office flooded back, and I swallowed down the anger that came with them, settling into the chair across from him. I stifled a cough, and my lungs burned like they regularly did nowadays. The room smelled just like him.

I knew discomfort with Mr. Jim. We had argued and fought and screamed when I was a teenager. I thought I could tear the walls down and allow him to pay witness to my fury. So yes, I had known discomfort with Mr. Jim very well, in fact. It was something that had been an ally back when my body was growing and changing around me while no one took the time to explain why. And yet it had never been like this before. I had spent my whole life tumbling and running away, then groveling back to Mr. Jim, but somehow this was different. Uncharted territory.

I explored his face for a while, searching for changes. The skin to be more weathered or worn, perhaps his hair a lighter shade of gray. I sought a difference in his countenance for which I could blame the lack of console I felt toward the man who had raised me. As a child, Billy had taught me that if I were to ever be late on my comings home or were up to no good and hadn't a way around a lashing, I ought to make sure I had a wound to show for it. While the sins of the flesh were forgivable, those of the heart were not.

But I found no change or injury on my dear Mr. Jim. At least not visible to the naked eye. His change of heart was now worn so sternly, just beneath the thin fabric of his work shirt, that I might see the taunting, ghostly outline. It lay there, not unlike the lingering scent of newly chopped pine uphill from a river. And with this, I no longer found forgiveness for his expatriation.

"Is there something you'd be needing from me, girl?"

I stuttered at his harsh tone. *Well, ought to get on with it then.* I attempted to take a deep breath. "Mr. Jim," my voice sounded weak. "I understand that you may not find my behaviors appropriate, but Billy—"

"Don't you dare make that comparison."

I was startled at his interruption. The look on his face was stone and fury.

I took another painful breath, "I—"

"I said, *don't.*"

I nodded despite my accumulating anger. I felt like I was swallowing a fist to push down the malice that inched up from my stomach. It was hard to gulp around, but I couldn't let those feelings reach my head because once they did, I knew all hell would break loose. Plus, it felt like there was too much inside me, and the exhaustion of it all took its toll.

"Your behavior is not only inappropriate but disgusting. Pathetic, even."

I ground my teeth.

"You have disgraced yourself, as well as my good name, which I have provided as protection your whole life. Spreading your legs for the first man who looked at you twice. It's childish. Have you no mind, besides the desires of your barely developed body? How self-obsessed and hedonistic can one girl be?" His voice quickly rose from a deathly quiet to roaring anger.

I preferred the roar. A roar was much more my style and easily matched. "Now, hear you me!" I bellowed in return, stepping out of my chair. "I will not be shamed for wanting to experience something more in life!"

"More?" he roared back, standing as well. "You fucking brat! You stupid little whore! Have I not given you enough? I have sacrificed every bit of my life for you. And this is the thanks I get? A slut for a ward!"

I shook at his words. I bit back the *why* that bubbled on my tongue. *Why had he done all of this? Should it not have been out of unconditional love?* I shrank back.

"What happens when he leaves? Will you just start taking up with someone else? Beg another man to fill your sheets at night? Bah!" Saliva launched from his mouth at the sound of disgust.

The room spun, and I placed a shaky hand on my forehead. It was cool, damp, and pounding. I looked up to the ceiling, and it looked like there were two. Lord, I felt awful. I took a shallow breath.

"You have become nothing but a disgusting traitor! You end it, and you end it now. Because hear you me, Magdalene, if you do not, if you enter this sort of relationship with someone like him, you'll never be welcome under my roof again."

My whole body went still at his words. I heard him huffing like a bull. I slowly brought my gaze back to him, hand holding my forehead so the cold pounding wouldn't spill out on him, though at this point, he deserved such a mess.

"It's Trixie," I whispered slowly.

"What?!" he barked.

I took my hand from my head to my chest and tapped myself. Part of me wished there was a mirror in the room, just to double-check. Make sure I was the one I thought I was. More cold sweat broke out.

"My name...It's Trixie. You called me Magdalene."

The room grew still, and Mr. Jim's face drew inward like he was no longer with me in the present. He was far away. After a moment, he collapsed into his chair. I shakily followed suit and gripped the arms of my chair, but I still felt like I was standing and swaying. I had not earned eye contact, which was fine because, now, I more than likely couldn't have maintained it.

"He asked me to marry him," I mumbled quietly.

I didn't look up at his sharp inhale. I closed my eyes and tried to focus on breathing, but it was like my throat was shrinking. I stuttered, my breath a bit high-pitched, and braced myself. I counted to ten and met his eyes. I couldn't read his expression, and for some reason, it brought tears to my eyes. That, and the bodily discomfort I was drowning in. A couple tears fell, and I attempted to wipe them away quickly and thoroughly so that none could follow.

"You're not..." His gaze shifted to my abdomen. "You can't be..." he trailed off.

"No, I'm not."

He leaned back, and the chair groaned in ironic relief. His shaky fist wiped the sweat from his brow. Perhaps it wasn't just me.

"And you're sure you aren't?"

I flushed furiously and nodded at the same speed. I had awoken that morning filled with shame at the staining between my legs and weak attempts to push Wallace out of my bed. Instead, he just swatted back at me, clucking his tongue all the while. He only left to fetch me a warm cloth, then, much to my surprise, climbed back into bed with me. I figured that was proof enough, but Mr. Jim didn't need to know the details.

Silence enveloped us. I longed for the everyday happenings outside of the room. I was the nymph Wallace had first mistaken me for and didn't belong here. I was invisible. *How could I explain that to Mr. Jim?* Those noises, that life outside the stale walls I grew up with that never welcomed me, that was what I wanted. When it came down to it, it wasn't about Wallace or even him. There wasn't a cataclysmic choice they thought loomed over us. There never had been. The imaginary choice the two of them agreed on was a faceless man holding two objects in his palms. One was a fish, and the other was a flask. I was left with my mouth wide open as he demanded that I choose one to be a dancing partner. Ridiculous. Mr. Jim and Wallace did not belong in the same category, and I didn't know how to dance.

"If you are asking for my blessing, I do not offer it."

I moved automatically, gathering myself out of the chair with a certain lack of grace that was out of character, even for me. My mind was blank while my body knew to leave. It gently urged me to go, with the loving understanding that wasn't in the man before me, who I most wished would provide it. I heard something close to me crash. I whirled my head around and stumbled a bit as blackness crept into my line of sight. The confused look on Mr. Jim's weathered face was the last thing I saw before the ground reached up to hug me against its cool, harsh frame.

Chapter 23

verything shimmered yellow, and my body tossed back and forth, but not of my own volition. My eyes couldn't focus, and made horrific shapes of everything that surrounded me. Two figures loomed over me as I lay in what had to be a bed as it absorbed each thrashing movement I didn't mean to make with grace. Everything around me swayed, and the room was foggy and nearly shuddering as if we were underwater. My eyes could not focus, no matter how many times I tried to blink. It was all too familiar and yet startlingly foreign.

My ears rang, and I barely made out the noises piercing my consciousness. My surroundings were too loud, bright, and harsh. My lungs that had carried air my whole life were ablaze as I worked to take a small breath. I coughed repeatedly. My coughs were damp, like each cough watered my horribly chapped lips. My lungs were filled to the brim, it seemed.

The pressure in my chest felt like something swirled in glorious patterns drowning me from the inside out—something like a fish. I had swallowed a fish. There was a salty, large, miserable fish caught in my lungs. Now, how on earth I got a fish in them, I had no idea. *Maybe one snuck in when I wasn't looking?* Sneaky bastard. I giggled deliriously at the thought of Tom Beau dancing in my lungs. He could perform a jig with Dev. Give the creature a top hat, and they could charge ten cents a show. I felt a warm hand on my forehead, and it scalded all thoughts of fish and show business right out of me.

"Trix, what is it?" Wallace's warm voice murmured, his words blowing across my face.

I heard a wretched sound of distress from the other side of the room and a soft voice speaking quickly. I couldn't understand what was said, but it didn't sound right. Nothing felt good, and distress was the metallic and bitter taste on my tongue. I was so cold, so I inched toward him.

"It's..." I tried but fell into a coughing fit.

His arms wrapped around me like a snake and hoisted me up. The pain from the coughing was duller at this angle, and I was grateful for it. The fit ceased, and I wiped the salty fish water from my lips, giggling in relief. It was so obvious. If I could just tell these people a fish was caught in my lungs, they could relax and *get it out.*

"The fish..." I continued, trying to whisper toward the figure that had to be Wallace.

I fell backward like an infant who could no longer hold my head up. Wallace righted me. My head lulled forwards, and my lips hit his cheek. I rested there for a moment and tried to breathe.

Slowly, Wallace nodded, "The fish?"

"The fish—"

I picked up what I hoped was my arm and lightly hit it against my breast. Right where my lungs were. Right where the fish was. The fish squirmed within me, and I was seized by another fit of coughing. Water streamed down my eyes. My arm was so heavy. Visions danced behind my fluttering eyes, and I coughed. *Spinning...spinning...was I swimming? Oh, god. I was drowning.* I tried to shake my head, shake the water from my head and stay afloat, but Wallace held me tightly. Everything was wet, I was freezing, and my body convulsed due to the cold water.

"Help," I whispered between coughs.

I heard another sob, this time much closer to me.

"She thinks she's got a fish in her lungs," Wallace's warm voice whispered.

I nodded helplessly. I focused intensely on the sounds around me, trying to regain control, but everything got dark again.

"Ms. Liz! Go grab the washing tub, get plenty of water, quickly!"

I heard shuffling, but as Wallace's words sank in, I thrashed about.

"No water!" I gasped, wiping everything wet off my face.

My words sounded clear again. "Wallace, no more water. The fish. He brought the water. No more..."

I sobbed as another cough shook through me, and a new presence came close. It was a dark and unfamiliar mass. I still couldn't see straight. But something about their fuzzy posture made me want to be left alone with my fish, survival be damned.

I sought out Wallace's stormy eyes and found them through the haze. I blinked past the water and tears and tried to hold his gaze through the surrounding shimmering darkness. I tried to block out the pain, discomfort, and lightheadedness and focus just on his eyes. I could find those eyes through hellfire. His eyes were made for me. Even as I tittered on the brink of drowning, I knew this had to be true. Perhaps if I stared at his eyes long enough, I could fall into them. Be a part of those eyes and him permanently. *Color didn't feel pain, did it?* I opened my mouth to ask Wallace that. *Would I still hurt if I simply became a part of him? Could that be an option?* But those eyes turned into slits and broke the concentrated stare I attempted to communicate through.

"NO!" Wallace shouted, blocking me from the dark foreign mass. Something twinkled like a diamond by its side, momentarily penetrating the dull light. Wallace covered me with his body. God, he boiled the water within me. It was delicious.

"Nae! Dinna come near her!" he bellowed. "Look at her! Look at her *lips*. She's got nothin' left."

Nothing made sense. Wallace did not want the man to cut me. But if he cut me, couldn't he get the water out? I struggled against Wallace.

"Cut me," I whispered meekly as I wrestled against my stormy-eyed devil. "Cut me...drain...the water..." I was very sleepy again.

I tried to force my eyes open as everything moved. I hadn't realized I shut them. My heavy head lulled from side to side, and blackness crept along the edges of my vision. I was so dizzy.

"Nae Trix. Nae lass, twill nae rid ye o' the water," Wallace murmured softly into my ear, pressing a gentle kiss there.

He held my head against his face. For a moment, the world slowed down, and my vision cleared slightly. I heard a sniffle and the sound of snot trickling out of Wallace's nose. His face was wet like mine, but Wallace was not drowning. Wallace was crying. And then my lungs blazed again. My body rejected all my insides with each hack. Like my lungs, spleen, heart, and *fish* were trying to escape. But I only needed the fish out. The rest were vital. This was really becoming a pickle. As the fish nearly made it to my lips, another figure, tall and gray, entered the room. The spinning room momentarily stopped. Mr. Jim. Mr. Jim would understand.

"Mr. Jim..." I gurgled, unintentionally swallowing the fish back down so I could speak. *Damn*.

His figure rushed to my side. I felt his weathered hand on my cheek. The one unoccupied by Wallace's warm head.

"Mr. Jim, you have to get the fish out," I rasped.

My voice sounded far away. Mr. Jim rubbed his thumb over my mouth, gently wiping the saltwater off. He understood. I felt his comprehension through the subtle heartbeat in his fingertip. My eyes fluttered in happiness. Mr. Jim understood.

"Yes, Trixie-girl. I'll get the fish out. Wallace, move aside. Doc, looks like we won't be needing you," Mr. Jim stated softly.

I once again struggled against Wallace, desperately seeking salvation.

"Nae!" Wallace bellowed once more, holding me tighter than ever.

This time, Wallace moved my body so that I was behind him. His arm was twisted, holding me so my chest pressed against his back. The fish did not like all this jostling, and I had to agree with its distaste.

"Dinna ye dare," Wallace growled.

"This isn't your decision to make, boy," Mr. Jim muttered back at him. "She's dying. And your time wasted on prayers is killing her faster."

My muddled mind ached once more. My vision got foggier as I riffled through their conversation.

"If 'tis nae mine, it bloody well 'tisn't yers," Wallace bellowed.

Mr. Jim's blurry figure backed up, much to my dismay. The room was painfully silent. The only sound was my disgusting, sloshing body. Wallace shifted his hold on me, but this time more gently. He pulled me back into his arms against his warmth, for which I was terribly grateful. The blankets were wrapped around me. I wanted to sigh in relief, but the fish. So, I reached out my arm toward Mr. Jim, to take comfort in his familiar rough hand as I drowned in front of him, but my fingers caught nothing. A bustle erupted in the room, along with a fluttering number of footsteps. I heard a feminine gasp. A floating red bit was suddenly in my weak vision. Dev. A shorter, plump figure was next to her, Ms. Liz, I supposed, and a massive figure behind them. *Billy?* I couldn't understand why everyone surrounded me. Nor could I remember what day it was or how this all began. I looked quite forward to the end of this.

"Will she make it?" Dev's soft voice trembled.

God, they knew this fish would kill me, yet they stood there doing nothing. I was so lost and suddenly hot. I tried to push away from Wallace, but he held tighter.

"We can only hope she will make it through the night," a solemn voice came from behind me.

"Everyone out," Wallace whispered.

The blanket slid off, and I was back to freezing. No sound of movement came. A growl came from deep within Wallace, where my head lay upon his chest. I choked again and faintly heard movement around me. The cold floor touched my feet, and I stumbled, hoping to land on something soft. A familiar warmth grasped me with weathered hands.

"Mr....Jim..." I croaked and then gasped for air.

"I'll not let her die," Mr. Jim whispered, pulling at me. I stumbled more.

"She ain't going to die, now go. She wouldn't want to be seen like this," Wallace replied.

I felt his hands at the straps of my chemise. Then Mr. Jim's grip was gone. I continued to shiver violently. Painfully. I was flying apart, and no one was doing much to keep me together—quite the opposite. My damp chemise was stripped off me, and Wallace picked me up. I let out a croaky gasp. Biting water encompassed me, and I threw my head back with a scream. I fought wildly against the strong hands that attempted to hold me in the water.

"Cold!" I managed to get out of my chattering lips. I shook so violently I thought my teeth would crack.

"We've got to freeze Tom Beau," a warm voice whispered close to me.

I shook but worked to stop flailing and concentrate. I'd do whatever it took to make this all stop. I grabbed at Wallace's warmth and tried to be still for Tom Beau to jump out. I opened my mouth, but a series of chokes strangled me with no apparition of a fish. Wallace's hands tenderly moved my body forward in the tub, and the next thing I knew, I was not alone in the water. He let out a little yelp and a laugh.

I focused on my breath. Wallace pulled me against his chest, and my mind felt clearer. I hung my head forward to let the water drip from my mouth. His fingers worked at my scalp, rubbing gently as if he could coax the water out. He murmured sweet nothings as the angry aching in my chest caused a sob to wrack through me. I opened my eyes and saw that clarity had returned to my surroundings for the most part.

I brought my fingers to my lips. My very damp lips. I was dizzy once again. I looked at my fingers, smeared with red, and I gasped as my vision doubled. I had never seen such a bright red in all my days. Surely the colors in Spain couldn't compare to this. Wallace's arms wrapped around my core, and his face burned in my back. His lips itched at the skin on my back as he seemed to be saying something.

"Wallace," I rasped, "Tom Beau is dead."

And then blackness, once more.

Chapter 24

aking up took ages. I floated just below the surface of reality, like the shallow bits of the Lil' Big that sparkled in the summer sunlight as they delicately lapped at the shore. Every time I got close enough to breach into the fresh air of the present, a soft ripple tenderly pulled me under. I hadn't the energy to fight it. In the way back of my mind, I wondered if I would stay at this halfway point for the rest of my days. The thought didn't worry me nearly as much as one would presume.

Where I existed was calm. Very calm indeed, and I had never experienced such a feeling before. If this was what death held, I had no issue accepting it with the utmost welcome and grace. Though I couldn't precisely place where I had been before my arrival to this quiet and unexpecting now, something told me it hadn't been pleasant. This happy little in-between was a reprieve from the exhaustive life I had been forced into. Where I was, I found to be wholly untouchable. Clean.

Ultimately, though, what pulled me out was something not entirely clean at all. Something very foul-smelling penetrated my self-diagnosed purgatory, and I was brought back to reality's surface with a jolt. My eyes flashed open, only to wince at the bright light of the room. Where I had been before was bright, yes, but not as glaring. Nothing there had been sharp. Piece by piece, I realized that here would always be much sharper than where I had been in every sense of the word.

After a few deep breaths, which resulted in a slight cough, I recognized that the foul-smelling thing that pulled me from my comfortable nothingness was, unfortunately, me. I groaned at that, and my throat reacted with a raw and dry seizing. I wiped my face and found it oily, wincing as my fingertips ran over an imperfection on the high of my cheekbone near my hairline. I blinked a couple of times more before rousing my weak body. My head ached something awful, and I needed water, but the smell of me was too distracting to pay mind to any bodily craving. Vanity was a blinding witch, and I rose from my deathbed. I padded over to my washing basin, splashing the cool water against my face. I grew dizzy and clutched the rim of the table.

I had fallen ill. I remembered quite literally falling in Mr. Jim's office. I remembered wrestling in the yellow light with Tom Beau and us drowning together, hands held tight. All the while, everyone watched. I clucked my tongue at their supposed lack of help. I dampened the cloth and gently rubbed it over my neck and chest, and gentler at the painful bump on my face, fighting the immediate urge to pinch the imperfection away. Slowly, I wandered around my room as I tried to put it all together. My door flew open, and I looked up lazily to see Wallace standing frozen in my doorway. Why, the man looked as though he had seen a ghost.

"What happened?" I croaked and hastily washed at my underarms.

Could he smell me from there? In one hand, he had a pitcher of water and the other a steaming tin cup. I gestured to the coffee with my chin.

"You've been in and out of a fever for nearly two weeks." His voice was quiet.

I grimaced at that. That would explain my ripeness.

"How do you feel?"

"Weak and smelly," I grumbled.

He laughed breathlessly at that. I set down the rag and walked over to him, reaching for the coffee. I inhaled the aroma deeply and glanced at him under my eyelashes. He looked worn. The deep and dark circles beneath his eyes and the lines around his mouth were grave. Wallace looked so afraid. I felt guilty but couldn't exactly bring myself to apologize for falling ill.

"That bad, huh?" I mumbled and took a long drink of coffee.

He shook his head and walked over to the vanity and set down the pitcher of water. Despite the coffee and that I hadn't left my bed in two weeks, I was exhausted. The coffee tasted like a miracle, nonetheless.

"As happy as I am to see you up, Trix, I think you should have a seat."

I made my way back to my bed. The air was stale, so I stuck my nose deeper into the cup of coffee to try and wash out the smell of sickness and all-too-sweet human flesh.

"Open a window," I rasped.

Wallace did as I asked. As I sat on my bed, I ignored how the sheets had a strange worn feel to them, a dampness that reminded me of humid air. I continued to drink my coffee. The air outside was a little cooler than I would have expected. Despite my sensitivity to the sunlight when I awoke, it was clear that the muted autumn sun was approaching us. Two weeks was a long time, after all.

And then Wallace was in my line of vision with a basin full of soapy-looking water and a cloth. The scent of lavender floated up, and I gave him my most earnest half-smile. Or I tried to. My mind still felt slow. He took the cup of coffee out of my hand and gently set it on my side table, where the Bible lay open. Carelessly so, as if someone had read it recently.

A quiet, unfamiliar voice that sounded nothing like Mr. Jim and everything like myself told me I needed to have a talk with the Man upstairs. Perhaps even grovel a bit, as I had been a foolish, horrible girl to Him. And despite it all, He had given me the strength to pull myself out of two weeks of near-death. I winced inwardly. Because I wasn't sure if I genuinely believed that, and disagreeing with my own conscience gave me a headache.

With Wallace's free hand, he turned my gaze back to him, letting one finger stroke down the length of my nose. He nodded at me sternly, more of an assurance to himself than to me. He kneeled in front of me, and I veered backward. He gathered my legs and pulled them forward so that I sat on the edge of the bed, plucking silently at the tie of my nightgown, swiftly removing it from my form. I glanced at my withered body and covered it immediately. Two weeks was a long time indeed. Wallace paid no mind to my evident discomfort as he unfolded me, pulling my naked body even closer to the edge. His smile was tight, and he tenderly washed me with the slowest of care.

"Everyone was quite worried," he explained conversationally.

I closed my eyes and leaned back onto my elbows, "hmming" in response. The smell of lavender, as well as the cool, fresh air, was soothing. But as he delicately bathed me, something itched at me. My eyes fluttered open and landed back on the open Bible.

"Why the Bible?" I drawled.

His hands didn't even pause as he let out a soft laugh. "Mayhap I took ye for a fanatic and wanted to impress the girl."

I met his soft stare. I cocked an eyebrow, and he chuckled with a quick wink.

A long while passed before he spoke again. "I was late for supper, yes?"

I wasn't following him in the least.

He laughed again. "The day we met. I was late and came in while everyone was seated and praying."

I nodded slowly.

"I had spent the rest of my day thinking about this dismissive, ethereal nymph, only to walk into a boarding house dining room and find her there. Seated, fully clothed with her face pinched together and head held high, and I thought, well, that's not right. That wasn't where you were supposed to be. You stuck out like a sore thumb, and everyone around you either didn't seem to notice or just didn't care to. And... 'twas hurting ye. The way ye looked at all of them and spoke to all of them. Ye were screamin'. They may nae have been able to hear ye, but I could. I just wanted to make it better. Ye made me want to be better."

I waited. He stopped washing me and looked down at the cloth in his hands. He spoke to it so lovingly. I envied that cloth.

"I don't know what it is, Trix. Lord knows you are as far from angelic as they get. But when I look at you, I want to be better. I want *us* to be better. Together. Suppose in the beginning, though, there wasn't much of a *together* for us. But I figured if I couldn't have you, the least I could do was better you."

I was quiet as he worked his jaw, clearly attempting to put words to his thoughts with slow words.

"Maybe seeing you, falling in love with you despite all your hurt, it made me feel like saying sorry. For what I had done in the past. And dammit, I just wanted to be better."

I let his words sink in. "So, God is supposed to make it better?" I questioned softly.

He smirked. "He's got a hell of a lot more power to do so than I."

He got back to washing me. I looked out the window and burned with the sudden desire to tell him what I had said to God. To come clean, to confess my proud, blasphemous ways. To truly lay my soul bare to Jayson Wallace and let him steer me back toward enlightenment. But I didn't know how to express how I felt. I didn't know how to say that while I was in my precious waiting room between asleep and awake, I hadn't seen a God. I didn't know how to explain just how alone I had been; that when I broke the surface, ain't no God was there helping me along. *How could I explain that the faith I had been told we were born with, the faith that was supposed to live inside us all, in me, felt broken?*

"You really believe in God?" My voice trembled as the question slipped out.

"Me and the Man upstairs? We go way back." I heard the smile in his voice.

I gave a dry laugh. "Where'd you find Him?"

"Find Him? Trixie-girl, He ain't hiding."

My gaze settled on the Bible one final time. I knew He wasn't hiding. I had dismissed Him, for heaven's sake. But before that, before our fallout... *Was it so incredible to wonder if God abandoned me long before I, Him?* My headache returned.

"There is a God, girl, believe me. He is up there, and He sees and knows all. But... He ain't as forgiving as us lowly group of sinners wish Him to be."

I fought the urge to swear as Wallace confirmed what I suspected. It was the nail in the coffin and the dirt on the lid, burying any hope I had for absolution.

"Let's just say the devil ain't the only one who likes making bargains."

Wallace dropped the cloth into the water basin and trailed his fingers, soft as feathers, across my abdomen. Tracing delicate patterns. Or perhaps just counting my ribs. I came up to my elbows to view him better, but he just carried on. His breath brushed my knees, and I caught gooseflesh.

"And I made enough o' those these past weeks betwixt the two o' them to say when our time comes, I might be a wee late meetin' ye at the grand gates o' Saint Peter," he admitted barely above a whisper.

His eyes flashed up to mine, and my breath caught. I was stunned momentarily at the raw emotion that sat in his eyes, unflinching and proud. As if, despite the steely confidence in potential damnation, he would do it all over again. He did not fear the debts he had dug himself into but faced them with near mockery. This strong man of mine made me want to be better, all the same.

"I'll wait for you."

It was the truth. I would wait for him. It was the least I could do. What would heaven be without my dear Jayson Wallace by my side? Besides, something deep in my gut told me I would be jumping through more than a few hoops to get there myself. But he didn't need to know that.

"'Tis a deal," he purred.

I warmed at his tone. And then he sealed it with a quick kiss upon the rugged, scarred tissue of my kneecap. Wallace's caressing hands left my body, and despite the weight of our conversation and my current state of exhaustion, I longed for their return. I sat up fully, closing my eyes as a head rush followed, and he slipped a silky textured wrapper around me. I was then lifted and placed in my rocking chair, with the blanket wrapped around my waist. He tucked me in like a child, as he always had.

I lazily opened my eyes and found myself in a black silk dressing gown with a lace trim that brushed the high of my neck. I trailed my hands along the delicate fabric and glanced up curiously at Wallace. He leaned down, bracing himself on the arms of my rocking chair so that he was eye level.

Wallace cocked his head until I fully met his eye. His lips twitched into a soft smile, and he then pressed those smiling lips against my own.

For a moment, with the warm and familiar pressure of his lips, two weeks of blackness melted away, pulling back the insecurity I felt toward the man who loved me. I leaned forward, and one hand reached tentatively to touch his chest. The heartbeat that lay beneath my palm and his fleshy casing pounded, and I understood that we felt the same at that juncture. Timid and a little desperate. Yet, once again, equals in the time we were given. The ability to share an emotion without having to speak burned me and blinded me with surprising desire.

I pushed closer to him, and with a small groan, he pulled back from me. He hung his head and breathed deeply, steadying himself. I leaned my cheek against the side of his head and breathed in the smell of him. My lungs constricted lightly at the action, and I gave in to a small cough.

He pressed closer to me at the sound, and his own breath shuddered. "Ye'll be the death o' me, girl, mark me words. If ye ne'er close those sad, angry eyes of yers again, twill be too soon. My soul canna take another second without their quiet fury. What I wouldna give, these past two weeks, to have ye cursin' hell fires upon me. I would have welcomed whichever damnation ye found fit, only to have ye awake and with me whilst ye did so."

My fingers clenched around the cloth of his shirt. I didn't have the words or the guarantees he wished for. My other hand reached up to press his head closer to my face, and I cradled him against me. Holding as tightly as I could, hoping that a firm grasp would be taken for honest reassurance.

"I love ye," he whispered.

I closed my eyes as something like ecstasy rushed through my veins, more potent than the roughest rivers. When Wallace proclaimed his love for me, I felt as if the world would lick cream out of my grubby palm. It was marvelous.

"I know," I sighed.

He gently drew himself back. My hand slid from his chest to the front of his pants, and he smirked down at me. I bit my lip at the warmth that pulsated there.

"Girl, I ache for ye like a man without water, without air. Despite yer sickly hue and ribs stickin' out so far they might poke me most violently, I fear that if I look upon ye too long, I will unman myself altogether. But alas, ye only just returned to us, and I'll nae exhaust ye with such monstrous demands."

He removed my hand, returning me back to myself. As I sat, neatly tucked into my rocking chair, Wallace silently busied about my room. He stripped my bedsheets, and I wanted to jump back into his arms and cover him in every type of kiss he ached for. He merely winked at me before heading to the door and calling for fresh linens. I stared at the red stain on the pillows. Not the vibrant red that struck out from my black dreaming, but instead a rusty and tarnished looking hue. It disgusted me to the point of nausea.

There was a commotion below in response to Wallace's call, and then multiple footsteps rushing up the hollow echoing wooden steps. I took a deep breath as a shrill call from Ms. Liz alerted her planned entrance, followed shortly by her physical apparition in my doorframe. The guilt kicked in once more as I took in her crazed eyes. And the dark circles that lingered beneath them, puffy and so unlike her. She clutched at the door frame as she took in my weak but wide-awake appearance. She whispered some form of thanks and closed those eyes of hers tightly. Billy-boy followed her, only to take one look before turning his back to me. Those paws of his tangled in his untamed curls, and he let out a massive exclamation.

I looked over at Wallace, not even needing to play up my helplessness, and he sauntered over to me. He perched himself on the windowsill with one warm hand resting on my shoulder. Mr. Jim pushed past Ms. Liz and Billy. To my shock, his face crumpled only for a moment at the sight of me. Why, the stoic man nearly cried. Composure was regained under his façade, and he hurried to my side just as Wallace's grip on my shoulder tightened.

Mr. Jim was on his knees in front of me, reaching out to feel my face in search of a lingering fever.

"She's still a little warm," he grumbled. He gave my cheek a pinch and a tight smile.

"But she's awake," Billy called as if they had not taken notice.

There was another bit of a commotion at the crowded door frame as a small man with graying hair and spectacles entered with a smooth leather bag. Dev followed but was held back by Billy. She shot him a look, but he kept her tightly by his side.

"Oh, for heaven's sake," I murmured in response to the number of people in my personal quarters.

I wasn't appropriately dressed, and despite Wallace's attempts to relieve me of my own stench, I needed a proper bath.

"If I may," the quiet doctor said as he shuffled Mr. Jim to the side.

Wallace stood, keeping one hand on my shoulder. Mr. Jim stood over my other shoulder with his arms folded grumpily across his chest. He was looking under his eyes at Wallace. The doctor mimicked Mr. Jim's actions, searching for a fever hidden deep within my skin. His cool hands then traveled to my throat, which he gently pressed against on either side. I hissed at the dull ache it caused. He frowned at that. The grip on my shoulder intensified, but I didn't have the heart to tell Wallace that his worry would leave a bruise.

The doctor continued to putter around me, prompting me to open my mouth and give him a great big "ah." After it all, the doctor stood slowly and addressed Mr. Jim directly. "She'll have to be relocated. For her own safety as well as the safety of you all. I know of a sanatorium that has opened just outside of Denver..."

"No," Wallace interrupted firmly.

"Mr. Wallace, for the safety of..."

"No sanatoriums," he repeated.

"Sir...I, I must insist, unless you are, yourself, a d-doctor, and have some better plan."

"Maybe I am. And I do."

We all waited impatiently for an explanation.

"I spent a year and a half at a ward in upstate New York. Within the first six months, I witnessed one hundred and fifty patients perish. I kept three under my specific supervision and care. All three recovered. It seems the help necessary for recovery includes a significant amount of one-on-one attention. Trixie'll get her help, but she won't be leaving my sight."

The doctor sputtered at Wallace, and he left his stance to take a much more protective one between the doctor and me.

"For the sake of others, the girl will have to be relocated," the doctor repeated tediously.

"Couldn't agree more. There's a cottage northwest of here, a bit run down, but the thinner air and the distance from the trains' smoke might do those crummy lungs of hers some good. I'll have it fixed up by the end of the week."

I pictured the Lil' Big shack fixed up. It was small and old, but the last time I had entered, it was stable enough. It had been warm at night when Billy and I hid out in our youth. I strained my neck around Wallace. The doctor gave him a sharp nod and headed for the door.

"How long will she be gone for?" Mr. Jim called.

The doctor paused at the door.

"The quickest recovery I've seen was six months, maybe seven," Wallace answered.

The doctor nodded gravely. There was a chorus of protests from everyone. My hands were clenched together so tightly that my knuckles were white.

"But surely it won't be so long. The girl is already better. Got gumption in her, she does," Billy stated proudly.

Mr. Jim must have shipped the doctor in from Denver, as he was obviously not from these parts. The dust hadn't even settled on him yet.

He adjusted his spectacles, then looked over at Billy, not even bothering to address his patient. "Yes, well, it's going to take much more than gumption, isn't it? The girl's contracted consumption."

I swore quite profoundly at that.

Chapter 25

I was warm to the touch and lightheaded by the time my room finally cleared, save Wallace and Mr. Jim. As the doctor departed my chambers, I couldn't help but note the serious look directed at Dev, as well as a more subtle nod toward Billy-boy. Dev's sad, bright eyes shot to mine with a deep worry that didn't become her. A woman with child couldn't risk proximity to consumption. Billy ushered her out quickly, looking back to blow me a kiss. Ms. Liz pointed out that I was all but skin and bones and that she ought to fetch me something warm from the kitchen.

"You plannin' on explaining this doctor nonsense?" I mumbled.

Wallace was uninterested. "I had a life long before you, girl."

Mr. Jim grumbled in agreement with that.

"Do you know of anyone else who has fallen ill here in town?" Wallace questioned.

Mr. Jim's shoulders went a little rigid before he gave my cheek another light pinch. "No."

Wallace couldn't rid himself of the suspicious expression that plagued his face the moment Mr. Jim walked into the room.

He placed his hand back on my sore shoulder. "They must not be showing symptoms yet. We ought to find out. Someone in town has to be the source. I've a better chance of saving two lives than fifty." Wallace's voice had taken on a stiff, analytical tone I hadn't heard before.

I attempted to picture my stupendously foolish man as a serious doctor. Suppose he did possess an oddly extensive amount of knowledge that pertained to almost everything. I felt Wallace's annoyance towards Mr. Jim's quiet lack of contribution.

"Jim..."

"The girl didn't get it from anyone in town," Mr. Jim insisted.

Wallace crossed his arms and fully faced Mr. Jim.

Mr. Jim ignored the defensive stance and smiled sorrowfully over his shoulder at me. "I got word of a tribe outside of Denver, frequented the trading post we..." He sighed. "It started the beginning of summer, but now they are dropping like flies."

I frowned, and Mr. Jim turned back to his beloved window. Denver was still a long way from here. Besides, I had never been. I was a touch frantic at the level of silent tension in the room, and when I glanced at Wallace with my tired attempts to understand, I nearly gasped. The man was venomous. If a mere glance could kill, Mr. Jim would have already been six feet under. Wallace's jaw was overtly pronounced, and he ground his teeth. He rippled in a fury. It was, in a way, as horrible as it was wonderful.

"Wha—" Before I could finish, Wallace swiftly reached down to rip off the blanket I had spent the summer unashamedly in love with, leaving me bare sans my new black silk.

Wallace threw it to Mr. Jim and spat at his feet. "If I could kill you..." Wallace whispered through clenched teeth.

I whipped my head pathetically between the two men before observing my blanket with slow comprehension—a trading post outside of Denver. Consumption was highly contagious, after all.

"Oh..." I murmured.

"Why did you get that blanket, Jim?" Wallace hissed.

"I got it for Trixie—"

"I understand that ye got it for Trix. What I am askin' is *why*? Why did ye have to get the girl a bloody blanket from the tradin' post?"

Mr. Jim said nothing, just looked back out the window.

"'Twas to comfort her? Hmmm? Keep the wee lass warm at night and thinking o' ye afore she shuts her bonnie eyes? Remindin' her each night 'tis yer world she's been brought her into, nae birthed into. We're ye plastering yer face o'er any lingerin' memories o' her mam and da? O'er those ye stole her from?" The room nearly shook with Wallace's roar.

"I told y'all, Chanteloup was a nomad! He left both my girls on his own, ya hear?"

"Aye, ye've said as much. But what if he returned?"

"Trixie is my girl, dammit!" Mr. Jim snapped.

"And ye made bloody well sure o' that, didna ye?"

"You come here, and you think you know...you think you understand th-the decisions...Do you think even if I did find Chanteloup's family, if they even inhabit these soils, they would have taken her in? Get off that high horse of yours! Ain't no folks gonna take in a stray. I took care of the girl. I knows what's best for the girl. I've done what's best for her, and I will always do what's best for her!"

A shuddering silence fell over the room where my ragged breaths were as loud as gunfire.

"Ye lied to me, didna ye? All those years ago. Back when..." Wallace took a visible swallow, and despite the hard set to his jaw, his tone was riddled with devastation. His attention flickered to me before he composed himself once more and faced Mr. Jim.

"Ye lied to me."

Mr. Jim did not respond.

I squeezed my eyes shut and covered my ears. I couldn't listen to this. My father had left. Mr. Jim told me my father had left me. That had been the end of it. That had to be the end of it. I opened my eyes to see the stern face of Mr. Jim. But he didn't look at me. No, he looked over my shoulder, somewhere far away. Lost, trudging through the unknown of what had been, as he was one to do of late. Behind the set in his jaw and the furrow in his brows, I glimpsed the unspoken sorrow. The endless what-could-have-beens. The longing for a dead woman. And the promise to protect her child at all costs.

I had to trust that what Mr. Jim had done was for the best. Because if I didn't, if I let the unspoken accusations Wallace hurtled at Mr. Jim take root...Well, I didn't think I could survive that. I *knew* I couldn't survive that. Mr. Jim had said once his word was law, and in that moment, that vibrant fork-in-the-road of a moment as we sat in my room reeking of sickness and betrayal, I decided it was. And ever would be.

Amen.

So, I untangled myself from my sitting position to stand and reach for the pitiful blanket. So obviously not made from hands of Northern European descent, the pattern seemed to quiver against the still of the air. The poor thing didn't deserve to be subjected to such horrors as the competitive anger of man. Wallace's grip on my shoulders bit into my skin and made me gasp, which then followed with a cough or two. He yanked me away from the blanket, placing himself between me, Mr. Jim, and the blanket. I glared at him with annoyance as well as honest exhaustion. His eyes were a little wild, and his skin color was stark in contrast. His jaw stayed set, and I noted the sharpness of his teeth through his tight snarl.

"Nae," he ordered.

My eyebrow shot up nearly to my hairline. I weakly attempted to struggle out of his ridiculous grip. To no avail, I whispered my plea and tried to reach down for the blanket once more. He jerked me up straight again and gave a little shake.

"What the devil is the matter with ye, girl? Tryin' to get yerself kilt?" He shook me with each word so that my neck felt loose, and my teeth chattered together.

My mind spun with the sudden movements, and it took me a moment to collect myself. "It's not like it'll make me sicker," I hissed through clenched teeth.

"Oh, ye ken that for certain, do ye?" Wallace snarled.

"Let her go, Jayson," Mr. Jim said gravely.

"Shut that bloody yap o' yers, else I'll be shutting ye up meself." The arsenic in Wallace's words dripped delicately down my spine like sweat from an exceptionally exertive day.

Wallace would rid me of the blanket. Knowing him, as I was beginning to, I figured he would set it aflame and dance about like a wild thing. Which was ironic if we all took a step back and reviewed our parts in this play. My gaze flashed to the bright, thick crumpled mess once more, and tears of sheer nonsense clouded my vision. I mouthed a repeated plea and reached a shaky hand up to place it on his cheek. His eyes closed lightly at my touch, and despite everything, the reaction warmed my heart.

Thoughts of love fluttered into my mind, as well as an immediate fear of them and their sticky, foreign nature. I pulled my hand away promptly, and Wallace's eyes flashed open. Fury returned to his countenance, and he released me with a bit of a push. He headed to the door, and I reached down to grab my blanket. I straightened too quickly and experienced another dizzying head rush. Mr. Jim's familiar hands caught me. I couldn't help but curl myself into him, attempting to create some desperate form of embrace. It had been so long since he had touched me. His arms wrapped around me as if maybe, just maybe, he had been missing me as I had missed him.

Wallace froze in the doorway, and I couldn't hold his gaze and withstand the cold, desolate pain exchanged for the lively beauty that usually resonated there. "We leave by the end of the week, girl."

"I'll take Trixie to the cabin. You're needed down here to handle the business," Mr. Jim ordered softly.

"More than ye?" Wallace scoffed.

Mr. Jim nodded in response.

Wallace laughed faintly and ran a large hand over his face. "Hear me now and hear me well. Until the day that I die, I will be by that girl's side. Nothin', nae ye, nor disease, nor God will stop me. Should ye try to separate us, I will find ye. With a vengeance that will haunt yer dreams and make yer sheets damp with piss and sweat. Ye will stay in town, Jim. And 'tis final."

Mr. Jim tightened his grip on me, and I felt Wallace's angry, possessive glare before he left the room.

Chapter 26

 nd just as winter arrived and autumn left, I found my love for Wallace had grown as a flower buds. It was tender and hesitant to reveal itself in fear of the surrounding environment. So it lingered in its fold, quietly on the cusp of a dramatic spectacle, building each day with crystalline precision. And once it was ready to reveal itself, it would leave the surrounding world breathless. If only for a moment.

Winter wrapped its tight grip around our throats as if the hellish summer's drought had never occurred. Wallace said weather was a fickle witch throwing us all for a loop no matter where you called home. Even in Andalusia.

My fever danced through my body, coming and going much as the shores of the Lil' Big lapped up and retreated in the springtime. Blood had not returned to my cough since the day I had woken from my deep sleep, and by early December, we had found the days without fever outweighed those with. My contact with anyone outside the cabin was nonexistent. Much to my delight, I found the transition into solitude from those who had surrounded my whole life more natural than expected. The secret guilt I had harbored about leaving them was slowly chipped away with time and space. Despite my health and complete lack of independence, I discovered an unfamiliar trust in myself. Just as a child learning to walk balances on those pudgy, newly found knees, I, too, was uncovering a stride with my head held high. Finding faith in myself was glorifying.

The cabin was small, barely possessing the basics to survive. But something about the single bed with just enough room for two bodies, the unsteady table with two chairs, the bookshelf, fireplace, and big brass bathtub felt familiar. The small space was, in a way, the closest thing to home I had ever found. The bed was shared, less so at first when Wallace nursed my recurring fever through the nights, but nothing more than sleep had occurred in its frame. I hadn't minded in the beginning. Especially when I finally started to get better. Pride had shone in Wallace's eyes when it became clear I had a chance of surviving, and his look filled up lifelong, seemingly bottomless holes in my heart. Though when the fever stayed gone for nearly three weeks straight, my body once again grew restless for another type of satisfaction.

My weakened frame made my attempts to physically seduce Wallace futile. The incorrigible man would give a high-pitched giggle and gently pat me somewhere that did not relieve anything. Instead, he told me stories of the life that we would build together. He whispered warm words of a salty wind that would coat my hair, worn loose around my shoulders at his insistence. And wines that made any tucked-away bottle of sherry Ms. Liz had taste like ash. He chuckled into my ear about all the babies he would fill me with, which earned him a swat or two. I knew as much about motherhood and having a baby as I did about why the sky was blue. I shared this with Wallace, and he just laughed, claiming it was so the ocean had something to match.

Wallace spoke, holding me closely with a dying fire in the hearth until Sleep reached for me, and I fought the pull she had at my eyelids with everything in me. Yes, despite my pride and fear, I fell in love with him quite desperately, indeed. But that bit of information was kept very much to myself. It wasn't any of his business, anyway.

Billy and Dev's wedding couldn't wait for me to recuperate. The event happened quite shortly after my relocation. I understood. Yet, for some reason, when Wallace brought letters from my family providing details of all the celebrations, I fell into a dark, angry sadness and couldn't seem to finish them.

I knew it was a very selfish thing. It wasn't fair for me to find joy in my distance and then anger at those I was distanced from for continuing their lives. But deep down, I suppose I wished for the freedom to go along my merry way, and perhaps leave them with a large hole that lingered until I returned. If I ever did. A certain, secretive desire to punish them for things they ought not be blamed for grew teeth and gnawed at my heart. Despite my joy of independence, I was hurt by how easily they continued without me; the confirmation of how unnecessary I had always been.

With shame and a flushed face from no fever, I confessed these layered emotions to Wallace. He didn't have the words to fix how I felt. But he was patient and listened through my stumbling attempts to explain how much it hurt to feel the need to leave the only ones I had ever known. Only to then be awash in their unexpected allowance of it. Their unbothered acceptance of my departure (the one we all knew would continue after my recovery) was tough medicine to swallow. Wallace told me that I was a selfish little thing, but that was alright. The plague of humanity was meant to riddle us with selfishness. As long as we admitted to it, we could consider ourselves in the clear for owing apologies. I received no letters from Mr. Jim, but Wallace and I did not discuss this fact. We kept the subject tucked in the shed out back. As if the winter chill could freeze the locks and therefore make it inaccessible to grab and poke and understand until the thawing, forgiving winds of spring.

Meanwhile, the snow came with full force, coating us in a lovely, frigid mess. I watched it come and fall and stay through the warped, cloudy windows, all the while, sitting on Wallace's lap as he read aloud to me, book after book. Time passed us by with a lazy slowness that, at one point in my life, I swore would have made me restless, but now left me content. I didn't know which day it was. Suppose I didn't need to know. I ached to be with Wallace as a man and woman were meant to be on late nights tucked away from the rest of the world, but I found quiet happiness in his presence. That happiness surprised me. I never thought I could sit still with another and not feel an itch upon my flesh or a chill within my heart that commanded me to run. Yet, I was beginning to find just that, and though I wiggled nervously in his embrace from time to time, deep within my soul, I did not want to leave him.

One morning, I woke to a cold bed, only to find Wallace had pulled a chair close to the bedside. Through sleepy eyes, I witnessed the most severe expression plastered across his face. His elbows rested on his knees as he leaned forward, hands cupped together as if within them was a precious lightning bug. He didn't meet my eye but sat transfixed with whatever was in his hands. The snow fell steadily. I didn't speak as I witnessed his countenance. I rolled to my side so that I faced him fully and held my head up in my right palm. I let my left drift close to where his hovered over the bed, but I didn't touch him. I waited for him to share his thoughts with me, which usually didn't take long.

He continued to stare blindly at his hands. I drummed my fingers on the bed and watched his solemn face. The wind whispered calming words through the cracks in the house, and the low fire still radiated a glowing warmth that kept me comfortable from any chill. Internally was a different story as I swallowed down the slowly building discomfort of

Wallace's prolonged silence. I wasn't sure if I had ever spent this much time with him awake without conversation. I was shocked that he was capable of it. I would have to remember this moment in the future when the man went on a rampage of endless talking. There was a crack from the fireplace and a lazy collapse of wood.

"It's Christmas Eve," he finally announced.

I had lost track of the days long ago, but I suppose it made sense. The last set of letters I had received raved about the baby's preparations and the holiday season.

I slowly nodded. "Alright. Merry Chris—"

"Marry me," he interrupted quietly.

Oh.

I stared at his hands. Stupidly aware of what he held in them. His gaze burned into me. Sweat sprung from my underarms as well as my palms. His hands opened slowly to reveal a shiny silver ring happily nestled within. I stifled a cough as my current and beloved state of reality shattered around us with his adoration-filled demand. It was a bit like I was falling. Like in a dream, where after a while, you stop fearing the fall. Instead, you're impatiently curious about the smack that awaits you at the bottom.

I slowly straightened up into a seated position and ran two shaky, sweating hands through my hair. Wallace didn't move, but his eyes followed me like a wolf to his prey. I fought the urge to scoot back from him. I gnawed at my bottom lip and watched the ring glimmer softly in the winter morning light.

"You've already asked me this." Was all my mind could think to say in an, unfortunately, scratchy voice. The consumption might have ever altered my voice, I was coming to realize.

"I'm no longer asking, Trix," he stated coolly. His eyes were unwavering.

I set my jaw and focused on my anger instead of the heaps of other emotions that lay just below the surface. "You can't—"

"No, *you* can't." I heard my teeth grind at his rude interruption. "You can't tell me that you don't love me. You can't tell me that you wish to be apart from me because if you did, you'd make yourself a liar. I am telling you to trust me. I am telling you to spend your life with me, because, girl, you are going to live. You are going to live full and well, and with me, goddammit. I'll nae return ye to Jim like a bloody borrowed cup o' sugar."

I looked back at the ring. In the low morning light, it glimmered scantily in those large-palmed, long-fingered hands of his. I peeped intricate etchings of delicate flowers and swirls of vines on sturdy silver in that glimmer. My hand twitched with a divided desire to either snatch the ring and toss it in the fire or slip it on my finger. I wanted both. He smirked as if he saw right into that part of me that wanted the ring with everything I had. Or at least half of that everything. As if he saw that small twitch of my hand and understood each swirling thought that circled my mind.

If I knew Wallace, which at this point, I felt as though I did, then I knew that half of me was more than enough for him. And how wonderful was that? Even when he asked for everything I had with the confidence of a man much more masculine or handsome or established than him, he still settled for my barely available parts. Those scraggly broken bits that didn't shine too bright in the sun and could easily cut him if he snatched at me from the wrong angle. He wasn't even discouraged by them. Instead, he saw hope where I felt broken. When every bump in the road felt like a paralyzing halt to me, he saw opportunity. And he would offer his hand through every step of progress I would have to take, should I decide to live that life I wanted.

I flexed my hand this time. He was right. I couldn't return to what I had before. There was no turning back, and the only option was to move forward. Or else I would become stuck in the ground like an old dying tree with roots too deep, too far set to stand a chance of survival.

A while back, Dev had made it clear that relations with a man could leave you trapped, but if you had the right man, maybe it wasn't such a bad thing. Deep down, I knew I wouldn't find a better man than Wallace. Not that he was a good man. But for someone like myself, he was the best man. *And when it came down to it, wasn't that all that mattered? To be with someone who could sit with you and tell you they didn't care how you lashed out or how drunk you got? At the end of the day, it was still you they wanted to be with?* The life of solitude I was so prepared for no longer seemed as comforting as it once did. With a ring, I would tie myself to Wallace with such severe permanency, God would probably chuckle. And without it, I was nothing more than a soiled good. One that nobody wanted in the first place. On top of all its ugly appearances, this misshapen apple also had a worm swirling about in the depths of its flesh.

So, I reached forward to his open palm so that my fingertips were painfully close to the ring. I bit my bottom lip and nodded with a heavy head. Wallace closed his eyes, and a soft, nearly sweet smile spread across his sharp cheeks like the slow drizzle of molasses. His hands flipped so that the ring fell onto the bed haphazardly, and he no longer cupped my tentative touch but fully grasped it. Wallace bowed into our hands, and I was confused by a powerful emotion that prickled beneath my nose. Suddenly, Wallace's shoulders gave a funny heave, and for a moment, I thought he had begun to laugh. A bit of an unorthodox, violent expression of emotions wasn't something to put past the man. I figured he laughed at our moment like a madman until I felt the warm droplets of water hit my hand enclosed between both of his.

From whichever source they originated, his tears became too much for him to handle, and triggered something deep within me. That prickling sensation was damning for me, and I cried with him. Perhaps it was out of relief. It was so brilliantly clear with this turn of events that I had reached the end of something. What, I was not entirely sure, but had assumed would trail behind me all my days. Perhaps I cried because I was bidding farewell to my lingering loneliness. Perhaps we both were. Maybe I mourned the loss of something, whether I liked it or not, I had grown to know so well.

I cupped his face to further extend the mutual emotion with more physical contact. I noted the specific texture of his warm tears dribbling down the harsh plane of his cheek, and another shudder passed through his body. My body responded with sniffles, which should have had me concerned about the unattractive nature of those noises in such a quiet room. But it didn't. He slowly straightened and transferred both of my hands into one of his. He reached out to grab the back of my neck and collide his mouth against mine. Our faces were stained with tears, nervous sweat, and snot, but we breathed each other in as if it were the last time, not the beginning of the rest of it.

Our clumsy mouths slowly regained some semblance of sexual order. Eventually, our lips and tongues and teeth were moving together with a familiar yet exciting rhythm. It had been so long since we shared a kiss of this caliber. The hand pushing the back of my neck closer to him grew more possessive as those fingers of his threaded through my hair and gripped for dear life. I couldn't help but give a sigh of relief as I was floored with dizzying pleasure. He clung to my entrapped hand in a nearly paralyzing grasp and pressed it against his rapidly beating heart.

Oh, how I had missed it all! I had missed this internal heat burning me up, not from a fever, but from a much more decided action. Wallace moaned against my mouth, and I bit his tongue playfully. A roar of pleasure shuddered through the man, and I wiggled a hand free to grip the collar of his shirt to pull him closer. To pull at him until we were once more one single being. One, and never two. I could not stand the thought of us, the beautiful and tarnished us, who surely would drown in their singular loneliness, becoming two ever again. It would soon be him inside of me, but I wished the roles were reversed so that I was the one curled within him. Only I wished to be inside him fully, entirely. Surely no one would complain, as we would take up less space in such positioning. Though I believed it was fair to say that I took up very little, to begin with. It had always felt like that small amount of space, minuscule really, compared to the grand scheme of things, was still always too much.

I was up on my knees, clawing away with the desperation of a Banshee, while Wallace just sat, somehow equally coy as he was out of his mind. I broke our lips apart to gasp for breath. Wallace's lips never left my flesh, and he quickly nibbled and bit and hummed and licked my ear in such a way that my lower stomach pooled with sinful heat. I cried out helplessly.

"Oh, Trix," Wallace whispered darkly against my warmed skin.

My nails bit into the hand that gripped mine, and his other slid slowly from my neck. Painfully slowly. I was starved for the air that fought with me by the time his rough fingers found the front of my sleeping gown. I hissed through the closeness in my throat and lungs. He traced my barely feminine lumps gently. Much too gently for my preference, and I tossed my head back in agony. He leaned forward to plant a dissatisfying sweet pattern of kisses on my exposed throat.

"What's wrong, girl?" he whispered softly before a quick bite of my skin.

I whimpered like a woman I had never met before and gripped his throat dangerously. He growled at that, and just as his actions finally became wonderfully rough, my lungs seized. Blackness momentarily danced around the corners of my eyes, and I reached out to grip anything that would reach back. I was out of his grasp. The next thing I knew, Wallace was behind me, rubbing soft circles into my back. I inhaled through my nose and pushed all the hot air that felt like it was boiling me alive out. Despite the chilly winter air, the memory of a fever that had wreaked havoc throughout my body left a sour taste toward any heat whatsoever.

As one of Wallace's hands rubbed my back, the other inched its way towards my throat to gently stroke. I enjoyed the tender moment as my lungs slowly calmed. I took three deep, clear inhales before turning to face him once more. He smiled a little sadly at me, and I just rolled my eyes, not wanting to wallow in it all. I was getting better. I wasn't perfect, but I hadn't been so in the first place. I was better. I slipped my arms back around his neck and attempted to pull him close, only to have him grasp my forearm and lightly break my hold, pushing me back to hold me at arm's length.

"Trix," he murmured.

I gripped the back of his hair tightly with the arm he didn't hold hostage. My soiled heart jerked at the sudden rejection. I bit my bottom lip as shocking tears sprung to my eyes, shaking my head jerkily.

"What?" I asked in a broken voice, feeling just the same.

Frustration and heartache sunk into the pit of my belly quicker than a fat raindrop. I pulled and then yanked Wallace's head by the back of his hairs up to look me in the eye. His eyes were kind—the sympathy, the pity, the raw and unwavering love that infected those horribly beautiful eyes of his. All of it made me sick.

"I canna," he whispered delicately.

My tears pooled over my lower lids and trickled down my cheeks. We had been so close. So close to how we had been. How we should be if it hadn't been for the damn ailment that lurked beneath my flesh and threatened my life. The damn ailment that still threatened my existence. And while I wished to ignore this fact, it was clear that Wallace, with a red-laced contradiction, could not.

My life was still so present in my fingertips, warming and cooling to each touch with a certain familiarity that scared off any fears of death I faced in the past months. But he did not know that. He could not feel the glorious, relieving betterment that was crawling through my veins each day. He saw the weak limbs and the pale, skinny frame and coughing spells that nearly put me under each time. And as usual, I didn't have the words. They were stuck at the bottom of my heart. They sunk lower with a settling disappointment that it could be a while before the man I loved would touch me again as a man touches his woman. As a man such as Wallace touches his woman.

I didn't have the words, but I had my body. Though I was new to this feminine creature nonsense, that ought to be enough. I leaned to kiss him, only to have his face turn so that I bussed his sharp cheek. I turned my head to meet his lips despite his wrestling, all in the wrong ways. I let a pathetic murmur escape my lips. He groaned in return. As if to say "no" was as difficult as it was to hear it. Still, he strained from my grasp, and I clung to him with the chilling reality that he was all I had left to hold onto. While he could reassure me with promises and lovely words that were as fluid as a stream in the middle of spring, I could not. All I could reassure his fears with was my body. Plus, I had missed him. I missed the feel of a man so impossibly close.

Mr. Jim had been right; I indeed was a wanton. *But was being a wanton so bad if you had a man wanting you the way Wallace wanted me? At a certain point, wasn't the shame and promise of hellfire worth it all?* So, I kept squirming, and he let me. I straddled him, clutching his face between my hands.

"No... Wallace...please—" I murmured between soft, wet kisses along the most vulnerable parts of his neck.

I curled my fingers into his thick, long hair and pulled precisely how he would my own. I bit down hard on the thin skin just over his Adam's apple, and he pulled back so quickly that my teeth came together with a harsh clack.

"Please," I whispered.

His beautiful eyes were closed tightly, and his jaw was clenched. A muscle ticked in his jaw. I had seen this look before—the look of the devil on his back. Or at least whispering sweet nothings in his ears. I would win this; I just needed to be clever. And no bout of ailment was strong enough to strip me of my most clever self.

"Please," I begged again, reaching out to gently stroke his lips with my fingertips. They parted slightly under my touch, and his brow furrowed deeper.

"Please...husband..." I murmured like the devil that pushed against his back and licked at his ear with a serpent tongue.

"Husband, please. Love me," I cooed.

As those sinful words left my lips, Wallace's eyes flashed open and wild. He pulled back to stare into mine deeply.

"Husband," I repeated with finality.

A cascade of raw emotions flashed across his beautiful face. I had him despite the crumminess of my lungs. I had him once more.

Chapter 27

I lay securely next to Wallace, basking in the aftermath. Relaxing in the wake of our great, explosive expression of liveliness. I clung to his warm vitality with a lazy joy coursing through my veins and heavy breaths. I trailed my fingers mindlessly through his chest hair. My fingers brushed over those funny markings, and I traced them with butterfly pressure, still convinced a marking so harsh in contrast had to be painful. But it remained flat, like a birthmark.

"Were you a sailor?"

He sighed and shrugged nonchalantly.

I wiggled my mouth in annoyance at his lack of an answer. I couldn't help but feel like the shrug was a taste of my own medicine. It was an irksome gesture.

"I have a gift for you," he sighed once more with eyes closed. He was in the ultimate state of relaxation.

"But—" I mumbled in protest before glancing down at my hand. He opened one eye. I furrowed my brow at my naked ring finger.

"Oh..." I murmured.

Wallace let out a bark of that high-pitched giggled, then swiftly untangled himself from me to find the ring. I grimaced and patted around the warm sheets a bit helplessly. I warmed as my searching quickly turned frantic when it was clear the ring wasn't merely tangled in the sheets. Wallace was on his hands and knees. I gnawed at my kiss-swollen lips.

It was irrational, but I felt the fool and swallowed the urge to dress and walk right out the door. My jaw clenched, and my knuckles ached in protest to my hands squeezed into tight little fists.

"Oh, Wallace," I groaned quietly, and my stomach sunk deeper as he let out an exasperated breath, continuing to search. He let out a dry laugh. "I'm so sorry..." I continued, feeling small. That quiet apology had him glance at me for only a moment. He rolled his eyes at my distressed state and went right back to searching.

"Quit yer bellyachin' girl, it didna sprout a pair o' legs and run off on us. And if it did, I'll buy ye another one. Hell, Trixie, I'll buy ye a different one for each day o' the bloody week should ye find that fit."

"I don't think I'll ever find that fit, Wallace."

He just grumbled a low, "We'll see," in response before a loud, giggling, "Aha!" erupted from his comically naked and halfway-under-the-bed form.

I bit back a smile as he scrambled into bed.

He feigned a look of seriousness with a touch of scorn. "Hand," he demanded.

I rolled my eyes and reluctantly offered my left hand, and he snatched it as if I had plans to yank it back at any moment. I was tempted, but I pushed that incriminating thought to the back of my mind. He slid the ring onto my finger, and he was all bright and shining and surprisingly *youthful* in the languid winter light. Briefly, he shone with vitality and potential, and the fine lines around his eyes disappeared. It was odd, as I had never thought he looked all that old before. If anything, I had consistently been unnerved at how alarmingly young he looked for the experiences he had packed into his life. But his eyes were worn with a solely aged shadow. And for a fleeting moment on the Christmas Eve of 1886, in the abandoned foothills of Colorado, that shadow lifted, making Jayson Wallace look like a young man.

"Well?" he prompted, lifting my hand for me to have a clear vision of the ring.

I glanced down at my finger clad in the shiniest bit of silver I had ever seen. I ran my left thumb over the intricate etchings that continued beautifully around it. Despite all its glory, I couldn't help but find the ring bizarre on my scarred, unpolished hand. I made a fist and released it, testing the feel with a ring now involved.

"Feels...different," I mumbled finally.

"Och!" Wallace cried out before grabbing my chin and crushing me into the most beautiful kiss, whose inspiration I was not privy to.

By the time he released me, I was nearly clawing at him once more. He growled in response to words I had not said. My gaze flickered back down to the ring. He tenderly stroked my cheek.

"Your gift," he repeated.

"But you already gave me something," I protested softly and fluttered my properly dressed finger at him.

He rolled his eyes. "Yes, and I can tell just how much you love it."

"Truly, Wallace, you already gave me a gift."

He gave me a sarcastic look. "I have enough self-awareness to know that a lifetime with the likes of me wouldn't be wished upon the foulest of folks. Let alone be considered a gift for my new bride."

I couldn't help but scrunch my nose up a bit at the word *bride*. He reached forward. He pinched my ugly scrunched-up nose between his thumb and pointer finger before hopping nakedly out of bed. I snuggled back into the bed. I rolled to my side and watched him rummage around the room, muttering to himself as if I had disappeared just as his back turned. He eventually remembered where he had left his parcel.

Snow didn't sound like anything. It never had, and unless the wind was roaring something mighty, it never would. It was a vain creature— that white, pure snow. She fell with grace and beauty, and—let's keep this bit between you and I, of course—a bit of stupidity. Despite all those vapid characteristics that faded away instantaneously with her arrival, no one ever expected her to say something clever. Yet she was loved so dearly. Meanwhile, thunder and his angry roar, wind and her painful wail, and hail with his imbecilic cackle, were so carelessly brushed aside. Passive aggressively grouped together in a box with a warning label written in a sloppy hand that read *ANNOYANCE*.

As I sat with all these cynical thoughts circling around my warm, post-coitus brain, I briefly understood the exact sound of the snow falling on us. There was a warmth in that stupid, frigid fluff. As there was an acute silence in its effortless beauty. And I was happy. Suppose I always figured happiness would be much more complicated than that. I wish now that I could have frozen my most perfect *then* in the snow and died with it there in the raw foothills of the Rocky Mountains.

There was a box in front of me wrapped with a bright red ribbon. I blinked my dry eyes and smiled up at a patiently waiting, naked Wallace. He humorously held the parcel in front of his nudity. I smirked as I reached forward, greedy for my gift as well as what hid behind. I sat up and put the gift in my lap atop the pooling of blankets. He folded his arms over his chest and stood, a little oddly, at the side of the bed as I made quick work of the bright red ribbon and tore into a box with a child's growing excitement. I spotted a pair of shiny, sharp metal blades with thick leather straps within my mess of a box. I tentatively reached in to lift one of the contraptions delicately, fearful of the silver blade.

They were surprisingly heavy, and the leather was stiff to the touch. They looked like elongated, slender animal trappings.

My eyebrows pulled together in confusion, and I gave him a wry and breathless, "Thanks?"

He chuckled and sat down on the bed with me. He reached into my box and grabbed the other dangerous gift. "The Lil' Big froze over, girl."

I waited for a better explanation, testing the weight of the metal once more. He looked at his blade.

"Jesus may have walked on water, but man sure can try."

I just stared, still not comprehending.

He rolled his eyes. "You skate on the ice."

"What?"

He giggled at my disbelief. "You put them on your feet and slide. Purposefully."

"No," I gasped.

"Yes, girl. You can. You can, and you will. You'll love it."

The fire gave a bit of a heave. My skin was covered in gooseflesh. He reached to take the skate out of my hands and put both back into the box. He placed the box beside the bed, then quickly pulled the blankets back over my body and pushed me into the sleeping position.

"Take a bit of a rest first, then I'll show you how graceful a scrappy little bit like yourself can be."

I was tired, despite my lack of activity. So I let him tuck the covers

tightly around me, kiss my somehow already closed lids, and I slept.

Chapter 28

he aroma of warm, smoky fat grabbed my wrists and yanked me from my sleep. There was a hollow aching in my stomach and a papery feel at the back of my throat. I was also horribly freezing. I pushed myself up from the pillows to see afternoon sunlight, and a fully dressed Wallace fixed and fussed about the hearth. I noted the little words he used to himself as if he were the only one in the room. I blissfully pulled my knees into my chest and wrapped my arms around them. Wallace had been gentle with me, gentler than I would have preferred. But to have him again was enough for the ever-fading now. My husband had been gentle with me. Husband...
husband...

"Husband," I whispered the word, testing exactly how it felt in each corner of my mouth.

"What was that?" Wallace called cheerily, looking over his shoulder with a sinister smile. I straightened a bit.

"Cold," I rasped. "I said I was cold."

He smiled wider, a knowing look in his eyes. Damn. "Well, you ain't gonna get warmed lounging about dressed in all but your skin. You're the original sin. I've grown to suspect that God created winter in attempts to keep the likes of you covered from the greedy eyes of man."

I rolled my eyes at his words, and with his scold, he paced over to assist me with dressing in my warmest.

"Let's not bring Him into this, hmmm?" I suggested all too sweetly.

By the time I had adequately dressed for another winter's day and was fed to the brim, the sun had passed his peak and seemed to ready himself for supper. After Wallace took my plate, he returned to putter about me, covering me with more layers than what would be necessary for the tiny cabin. I was wrapped and tucked with every piece of wool and leather available before Wallace dropped to his knees and slid a thicker set of stockings over my legs. I savored the feeling of his warm fingers touching the soft-covered bits of my flesh, despite lying naked with him only hours before. His hands on such a private area felt scandalous. I bit my bottom lip and looked into his stormy eyes under my eyelashes. He grinned and shook his head before sitting on the backs of his heels.

"Should have never given into you, girl. I've created a monster here. Keeping you nice and satisfied'll become a full-time job for me. But I suppose a man must do what a man must do, and the thought of you growing bored and finding comfort in anyone else strikes the fear of God into me."

It was pointless to reply. He always found a way to talk to me like he was simply talking to himself. It made me feel like I was there in his mind with him. And it was cozy, I had to admit. He reached for the box and lifted a terrifying metal skate. I winced as he grabbed my foot, and fluidly slid it into a pair of boots I didn't recognize. It was quiet as he tightened the laces so that my feet were snug, and my ankles couldn't move about. After the boots were on, he made work of attaching the blades to each bottom securely. He leaned forward to place a kiss on each of my knees before standing quickly. He offered his hands to me, and I shakily slipped my mitten-clad palms into his.

He helped me up, and I gasped at the sensation of standing knives. I tipped backward a bit, and Wallace caught me. Despite how tight the boots felt around my ankles when Wallace laced them, I was significantly off-balance standing, and my ankles quivered in the boots. It was like I was flailing about, and it took a full minute for me to find a sense of security in my stance. Wallace was patient with me and gently let go of my hands once I had my bearings.

"There you go," he whispered.

I reached for him fearfully, and he didn't shame me for it but met my reach with a firm grip. A cold sweat broke out along my hairline. "Wallace, I can't do this."

He just smirked and clucked his tongue. "Sure, ye can. If yer well enough for a bit o' bed sport with the likes of a man as *poetically* in love with ye as me, yer well enough to learn a bit o' skatin."

I scoffed at his teasing tone and focused on balancing myself. I loosened my grip on him. He released me and took a large step back. I inhaled deeply and closed my eyes, searching for something deep within me that was strong enough to steady myself. I found it somewhere near where I figured my liver was, and I was still.

I flashed my eyes open at Wallace, and he gave me a soft clap. "Alright! Let's get you on the ice."

My eyes widened, and the next thing I knew, he swept me off my feet and took us outside. The winter air bit at my skin, and I buried my face into Wallace's neck. His untied hair whipped around us in the gentle winter breeze, and I took in his scent to calm myself for whatever this nonsense he insisted on would be.

"Why are you carrying me?"

"I'm just helping you out. I won't have you breaking your ankle on solid ground before you get a chance to be on the ice."

I blanched but kept my mouth shut. Wallace plopped me on my feet, and I reached out to steady myself from his unashamed carelessness. I huffed at him as my skates cut into the frozen, snow-clad earth. Wallace was correct. The Lil' Big was coated in snow, as well as what seemed to be solid ice. I shivered.

"Why am I doing this again?" I grumbled.

Wallace snickered and let go of my hands, heading the few paces to where the ice began. Much to my horror, his intentions of standing on the ice were clear.

"But what if you fall?" I protested nervously.

"I'll get back up," he said confidently before stepping back onto the frozen body of water.

He glanced quickly over his shoulder before facing me and reached out his hands. I made small fists in my thick mittens and held them rigidly against my breast. My body was tight from the fear and wobbling I would experience due to the preposterous blades attached to my feet. I glanced down at my boots, and he did the same, taking a deep breath, which felt like it was much more for me than him.

"What if *I* fall?"

He looked up at me and gave me a wolfish smile. "Then *you'll* get back up."

The wind picked up a bit and swirled the snow around us in the loveliest way. Dancing with elegant, nearly invisible arms, which reached out as if she wished for both of us to take her hands and join in the mystical movements. I peered around the wonderland that had become of my Lil' Big. It looked nothing short of a fairy book, and even the shabby cabin that we (Wallace) had turned into a home looked elegant in the winter white. There was something very safe about the frigid, dead beauty that surrounded us. Amid all that glorious death, I was alive. At least for now, that was. I was getting better, and with the help of Wallace, confidence bloomed in my quiet, tarnished soul that I could continue to get better. He didn't push me but waited as my mind did its tiny swirls in an attempt to make itself up. His patience was warm. I finally took his outstretched hands. He gripped me tightly, and I slowly shuffled forward.

"That's it, girl—baby steps to me. Now don't take steps when you get on the ice, though. You'll fall something awful if you do. You gotta remember to slide. Don't be scared. I won't let anything happen to you. I won't ever let anything happen to you, Trixie-girl."

I nodded mechanically at his kind words. The moment my blade touched the ice, I froze up and flinched violently at the unfamiliarity. I flinched harder as the feeling of falling backward seized me. He clenched my hands, and in that sturdy, constant grip of his, I found a calm sense of center and ceased with my jerky movements. My eyes flashed up to his, and a nervous giggle escaped my lips.

Wallace laughed. "Hardest part is over," he whispered.

I peered into his eyes, too scared to look down.

"Okay. I'm not going to let go of your hands, but you're going to come with me, alright? Bend your knees a little. I'll pull you."

My brows furrowed in preparation. I gripped his hands with everything I had as he directed me across the ice. I held myself taut so I wouldn't flail about and knock us both down but couldn't help jumping at the sensation of sliding on these blades of his. Despite the winter chill, a trail of sweat ran down my spine from what had to be nerves.

Wallace kept my eye and matched his breathing with my own inaudible huffs. I slid over the frozen Lil' Big effortlessly while a cry of surprise and joy escaped my lips. It was like flying, only on the ground. And slower than a horse. More so like walking fast, but without a foreseeable interruption. But for reasons beyond my own understanding, I felt like a god. The cold wind pinched my nose in response to my blasphemous comparison of being anything more than a runty mutt, but I couldn't be bothered. He kept us close to the bank, making a pathway of long, skinny ovals as my legs warmed from the continued bend of the knees. It was a freeing feeling. We said nothing to one another other than a giggle, and I felt like a child.

"Okay, Trix, I'm going to start to let go of your hands," he said all too quickly.

I bubbled a protest, and he laughed as he carefully turned us so that he was walking/sliding back toward a solid ground with more traction.

"You're going to push yourself. Keep your feet like a duck and hold that bend in your knee. Go one leg at a time. It'll make sense once you just start. Whatever you do, don't try to slide with your knees locked. You'll be on your ass faster than the devil." He grinned at me and slowly released my hands, a couple feet from the bank.

I froze and slid only a few inches before coming to a weird, shaky halt. My arms flew out in wild circles to regain some semblance of balance. Wallace slowly scooted backward with his arms outstretched. He was awkwardly crouched, almost like a creature, as he crept to solid ground. I clenched my hands into fists and gawked like a deer caught in a damning snare at Wallace's retreat. I swallowed down building frustration. He laughed at the expression on my face, and I gritted my teeth. He was playing me the fool, dolling me up in these contraptions, and abandoning me. As I unclenched my jaw to tell him that, his eyes went wide.

In a rush, his arms flailed outwardly as mine had as if there was something to grab onto. Somehow his creeping failed him as his feet slipped out from underneath him comically and he fell to his rear. I instinctively reached out to aid him only to freeze, understanding once again how unstable I was.

Wallace sat on the ice, legs sprawled out and gasping a bit before watching me in my frazzled state of concern. I shuffled on the ice with a little bit of rocking back and forth but somehow kept myself upright. He lifted one hand as if that could stop me, and his eyes shifted side to side, his face the image of concentration. He looked as if he were waiting for something. The sun sunk slowly around us, painting the scene an eerie bright in its fleeting moments. The look of concern on his face told me not to breathe. I fretted over a potential injury until he finally met my eye.

Wallace burst out laughing. He sat with his legs sprawled out, leaned back, and let out the longest, most beautiful string of high-pitched giggles I had ever heard from him. I stayed frozen at the sound for a beat before finally joining him with a sense of relief. He lay down on the snowy ice and made snow angels as he continued to laugh at his clumsy self. The man was indeed the most ridiculous human being I had ever met.

My laughter ceased before his, and twilight drenched us. It was as if the last rays of the sun had glimpsed all the carefree, childlike wonder my dear Wallace and I had, and the sun was caught turning on his heel, running to join with a pair of his own ice skates clenched between a glowing yellow fist.

Wallace sat up and brushed the snow from his gloveless palms before arranging himself in a more mature, contemplative seat. One hand fisted beneath his chin as if he were thinking on something quite draining before he lifted a finger and swirled it.

"Proceed," he commanded stiffly.

I giggled before confidently placing my hands on my hips.

"How do I do it again?" I asked, feeling lighter after our bout of silly.

He told me exactly how to move my body, and I listened intently as the sun gave up his pursuit and the wind rustled with more gumption than before. I took one deep breath, shuffled shakily so that I faced the long path that he had made for me, and pushed myself forward.

I glided roughly, just as Wallace said, "Now your other foot, girl."

I did as he instructed, and slowly I felt an intrinsic pattern inside me projecting my body forward.

He called out a soft cheer as I slowly but surely skated across the frozen Lil' Big. I slid back and forth, nervous on the turns, until my body found a timid familiarity in the repeated motion. It didn't take as long as I thought it would to perfect a gliding speed that left me breathless as the soft winter air whirled. Every now and then, I hit a rough edge or jerked with sudden uncertainty. A thrill of fear shot down my spine rapidly, only to have Wallace cry out for me to keep my knees bent. And each time he called out with advice, I regained myself. It was lovely to feel in control of my body after spending the past couple of months a mere victim of it. I was getting better.

I came to a jerky stop before lifting my arms above myself in a proud show of victory. He clapped his hands together reverently, and I gave a wobbly bow before jerking upright and nearly landing on my rear just as he had. I giggled. Wallace's face shone in the moonlight, and for a moment, the air was too thin. Skating about was a bit of work, and work itself was foreign to those weakened muscles of mine. I bit my lip and surveyed the dark yet somehow shining, solidified body of water from my childhood. To my left, in a looming shadow, sat the boulder where Wallace and I first met.

The memory felt like two lifetimes ago. I didn't recall who I had been before Wallace. The love that came with him was a bright, illuminating kind that showed me a world I never knew existed. A world I thought would never be for me, that I would be left ignorant to until my body rotted in the same lifeless soil I had spent my entire existence gracing.

With him came strength. With him came the expectation of being more than I was and accepting the skin I was born into. It was a fire beneath my heels that was pushing me forward daily. It was warm without being hot. I could touch the cast iron and not burn but absorb a certain power from the surrounding heat. The walls I had always been told surrounded me, that could only be penetrated through quiet, consistent lies held no foundation in a world with Wallace. Shame for being born outside of what was considered right did not exist between us.

I should have told him that I loved him then.

But his attention-seeking voice interrupted any chance to. "I thought it had all come to an end." He gestured to the boulder with his chin and looked back at me. "The day I met you. I thought I must have finally died and gone onto whatever came next."

I waited for him to continue. He always seemed to.

"I had shown up in another place, tail probably tucked between my legs, ready for another bout of great, soul-crushing nothing. I was sitting on that rock of yours, a fact which was unbeknownst to myself at the time, shaking the gates of Saint Peter and demanding entrance. Then, out of the glittering sludge you now stand upon like a half-assed depiction of Jesus Christ, emerged a nymph. Slick and naked and *glitter-*

ing with droplets of water that clung to your perfect flesh, that I envied most earnestly. You opened those eyes that I swore—no, I swear—were a gift from the devil himself to help tempt man. For though he is a fool, man is not fool enough to fall for another ruby red apple of temptation. Any man with anything between his ears would know to run from you because your eyes are the warning of the second coming, my most terrible love. You're a trap. Temptation itself. And I sat there, watching you, thinking how on earth, after all this time, had I earned an afterlife so glorious it could involve even the mirage of such a thing."

I studied the boulder while he described our meeting as though I hadn't been present. Suppose in a way I hadn't, at least from his clouded set of eyes. His words warmed me.

"Why did you come here?" I finally asked as Mary Moon entered our conversation to shine proudly on us.

"To work with Jim. There was a debt that needed to be called in," he answered in a surprisingly dead tone. His voice altered from something so soft and loving to hateful malice.

"How long have you known Mr. Jim?" I prodded.

"Too long," he said with finality.

I never could let sleeping dogs lie. "What does that mean?' I prompted.

The burn of his gaze tempted me to match his eye as the equal I felt I was. "I do not wish to discuss your Mr. Jim."

It was a dirty accusation, and my eyes flashed to him. Frustrated heat built where my crummy lungs were supposed to be. "If you have such a distaste for him, why did you decide to work for him?" I shot back.

"With."

"Huh?"

His eyes burned until I realized my mistake and mouthed a dumb *oh*.

"I did not know then what I do now. I did not understand. If I had—"

I waited. The moonlight shone brightly across his sharp, tormented face.

"If I had, I would have come sooner for you, girl. You have to know that." I took a deep breath at his confusing words.

"I don't know what that means," I confessed.

"I know," he whispered sadly.

"I wish you for once would just tell me what you mean." I tried to bite back the snap in my voice, and he let out a crude laugh.

He was the portrait of a crying clown with a painted smile. "And here I thought you loved me for my wit."

I looked back at the boulder.

"Tell me, girl, if it is not my wit that sets your loins aflame, what is it? My tender heart, perhaps? My charitable soul? Or, could it be," he feigned a gasp that made my eyes flash right back to him, "my stunning physique?"

I couldn't contain my laughter as he looked at me with mock horror, a hand coming to his heart as if it were beating as rapidly as a virgin's.

"You're impossible," I said and rolled my eyes. He still did not answer my question, and it hung limply in the air. I took a deep, shaky breath. "Will you ever explain it to me?"

I couldn't help but note the exhausted desperation in my tone and shuffled on my skates, insecure about the palpable hatred shared between the two men who meant the most to me.

"Yes," he said gravely, "when you are better."

"I'm getting better," I retorted like a small child.

He laughed softly at that. "I know ye are, girl. But ye ain't better quite yet. I will explain it all to ye once yer better, and we can get ourselves outta here. Put a couple o' oceans and countries between us and yer *Mr.* Jim."

My breath stuttered. I knew we would go. I knew that there would be nothing left for me in Wicker Soul, with my relationship with Mr. Jim torn into decorative ribbons. I had never wanted to leave with him, despite all his promised plans. With the clarity of our newfound distance, I wondered if those promises resulted from care for me. Or the weight of a guilty conscience due to my poor late momma. Nonetheless, I was depressed at the thought of leaving Mr. Jim.

I had wished for freedom. I wished for those strings that bound me to him to be cut as swiftly as the strings that kept me from controlling my own limbs, and my own fate had been. I had demanded my wishes with the pride of someone who had a right to them. Those wishes were the debt God owed me. Or they, at the very least, would cancel out the debts He had let me be born into. But I had not known how heartbreaking those mutinous wishes of mine would become, should they ever be granted. No one ever warned me that life's bittersweet moments wouldn't be balanced on the golden scales of justice. Sometimes the bitter outweighed the sweet. I fought the urge to pull at my hair in frustration. I couldn't stay, but now I realized just how scared I was to go.

"Wallace, what if I don't want an ocean between Mr. Jim and me?" I suggested with a quiet reverence. Or at least I tried to. Just as the damning proclamation tumbled out of my dry mouth, a handful of interruptions coincided.

Firstly, a loud noise like the splitting of a tree rang out, jolting a shock through me. Secondly, a searing pain bit through my left palm and threw me off my skates and onto the ice with a mighty tug. And thirdly, the ice that I so violently landed upon gave a low, odious groan before collapsing beneath me. It happened all too quickly as I searched in shock for the face of a terrified Wallace. He scrambled to get to me as I sunk into the surprisingly turbulent waters below. My last sight above water was his horrified face, and he screamed something I couldn't comprehend.

I was sucked below the surface swifter than I thought possible, and the water's sharp teeth bit into my skin, causing me to gasp and take in more of the razor-sharp water. I choked and tried to push myself back up, but I couldn't figure out which way that was, and my left arm was oddly paralyzed by my side, tangling in my sodden skirts. As the water quietly sucked the mobility out of me, my fuzzy mind clung to one singular realization. After the hellfire of a fever I faced months before, I had always thought death would be hot. I was wrong. Death was cold as ice.

Chapter 29

I startled awake to muffled cries, only to be flooded with delirious relief. The cries that permeated my sleep brought back memories of my most feverish state. When those who cared for me huddled around my bed and sobbed into it. Little did they realize, I hadn't any need for their water because I was drowning well enough on my own.

Drowning.

Was I still drowning? Had I ever stopped? Had I not been in a constant state of treading since my offensive nudity sacrificed to the sun had driven a clever blackbird to take its own life that fateful day six months ago? I shook my head quickly. *No.*

I was getting better. The fever had stayed gone. I opened my eyes only to wince at the somehow low, sharp candlelight. I woke alone, with no loving eyes welling up beside my bed. Instead, muffled cries arose from the corner of the room next to the fireplace. It was Wallace, with his head in his hands. Sobbing. Ragged, heaving, shaking sobs. I winced as pain shot from my hand and ignited through my heart and head. It faded as quickly as it started, not dissimilar to a growing pain, and I breathed through a groan. Despite the state of Wallace and the remarkable jolt of pain, I was thankful for his mewling, which pulled me from my slumber. My vision narrowed into a squint as I tried to tie together the events of my horrific nightmare.

There was something freezing cold. Then something that felt like nothing at all, but also everything at once. A blinding light and the enveloping warmth of climbing into a soft bed after a long winter's day. Peace. Then yanking, ripping blackness. A dark, devilish man. No, not devilish, *the* devil. A nod from his horribly beautiful face, sharp and angelic. Followed by something that sounded like an inhuman scream. I whirled around to find myself alone. In a room of blackness, surrounded by shimmering walls that did not particularly offend me but danced and dazzled around me in the most distracting way.

Fear.

Heinous, unadulterated fear is what the dream had been. It was like every move I made during this dream, every step, pause, or breath was not of my own volition. I stood in line and kept getting pushed forward despite my clawing attempts to remain still. To return to that soft, warm space that smelled familiar. Like soap made with rose petals. And then Wallace's sobs had woken me up.

Had I had too much to drink? I covered my eyes and tried to recall, only to wince once more in reaction to any pressure on my left hand. I quickly assessed the back of it for an injury as the feeling faded. I sat up fully and made a bit of a rustle.

"How do you feel?" he croaked without looking at me.

I wished to comfort him. Wished for him to comfort me. Something had happened, and now, it was clear we stood on the banks of the Lil' Big with a long line drawn in the sand, separating us.

"Odd," I answered honestly.

He nodded, placing his chin on folded hands and leaning closer to the fire. "That...that'll pass."

The fire crackled around us, and I picked at my quilt. Waiting for further explanation about what exactly I could expect to pass and what caused it in the first place. I didn't feel ill. Despite my lightheadedness and fragmentary, out-of-body feeling, I knew the fever had not returned. It hadn't wrapped its fiery hot fingers around my veins and pulled me back into a dumbfounded madness like it had before. I had been getting better. I *was* getting better.

"What's the last thing you remember?" he inquired, his voice barely above a whisper.

I wanted him to face me. I wanted to see the whites of his eyes, so I could find a way to comprehend his cold, pain-ridden tone.

I stared at his back until my eyes grew dry. "The Lil' Big. Frozen over," I finally stated. *How long ago had that been?*

I watched him nod. "What else?"

I flinched at the memory of a deafening crash. "Something broke." I clenched and unclenched my hands repetitively. My nail beds grew too heavy for my fingers to support.

"The ice broke," he stated flatly.

Everything rushed back. I fought against a shiver as I momentarily was returned to the awful, icy depths. I remembered the look of horror on his face and how he reached out for me. At the time, he had seemed too far. At the time, everything seemed quite hopeless. And then, just before blackness had wholly enveloped me, an odd peace washed over any fears. Acceptance perhaps. A flash of unconditional comprehension.

"You saved me?" I asked with an incredulous smile.

A cruel laugh erupted from him, and his dead eyes found mine. "Nae girl. Nae, me bonnie wee Trixie-girl. I didna."

I was dumbfounded. Perhaps I hadn't known him for a lifetime. But I had known him well enough to understand that when he spoke in that funny, almost gurgling accent of his, I ought to pay proper attention. Because good or bad, that meant whatever guard he had up was down, and perhaps something very exciting was on the precipice of occurring.

"Wh—"

"I didna get to ye in time," he interjected, "I couldna get to ye in time. I tried to. But I... I'm so sorry."

I felt cold. "What do you mean...in time?" I asked slowly.

He was broken but still as handsome as all sin. I had never seen Wallace sad before. Not even when I had rejected him and hit him and hated him. I had seen him melancholy. More than once. But each wave of his melancholia still brought fine, kind crinkles at the corners of his eyes and a caustic sense of humor that both ignited and delighted me. I did not care for a sad Mr. Wallace, I quickly came to find. Whatever was powerful enough to make Wallace truly, properly sad was powerful enough to terrify me.

If he claimed he hadn't gotten to me in time...

I patted the bed with both hands to make sure I was really there. The quilt depressed with my fundamental, human pressure. I was wholly present, taking up weight and space as always. I patted my chest. I took a deep breath, and though I couldn't say that I felt any better than I had this morning, I didn't feel worse. I was entirely present in my betterment. And that didn't make sense. Because if I had nearly drowned, indeed I would feel worse, not better. That striking comprehension made my stomach toss like the ground moved from beneath me.

"Wallace," I said, "what on earth are you talking about?"

I don't know how long I waited for him to speak.

"I was born in 1521."

The fire cracked. My eyes narrowed. I waited patiently for him to make sense of his nonsense, as it was clear now that we played one of his lyrical games.

He continued soberly. "When I was a young man, somethin' happened to me. Somethin' that I still canna explain. Trix, I—I canna die."

I pursed my lips and fought an awkward fidget. I opened my mouth to say what, I did not know. Therefore, I closed it dumbly.

"I canna grow old. I canna retain injury, nor contract ailment. And now neither can ye." He took in my expression, Lord knows what it was, and wiped a hand over his face. "I'm nae the only one. 'Tis... 'tis like a sickness. And I *gave* it to ye."

My face scrunched up as I attempted to decipher where the punchline was and how I must have missed it. I tried to produce a forced smile in response to his story. My dancing smile was not well received because he looked away from me. Though the man was babbling, and his tone lacked the concrete humor that was usually laced throughout each prepositional phrase. Such a farce was not like his usual teasing nature. There was always a punchline. A great *aha* that tied his stories together with a polite bow. But this did not come. Which meant somehow the man thought himself serious. I remembered his comical slip on the ice. He had gone down hard.

"Wallace, you fell earlier," I began gently, attempting to disguise the suspicion in my voice with care. "Perhaps you hit your head on the way down? Why don't you come to rest for a bit?" I continued, softly rubbing the open side of the bed that I had utilized only moments before to prove my vitality.

He stood up too quickly, and his chair abruptly turned over. He let out a barking, desperately bitter laugh, and his gaze raced about the room. He seemed incapable of landing on anything of interest and did not even look at me. He ran his hands through his loose hair and pulled it in exasperation. The whimpering firelight threw horrific shadows over his sharp features. The harder I watched him pull at his hair, the more cinched his face became until his eyes snapped shut in what I believed was pain.

I leaped out of bed at that and rushed to him. I gripped his hands and tried without avail to loosen his grasp. To free his poor, abused scalp.

"Wallace, stop this!" I cried. My voice was uncharacteristically shrill as something more profound and heavier than dread filled me to the brim. "Please," I whispered brokenly as my tugging turned into clawing at his relentless hands.

His eyes flashed open and were filled with something ghastly that mimicked whatever I felt. I quickly released his hands and tried to step back from the mad man he had transformed into before my eyes. He reached out and gripped my shoulders, giving me a teeth-rattling shake. I fought to keep my focus as my neck snapped backward and forwards. I tried to flinch away, but he did not let up with his biting hold. Terror racketed through my body, not exactly because of how rough he was, but because my emotions were apparent on my face. And he was ostensibly oblivious to them. He was, for the first time, it felt, entirely ignorant of what I was feeling. That is what terrified me.

"Wallace, you're hurting me," I finally gasped.

He immediately released me with a careless toss. I stumbled back a bit, gripping at the short posts of the bed to sturdy myself. I took a ragged breath in, and it sounded like gunfire in our silence.

"No. I'm not. At least, not really. That's what I am trying to explain to you. I can't hurt you. Not anymore. Not physically," he hollered in a manner I had not suspected him capable of.

The quiet, once sanctimonious cabin quaked and shrank at his outburst.

"The ice broke, and you fell in. I tried, but I couldn't get to you in time," he repeated, over-enunciating his words as if I misunderstood him. "By the time I did, it was too late. You weren't going to make it. You couldn't—" He broke off with a ragged breath. "You were dying. And I couldn't let you."

I clutched tighter to the bedpost. I rambled automatically as the room became much too small and began to sway. It wasn't possible.

"No... no. Wallace...I'm fine. I'm—I'm better. I'm not—"

I was getting better. I didn't have the correct words to explain that I was so obviously alive in front of him.

"You're something, alright. But better, I couldn't say," he agreed bitterly. "You were getting better, Trixie-girl. Up until that ice broke from beneath you and sucked you down. Then, my love, you most certainly lost any chances of continuing that betterment you hold so dear. I couldn't get to you in time. The water was so dark and deep. When I pulled ye up ye were nae breathin', and ye hand was nearly blown apart and I dinna ken, I couldna...I just acted. I'm sorry. All I could think was *not like this*. I could nae let ye die like this. Not when ye had fought so hard...when ye had agreed—" He began to fall apart once more.

I couldn't help but reach toward him in sympathy. He was losing it from such a fit. His eyes then fixated on my outstretched hand.

"Yer hand, it pains ye, aye? Look at it!" he bellowed.

I mechanically lifted my hand, and without being prompted, I turned it around to view. Air gushed out of my lungs. I stumbled as I gripped my wrist to hold it steady as my vision doubled. My eyes flashed to Wallace's, then back at the horrible mess that had become my once calloused, but clear, left hand. Identical to Wallace's his chest was a large, neat, black mark on my palm.

"What have you done?" I whispered.

I ran a thumb over the dark color, but nothing happened. Then I rubbed at the marking hysterically, in hopes that it would blend and bleed as an ink stain did. But the lines stayed smooth. I tried even harder but to no avail.

"What have you done?" I repeated, my left hand going to my throat. I could not look at that marking any longer.

"I...I made ye... I told ye... Yer like—" His stammering was disgusting.

His sadness was disgraceful, and his loyalty transparent. He clearly couldn't find the words, so instead he acted. He walked directly to the table where a glass innocently sat. With a quick snatch of the hand, he smashed the glass against the table. I jumped. With concentrated intention, he sifted through to find a huge, looming piece.

I clutched the bedpost and watched helplessly. The sinking suspicion of what he would do ravaged my already overwhelmed mind. He forced me to witness him dig a gnarly shard of glass traumatically deep into his left hand. My knuckles grew white from the grip I had on the bedpost as a scream ripped out of me. Crimson blood pumped down his arm, and he continued to dig the glass into his palm. A soft, nauseating, squishing sound echoed in the cabin. His teeth were slammed together and bared with an animalistic carnality. His nostrils flared as he pulled the glass with a grotesque jerk out of his mangled hand.

A bride would go to him, bind his hand and kiss it well, and tell him whatever was broken we could fix. But I was glued to the bedpost. He held his disgusting hand in clear view, and I couldn't look away from it. His hand held the same hypnotizing draw that the mangled skull of the dead blackbird had so many months ago. My stomach lurched, but I needed to see it. I opened my mouth, but nothing but hot air came out. I didn't know what to say, but I had to say something. I slowly blinked, and when I opened my eyes, another necessary gush of breath rushed out of me. Because the gore on his hand was gone.

I fell to my bottom. His left hand was as smooth as a baby's butt. The bedframe pressed against my back with sharp pain, and I heard the blood in my ears. It was the work of the devil. Because despite how madly Wallace spoke, I knew I was not mad despite how mad I felt. I saw him drive a piece of glass through his hand, violently.

"Tell me what you did," I whispered.

He took a step toward me, and I pressed even further away, clinging with one hand still on the bedpost and the other wrapped around my legs protectively. He stopped and lifted his two beautifully smooth palms to me as if to say he meant no harm.

"Trixie-girl... Ye wer—"

"No!" I roared, standing up on shaking, jerky knees.

It was devastating, really, as I had just recently found such confidence in those joints. I kept the door to my back, and Wallace continued slowly to step toward me. I shifted my placement so that his only option was to stand on the other side of the bed. If he wanted to, he could reach out and snatch me with ease, but the small space between us gave me a false sense of comfort.

"Explain to me what you did!" I snarled.

"I dinna ken! Ye were just lyin' there, and I knew ye were dyin'. I started to beg. I asked, and the next thing I ken—"

My nightmare came rushing back. A wicked smile. A devilish smile. "*Who* did you beg?" I demanded through gritted teeth.

We both knew the answer. Or the lack thereof. Ain't nothing good could come from that type of prayer. Ain't no God, especially the one I demanded to cut ties with, answer a prayer like that. Never had. Never would. Never will.

It was odd. I hadn't thought much of the devil. Maybe it was because I had spent a childhood under the care of a matron who used the threat of the devil to try to shape me into the young woman I would never be. Her tales were so spectacular that the devil took the shape of a colorful, cartoonish character in my mind. Mischievous, much like myself. Perhaps my devil had even, at times, felt like an ally. Someone equally small and wild and red and up to no good. But never was he an actual demon. *How funny was it now to be standing directly in front of the devil in human form?* I preferred my spiteful little red man.

"Take it back," I ordered around numb lips as I gazed at the perfect skin of his palm, still held out to me like an offering. Taunting me.

He reached for me, and I jerked away. I recoiled to the wooden bed frame closer to the door and held my open, marred palm to him to match.

"Take. It. Back," I repeated through gritted teeth.

"Trixie... Girl... I canna—" he murmured.

I spat at him, the devil incarnate, and bared my teeth to him in de-fense. "Yes, you can. You did it. Undo it!" I barked.

Panic rose within me at breathtaking rates and fueled my rage. I couldn't take my eyes away from his perfect palm. The room swirled around me, and I reached out for that beloved bedpost once more.

"Trixie... take a deep breath... 'twill be alright," Wallace said in a shaky voice.

It broke a bit. His lie was more fragile than a fallen leaf.

"Wallace, just fix it, alright. I don't want... I don't want to be like that. Like you, I would rather—" My voice closed around the word *die* reflexively.

What he claimed he had done, it wasn't possible. I had to prove that to him. I paced over to the table. Whatever he was, I couldn't be. *Some-one would have stopped it, wouldn't they have?* God would have—

Oh.

Right.

Well, it was safe to say that bridge was nothing but water-sodden ash now, wasn't it? Just as well, I was never known for my timeliness. A tardy apology was a fitting end, all and all.

Erratically, I reached for an enormous shard of broken glass. With a certain lack of grace, I held it up to my breast, directly above the heart that he believed would treacherously pump forever. I would plunge it into myself and die at his feet, just to prove him wrong. To prove the newfound terror that coated my veins wrong. To remove myself from the stale air that now surrounded and snuffed out the love that once permeated these four walls.

"Trix, please don't make me watch that," was all he said.

He did not stop me. He did not even reach out to touch me. No, instead, he took an exhausted seat on the bed. Because he did not need to. I was not in danger. If he was correct, I was no longer ever in danger. I pushed the glass, nonetheless, refusing to accept the hideous reality at hand that was sinking in. A hiss of pain escaped my clenched teeth as the sharp edge slowly broke my skin. A brief flash of ecstasy came with the confirmed pain. Wallace watched with what must have been the weight of the world on his shoulders. I kept pushing the blade into my soft and boney breast and watched as tears pooled in his eyes. Salient pain rushed through me. I released the glass, and it clattered to the ground.

That look in his eyes, the void of sadness, but not concern, was enough. He was silent—truly, utterly, tremendously silent—for once. Tears fell, and then an odd, strangled wail erupted from him. He reached out to me. I swallowed a sarcastic scoff. As if I would go to him. As if I could. My left hand reached up to my chest, where I had cut myself. I felt the warm damp stain and the tear in the chemise. But beneath, the skin was smooth. Unaffected. Permanent.

I stared in disbelief, as well as horror, at the broken face of Jayson Wallace, who sat on the crumpled bed with tears streaming down his face and both hands outstretched. Palms forward as if there were something he could give. Something that neither of us could see. Something other than the clean, scarless flesh that proved his divination right. I was disgusted with the pathetic scene that he attempted to play out. *So, he could cry?* I was ever-altered, changed, disgraced. Broken. *He broke me, and it was he who sought my comfort?* The burden of my sex was as much a part of me as my skin. I stumbled backward.

My burning hand searched blindly behind my body for the door handle while I clutched my throat with my right. I hissed as the left met the cool knob and a jolt of something like pain, but not quite, singed from it.

"Trix—" Wallace croaked as I weakly yanked open the door, and the frigid night air whistled in.

"No," I whispered in an equally broken voice, then turned to run into the night.

Chapter 30

he snow and cold, rough ground felt like needles against my bare feet. But gone was any genuine care for the pain. If what Wallace told me was true, if what I *saw* was real, what I *felt* was true, I needn't worry about any frostbite or wearing the skin over my heels down to the bone. I needn't worry about anything else, ever again. That thought, that incomprehensible everlasting, ripped a sob out of my gasping throat. My mind spun as if I ran through a nightmare, one in which my feet felt foreign and useless. I jerked in one general direction with each push forward, impossibly out of control, but somehow still moving. My sobbing didn't slow me down, and each spike of pain that reverberated throughout my body faded all too quickly. The spots that stung vibrated with something less like pain and more like an unwelcome tickle before fading into a healthy balance of normalcy.

The screams of the freezing winds hurt my ears emotionally, not physically. I comprehended that I was uncomfortable, as opposed to tangibly feeling so. I continued to push those newly useless muscles and bones forward in a run. I ignored the branches and brush that I barreled through. Ignored the way they pulled at me and shredded my skin as if to hold me back. Begging me to return. The hounds of hell nipped at my trailing nightgown. I ran desperately toward the fleeting salvation ahead of me that, somewhere down the line, I had forgotten to ask for. That I had demanded to be freed from. God tossed His mighty sharp rocks and ice patches and thornbushes at me—a physical rejection. Yet still, I pushed forward, toward the only thing my soul needed. Forgiveness.

That was the funny thing about faith. You never realize how much you have until damnation is licking at your cold, calloused heels. I pushed myself further, and my path was lit by the large, full of mourning, Mary with eerie slow-moving clouds that made everything flicker in and out of sight like a candle exposed to too much wind or breath. Driven by something instinctual, I had no idea where to go or what to do, but an itch led me down a familiar path.

My fist banged on the door, hard enough to bruise. I didn't call out, despite the gaping of my mouth. I was breathless and didn't have the words, even if I hadn't been. I kept banging on that damn door and noted relief when rustling voices echoed from behind it. The door swung open quite dramatically, and I nearly stumbled into the room. I gawked at a surprised yet impressively snarky looking naked woman without a hint of recognition. She pursed her lips and leaned a shapely hip on the door frame, crossing her arms over her breasts.

"May I help you?" she drawled as she looked me up and down.

I continued gawking, shaking in my wet from the snow and sweat. I knew the white of my gown clung and had acquired a certain level of transparency through my travels but I couldn't be bothered with that. I didn't take time to mimic her actions and inspect any lower than her breasts. All I would find was a shapelier, more expertly crafted version of what I also had. I noted that my perceived dismissal of her wonderfully naked figure caused a hint of distress in her eyes. Disappointment, perhaps. She scoffed at me, and I stared beyond her into the low-lit apartment. My left hand stayed frozen in place. My gaze flashed back to the whore's as she suspiciously eyed my left hand. My aching, newly marred left hand that I held half clenched in front of me as if another door would need pounding upon any minute.

Her pretty eyebrows furrowed, and she looked over an elegantly feminine, in an obvious sort of way, plump shoulder. Mr. Jim came into view, his rumpled denim shirt half-buttoned, with a small, blond woman clinging to him from behind. She was as small as me. His eyes looked bored as he assessed me in the doorway as if I had been expected, drenched to the bone in only a nightgown. The pale hands of the small woman trailed delicate patterns on Mr. Jim's exposed skin. She played a bit of hide-and-seek with his shirt's cloth in the most distracting way. Briefly, I pondered if I had ever seen Mr. Jim's bare chest before. Indeed not, at least not in a such a manner. It was clear he had been an impressive being back in his prime, but I already knew that. Evidence of drink and age tainted his sinewy frame.

"Whaddaya doing here, girl?" Mr. Jim grumbled drunkenly, shocking my gaze back up to his unfortunately droopy one.

I didn't need to take a step closer to know that his breath reeked of whiskey and something altogether foul in nature. I held his cruel eyes, breathing harshly through my nose. I opened and closed my mouth, nearly gasping for air, but words failed me like a fish out of water. *Tom Beau would be pained at my discomfort, wouldn't he? He would understand.* My attention drifted off to some uneventful corner in the room. I shivered in the realization that not too long ago, I had been welcomed by the icy hands of mishap into his frigid living space. I hadn't even taken the time to bid him a hello or farewell. Not very thoughtful of me.

"Trixie!" Mr. Jim snapped, pulling me out of my delirious musings. There was sobriety in his angry eyes.

"Hmmm?"

My fear and confusion gripped my throat once more. I glanced behind to make sure nothing had followed me here before facing my audience again and noting that the little woman's lovely pale hands had halted. They ogled me as if I had grown three heads, and I felt the plump one's soft breath blowing across my forehead. She smelled like an odd combination of cheap flowers, sweat, sex, and liquor. It was altogether quite lovely.

"Are ya hurt?" He focused on the small bloodstain in the middle of my chest.

I didn't know how to answer that question accurately, so I just shrugged.

Mr. Jim's eyes flickered to my raised hand, and mine followed. I don't know what made me do it. My mind was still trying to claw its way out from the delusional fog permeating it. The only thing that made sense in that moment of heightened everything was to uncurl my left hand and show Mr. Jim the marking upon it. Words had left me, perhaps permanently. My mind was incapable of creating a single thought to even consider a proper explanation. Somehow, surrounded by the whores and the frigid cold and the fear of God choking out any rhyme or reason, I figured Mr. Jim knew what to do.

So I uncurled my left hand and waited for the world to end and begin anew with the precise, comforting clarity only the trust found in a father figure provided. The face of the woman standing closest to me clouded over in confusion, and she looked at Mr. Jim. A flicker of something danced across Mr. Jim's features. Something like surprise, but still too drunk to be entirely such. Other than that, he did not move. My hand shook as I held it up for him to pay witness. Then he nodded. A quick, tight jerk of his chin down that wouldn't be visible to the naked eye of a stranger who had not grown swaddled in the stifling blanket of this man's equal parts care-to-wrath.

"Get out," he ordered quietly, terrifyingly.

He held my gaze with a sharp intelligence that broke my heart. He knew. Tears pooled. I didn't know when I had stopped crying, but I was crying again as if I always had been. Behind the initial shock that Mr. Jim knew exactly what was going on, I began to understand that perhaps nothing would be earth-shattering to me from now on. Because nothing would shatter the earth. It was simply going to keep turning past the end of time, with me still on it.

"Ya, go on, girl, git," the beautifully plump one hissed.

She clearly wasn't the brains of the operation

"Not her," he growled without moving.

Both women regarded him in shock. I watched as the small woman's pale arms retracted from her possessive embrace around Mr. Jim's uncaring form, like two frightened white snakes.

"Jim—" the plump one cooed, walking with stunning beauty, all curves and movement and sheer femininity.

As she reached for him, he quickly raised an arm to strike. Both women shied away and covered their faces. It made sense, as what they had to sell was directly related to just how lovely those faces looked. With their retreat, Mr. Jim reached into his pocket and pulled out a bag of monies and dumped them onto the floor. They crawled on their hands and knees, collecting their dues as the candlelight danced across their soft naked flesh. With their payment sufficiently accounted for, the women silently dressed and exited the room. Neither woman dared to touch me as they slithered around my posture in the doorway.

Mr. Jim waited for the door to shut before he slowly began to undo his shirt's remaining buttons. Every muscle in me clenched as I watched him shed his own shirt. For a brief and terrifying moment, my mind returned to precisely what he had been up to prior to my arrival. An unease that I had never experienced coldly trickled through me. But then he slowly revealed a stark black marking in the middle of his aged bare back.

Nausea washed over me. I swallowed it down. Comprehension of everything, every detail of what had been, what was current, and what would come, violently tumbled into my mind. For one glistening moment, it was all so clear. Blindingly so. The sordid, rusty blade of truth had sliced through my oily eyelids, leaving them finally, permanently open. It burned.

The nod. The sly, dark, incomprehensible nod from my dreams. The terrifyingly *familiar* face danced in front of my open eyes once more. It blocked any visage of the reality around. And then blended into the reality around. Reality and wonderments and nightmares blurred together in one horribly bright, hateful truth. Until the end of time, the devil would lurk in my dreams. Haunting me, not because he had become a part of me, but even worse, because he had paid witness to me. He had approved of me. And God had mourned. Helplessly calling out from the rafters in the Court of Free Will, Proud Choice, and deliciously selfish Human Error.

Misery did not love company, so it seemed. The realization that Mr. Jim, a cruel and confusing man, but nonetheless *my* cruel and confusing man, had seen and felt the same scene caused me to fall to my knees and scream. I sobbed and clenched my left hand, attempting to see the marking through my useless gaze. He was behind me, clad once more in his shirt, thankfully, and held my shaking self against his warm chest. Nonsense bubbled from my lips, and he nodded against the top of my head. I clung to the arms wrapped around my body and dug my fingernails into his flesh in a desperate attempt to keep him with me. To never leave me. To never leave me a lonely victim of the fate into which I had fallen with the grace of a skinny newborn calf. I sold my soul, or whatever I had left that kept me neither above nor below, to Mr. Jim. There, on that dirty floor, still warm from the soft bodies of the whores who so recently crawled across it.

We stayed there for God-knows-how-long. My eyes did not dry, but the screaming sobs died down. This seemed to be only because, despite my body's new capability to be unaffected by any ailment, my scratchy voice had gone entirely hoarse.

Mr. Jim shifted so that his arms could slip underneath my knees. He lifted me like a child and brought me over into a worn chair by the fire that roared amicably. "We've gotta go, Trixie-girl."

Other than that, he didn't say anything. He didn't ask any questions. He didn't make me explain anything. He just wrapped me in a blanket and put a glass filled to the brim with an amber liquid in my right hand and told me he would be right back. I waited for no more than twenty minutes before he barged through his door and presented a travel bag full of my belongings. I presented an empty glass. We continued to not speak, and I dressed properly. He packed quickly.

Meanwhile, I poured myself another three fingers of whiskey. The burn that trailed down my throat comforted me. As did the euphoric lightheadedness that followed. By the time Mr. Jim felt himself to be collected enough, I was drunk. But he didn't comment on any of that. Our movements were a whirl of candlelit nonsense as he rushed me out that door, bag in hand and mittens on snug. Snow fell softly around us, and I looked up to the late-night sky, as Mary Moon showed Herself to smile sadly down at me without the infringement of clouds. I opened my mouth and stuck my tongue out to taste the air as no snowflakes fell this evening. So maybe just Her. Mr. Jim took my elbow and pulled me to the stables.

After a beat of flustering business such as saddling and loading up the beast, I was then hurled upon a grunting Butterbiscuit and tucked in with a large blanket. Mr. Jim hoisted himself to sit behind and held me protectively before we took off into the cold winter's midnight. We rode through the remaining night and morning in silence. To my quiet surprise, Butterbiscuit made the trip with only one break, lasting no more than an hour.

Denver seemed sleepier than I had thought it would be, but that very well could have been due to the hour. The city was brown and gray, with more smoking chimneys than I could have ever imagined. The chimneys weren't warm and cozy and full of burning promise, but instead tarnished and tired-looking, on an equally tired morning. I looked across the city with an empty heart. Nothing I pictured seemed to be as it was, and I had never felt more out of place than I did when we stopped in front of a large building in a city that offered imminent departure.

Mr. Jim checked us into a boarding house a stone's throw from the station. I was immediately put into bed with the soft chiding that sleep on a train would not prove fruitful. He drew the curtains tight to provide an ideal sleeping environment. I twisted the cold ring on my finger, mindlessly. If Mr. Jim had noticed, he hadn't said anything about it. Despite the amount that I had drunk, my hangover had already come and gone with a speed that made me nauseous for entirely emotional reasons.

"Mr. Jim?" my lips mumbled as I stared at the ceiling.

My throat felt raw, but that had to have been from the weight that lingered within it. The candlelight flickered across the ceiling of the crummy hotel. He stopped his busying about to look at me.

"Hm?" he softly prompted, coming to sit on the end of the bed. The bed groaned with his weight. He made no move to touch me, just continued to wait patiently for me to continue.

I took a shaky breath. "Does it ever stop?"

Silence followed for only a moment, like most conversations with him seemed to. But finally, I got the half-assed response I ached for.

"Does what stop, girl?"

My mind slowly worked on attaching words to at least one of the emotions I was experiencing. I clung to the corpse of who I was, and I was left unattached and lost—a loose soul, bouncing around for a place or personality to settle back into.

"The Big Hurt." I couldn't breathe for a moment and then could breathe all too easily. It hurt. My lungs were on fire, and for the first time, only words could ease the burn. "I'm...floating. I am above my body... apart. But I can still feel everything that is happening to it. My life is slipping through my fingertips and toes. They hurt, Mr. Jim. They hurt as if..." My voice cracked.

"As if?" he quietly prompted.

"As if despite my *wondrous* new circumstances, I am bleeding out, and no one can see." I looked at him now.

He bravely met my eyes even as they betrayed me, pooling with tears.

"As if I'm screaming, and no one can hear." A sob shook its way through me and poured out like the Flood. "Can you hear me, Mr. Jim?"

My voice was hysterical, and my vision useless. The tears wouldn't stop. Rationality was rejecting all that had happened repeatedly, like some form of a vengeful virus.

Mr. Jim did not respond for a very long time. Finally, he reached out to settle my erratically twisting finger. His fingers grazed the lovely ring.

"You really loved him?" he asked quietly.

I squeezed my eyes shut as a surprising shot of pain seared my chest. There was a reason heartbreak was named thus; the emotion was no good for one's most notorious organ. I nodded. Mr. Jim would have to be the keeper of my most hidden secrets, so it seemed. He hoisted himself off the bed and walked closer to me. He placed his hand next to my head and leaned down. I smelled the tobacco and whiskey and dust that always clung to him.

"Then, no, Trixie-girl. It never stops."

I squeezed my eyes tighter and nodded once more, believing him wholeheartedly.

His rough hand found its way to my face and stroked the damp cheek. My eyes flashed open despite their irritation at the rare show of affection.

"When someone breaks your heart, they take things from you. And as much as I wanna say it's all in that head of yours, it ain't. Those things that they take? Some of them grow back on their own with time. Others don't. And that's all right. Because God gives us plenty more than we need. And just as man can live withoutta kidney, you'll find you can live without those things."

On that note, Mr. Jim blew out the candle.

And I slept.

Acknowledgements

I want to say thank you to my friends and chosen family, who have pushed me through this process. I would have given up if it were not for you all believing in me when I couldn't believe in myself.

To A, I guess I just love you so very much and you inspire me.

To B, for being a fellow writer and helping me, even though you're so much better at it.

To J, for reminding me that I am loved and valid every single day. At 12 years old, you were my Billy, and still are.

To BJA, the cover design is everything I wanted. I'll buy us that house one day, I promise.

To my daddy who once threatened to burn my manuscript if I kept hiding it: harsh, but I get it. To my momma who read every single thing I gave her, and takes every call, Moon and back. To Grandma Cat for being the greatest librarian/baker that ever existed, and teaching me that it's alright to be sad even when you don't know why. To Grandaddy for reading Edgar Allen Poe to me when I was probably too young, you and daddy are the reason I am such a creepy little thing, and I wouldn't have it any other way. To Papa who fed my imagination (I'll write about Charlie one day I promise). And to my Grandma who taught me to never let a man tell me what to do, that we are the smartest people in the room, vanity is the greatest sin, and to never, ever ever give up. I miss you every day.

To the team at Cup & Quill, thank you for helping me create something legible out of the, at times, mindless ramblings I called a novel. Rebecca Stohler, you were the first person outside of friends and family to read my novel, thank you for that.

To Jessica Hammerman and Isaac Peterson of Emerald Books, thank you for your help editing, I wouldn't have this novel ready without you!

To Mr. F, for teaching me, reading *Franny and Zooey* to me, and pushing me to keep writing after reading a small excerpt I sent to you when I was drunk in Amsterdam.

And to my ancestors. To come from such a long line of resilient women is an honor that deserves few words, other than thank you. Thank you for your sacrifices, and for paving the way for someone as scrappy as me. I hope I have made you all proud, this is for you.

Made in the USA
Coppell, TX
13 April 2021